Bitter
Magic

A Demon Trappers® Novel

Bitter Magic

A Demon Trappers® Novel

Jana Oliver

 Nevermore Books

Published by
MageSpell LLC
Coimbra, Portugal

Bitter Magic
A Demon Trappers® Novel
ISBN: 978-1-941527-28-3
Copyright © 2024 Jana Oliver

Cover Art courtesy of JoY Author Design Studio
Angel Wing Graphic used with permission of
Macmillan Children's Books

To

my husband

Harold Buehl

who was there when it counted

The old world is dying,
and the new world struggles to be born:
Now is the time of monsters.

~ Antonio Gramsci

ONE

July 2019
Atlanta, Georgia

The cemetery was too quiet. There was no rustle of a breeze, no noises from the neighborhood nearby, and even the traffic sounds from the city were muted. It was as if there were no one else in the world but the dead, and Katia Breman.

Experienced demon trappers didn't spook easily, and it wasn't as if Katia was unprotected. A large circle of twinkling candles and Holy Water had been laid onto the ground around her, then charged with a prayer to keep her safe. That same circle guarded the recently deceased Albert Means, who was tucked into his casket, inside a vault, and then under six feet of red Georgia clay.

To her dismay the dead guy's widow had dropped by for a visit right after Katia had begun her "shift." Mrs. Means was a woman in her mid-fifties who talked a lot and listened even less. She'd gone on and on about how nice her husband's casket looked at the funeral. Not that she missed the man she'd been married to for over thirty years, not that she was grieving his loss. No, it was all about appearances.

According to the widow, Means' heart had said, "That's it, I'm done" during an appointment with his accountant. Which made Katia wonder just what the accountant had told the guy, but she'd been polite and not asked that question. Finally, Mrs. Means had ended her self-obsessed monologue and left Katia in peace.

Now the cemetery's eerie stillness made her wish she weren't here on her own. It'd been almost six weeks since she'd made her solo journey from flat and hot Kansas to steamy and buggy Georgia. And nothing about those six weeks had been normal. Tonight wasn't any different.

Sitting vigil to prevent a necromancer from making off with the dead wasn't Katia's usual job. Mostly, she trapped Hellspawn or helped the city's lay exorcist pull demons out of people. Despite what Master Riley Blackthorne claimed, protecting the newly dead wasn't a skill every trapper needed to know. Still, when you were a journeyman trapper you did stuff that didn't make sense.

At least Katia was being paid to be here, which was why Riley had recommended her when the grave watchers' schedules got shifted around due to illness. The old guy who'd been watching the grave before her had been thrilled to move to an earlier time, escaping the midnight shift, as he called it.

Ten dollars an hour for a ten-hour shift got her closer to a deposit on an apartment, and there would be no demons involved. Other than the unnerving quiet, this gig was the graveyard equivalent of watching paint dry.

"It's a dead-end job, but someone has to do it," she muttered. And now she was talking to herself.

If she were honest, Katia didn't care much for the cemetery, the kind that mandated that all the headstones were flat and slightly below grade so the big mowers could roll right over the top of them. That felt like disrespect to her.

Her much-beloved grandmother, after whom she was named, had been adamant that the dead should be respected, mostly because if you dissed them they had ways to get even. Katia had never known what her gran had meant by that, and now it was too late to ask. At least her grandmother's grave had a genuine marble headstone and pretty flowers that bloomed right up to the first Kansas snow.

As the hours crept along, Katia used her phone to research how necromancers could "buy" the dead right out of their graves. From what she could find on the internet, it was hinted that there'd been money slipped under the table to certain powerful lawmakers, and only then had summoner friendly laws been passed to allow just such transactions. No matter where you lived, politics was all the same.

Legally the necros were allowed to call the deceased from their grave after the first sundown following the death, providing the family approved of the reanimation. Or the deceased if arrangements had been made before they took their last breath.

Which made Katia wonder what would happen if the deceased wasn't buried by that first sundown. Could they still be summoned by a necro? The key thing was that the corpse was "presentable," which left out such things as car accidents, major burns, and demon attacks. According to Riley, not all the reanimations were legal. Some were outright theft.

The exhumed were sold or leased as servants of some sort. Most became domestic employees, as if there weren't enough humans of the breathing kind who needed a job. The dead didn't have labor unions and so they were usually paid very little.

Others were reanimated because of their skills in life, like a particularly talented corporate attorney or an artist. One author had been brought back to write two more bestselling books before being returned to his grave. According to the internet, the legal ramifications of that postmortem scribbling were still bouncing around the courts. Lawyers gotta lawyer, as her gran would say.

The Deaders, they were called, were useful for about six months to a year, depending on the postmortem maintenance skills of the necromancer involved. The whole idea made Katia queasy.

It was just past four when she was about to stretch out on the sleeping bag Riley had loaned her, when a light approached, dutifully bobbing above a necromancer like a mini spotlight. This had happened four times during her shift, and the first time she'd nearly freaked out. Summoners weren't that common in her home state, but they seemed to be thick on the ground here in Atlanta. Just like Hellspawn and mosquitoes. To her relief, the widow had been insistent that *Dear Albie* stay below ground. That's all Katia needed to know.

She relaxed as the summoner drew closer because this one she knew. She'd met Alex Greene during her first unforgettable day in Georgia's capitol, a day that nearly ended with her checking into Hell, forever. She'd also met his uncle, Mortimer Alexander, a very senior summoner. She liked them both even though she detested what they did for a living. Still, Alex was younger than her and him being here on his own was odd. She'd not thought he was far enough in his training to perform a reanimation without his uncle's help.

Alex stopped just outside the circle, studied the protective ward, then frowned his displeasure. The ward wasn't going anywhere unless she broke the circle because Riley had taught her how to set it properly. It immediately spat bright flames at him when he stepped too close. Alex retreated, his frown growing.

After a long pause he said, "I'm a summoner," pointing at the black robe he wore.

Well, duh. Of course, Alex was a summoner. They'd spent time together at his uncle's house, and then met up again at a local trapper's convention. Had he forgotten her already?

Besides his cluelessness, the black robe bothered her. Earlier in the week she'd listened in as Riley had patiently explained necromancer rankings to her current crop of apprentice demon trappers. Most newbie summoners rated a pale gray robe because their magic was very weak, and that's what Alex wore the last time she'd seen him.

His uncle, on the other hand, had earned a black robe because Mort's magical prowess was seriously badass. From what she'd heard that required years of study. Either Alex was yanking her chain or . . .

"What's your name?" he asked, his eyes on Means' grave, not her.

Working with Hellspawn had taught Katia that names had power, so she offered her mom's instead of her own.

"Susan," she said.

"Susan, I want to make you an offer."

Black robe, doesn't know me, hasn't introduced himself like the others. She'd bet a glamour spell was involved, a strong one if she couldn't sense it. But why impersonate Mort's nephew?

One of the scars on her left forearm began to itch furiously, and the intense discomfort made her look away for a moment. When she returned her attention to her visitor, he now sported a faint hazy outline, the spell he was using to alter his identity.

Nice try. "The widow doesn't want Mr. Means reanimated. So, thanks, but no thanks. Now if you'll head off, I can get some sleep."

"If I reanimate the corpse, you could have the rest of the night off. I'll even double what they paid you."

And now he tries to bribe me. "The dead guy's name is Albert Means. He has a wife and two daughters," Katia replied, because the missus had been extremely specific about all that. "Even in death this man deserves respect."

The fake Alex's frown deepened further. "You are going to be a problem."

She huffed. "From what I've been told, that's my purpose in life."

The summoner pushed against the barrier again, causing it to glow brighter. "You will break this circle, or *I* will."

The voice had taken on a level of menace now, as well as ramped-up in power.

So not Alex.

"Here's a counteroffer: You leave now, and I won't report you to the Summoner Advocate. I'm sure he'd *love* to know you're all glamoured up as his nephew."

The necro's eyes grew darker. "That was a mistake, *Susan*."

Katia felt the spell begin to grow around him. It started out small, then built, and built even more as it pulled on his power. His eyes were closed, his hands raised, the robe flowing around him. And then the spell exploded, flowing outward across the cemetery like a windstorm.

Flat gravestones erupted from the earth and rushed toward

the circle like incoming missiles. It took all her courage not to move, not to panic and run. She'd been inside a Holy Water circle while in Hell, and it'd kept her and Simon Adler safe. This one would hold. It had to.

A gravestone hit the ward, then another, and it felt as if the ground shook with each strike. With each assault the circle flared bright white and repelled the magic attacking it.

"Let me in!" the necromancer shouted. "Let me in!"

The words burrowed into her mind, demanding she walk through the protective sphere, causing it to fail. Once it was gone, so was Means. "Come to me now! I command it, Susan!"

The vicious mental assault drove Katia to her knees, causing her to rock back and forth as the pressure only built within her skull.

"No," she whispered, her voice cracking. "No."

She thought of the exorcist, and what it had taken for her and Simon to survive in the pit. What it had been like to stand in front of Lucifer's throne. How terrified she'd been, how sure she'd never see her family again.

This is only a necro.

Katia forced herself to rise, her head pounding and heart hammering. She scowled at the magical threat, ignoring the chaos of utter destruction raging around them.

She gulped a breath of damp air, stubbornness overriding every other emotion. Crossing her shaking arms over her chest, she glared at him.

"Aren't you done yet, dickwad?"

The necromancer howled, and for a moment it sounded unearthly, almost inhuman. Then with an air-sucking pop, he vanished.

She waited in case this was a feint on his part, but he did not reappear. Finally, Katia began counting slowly to thirty, then to fifty. When she reopened her eyes, she found the cemetery unchanged—no uprooted trees, no gravestones littered across the ground. That incredible display of magic certainly hadn't been Alex the Newbie Necro.

"Yeah, it's a dead-end job," she muttered, then shook her head, her heart still beating too fast.

One thing for sure, the hundred bucks she'd get for tonight's vigilance wasn't nearly enough.

†✶‡✶†

After pacing around inside the circle to burn off her anger and the residual shakes, Katia finally dropped down on the sleeping bag. Why hadn't the summoner been able to force her to break the circle? Was it because of something she'd done?

"No, I was damned lucky." There'd been no other reason. Somehow she'd kept Means safe and saved herself from one helluva butt chewing from his missus. "Go me."

Once the threat departed the night sounds had returned, including a dog barking somewhere in the distance. An owl hooted in response, as if they were having a conversation. Katia finally laid down, putting her hands behind her head, trying to relax. The moon peered down through the trees, casting a pale light on the gravestones. It was still warm, a typical July night in the Deep South. The occasional whine of a mosquito came from outside the circle.

Katia must have dozed off because she woke to a car door closing in the parking lot further up the hill. The sun was up, and a quick check of her phone said it was nearing eight and the end of her shift.

How she could have slept after that nocturnal horror, she had no idea. It had to have been the stress, nothing more.

The figure trudging toward her was Katia's boss. Master Riley Blackthorne was six years younger than her. She had shoulder-length auburn-brown hair and eyes that spoke of deep personal loss. Katia could not imagine what it was like to be orphaned, married, and already a master trapper at eighteen. Or what it had taken to survive all that had happened to her.

But was this really her master? It would be hard to tell because Riley was also a summoner, so magic was in her blood.

Whoever this was, came within thirty feet of the circle, then abruptly halted. She took a deep inhalation, then executed a slow three-hundred-and-sixty-degree turn.

When she was facing Katia again, she said, "Wow, now that's some power. What happened last night?"

Katia rose. Her scars weren't itching, her version of a "something's not right" warning system. Still, she was on edge.

"Prove to me you're Master Blackthorne."

If she'd expected Riley to be upset at that demand, she'd have been disappointed.

"Smart move, because I can guess why you're asking." Riley took a deep breath. "You are Katia Breman, previously of Lawrence, Kansas. You were sent to Atlanta because they thought you were a problem child for their Guild."

"Lots of people know where I came from and why," Katia said, hedging.

Riley cocked her head. "Last night must have been a bitch or you wouldn't be so skittish." She nodded to herself now. "Okay. Because you are a special soul, you spent quality time in Hell with my favorite lay exorcist, saved the lives of three boys, and lived to tell us about it. How's that?"

There was no hazy outline, nothing that made Katia's hackles rise. This was the real deal.

"Thank God, it's you," she said, then sighed in relief.

Riley took a quick look at the grave. "Mr. Means is still in place, I see."

"Yes. It got damned ugly there for a while."

Her master shook her head as if trying to clear it, then created her own circle of protection out of nowhere, without all the bother of using Holy Water. It blazed up around her as she parked herself on the grass. After another deep breath she said, "Ah, that's better."

"What are you feeling?" Katia asked.

"Residual magic, the really strong kind. What did you feel?"

"Something weird. It made my scars itch. At least, the big one on my arm. That's usually the one that warns me something bad is going down."

Riley eyed her. "You sense a lot more than most folks."

"My grandmother was like that. Drove my parents nuts. They're firmly in the 'weird stuff doesn't exist' camp."

"Even after your brother was almost killed by a demon?"

Katia shrugged. "Yeah. They're still denying all that but failing badly."

"Well, considering what you were up against last night, I'm thinking your itchy early warning system is a good thing. Anyone else, and we'd have to call this guy's widow with unbelievably sad news."

Another car door slammed, most likely Katia's replacement. They both watched as the woman unloaded items from her trunk, then closed it with a pronounced thump.

"Is she for real?" Katia asked.

Riley nodded. "There's no glamour." She looked back. "How much of last night do you want to share with her?"

"A warning, but not too many details. I think some of it's going to cause problems when it gets out."

That earned her a thoughtful pause. "Then you tell her what you think she needs to know, and you can tell me about the rest in the car."

Katia kept another sigh of relief to herself. Her previous job in Lawrence had been a bitch after her first master had died unexpectedly. Master Griffin had been fair and great to work with, but her second master made her job impossible. Plus, the ass had been pocketing most of her wages, claiming it was the National Guild that was slowing up her payments.

Due to those lies, she'd had to sleep on friends' couches or in one of the trappers' "bolt holes" because she didn't have enough money for rent. Or much food. Because of issues with her family, and her own stubborn pride, Katia had been on her own. Then she'd been sent to Atlanta and everything had changed. Really changed.

Because of all that, Katia was still waiting for Master Blackthorne to go bad on her. Not likely, but trust didn't come easy, even when your new master was legendary in the trapper world and wielded magic like most people took a deep breath.

"Good morning! I'm Gloria," the new arrival called out. She was older, probably in her early seventies with short silver hair. She toted a small hamper, a folded beach umbrella, and a turquoise lawn chair. "Looks like the weather is going to be hot again today. Lower nineties. No surprise there."

"Hi," Katia said, glanced at Riley and then back at the lady. "You should know that there was a summoner here last night who didn't follow the rules."

The woman came to a halt, all the gear still in hand. "How bad was it?" she asked.

"Bad. He tried to break the circle. Really tried, if you know what I mean."

"Ah, one of those. Well, I know how to deal with them. Luckily, they're not as powerful during the day."

Riley raised a skeptical eyebrow at that assumption.

Katia's replacement waited at the edge of the circle until she'd recited the phrase that allowed her to cross over it, providing she meant no harm to those inside. Gloria sailed right through, and while Katia rolled up the sleeping bag and tied it, the other grave watcher set up her lawn chair and umbrella. She sank down into the chair, then donned a pair of sunglasses as well as a broad-brimmed hat. She looked like she was ready to spend the day at the beach rather than in a boneyard.

"Anything else I need to know?" she asked.

Katia shook her head. "Just be careful. The necro was really powerful."

"Okay, then you're free. Have a good day." Her replacement pulled out a book, thumbed to a particular page and began to read. From what Katia could tell, it was an historical romance by someone named Burrowes.

Katia carefully crossed the circle, feeling the tug as she stepped outside its protection. Riley took possession of the sleeping bag, leaving her the small cooler and her own trapping bag.

Neither spoke until they were in the car and headed toward the heart of the city.

"So, what really happened?" her master asked, giving her a quick glance.

Katia took a deep breath, organizing her response. "First thing, the other necros introduced themselves. He, or she, didn't."

"Not smart. They're required by the Society to do that. Go on."

"He made himself look exactly like Mort's nephew, but his voice was wrong, and he was wearing a black robe."

"What?" Riley blurted, jerking the wheel. Fortunately, no other car was near them at that point. "That's not right. The Summoners Society goes ballistic if you do that."

"Yeah, well this necro's glamour was really strong, and his illusions just flat out incredible. It looked like every gravestone and all the trees were attacking the circle."

"I've seen that happen. You never forget it."

"I sure won't. Then he tried to get inside my head. It felt like he was using a pickaxe on my skull."

"How'd you fight him off?" Riley asked as she stopped the car behind a school bus.

"I thought of Simon and our time in Hell. That necro had to stand in line to scare me like that trip did. I still have nightmares about it. I know Simon does."

Riley nodded, then didn't say anything further until they reached the next stoplight. From the line of cars waiting for it to change, it wasn't going to be quick. "How fried are you?"

"I'm tired, but I want to know what happened last night. The magic he threw around was big time, and if he does it again, someone might get hurt."

"That matches what I felt. Whoever that was wanted you to panic and break the circle." Riley looked over at her, smiling. "You showed them just how tough a trapper can be. Well done, Journeyman Breman. Well done."

The unexpected praise pushed back a little of Katia's exhaustion. "What do we do about this?"

"We tell Mort, first thing. Mostly because he's the Summoner Advocate and because that idiot used his nephew as a head fake last night."

"I didn't tell him my real name. I gave them my mom's."

"Always an innovative idea. Just like demons, summoners can get into your mind easier if they use your full name. Well, except in my case."

Katia pulled out a bottle of water and took a long sip. When the bottle went back into her trapping bag, she just had to ask, "Why *do* the fiends call you Blackthorne's Daughter instead of your real name?"

"Because my dad gave up his soul to the Prince to keep me safe. He got it back, but that's why."

What?

Katia tried to process all that, but it was early in the morning, and she was still messed up from the attack overnight.

"Okay," was the best she could offer. "I'm too out of it right now, but some day I'd like to hear how all that happened." She hesitated, then added, "If you're okay with that."

"I am. You need to know my history, just like I need to know yours."

Of course she did. And part of that history Katia wasn't ready to share. If ever.

"You know one of the things I like about you?" Katia shook her head. "You're honest even if you think it might make you look bad. Not everyone is able to do that, especially after the jerks you had to put up with in Lawrence."

"Some folks would call bullshit on that."

"Some folks are idiots."

She laughed because her boss had a point. "How pissed off is Summoner Alexander going to be when we tell him what happened?"

"*Majorly* pissed off. I will make sure that none of that anger goes your way, not that Mort would do that anyway. The other summoners? They can be dense sometimes."

"Oh great. Dense people with magic. What could go wrong?"

Riley chuckled. "You're about to find out." At Katia's grimace, she added, "Summoners do steal corpses, but the ones in Atlanta know not to go there because Ozy is not someone to cross."

"Who?"

"Lord Ozymandias. Not sure if that's his real name or if he's just a fan of Shelley's depressing poem. He's probably the most powerful summoner in the eastern U.S. Maybe the entire country. Anyone with a brain does not cross him.

"His lordship made a big mistake last year, and he's keen that nobody else is that stupid. If you summon a demon, he'll snuff you. He's not much nicer to those who body snatch, either."

"Snuff? Like kill?" A nod came her way. "So, what happens if you steal a body?"

"Ozy pulls the magic out of you. Literally. Most go insane."

Holy shit. "Then why would a necro risk their life for one dead guy?"

"That's a really good question."

When they'd entered Little Five Points, it took Riley a while to find a parking place. This was Katia's second time in this part of Atlanta. When she was fresh off the bus from Lawrence, Simon had brought her here. That day was still a blur, but she remembered the strange sensations she'd felt as they walked to the summoner's house.

There was significant magic in this neighborhood, but a blend of many distinct kinds, like a complex perfume. According to the exorcist, L5P, as it was called by the locals, was home for witches, necromancers, and various Pagans. Magic was a given here.

"Don't you have to let him know you're coming?" Katia asked as they walked under the copper arch that led to Mort's house. As usual that arch vibrated, which was just creepy.

"Usually I would call ahead, but not with what happened overnight. He'll want to hear about this as soon as possible. I didn't want to just send him a text."

That made sense.

The café on the right was open and the smell of something delightfully delicious wafted out to greet them. Katia's stomach weighed in on that, but now was not the time. The New Age shop on the left was still closed. In the building just beyond it, the sign that had announced a new bookstore was gone. Instead, a new notice said a mini grocery would be opening soon. The name of the business: *Odin's Pantry.* This was definitely L5P.

As the walkway split into two, they headed down the left lane toward Mort's house. When they reached a bright purple door, Riley knocked. She waited a decent interval and was about to knock again when it opened. Katia had expected to see the necro or his nephew Alex, but instead it was a thin woman with curly hair and black glasses.

"I'm Summoner Blackthorne and we need to speak to the Summoner Advocate," Riley said politely. This had to be one of Mort's reanimates, and from the way she spoke, not someone her master knew.

"He isn't here," the woman replied solemnly.

"Can you tell me where to find him?"

"He is at the Summoners Society."

Riley's brow furrowed. "Okay, I'll send him a text message. Is Alex home?"

"No. He is with his uncle."

"I see. Thank you for your help."

Another nod and then the door slowly closed.

"She does really well," Riley said as they walked away. "Not all reanimates are that sharp. But then Mort is exceptionally kind to his people."

"I still think it's strange."

"It is, but trapping demons or exorcising them is strange too. It all depends on how you look at it."

"Do you summon the dead?"

"No," Riley said, shaking her head emphatically. "Not my thing. My dad was called out of his grave, and I can't do that to anyone else."

"Oh." There was so much Katia didn't know about her

master.

"You heard from Simon yet?" At her nod, she added, "Is he still at the monastery? It's hard to tell from the pictures he sends me."

"No, he's done his meditating with the monks thing, and now he's hiking in North Georgia somewhere. And he's training at a dojo. He sends me a lot of pictures of wildlife." She sighed. "Mostly squirrels."

Riley chuckled. "You get squirrels, I get pictures of trees. Lots and *lots* of trees. I still can't believe he's really *on vacation*."

"He didn't have a choice. The dude at the Vatican told him to take two weeks off. It *wasn't* a suggestion."

"Ah, I wondered."

"Honestly, he needed it," Katia admitted. "Simon's been really tired lately."

"Then it's good he's where he is. I'll keep smiling every time he sends me another tree."

"I'll do the same with all those damned squirrels."

When they reached the car Riley paused to fire off a text, then tapped her foot while waiting for a reply. Katia leaned against the vehicle and yawned.

A ping sounded. "Well, Mort is in a meeting at the Summoners Society which means the crap has already hit the fan, as my dad would say."

"Do I need to be there?" Katia asked, crossing her fingers. *Please say no.*

"Yes, they'll want to hear what happened."

"Damn," she muttered.

"Yeah, damn."

TWO

The solemn tranquility of the monastery had given way to the majesty of the deep forest. Or so Simon Adler told himself. No matter where he was, he truly needed this sabbatical, a respite from exorcising Hellspawn even if it meant communing with trees, wildlife, and the occasional hiker.

Simon had spent five days in prayer at the monastery, examining his life, and his soul. The monks had understood that need for silence, so he'd been left alone unless he wished to speak with someone. Though some might think such contemplation was easy, it was anything but.

First, he'd had to shut off his chattering brain. It kept bringing up memories, some good, some unbelievably bad. Once he'd calmed it down, he'd assessed his life and relationships, his personal biases, and his job. Not all the revelations he'd received were bad. Some had been genuinely surprising.

He had to admit that he'd made progress since his near-death experience the year before, but he had a long way to go. That was what being human was all about. He was less judgmental, which was good. He also knew that he still had blind spots, and those troubled him.

In his personal life, Simon realized how much he'd been avoiding conflict with certain members of his family. Part of that hesitancy was to maintain familial harmony, but often it was just chickening out because he didn't want to face the pushback. That wasn't fair to him or the other members of his family.

The Old Simon had often wondered if a monastic life was his calling, but the New Simon recognized that wasn't his thing. Celibacy was a choice, and it wasn't going to be his. He'd learned that in Ireland during last year's sabbatical. Now he exorcised demons and was good at it. All things in balance, as they say.

This week he was hiking in the Blue Ridge Mountains in the northern part of the state, checking out various trails, building up his stamina while chilling out. He liked hiking, but it seemed odd to be trudging along without a bunch of siblings under foot. And all the noise that went with that Herd of Adlers, as his dad called them. Like most Dad jokes, it was lame, but Simon still smiled every time he thought of it.

The Adler clan totaled eight children, neatly divided between males and females. The last time he'd been hiking in this area it'd been with the whole family, ten of them total, plus two energetic Golden Retrievers. That meant two minivans crammed with food and gear. He'd been sixteen at that point, his eldest sister, Deanna, twenty-three, and the youngest, Misha, was still a baby. Now Dee was twenty-eight and Misha was six. Time really did fly.

This trip it was just him, and for the first time in Simon's life he missed being with people. He missed Katia and Riley. He could just imagine what they'd be like on this hike. He suspected Katia would love being out here in the wilderness. Riley, not so much. She was a city girl.

But he needed time away, which was why he was doing his best to not check his emails and texts until the end of each day. It would be so easy to get sucked back into their lives and miss the whole point of why he was not exorcising demons at the moment.

Rest, relax, reconnect. That had been his mantra since his superior at the Vatican told him he needed a sabbatical. Father Rosetti was right: Lay exorcists burned out all too quickly, and even Simon saw the warning signs in his own life.

He hiked along savoring the fresh air and the lack of fiends trying to kill him. The kinds of things other people took for granted. But not for a lay exorcist. Which is why he'd also been attending classes at a nearby dojo, honing his skills in combat. Again, all things in balance.

Ahead of him, poised in a tree, was a colorful bird. His sister Amy would know exactly what kind it was, but he wasn't into that kind of thing. Since it was so pretty, Simon pulled out his phone and took a picture. He'd send it to Katia tonight. That's what he'd done for the last few days, along with a lot of pictures of squirrels, just to mess with her head.

She'd always send back an amusing comment, and they made him feel good. He truly missed her, though he'd yet to tell her that. They'd become friends far quicker than either of them had expected, but being sent to Hell's living room together would do that. Katia could have easily sold him out to Lucifer to save her brother's life, but she hadn't. It was that courage, that inner fire, which had made her special in his eyes. Maybe someday he'd tell her that.

A sound on the trail behind him made him turn. Then he blinked. The figure approaching him wasn't a hiker, or a birdwatcher. This one had white wings. They weren't out in full display, but he could see their tips just behind her shoulders. Brilliant blue eyes, somber expression. That narrowed down what this might be.

"Divine," Simon said. Whether it was a Fallen or one of Heaven's crew he wasn't sure yet.

"Simon Michael David Adler," the figure replied.

It appeared as a short female with bright blue eyes, mahogany skin and long, pale blonde hair. She wore a green gown, the color of new grass, which was knotted at the waist with a piece of worn rope. Perched on a shoulder was a small tawny owl who studied him soberly.

He'd thought he'd caught a glimpse of her before, though he hadn't been sure until now. "You followed me from the monastery."

She nodded in reply. The owl swiveled its head around to check behind them. A chirp came, then it turned back toward Simon. Owls always fascinated him, this one especially.

"You train in war while seeking peace," the newcomer said.

That was one way to say what he was doing at the dojo,

along with all the prayer and exercise.

"I am doing that, yes."

The raptor ruffled its feathers.

"Trust your instincts, Simon Michael David Adler. Matters are in flux so you must be on your guard. There is danger for you and the ones you care about. Do *not* assume your eyes are lying to you."

Before he could reply the pair vanished, leaving behind only the trees and the hiking trail. The angel was one of Heaven's crew as there was no bait offered to try to secure his soul.

"Thank you, Divine. May you and your companion be safe in the Light."

In the distance he heard the hoot of an owl, causing him to smile.

Instincts. Be on my guard.

Simon gave a sigh and continued his hike. He'd always trusted his instincts, but now he would be doubly vigilant because the Divine's warning wasn't just for him, but also for those back home.

†✳‡✳†

Riley had been to the Summoners Society so often that it didn't really register any longer. Not so with Katia, who stared at the building as if she wasn't quite sure what to make of it. And when Riley removed the long dark-blue robe from its vinyl case in the car's trunk, and pulled it on, her journeyman's eyebrows rose.

"At the Trappers Guild, I'm Master Blackthorne. Here, I'm Summoner Blackthorne." She pointed at her robe. "You always dress for the part you're playing, wherever you are."

"That sorta makes sense. What are these people like?"

"They're like trappers. Some are nice, some are not. You're here with me so if someone hassles you, I will get in their face, depending on the color of their robe. If the robe is darker than mine, Mort will step in. You're good, no matter what."

The trapper gave a quick nod, then went back to eying the

building. That intensity was one of the things that Katia was known for. She rarely missed the minute details, which is why she was so good with the Trappers Guild paperwork. It might also explain why she was more tuned into the supernatural than most.

"Any more trouble from your former master?" Riley asked.

A sigh returned. "Master Kelly kept sending me nasty texts. I blocked him so he switched to emails. I blocked him again."

"Well, that doesn't surprise me. I've heard, *unofficially*, that the National Guild has done a full audit of the Lawrence Guild's finances."

"They found something, right?"

"They'll have the results in a couple of days. My guess is that Master Kelly is going to have a lot more to worry about than you."

Katia's face lit up. "That totally works. I wonder how many other trappers he screwed over. Besides me, that is."

"We'll know soon enough." Riley turned her attention to what awaited them inside. "Let's get this done. I have apprentices to train, and you need to get some sleep." She hadn't missed the dark circles under the journeyman's eyes, or the frequent yawning.

"Yes, please." Followed by another lengthy yawn.

The three-story gray stone building that was home to the Summoners Society appeared to be in excellent condition. "How old is this place?" Katia asked.

"Civil War era," Riley replied as she pushed open one of the front doors.

The interior was just as old as the exterior, but still nice. They were met with a spotless granite floor, soft paint colors, the whole works. Somebody had spent money on this place.

"Pretty fancy, huh?" her master said. "It managed to survive General Sherman's occupation. I'm glad it did because it's rather grand. Oh, and we'll be met by a butler. Summoners are a bit old-fashioned."

Further away, sitting at a desk, was a black-suited gentleman. When he signed them in he studied Katia's trapping license without comment. Then returned it.

"Where may I find Senior Summoner Alexander?" Riley asked.

"He's in the boardroom, Summoner Blackthorne," was the polite reply, though the man was still watching Katia closely.

"Thank you, Rogers."

Katia trailed behind her master as they headed deeper into the building, the hem of Riley's robe making swishing noises on the stone floor. After a couple long hallways, each lined with brass wall sconces, her master finally stopped at a door, made a gesture in the air, then waited.

"I let Mort know we're here."

A brief time later the door opened and Mort stepped out, closing it behind him. Unlike the other times she'd seen him, his face was drawn, as if whatever was happening inside that room was going badly.

"You said you have something to tell me about the reanimations last night," he said.

"Plural?" Riley said. He nodded. "Well, we're here because of what went down at Brentwood Cemetery. You need to hear this because it involves Alex."

Mort frowned. "Let me guess: My nephew broke a circle and stole a corpse."

Riley blinked at that news. "No, he tried to, though. That happen somewhere else?"

"It did. One of the grave sitters had to go to the emergency room because of it. The mayor called his lordship. You know what that means."

"Yeah, I do."

Katia could just guess how that conversation went.

Mort concentrated, then nodded as if he'd heard something they hadn't. "Lord Ozymandias wants you to report what happened last night." He was looking directly at Katia now.

"Okay, we're on." Riley said. "Remember, we have your back. Show respect, but don't take any crap."

Katia stifled a groan as Mort ushered them into the boardroom, a long and narrow space with a polished black oval table set in the middle. The walls were a muted gray and there were no colorful accents anywhere. Katia wasn't sure if that was a power statement or a lack of decorating savvy. The room smelled of coffee and aftershave. She did a quick nose count: Seven necros, including Alex, the real one this time. He was noticeably pale and his eyes radiated fear. A faint bruise sat on his right cheek.

One necromancer immediately caught her attention, an older man with silver hair and oddly colored eyes. He wore a black robe, and the glowing green sigil in the middle of his forehead said he was someone powerful.

"Lord Ozymandias, my fellow summoners," Riley began, confirming her guess as to his identity. "This is Journeyman Katia Breman of the Atlanta Guild. She was grave sitting last night and was attacked by a summoner. She is willing to provide information about that attack."

"Your timing is fortuitous. Join us," Lord Ozymandias said, gesturing.

They filed down to the end of the table, then took their seats. Katia dropped her hands in her lap, then realized her fists were still clenched. It took effort to relax them. It wasn't her on trial here, but she knew exactly how that felt.

"I don't see where we need to hear anything further," a summoner said. He was younger, with light brown eyes. His robe was dark brown which meant he had significant magical ability, but not at the level of Summoner Alexander or the dude with the glowing forehead.

"I have already told you it wasn't me last night," Alex protested.

"Three grave sitters described you exactly. I'm sure the fourth would if she wasn't in the hospital."

Katia gave her master a quick glance and wasn't surprised to see Riley's annoyed expression.

"Your observations are duly noted, Summoner Vazio." The most senior necromancer turned toward Katia now. "Please tell us what happened last evening, Journeyman," his lordship commanded.

Katia cleared her throat, then told her tale. As she did, she watched the faces of the necros. Most appeared willing to listen, but two of them did not. Alex kept his attention on her, while Mort had his eyes closed as he listened intently to her report.

"The summoner who attacked the circle looked like Summoner . . . " She'd blanked on Alex's last name.

"Greene," Riley whispered.

"He looked like Summoner Greene, but it wasn't him. His voice was wrong and there was a hazy outline around him."

"You saw a glamour?" Mort asked, his eyes open now.

"Yes."

"I doubt that trappers are that sensitive," Vazio said. Then he seemed to realize he'd dissed her boss. "With a few exceptions, of course."

"Most aren't," Riley cut in. "Journeyman Bremen has a gift for seeing through glamours and illusions."

"Really," was the flat reply. He might as well of called her master a liar.

"I'm not sure if that is enough to convince me," another remarked.

"I can see Divines, as well," Katia admitted. "It's just something I'm good at."

"That's rather hard to test, don't you think?" Vazio replied, folding his arms on the table. He seemed to be the most insistent that Alex had been the culprit.

"Not really. I've seen three in Atlanta already. Master Blackthorne can confirm that."

Riley gave a nod.

"I'm sure that might be the case, but you're the only one who claims it wasn't Apprentice Summoner Greene last evening. We have four corpses stolen and someone must be held accountable."

"As I have said, repeatedly, Alex does not have that kind of magical capability. He's barely handling illusions at this point," Mort insisted.

"When I arrived at the cemetery this morning, I felt the residual magic from the attempt to break the circle," Riley added. "It was immensely powerful. It's not anyone I've met in this society."

"Well, in some ways that's a relief, but it will make our task harder. I will examine the magical signature and see if it is familiar."

"It was already fading by the time we left, so you might not be able to sense it."

"Very convenient," Vazio replied.

Riley gave him a frown. "It wasn't Alex. That means someone is masquerading as him and stealing the dead. Next time this thief might show up as you. Is that what you want?"

"Ah . . . " Apparently, that hadn't occurred to him. "No, of course not."

Ozymandias cleared his throat. "Then we must find who this is and stop them. The last thing we need is the public thinking we're reanimating corpses without permission." He looked over at Riley now. "May we count on the Trappers Guild's assistance with this?"

"Of course. The Summoners Society has watched our backs often enough so it's only right that we help you anyway we can."

"Thank you." Those strange eyes moved to Alex now. "You will remain at your uncle's home until further notice. If you must leave, you are to be accompanied by a summoner so they can testify as to your whereabouts. Do you understand?"

Alex swallowed hard, then nodded.

One of the attendees, a woman, shifted in her chair. She was older, her dark hair up in a soft bun. Katia wasn't sure where her dark red robe stood in terms of the power in this room, but something told her this one wasn't to be messed with.

"Lady Torin?" his lordship asked. "You wish to weigh in on this matter?"

"I do." She looked at Alex now. "Perhaps it would be best if

Summoner Greene stayed at my home. That way there will be no questions as to impartiality."

His lordship appeared pleased at that suggestion. "I agree. That way no one may say his uncle allowed him to wander around unsupervised while we sort out this matter."

"I'll do whatever you need," Alex said. "I can't even get a glamour spell right at this point. Someone else is trying to frame me, and I want that bastard found."

"Language," Vazio cautioned.

"I'd call him worse than that," Lady Torin replied, and Riley nodded her agreement.

"Is this somehow retribution against you, Mortimer?" one of the necros asked.

"I don't know," Mort admitted. "I haven't annoyed anyone recently, but we summoners have very long memories."

"And we hold grudges," Ozymandias said, looking directly at Vazio at this point. He tidied up the papers in front of him. "I believe Summoner Blackthorne and Journeyman Bremen are no longer required at this meeting. The rest of us need to remain. We have *much* to discuss."

As Katia walked past Alex's chair, she heard a murmured, "Thanks." She touched his shoulder, then followed her master out the door.

Tempting as it was to vent, Katia held her silence. There were so many dynamics bouncing around that meeting room, and not all of them related to who was ripping off corpses.

As they walked across the parking lot to Riley's car, Katia finally allowed herself to relax. "I know they don't spook you, but those guys are way scary. At least to me."

"They can be. There's a lot of power in that room."

"Alex didn't do it. I know that."

"No, he didn't. You saw that bruise on his cheek?" Katia nodded. "He was learning how to do glamours the other day and one backfired. He's nowhere near the level of the summoner you battled at the cemetery." She paused and added, "That one was stronger than Mort, which is very bad news."

Stronger than the Summoner Advocate? That was scary.

"What happens now?"

"I'll drop you off at Simon's so you can get some sleep."

"Sounds good." Food, sleep, then maybe even more sleep.

Riley's phone rang. "Blackthorne." Her expression went from alert to surprised. "Ah, we're at the Summoners Society. I can be there in about twenty minutes." A pause. "Okay, thanks."

As she removed her robe and carefully packed it away in its case, she seemed pre-occupied.

"Trouble?" Katia asked.

"Maybe. The cops found something strange downtown. They want it checked out." Her master thought for a few seconds, then shook her head. "Probably nothing important. The police aren't good with odd stuff, so they call us when they don't know what to do with something."

"It's out of your way to take me back to Simon's. Can you drop me near a bus stop and I'll figure it out from there?"

"Okay, that I can do. There's one a few blocks from here."

From Riley's tone, there was more going on downtown than just something odd, but Katia didn't want to ask. Meeting Atlanta's most senior corpse collectors had been scary enough.

† ✳ ‡ ✳ †

Getting back to Simon's house took bus time, some more bus time, and then some walking. Though she was tired, the exercise seemed to help clear her brain fog.

Hopefully, the summoners would find their thief, deal with the fool, and then Alex could go back to learning newbie spells. At least it looked like Mort trusted Lady Torin to watch over his nephew, so that was a relief.

Katia hadn't intended on staying at Simon's house while he was on vacation, just checking the place daily, but then her plans changed. Right before Simon headed out, Grand Master Stewart had flown off to Scotland to visit his family. Then Mrs. Ayers, his housekeeper, announced that while he was away they were having the old house painted, interior and exterior.

Mrs. Ayers had assured Katia she could stay during the renovations, but she knew the paint smell would drive her out. After a long night of trapping or exorcisms often the only time she could sleep was during the day. That wouldn't be possible with painters tromping around on scaffolding and making lots of noise.

Simon immediately came to the rescue. He'd *insisted* she stay at his house, especially since she was going to be watching the place anyway. The plan worked great: She was out of the painters' way and Simon's elegant old Craftsman house was a great place to crash. And though she loved living at Grand Master Stewart's home, it was nice to be on her own. The only downside was that she had to cook for herself. She missed those massive breakfasts Mrs. Ayers insisted on making for her and the grand master. The food was so good Katia was regaining some of the weight she'd lost in Lawrence, one stack of pancakes at a time.

Pausing at the end of the driveway, she retrieved Simon's mail. Today it was a large brown envelope from the Vatican, it felt like a magazine inside, and a smaller envelope from Ireland. No doubt he'd appreciate both.

Simon's week away had given her time to think about her future here in Atlanta. She knew she wanted to stay because Lawrence didn't do it for her anymore. Too much family drama and too many bad memories with the Guild there. Atlanta was a fresh start and so far she hadn't screwed that up.

It was time for her to find an apartment. She'd been held back by the lack of money, but a few days ago most of the wages that her former master had stolen had appeared in her bank account in one very satisfying chunk. The National Guild had forwarded an accounting of those funds, and promised to send further amounts, as necessary. No doubt once the audit was complete.

Karma really did exist.

But housing was expensive here, so she'd need a roommate. There'd been roomies over the years because of finances, but she preferred being on her own. That was one of the reasons she envied Simon's living arrangements.

"Lucky guy," she murmured as she walked up the driveway. The day was already heating up, so being inside in the air conditioning was going to feel good. In many ways the weather here was just like at home; hot, humid, and likely to stay that way. At least until fall.

Katia had just reached the front porch when her phone pinged with an incoming email. To her surprise, it was from one of the landlords she'd contacted late last week. He'd be happy to let her see his apartment, but she reread the next line, twice.

"Viewing fee?" she said, frowning. "Fifty bucks to see your place?"

The email stated the fee would be credited toward the first month's rent if she decided to sign a lease. If not, he kept the fifty.

"No way. What a scam."

Grumbling under her breath, she tucked her phone away, let herself in the front door and disabled the alarm. As had become habit, she took a very deep breath savoring the smell of the house. The old wood floors had a scent of their own, as well as the bouquet of flowers on the dining room table. Flowers that had been waiting for her the first day she'd moved in. Bit by bit Simon was claiming this space as his own, and that gave her more joy than she thought possible.

He deserves a home, a place that gives him peace. And so do I.

Of course, the first night she'd stayed here she'd checked out every room. She told herself it was to ensure all the windows were securely locked, but in truth she was just nosy, as her grandmother would say.

Simon's bedroom was larger than the other two, his king bed neatly made with a duvet in light and dark gray stripes. The pillowcases were deep red, which made for a nice contrast. The room was a pale gray and a large crucifix hung on the wall opposite the bed, the last thing he'd see at night. Just what you'd expect for a man who worked for the Vatican.

His bathroom had a tub and a separate shower, all in white tile with blue accents. That was pure luxury. No doubt he needed the tub to relax after a long day of yanking Hell's assholes out of unsuspecting people.

His kitchen always made her sigh in envy as the former owner, one of Simon's relatives, had spent a lot of cash installing the latest appliances. Unlike most kitchens, the counters were almost empty with only a toaster and a coffeemaker in one corner. The rest was a length of pristine multi-colored marble.

The media room at the rear of the house had a big screen television and comfy chairs, but not much else. The television was a recent addition. That room had a slider that led to a backyard with tall cedar fencing on three sides. *Cedar.* She knew to the penny how much that stuff cost because she was a third-generation landscaper. Simon's uncle must have really loved this place. And now it was his.

Two lawn chairs leaned against the side of the house, and there was a brand-new grill tucked under a shiny black cover. The one thing that bugged her were the bare flower beds. Two long raised beds, one to the left, the other in front of her. Not one flower. Even in the corner where a statue of the Virgin Mary had just been added. Maybe she could help him with that.

Katia had just made it back into the house when she heard a noise at the front door. It sounded as if someone was trying to unlock it. The noise ceased and someone swore under their breath.

Swinging open the front door revealed a young woman a few years older than her, with shoulder-length blonde hair. Her eyes were the same bright blue as Simon's and she had the same cheekbones. It was a good bet she was in one of the family photos on the dining room wall.

"You're not Simon," the woman exclaimed, her surprise registering more as indignation than anything.

Katia resisted the temptation to be a smartass. "I am not. Can I help you?"

"I'm Deanna. Simon's eldest sister."

Katia didn't know the personal dynamics of the Adler clan, but she'd heard Simon mutter this sister's name a time or two. There always seemed to be an edge to it when he did.

"Hi. I'm Katia."

That earned her a frown. "I couldn't open the door. Is something wrong with the lock?"

"No, it worked fine for me."

"Is Simon here?"

"No, sorry he isn't. I'm housesitting for him."

The lady didn't seem to know what to do with that statement. "He's not here? Where is he? Why didn't he tell me he was going somewhere?"

Because he didn't think you needed to know?

"He's on sabbatical. He'll be back in a few days."

"But what if I need to talk to him?" the woman demanded.

"Your mother has his contact information," Katia said, hoping that would defuse the situation before it got ugly.

"But why are *you* here?"

"Because he asked me to watch his house?"

Like I already said?

"But who are you? Are you dating my brother?"

This was the Spanish Inquisition, Atlanta style.

"No, we're not dating. I work with Simon and that's why he asked me to housesit."

"You can't work with him. The Vatican doesn't allow women to do that."

Katia's patience was fading, fast.

"Yes, but a demon trapper *can* watch your brother's back during an exorcism, which is what I do. If there's nothing more, I need to get back at it." Or in this case, food and a long nap.

Deanna seemed utterly confused, as if this wasn't something she'd ever encountered before. Every family had that one busybody, as her grandmother called them, someone who'd designated themselves as the center of that familial universe, and upon whom all others must depend. She guessed that was this lady's role and probably why Simon muttered under his breath when her name was mentioned.

"Well, I'll call him," his sister announced. "That way he can verify you're supposed to be here. You could be anyone, you know?"

"He probably won't answer since he's on sabbatical. Call your mom. She'll straighten it out for you."

"You better be who you say you are."

"Luckily, I am."

And then Katia shut the door because she'd had more than enough.

There was another swear word, followed by a "Why didn't he tell me?" A short time later a car door slammed and the sister departed.

"Well, that was special," she said, shaking her head.

Tempting as it was to email Simon about the visit, Katia held off. He was on vacation, one he desperately needed, and she would do everything in her power not to ruin it. Besides, she bet she'd be seeing the Annoying Sister again. People like that just didn't know when to back off.

THREE

After a few hours' nap, Katia made her way to the trapping office, and then promptly volunteered to help Riley with her apprentices during their trip into Demon Central. For Katia, it was always fun to watch her boss in training mode. From what she'd heard, both of Riley's parents had been teachers so she was hardwired for this.

"Grade Three Hellspawn, especially Gastro-Fiends, are totally disgusting," her master said. "They will rip you up in a heartbeat if you're not paying attention. If you doubt me, both Katia and I have scars to show you."

The apprentices, Tim and Mickey, were riveted on what their master was saying, not blowing her off like some might. Always a good thing when the Hellspawn you were trapping could make a meal of you in minutes.

Katia really liked these guys, though they were nothing alike. Tim wore black, round-rimmed glasses and was anything but athletic. Mickey could have been playing pro football for a living. And yet the two of them riffed off each other like they'd been friends for years. Sort of like her and Simon.

Thinking of him always made her smile, which meant she wasn't paying attention to their surroundings.

"Any special tips, Journeyman?" Riley asked.

Of course, her boss had noticed that Katia had spaced off.

"The things have one track minds—food is what they live for. Doesn't matter what it is, if they think they can eat it they'll give it a chomp. The trick is not to be their next meal. They don't seem to be that bright, but they're devious and that gives them an edge."

The two apprentices nodded, then each looked around as if a Three was about to pounce on them.

"Let's see if we can scare up one of these monsters. You two will watch as Katia and I trap it. Next time around we'll have one of you give it a go," Riley explained.

"It'll be fun," Katia added, just for devilment.

"Yeah, fun," Tim said, eyeing the scars on her arms.

In the past she'd hidden them, but not now. As Riley had said, the marks were something to be proud of. It'd just taken her a while to realize that.

They went at least three blocks into the center of Atlanta and didn't see one Gastro-Fiend. A rat scurried by, then another, each intent on its own ratty business.

"If the rodents are doing their thing, there isn't a Three nearby," Riley said, shaking her head.

"Master Jackson said there's been fewer demons in the last couple of days," Tim said.

"Looks like he's right."

A strange pop came from the alley they'd just passed, followed by an unearthly chuckle.

"What was that?" Mickey asked, looking around.

Katia had heard that sound before. It'd been in an apartment building where she and Simon had exorcised a fiend out of a bestselling author.

She gave Riley a look. "That sounded a lot like a Big Mouth."

Her master's eyes widened. "You sure?"

The eerie chuckle came again, this time louder.

"Oh yeah, I'm sure."

Riley immediately sobered. "Okay, change of plans. If Katia is right, this is a new *Grade Four* demon, so not at all something you want to tackle. The National Guild is still working on the official name for the monster because it's just so freakin' strange."

"I'll check it out. Maybe I'm wrong," Katia offered, making her way into the alley. Behind her Riley began moving her apprentices out of harm's way.

The scar on her arm twitched. Then a Hellspawn slowly trundled her way.

"Oh, shit," she said under her breath. "It's a Big Mouth," she called out. "And it's about to start cloning itself."

"You think it's a trap?" Riley asked, at her side now.

That was a good question. "Maybe."

No matter how you looked at it, Lucifer's latest creation was just bizarre even by his Hellish standards. Taller than Katia, well over six feet, it really did resemble a big lime green beach ball with spindly flamingo-style legs. Then there were the tentacles, three on each side, which had flesh-ripping teeth along their entire length. At least its eyes were amber, not the fiery red like most demons.

It was as if the Prince had been really bored one day and decided to create a new Hellspawn based on whatever spare parts he had left over. The bizzarro result was the abomination waddling down the alley toward them.

"What the . . . ?" Mickey exclaimed.

The demon kept moving closer, its mouth widening as its body started to glow an unearthly red. The thing was about to reproduce.

Katia extracted a Holy Water sphere, then gave Riley a quick look. "Toss and run?"

"No," her master said, shaking her head. "I've got an idea." She grabbed onto the sphere and trotted back to where Mickey stood, and then whispered something to him.

The apprentice grinned. "You got it!" he said, adjusting the sphere in his hands.

He took a few steps forward, almost even with Katia now, then tossed that sphere at the fiend in an impressive overhead arc.

"No way," she murmured.

As he had no doubt planned, the sphere dipped down just at the right moment, then ploughed directly into the fiend's huge mouth. A crunch, a choking sound, and then before Katia could yell a warning there was a muted explosion.

The last time this happened the sphere triggered the same response and had fountained bits of demon all over a building's lobby. And Katia. This time something contained all that, a clear bubble that seemed to glow from within.

It took a moment to realize that her exceptionally talented boss had created the magical equivalent of a snow globe. Except now the interior of that globe quickly became obscured with severed tentacles, stringy pieces of gnarled fiend, and whatever gawd awful stuff lived inside that beast. Katia swallowed, twice, to keep from hurling.

The magical bubble slowly shrank as the interior's contents flamed and turned to ash. Then it vanished and the ashes landed on the alley's grimy pavement in a neat little mound.

"*That* was damned impressive," Katia said as she shot a thumbs-up at Mickey. "Dude! Wow!"

"I agree," Riley said, grinning. Then she turned back to her apprentices. "This is the second one of these things we've seen so far. We haven't figured out a way to trap them yet. That may not be possible, like with the Geo-Fiends."

"So that's all it does?" Mickey asked.

As Riley explained the birthing process, how it cloned small ravenous versions of itself in a matter of minutes, Katia wandered down the alley. The ashes were all they had to prove there'd been a demon, so collecting a trapping fee wasn't going to happen. Still, it'd been a great learning experience for the newbies and no one had gotten hurt.

"Ah, that was cool and all that, but what if you're not with us when one of those obscenities shows up?" Tim quizzed.

As the master explained the "slam dunk" method, Katia noticed movement further down the alley. A familiar figure stepped out of the dingy brick wall; a figure that could only be described as otherworldly.

The first time she'd seen her was at the TrapperCon convention. The Lady, as Katia called her, had brilliant red hair adorned with green ferns and alabaster skin. She was Katia's height and of slight build. Now she looked weathered, the ferns dying, her face no longer pure white but a sickly gray. As if she'd been ill.

"Are you okay?" Katia asked, stepping forward.

The Lady hesitated for a moment, opening her mouth as if to say something, then shook her head. A few seconds later she vanished into the wall beyond.

Since the others were engaged in a lively discussion of alternative tactics to take down a Big Mouth, Katia made her way along the narrow passage to examine where The Lady had entered and exited. Both were solid brick walls. And yet on the ground between them was a single fern. As she watched, it rapidly wilted, then turned to dust.

She is real.

The Vatican didn't consider skills with a bladed weapon important for an exorcist, but Simon had quickly learned otherwise. Often he found himself up against incredibly lethal Hellspawn, so anything that evened his chances of survival were vital. He figured if Rome's Demon Hunters used melee weapons, so would he. He'd fought with a sword before, had even killed an Archfiend, but he knew he needed to up his game. The last few days' private training sessions had shown him just how much more he needed to learn.

Now, despite a long hot shower and the over-the-counter pain meds, he still ached. Given the intense workout he'd received, this was expected. The other thing he'd learned was the dojo had an instructor who was proficient with a bō, a staff used in Japanese martial arts training. And that the instructor had a class tonight.

For the second time today Simon entered the training center. To him, it smelled of hope and sweat. As he walked through the building he passed a Tai Chi class in one of the rooms, slowly shifting positions in concert with their instructor. More hunting brought him to the room where the bōjitsu class was just beginning. With a nod toward the instructor, he took a seat on the floor, leaning against the wall. Then shifted around until he found a way for his sword arm not to cramp.

The class lasted for an hour and at no time was Simon bored. This martial art fascinated him because it was something that Katia loved. He only knew about that because Riley had told him that the trapper's birthday was coming up, and then she'd sent him a video of Katia working out with her staff. It'd been filmed while she was still in Kansas, well before events had taken so much of a toll. Back then she'd looked healthy, not skinny like now, her hair shoulder length.

Katia had mentioned that she'd had to pawn some of her belongings so she'd have money for food and a place to stay. Since it hadn't come on the bus with her from Lawrence, he bet the bō was history. But maybe he could change that.

As Simon observed the class he'd learned a few things: Not only could the weapon be lethal, but Katia was more advanced than these intermediate level students. Yet another surprise.

After the class ended and all the students had cleared out, he made his way to the instructor. She was putting away the practice staves. She was an Asian lady, probably in her forties, and had an intensity about her that reminded him of Katia.

"Excuse me. I have a few questions about using a bō. Do you have time right now?"

The instructor smiled. "I do have time. I'm Himari. And you are Simon from Atlanta. I heard you did well in sword practice today."

He groaned, gingerly moving his right arm, and trying not to wince when it complained. "I think I overdid it."

"We all do that from time to time. It's how we learn. What do you want to know about the bō?"

He pulled out his phone and showed her the picture of Katia with her staff. "My friend had to sell hers because of, well, financial problems. I want to buy her one just like it. Is that possible?"

Himari studied the image. "Yes, it is possible. Is she a new student or does she have some experience?"

"I'll show you."

Simon pulled up the video while sincerely hoping Katia wouldn't mind him sharing it. Then tried not to fidget as he waited for the instructor's verdict.

Himari watched the video, twice, then nodded. "This young woman is skilled. She has spent many hours in training."

Did Katia know how good she was? Maybe not.

"Are there ones that are shorter? Katia's a demon trapper, so carrying around a long staff isn't always an option."

The instructor handed back his phone. "Let's go to the weapons room and I'll show you what your choices might be."

"That would be great. Thank you."

A short time later, Simon had been shown all the various options, along with a spirited demonstration of each by the instructor. The lady was very good, and he resisted asking just how many years she'd been perfecting her skills.

"Trappers sometimes use a steel pipe to stop a demon." He pointed at an expandable metal staff. "Do you think that would be strong enough?"

"It can be, depending on which type of Hellspawn," the instructor replied, giving the bō a test spin. "Some do not like these because they feel the balance is off. Yet I know a trapper in Chicago who uses one. He says he likes it better than a steel pipe. More versatile in terms of attack points."

Which made sense. If you could drop a demon to its knees or on the ground, you gained the upper hand.

"But it is also more flexible and that can be an issue. It all depends on who is wielding it."

He had no doubt Katia would work around any limitations. "Okay, then I'd like one of those."

"Which color?"

"Ah, blue." Katia loved that color and the accents on the pipe would make it stand out. "And I'd like to have one of the traditional wooden ones, too."

The instructor raised an eyebrow. "This must be a very good

friend of yours."

The trapper from Kansas was more than a friend, Simon knew that now. It was one of the revelations he'd had during his retreat.

"Katia has saved my life more than once. I'll never be able to repay her, no matter the cost."

"Then you are a trapper, too?"

"Yes." Among other things.

"Ah, but perhaps it is your friendship that is the repayment, not the material items?" the woman asked.

It was an incredibly insightful comment, and Simon took it to heart.

"Perhaps you are right."

"How tall is she? That matters in terms of the length of the staff."

"Almost as tall as I am. The top of her head reaches my nose."

With a knowing nod Himari took him to the dojo's office. To his relief they had both staves in stock, so he paid for them, repeatedly thanked her, and then headed back to his hotel room with his purchases in hand.

Later that evening, sitting up in bed with a cold pack on his sword arm, he couldn't stop smiling. He might still be tired and sore, but he had just found two great birthday presents, ones Katia would never expect.

Now he couldn't wait to get home.

Once again, Katia found herself at the cemetery to watch over the still-deceased Albert Means. No one had called in sick this time, but there wasn't a line of folks eager to tangle with a necro after last night's adventure. So here she was because she needed the money. If the necro showed up he was in for one helluva tough time because Riley was sitting vigil with her. Her master had also insisted that Katia would get the entire vigil fee.

"We might get lucky and nail this sucker," her boss said, grinning.

Or not.

The cemetery looked no different than the night before, though fresh flowers had appeared on a nearby grave. When Katia paused in front of it, she realized one of her feet was resting on the grave itself. She stepped back immediately.

"I am so sorry. I didn't mean to do that." As if the dead could hear her.

It was a Breman family thing—you didn't walk on a grave. This one had a vase buried partway in the recently disturbed soil. There was a bouquet of yellow roses inside, though the petals were already beginning to droop.

"Anna Lee Lanier," she murmured, reading the temporary placard that announced the deceased's particulars. A check of dates of birth and death said she'd barely made her twenty-eighth birthday and had died three weeks earlier.

"You can't see them, but the roses are beautiful. Someone misses you very much." A faint breeze blew across her face now, as if in acknowledgement.

Katia headed off toward Means' grave, eager to catch up with Riley. The current grave sitter was a young man, probably in his late twenties. He had a pale complexion, wavy dark hair, and glasses. Then he sneezed, twice.

"You have a cold?" Riley asked.

He nodded. "I should have been here yesterday afternoon, but I was too sick." He gave Katia a long look. "You were on the news today."

"Yeah, I bet I was."

The guy quickly stashed his empty juice bottle into a ratty khaki backpack, then rose. Reciting the phrase that allowed them to cross the protective border, he gave the grave one last look and then headed across the cemetery grounds without another word.

"What a cheery dude," Katia mumbled.

It took them a few minutes to get their gear set up, then they reset the circle because Riley wanted to enlarge it. Katia let her go for it because it certainly wasn't her that wielded magic in this duo.

Once the Holy Water and candles were placed and the new circle glowing away, Katia relaxed. The night was nice, she was earning money, and Riley was always full of interesting stories. They laid the tarp on the ground, then rolled out the sleeping bags. Once she was parked on hers, an unsolicited package came her way, one that contained strawberry Pop-Tarts, of all things.

"It's tradition, sort of," Riley explained. "Simon loves them, so we shared his supply when we sat vigil for my dad."

She knew that Simon had a fondness for those things, but there was a lot more in that explanation than just a memory. Maybe now was the time to find out just what had happened between them. "He said you two dated for a while."

"Yeah, we were just starting out and it was going really good and then, well, Hell messed us up," Riley admitted, her voice sad now. "Part of me is bummed it happened that way, but the other part knows that's why Den and I are together now. Simon's okay with how it all fell out. Well, at least once he stopped feeling so guilty about it."

"He still does a little, I think."

A nod returned. "Our exorcist carries a lot of guilt. He's getting better. You know, I actually cheered the first time I heard him swear."

Katia laughed. "He mumbles 'damn' every now and then, and I've heard him use the 'f' word once. I'm a very bad influence."

"Good for you. Simon always needed to loosen up. He's a much cooler person now." Riley eyed her. "He seems more at ease. Well, except for all the silly tree and squirrel pictures."

Katia had a theory about that. "Any chance he's just sending those to mess with our heads? Is that possible?"

Riley opened her own Pop-Tart, then hesitated before she took a bite. "You know, that makes sense. The old Simon—*no way*. I think the new one has some mischief in him. You don't see it very often, but it's there."

"Hmm. Maybe one of these days he'll start wearing

something other than those boring white shirts. He looks like he time-traveled here from the 1950s."

Riley laughed. "He does!"

"Simon works out and has serious muscles. He doesn't show them off, but they're there."

"Noticed that, did you?"

"I did," Katia admitted. "He's damned handsome. But you can't tell him I said that. It'd embarrass him." *And me.*

"I won't. Oh, Den mentioned something about going to a new BBQ place. Mama Z's is still his fave, but he says it never hurts to try something new. You and Simon could come with us, give my husband all sorts of grief about how Southern barbeque just isn't like the Midwestern kind."

Katia grinned, liking that idea. "That works for me." She finished her Pop-Tart before rearranging herself on the sleeping bag. "I'm not used to this. The joking around, you know? My parents pretty much shut me out when my brother got hurt, and then my job sucked after my first master died. It was damned grim there for a while."

"And now you're in with a bunch of oddball Southerners who shout a lot and make fun of each other." Riley smiled back at her. "You're doing just fine, Journeyman Breman. Don't let anyone say you're not." She paused and then asked, "Did you get the notice about the Guild meeting?" Katia gave a nod. "Good. You'll get to meet some of the others. Sadly, not all are house-trained."

She snorted. "That bad?"

"A few are seriously not good with females in the Guild. They gave me a megaton of crap when I was an apprentice, even when my dad was alive. There's more of us now so they've just had to suck it up. You'll hear lots of bitching and some smart-assed remarks. Ignore it unless they cross a line or get too lewd. Then nail them." She eyed her. "Unlike your last Guild, here you have backup."

"Still getting used to that," she admitted.

"I had backup, you get backup. That's the way it goes here."

They fell quiet after that. Riley began texting with her spouse, so Katia researched the occupant of the new grave.

Anna Lee Lanier. Born 1991 Died 2019.

Then she found the newspaper article. "She was murdered!" Katia blurted. At Riley's puzzled look, she pointed toward the grave in the distance. "The lady down there. I found a news article. Her husband was arrested. He says he's innocent."

"Man, that sucks. I wonder if he really did it."

"Isn't that what Alex wants to do—call up the dead to find out what really happened to them?"

"It is. That might be even harder for him now after what happened last night. Mort managed to keep his name out of the news, but summoners gossip like anyone else."

"So, he's toast just because of that lying necro?"

"Who knows? If we can get Alex free of this other nonsense maybe we can track down her killer. At least if her husband didn't do it."

He would not hurt me.

The voice was so quiet Katia almost didn't hear it. She glanced around but saw no one. Riley was texting again and didn't act as if she'd heard anything odd, so Katia shrugged it off and closed the news article on her phone. She was just going to freak herself out if she kept this up.

After her master finished her conversation, she laid down on top of her sleeping bag, wished Katia a good night, and curled up. She made it look so easy. Katia eventually stretched out on her own sleeping bag, staring up at the stars. They weren't as bright here, too much light pollution even in a cemetery.

As she drifted off, she swore she heard that voice again, though what it was saying was so quiet she couldn't hear all the words. Not knowing what else to do, Katia whispered, "Rest in peace."

Not yet. Not yet.

FOUR

Something magical bumped against Riley's mind and she opened her eyes, blinked, then slowly sat up. The cemetery was as dark as one would expect in the middle of the night. Darker, because the streetlights near the parking lot were out. They hadn't been that way when she and Katia had gone to sleep.

Another tap on her mind, though this time it was more like someone shoving on a locked door rather than politely knocking.

"Katia?" The journeyman was upright in a heartbeat, which said she hadn't been sleeping soundly. "We have company."

"The necro?"

"Yes. Best to let whoever they are do their thing. We're fine as long as we're inside the circle."

There was the crinkle of plastic as Katia took a long swig from her water bottle. "Do you recognize the magic?"

"Same as last night."

"Back for more, then."

Except this time, she was here.

The summoner floated out of the dark, skimming just above the grass. It was an impressive blending of glamour and illusionary magic, all black flowing robe and distant thunder. Hollywood would have loved it. He, or she, hadn't bothered to look like Alex. This time it was Mortimer Alexander.

"Dumb move," she muttered.

Riley pushed through the glamour and a faint impression returned. Male, maybe forty or so. He came to a halt a few feet from the Holy circle, his eyes on her and then moved his attention to Katia.

"Your name is not Susan. You lied to me," he said.

"Seemed only fair since you lied to me," she replied, steel pipe in her hand now. Protective circle or not, Katia Breman was always prepared.

The necro frowned at her. "I do not like liars."

"Oh, the irony," she replied, then yawned. "Don't you have something better to do than creep around graveyards in the middle of the night?"

Riley chuckled. "That is kind of the default setting for summoners, actually."

The necro's attention shifted to her now, along with a more insistent mental shove. She batted it back like a tennis ball causing the sender to blink in surprise.

"Don't be rude," she said. "You have no claim to this corpse. You need to leave. You know it's a violation of the summoner oath to reanimate the dead without their permission."

It was one of the first rules you learned when you began your training, and it was pounded into your head from then on just in case you hadn't been paying attention the first, or the tenth time.

"And if I have permission?" he asked slyly.

"Then we wouldn't be sitting vigil over the late Mr. Means."

"Who are you to challenge me?"

"I'm Summoner Blackthorne. I'm also a master demon trapper. And who are you?"

The smug expression didn't fade. "No one you would know. But you will after tonight."

His spell struck the circle hard, causing the protective sphere to flare bright white as it repelled the onslaught.

"Not happening!" Riley said, immediately reinforcing the sphere.

For a time there was a give-and-take of magic, though Riley already knew that this guy was much stronger. The Holy Water circle was all that kept him at bay.

As if he'd come to the same conclusion, the summoner abruptly changed tactics and spat out a single word that made her ears throb in time to her heartbeat. A rumbling came from behind them, but she didn't dare break her concentration to see what was happening.

"The grave's opening!" Katia cried out.

"What?" Riley spun around to find Means' plot churning like a team of energetic moles had taken residence. "That's impossible!"

The dirt blew straight up, then pummeled down onto them in fat red chunks. A large piece smacked into Katia, and she crouched down, belatedly covering her head. A sharp crack broke the vault's lid into pieces and then the casket lid flew straight up out of the hole and against the Holy Water circle like a guided missile. The impact blew the ward apart. Dirt and pieces of the casket's lining rained down around them. As the debris settled Means climbed out of his grave, then looked around, confused.

"You're mine now. Get over here," the necro said, waving him forward.

The dead man marched away from his grave, surprisingly quick for a corpse, ignoring Katia's feeble attempt to grab him. Means had barely cleared the remnants of the circle before he and the summoner went skyward in an acrid cloud of blue-black smoke.

"Oh, no," Riley muttered.

Purple and black arcs of magic seethed around them, making Katia's head roar and her chest tight. Riley was on her knees, her head bent, blood dripping from her nose. Some of that strange purple undulated across her master's fingers as she reached toward the ground. The moment she touched it, the magic flowed downward into the earth.

Katia's eyesight faded as the pounding in her skull increased. She lost her balance, falling forward, palms skidding in the grass. It was then she felt it, the persistent tug of the earth. To her astonishment, the spell's magic flowed down her arms and through her fingers.

As much as it hurt, she forced herself to stay connected with the ground, not allowing her fingers to curl in agony. Instead, she dug deep into the grass and then into the dirt.

Her body seemed to crackle as wave after wave of the powerful spell searched for an outlet. Whatever was inside her was beyond description, like someone had stuffed her full of fireworks and then lit them off all at once. She swore she saw intricate patterns in the purple mist and could hear the earth groan as the magic descended into it.

There was a low moan. It had come from her. Another moan, this one from Riley. Time passed, though she had no idea how long. There was only the endless rippling agony.

"That's it, just let it go," her master said from somewhere near her. "I'm sorry I can't make it go away any faster."

"Hurts."

"Yes, it does. Why didn't you tell me you knew how to ground a spell?"

"I . . . don't."

Katia's head bowed even more, connecting with the grass and the earth now. With her skin touching the soil, more of the magic pushed its way out of her, pulse by painful pulse.

Time passed. Hours. Decades. And still the purple flowed out of her.

"You taught her how to ground a spell?" That was Mort's voice, so apparently her boss had called for backup.

"No," Riley replied.

"You didn't?"

"No," Riley repeated, this time with more emphasis.

With a great deal of effort Katia raised her head to find the senior summoner kneeling on the other side of her. Some distance away was the older summoner, the strange one with the sigil on his forehead. Lord Ozymandias. Above him bobbed a glowing orb, a match to the one that hovered above Mort.

"Here, you need this," Riley said, holding out a few tissues. "Your nose is bleeding."

Katia managed to sit up, then she jammed the tissues against her face.

God, my head hurts so bad. The worst hangover in her life—

the night of her senior prom and too much tequila—was just a mild ache compared to this.

"You didn't show her how to ground the backlash," Mort said, as if that needed repeating yet again.

"I didn't have time. The circle just blew apart. *From the inside*."

His lordship swiveled around now, staring directly at Katia.

"Journeyman Breman, do you have any magical talent in your family?"

Did she? "No. Not like you guys." She was tempted to blow her nose to clear it, but something told her that wouldn't be wise. As it was, it burned as if someone had poured acid into both nostrils.

"And yet you see angels," Ozymandias said.

"They glow really bright. Hard to miss them."

Then his lordship was right in front of her, eyeing her intently. "Then how did you know how to ground the backlash?"

She guessed that was what had nearly blown her head off. "I saw Riley doing it. I figured I could give it a try. I just had to get that stuff out of me."

"Ohhh . . . " Mort murmured. He shot a surprised look at the senior summoner, and a nod returned.

"I can relieve you of the headache if you permit me to touch you," Ozymandias said.

"Ah, sure. Go for it. I swear my eyes are about to fall out." At least her nose had finally stopped bleeding.

"Close them for me."

When she complied there was a faint touch at the center of her forehead and then the agony melted away.

Her eyes snapped open. "Oh, God, that's better," she said, blinking in astonishment. "Thank you."

"You think she's a *chaîne*?" Mort asked.

"Must be, though there aren't that many of those around."

"A what?" Riley asked.

"Chaîne. The word is French and means, well, chain," Mort said.

As much as she appreciated that her head no longer hurt so bad, Katia didn't like being left out of the conversation. "Ah, sorry, but right now you're making zip sense."

"A chaîne or channel is someone who can ground spells, and in this case, a backlash, like what you just went through," Mort explained. "But that person is usually incapable of performing magic. It's an odd trade off."

"Okay, so I did a thing. No clue how, but all that glowing purple stuff is now pretty much gone. What's the big deal?"

Mort rose and then dusted off his robe, thinking through his response.

"The big deal is that you managed to offload the blowback of an immensely powerful spell. That's impressive, especially without training."

"Go me," she said, and winced again. The headache was better, but her muscles felt like she'd run a marathon. Riley looked like she felt the same.

"When this all settles down we'll put you in touch with someone who can help you with this ability. There is some . . . training involved," Ozymandias said. He traded a look with Mort. There was a lot not being said about this so-called training.

"Ohhhkay."

She'd just wanted to watch over a dead guy and earn some money. It should have been no big deal, at least until the corpse thief had ruined the whole thing.

"How could that necro pull Means out of his grave when the circle was up?" she asked.

Riley shook her head, then winced at the move. "Don't know. I have a lot of questions about this whole gig."

"We all do. I'll notify the widow," Mort said. "As Summoner Advocate it's my job to deal with this kind of thing."

"Even if the summoner isn't a local?" Katia asked.

"Even then. To the public we are all one and the same—grave robbers. This will only reinforce that stereotype once the news gets out."

"Is Alex still at Lady Torin's? I don't want him blamed for this," Riley asked.

"He is. He's safe there. No one messes with her."

Lord Ozymandias turned his back on them again, staring off into the distance as if trying to sense where their thief had fled.

"I think Means knew this was going to happen," Katia said as she stood on wobbly legs. It took a bit to get herself steady. "He just popped out of that grave like it'd been all planned. Or maybe it was because the necro put a spell on him or something."

"If he arranged his reanimation, his widow should have known about it," Mort said. "There's loads of paperwork that has to be signed and notarized beforehand."

"It appears we have a mystery," Ozymandias said. He cocked his head. "This might be a good time for me to depart. I have . . . inquiries to make. We'll have another meeting this morning at nine."

Then he was simply gone.

Katia's mouth dropped open, though the others didn't seem bothered by the summoner's abrupt exit. Had he even been here for real? Before she could ask that question, she heard the slamming of car doors as voices rose from the parking lot. One voice was familiar and decidedly angry.

"Oh no, that's Means' widow," she said. "This is so not a good thing."

As the lady marched down the hill from the lot, an older man at her side, she demanded, "Where is he? Why didn't you protect him?"

"How does she know her husband had been corpse-napped?" Riley asked, keeping her voice low. Not that the approaching pair would hear them with all the noise Mrs. Means was generating.

"That's a very good question," Mort replied.

When she finally reached them, he took the lead, his expression solemn.

"Mrs. Means? I'm Mortimer Alexander, the Summoner Advocate for the City of Atlanta. I am deeply sorry to say that your husband's body has been . . . reanimated without permission."

"I know!" She glared at him, then turned to the man next to her. "Take pictures of this atrocity. My poor Albie has been stolen and someone will pay for this."

The word "pay" stood out more than all the rest.

"I was just about to notify you. How did you find out this happened?" Mort asked.

"Someone called me. Told me my husband of thirty-two years had been stolen. It's an outrage! An outrage!" she said, launching a fist into the air for emphasis.

The only person who could have notified the widow was the guy who stole the corpse. Why would he bother?

"Oh, great," Riley murmured as a patrol car pulled into the lot.

Knowing this was going to take forever with the cops involved, Katia began to collect her gear.

"You! Stop! Don't touch anything. This is a crime scene."

She would have expected that warning to come from the cops, but instead it was the man who'd arrived with the widow.

"I'm getting my cellphone," she said, ignoring the dude.

She found it a few feet away and fortunately her habit of buying an extra tough case had saved the thing from being so much scrap. After blowing off the dirt, she swiped the screen and it came to life. "Thank you!" she whispered.

Her eyes returned to the grave, or what remained of it. It was a wreck, the flowers strewn in all directions, though the temporary name plaque had somehow weathered the destruction. As she reached over to pick up her water bottle, she found the widow in her face.

"What are you hiding?" the woman demanded.

She sorta felt sorry for the lady, but that sympathy was nearly gone.

"I'm getting my water bottle, okay?"

"You sure that's just water? Have you been drinking? That'd be about right. Drinking and not paying attention. Not keeping my husband safe."

Don't scream at the widow, don't scream at the widow, don't—

"Mrs. Means," Mortimer called out. "The police would like to talk to you."

With a huff the woman headed toward the cops, both of whom looked like they wanted to be anywhere else. Katia knew how that felt. As Mrs. Means carried on, and on, she rejoined her master. They both sank down into the grass, exhausted from the magical assault and all the drama.

"This is going to be bad," Riley said, keeping her voice down. "Cops don't usually get called out on these kinds of things. It's always an internal summoner matter."

Katia shot a glance at the widow's companion. "And her buddy's filming all this with his phone. Look at her, she's wearing *makeup*." She glanced down at her own phone's display. "At two-thirty in the morning? And those clothes? If someone called me to say my husband's body had been stolen, I'd throw on the first thing I could find and run my ass right out the door. I swear she knew this was going to happen." Then it hit her why. "I bet there's going to be a lawsuit. Wait and see."

"Yup," was Riley's only reply. And even that single word held a sharp edge of barely restrained anger.

It took another quarter hour before the Widow and her henchman left the cemetery. By that point she'd been nasty to Mort, accused her and Riley of all sorts of ugly stuff, then started in on the cops. It was at that point her buddy suggested they leave. Riley and Katia rejoined the others as the car pulled out of the parking lot. There was a group sigh of relief.

"Sorry about that. Unfortunately, it comes with the job," Mort said.

"Same here," one of the officers replied. He looked over at them now. "You're Riley Blackthorne. I remember you from that demon attack downtown. The one near the capital. You were with some dude with wings."

"That was me."

"Do you usually grave sit?"

"No. Katia had a problem here last night while watching over this grave. Same summoner. Tonight, he came back for seconds. I thought being here might make a difference. It didn't."

The cops traded looks. "We'll need to get a statement from you ladies."

"Could you also do a couple quick breathalyzer tests as well?" Mort asked.

"What?" Katia said. "We weren't drinking."

"I know. But this way it'll go in the official report. Never hurts to be thorough in case someone decides to make an accusation down the line."

"Exactly," the older officer replied, nodding.

"Go for it," Riley said.

After the tests, which proved neither of them had bothered with any booze, the younger officer led Katia away from the others and started asking a lot of questions. He was cute, in a cop sort of way, but still his questions rankled.

"Anything else you can tell me about why this evening went wrong?"

"Not really. The circle should *not* have broken. Master Blackthorne was *reinforcing* it. But then the coffin exploded, and Means was outta here," she said, jerking her thumb over her shoulder. "No way that should have happened."

The officer looked over at the grave, then back at her. "Is there any reason that Master Blackthorne would want this body to be taken?"

Katia was a second away from roasting the guy, then realized he might be trying to help. "No reason at all, because anything that happens with her is big news. The last thing she wants is any more publicity."

The officer nodded in agreement. "Okay, that's it for now. If there are any other questions, a detective will contact you."

"Thanks. Sorry you got stuck with this."

He rolled his eyes. "Same for you."

As the police inspected the desecrated grave with Mort, her boss angled her head toward the parking lot. They headed up the hill, toting their gear.

"Your butt-kicking headache will be back in a few hours," Riley warned. "Drink a lot of water. It'll help. Sorta." She glanced back as the three men stared at the open grave. "I am so glad I was here tonight."

"Me too."

If not, Master Blackthorne might have been on the phone to Katia's parents with the astonishing news that their eldest daughter had gotten herself snuffed during a grave robbery. One thing for sure, her obituary would have been front page news back home.

FIVE

Simon wasn't exactly sure what pushed him to return to Atlanta three days early, but the urge had started in the middle of the night. He'd awoken from a nightmare, the details of which he couldn't remember, then he couldn't go back to sleep.

Staring at the ceiling of the hotel room hadn't worked, neither had more pain meds. After over an hour of trying to work out why he felt so uneasy, he rose, packed, and checked out of the hotel. The sleepy front desk clerk looked as tired as Simon felt.

A quick stop at a Waffle House got him breakfast and sufficient caffeine to fuel him for the trip home. As he finished off his second cup of coffee, he cancelled his hotels for the remainder of the trip, then sent an email to the dojo letting them know he wouldn't be back, at least not this week. He pleaded an emergency in Atlanta which really wasn't a lie because that's the way it felt. His original plan to spend a day in Asheville and then one in Chattanooga could wait. Simon had to get home *now*. He was in his car, headed south even before the sun rose.

This urgency was not because of the five voicemail messages from his eldest sister. Simon had listened to the first one and found it to be Deanna's usual litany of complaints, at least when it came to her younger brother. He ignored the others.

A little after seven he was only a few miles away from reaching the interstate when his phone rang. When a name appeared on the phone's screen, he smiled. This was a call he'd always take.

"Hi, Mom," he said.

"Hi, Son. How goes it? You hiking today?"

"Actually, I'm almost back to Atlanta. The sabbatical helped, but I decided to come home."

There was a long pause and then, "Oh, okay. I'm glad they finally made you take time off. You work too hard." There was another pause. "Deanna has been trying to get ahold of you."

"I saw that. What's up?"

"She went to your house and found you were gone. Your exorcism partner told her that you were out of town. Dee was very unhappy that she hadn't been informed about your vacation plans."

"My sabbatical was none of her business," he said.

"I told her that. But you know her. And she's upset because your front door keys don't work now. If I need a new set, just drop them by when you have a chance, okay?"

The keys his sister had were an old set from their uncle, the previous homeowner. Dee had them because she'd watched over the place when Uncle Thomas went on vacation a couple of years back. When Simon had bought the house, he hadn't thought about reclaiming them. He hadn't cared.

Until recently.

"Your set are the right ones." He might as well tell her all of it. "Dee was in my house a few weeks back, moved around some furniture, threw stuff out of my refrigerator. She left a note that said I really should take my garbage out more often. I changed the locks the next day."

"Oh, that sounds like her. I'm sorry about that." There was a long sigh down the phone. "I don't know what to do with her, Simon, I just don't. She's got to be involved in everything."

Came with being the firstborn in a long string of kids.

"I am not going to be nice this time, Mom," he warned. "I am done with her interference."

That was The Old Simon. The new one had far less patience.

"Tell her to back off. She won't listen, but it's time she knew that she can't run over people. Your dad and I will stand behind you on this."

That was reassuring. "Thanks, Mom." Then he remembered the other issue. "Oh, I got Katia a birthday present. It's a wooden staff and it's almost six feet long. There's no way I can hide it if she's home this morning. Can I stash it at your house?" The other one he could hide in his trunk.

"Sure. Bring it over."

"I'll stick it in the garden shed. I can just imagine what might happen if one of the sibs found the thing."

A laugh came down the line now. "Yeah, put it in the shed. I'll be out this morning, but you know how to get in the gate."

"Thank you. Ah, sorry, but I'm almost at the turnoff to the interstate. I'd better focus on my driving."

"It's good to talk to you, Son. Call when you can. And bring your Katia over one of these days. She sounds like she can hold her own with this family."

"Oh, believe me, she can."

"Love you. Bye!"

He returned the love and then a short time later merged onto the interstate.

Deanna didn't mess with their four youngest siblings because they were still at home. The two older than Simon were safe as well: Amy was a legal secretary and had a toddler of her own. Joshua was in the Army and based in Germany, so their eldest sister couldn't order him around. That left Simon and his choice of professions, neither of which Deanna approved of.

"Time to set some boundaries," he said.

Then he upped his speed a bit. He needed to get home. Once he saw Katia, everything would be fine.

After a quick stop at his folks' place to stash one of Katia's presents, Simon headed home. When he pulled into the driveway he sighed in relief. Everything looked fine, nothing to indicate anything was wrong. Now he wondered if he'd overreacted.

"No," he murmured. Not after that conversation with the Divine in the forest.

The car Katia had borrowed from Grand Master Stewart was

here, so she was probably asleep after a long night's trapping. He turned off the engine and sat there for a time, enjoying the idea of being back home. The lawn looked like a landscaping pro had mowed it, which was the case. She'd also washed his windows, something he'd intended on doing one of these days.

Once he got his luggage out of the trunk, leaving the collapsible bō tucked under a blanket, he debated whether he should text Katia before walking into the house. But if she was sleeping, he didn't want to wake her.

The decision was made for him when the front door opened and she stepped out onto the porch. She looked like she'd been up all night.

"Simon?" she asked.

"Hey!" he said, then carried his luggage up to the porch.

"Is something wrong?"

"No. I was just ready to come home. I didn't text you because it was early, and I didn't want to wake you."

A lengthy yawn was the reply. "Yeah, it was a really long night."

He followed her in the house, which smelled of furniture polish. She'd gone to extra effort on his behalf and hadn't even known he'd be home today.

As he closed the door behind him, she yawned again. "I need a shower." Then she was in the guest room, the door closing behind her.

It wasn't quite the reception he'd hoped for, which told him something had happened. Something bad. Katia wouldn't usually blurt out those kinds of things but saved them up until she was ready to tell him. They were a lot alike.

Just as he was about to feel sorry for himself, her bedroom door opened.

"Welcome home," she said, sending him a faint smile. "I missed you."

Then the door closed again and everything was better.

†✵‡✵†

Katia did not hurry through her shower because she needed time to think of her next move. If she told Simon what had happened at the cemetery, he'd feel obligated to help her in some way. That wouldn't be fair. This was his sabbatical, the one he'd earned with every horrific demonic exorcism. And yet, part of her wanted him to be there, to give her advice, to watch her back. He made her feel safe and that was an amazing, and utterly unnerving feeling.

She found him in his recliner, thumbing through the mail he'd received from Rome. He looked up, studied her, and then set the magazine aside.

"The house looks great. Thank you."

"I had some free time."

"That I doubt. I mean, you washed the windows. That's definitely beyond the call of duty."

Katia shrugged and then plopped down onto the sofa. "Ah, since you're home early, is it possible for me to stay here a couple more days? The painting at Stewart's house is going okay, but they found stuff that needs repaired so they're behind schedule. If it isn't okay, I can try to find somewhere else to crash. Maybe a bolt hole. You folks have them here, right?" Lawrence had one, a place on Holy ground that was safe from demons. Not fancy, but it'd give her a place to stay until Stewart's house was livable again.

"There are a few bolt holes, but you don't need to go to any of those. You're welcome here as long as you want, Katia."

"It won't get you in any trouble with your bosses?"

Simon puzzled on that. "My house, my rules. I do have a clause in my contract about indecent behavior, but having a fellow demon trapper stay here doesn't count, at least as I see it."

"A female trapper would be okay? I don't want you to get in trouble with those guys."

"I don't care," he said. "And if it were a problem, my parents would happily take you in. They have a few extra bedrooms nowadays." He paused, then asked, "Would you like to tell me how you got the cut on your forehead, or am I supposed to act like it's not there?"

Katia almost laughed, but he was being so serious she didn't dare. Simon would find out eventually because someone would tell him, or he'd see a news report.

"I was grave sitting the last two nights," she began, and then the whole story poured out before she could stop herself. The further she got into it, the more his eyes widened.

"The necro blew apart a Holy Water circle with Riley *inside*?" he said. "That's . . . unreal."

"Yeah, it was. Major magic got slung around last night. Seriously bad stuff. Knocked both of us on our asses."

"So that's why . . . " he murmured.

"What?"

Simon shook his head. "What are the summoners doing about this?"

"I'm not sure. I got home late and crashed. I haven't heard from Riley yet. I'm guessing the necros are pitching a fit because it's looking bad for them. One thing for sure, Alex does not have that kind of power."

"No, he doesn't." Simon leaned forward in the recliner, rubbing his face.

"Look, I don't want you to get involved in this," she said. "You're on vacation. You know how it is; this weirdness will just take over. It's not part of your job description."

He looked over at her, puzzled. "You don't want my help?"

Oh God yes, she did, but not when he needed to rest. Needed to get his head in the right place.

"You were exhausted when you left town. You were running at about half speed of what's your norm. It was getting harder and harder for you to do the exorcisms, and the demons could tell. So no, it's best you *do not* get involved in this mess no matter how much I'd love the help. Riley, the grand masters, the summoners, they'll work this out."

He blinked, then leaned back in the recliner. "You're right. I'll stay out of the way unless you ask me to help, or something goes really wrong. Then I'm in one way or another. I won't let you get hurt just so I can have some R&R."

The steel in his voice said this was his line in the sand.

"Okay, we got a deal." Time to switch topics. "Have you had breakfast?" A quick nod returned. "Well, I haven't so let me go find something to eat."

He picked up the magazine and returned to his reading. Or at least appeared to. Now that she knew him better, she bet Atlanta's lay exorcist was quietly working out how to help her without her knowing.

You should have stayed in North Georgia with the squirrels.

"I hate this part of the job," Riley muttered as they waited for the council meeting to begin.

A glance at Beck said she'd be getting no sympathy from him. With Grand Master Stewart out of the country, it had fallen to her husband to be the dude in charge of all the stuff that grand masters do in Atlanta. At least it wasn't the entire East Coast. Not yet.

Besides Mr. Means' body waltzing off in the arms of the rogue necromancer, six more corpses had risen from their graves and been carted off. All the other grave sitters had been experienced, not a newbie in the bunch, and yet every one of them had failed in their task.

And just like Means' grave two of the others had blown up, knocking out the protective circle that should have kept the deceased safe. Now Atlanta's Powers That Be were demanding answers and it was up to Mort to supply them. Since he'd taken on the denizens of Hell for her, Riley was returning the favor. Though to be honest the mayor and others in charge of the city weren't nearly as bad as Hellspawn. Just annoyingly persistent.

"Is this going to be the new thing, summoners stealing peoples' bodies?" one of the city council folks demanded. "What's next? Raiding funeral homes?"

The man's tone was disrespectful, especially when it was

aimed at a member of the magical community. No wonder Beck came home bitching under his breath after one of these meetings.

"No, this is not the newest thing," Mort replied evenly. He wore a suit and tie, not his usual black robe, and sat behind a table facing those same city authorities. "We are investigating why this is happening, who is performing these illegal reanimations, and then we'll deal with the offender."

"What precisely do you do with these people?" another council member asked.

"The punishment requires that the offender's magic is stripped from them entirely."

"You make them like the rest of us, then?"

It was a loaded question, one that implied that *the rest of us* were somehow lower on the evolutionary scale.

"For a summoner, having their magic ripped away is traumatic. It damages the person for life. At that point, we turn them over to local authorities and they can be charged according to the Georgia code. Without their magic, they are not a threat to anyone." He hesitated, then added, "Some do not survive the removal of their magic. For those who do, insanity is often the result."

"So, we'd be given someone who is crazy and expected to deal with them?" This was the first questioner who was getting under Riley's skin. She could only imagine what Mort thought of him.

"Often the former summoner is found to be too mentally damaged to stand trial and they are sent to an asylum for the remainder of their lives. To be honest, they don't tend to live that long after their magical essence is erased."

He'd kept his cool, so far. But then that was Mort's thing—cool—until someone repeatedly got in his face. Hopefully, none of these people went that far.

"The guy in the gray shirt is talkin' about runnin' for governor," Beck whispered in her ear. It was the same guy who'd been jabbing at Mort. Someone eyeing public office usually craved publicity and wouldn't care if that publicity damaged anyone else along the way.

"Is it true that your nephew is involved in these grave robberies?" Mr. Gray Shirt asked.

"No, it's not true. Initial reports indicated that the thief resembled my nephew, but it appears the summoner was using glamour magic." There were a few blank looks at that. "A glamour can be used to imitate the appearance of someone else."

"You mean someone could look like me?" a different councilperson asked.

"Yes. That's what happened with Alex. He is just starting his training and has none of the skills needed to reanimate a deceased individual. That requires significant ability."

"You have that ability?" Mort nodded. "How many of you in Atlanta can do that?"

Their friend shifted uneasily. The necromancers were keen to keep certain information private, like the number of summoners in the city for instance. Though that was a matter of public record if someone went digging for the information. How many of them were proficient at reanimation wasn't something the Summoners Society wanted public.

"In the major metropolitan area, twenty-eight of us are actively seeking reanimation contracts at the moment."

Clever. He'd not said exactly how many could perform that magic, only the ones that were currently doing the job. Twenty-eight summoners in a region that encompassed over six million citizens? No threat at all.

Except one summoner was not playing by the rules and that meant all of them would suffer the consequences.

"We intend to find this person and stop them," Mort continued, his voice harder now. "This is an abomination, and it will not be tolerated."

"It might be said that reanimating a dead person is an abomination."

"They are certainly circumstances when reanimations are uncalled for. There are circumstances where the funds received assist the deceased's family after death. Every situation is different."

"Maybe it's time someone introduced legislation to make this illegal." No surprise, it was the guy eyeing the governor's office.

"Respectfully, that is a debate for another time," Mort said. "Right now, it is the Summoners Society's *primary* goal to find this person and stop them. We can argue about the rest later."

"You make it sound like what I propose is a waste of time."

"What I know, sir, is that over the last two days I've spent many hours with family members as they mourn yet another loss. They demanded to know why their loved one was no longer laid to rest. I had no answers for them, but soon I will. By God, *I will*."

The force behind his vow crackled in the air.

Mort tidied up the papers in front of him, and to his credit his hands did not shake. "Are there any more questions?"

The mayor looked around, then shook his head. "Keep me in the loop on the investigation. Don't hesitate to call the police, if needed. Do what you must to stop this, you hear?"

Mort nodded and left the room. Riley gave her husband's hand a squeeze and then followed the summoner. As she reached the door she heard Beck being called forward to talk about how the National Guild was handling illegal demon trapping in the city.

Since Master Harper would be a wrecking ball in these hallowed halls, the problem fell into Den's lap. They knew him from before he became a grand master, so in some ways they trusted what he told him. Most of the time, that is.

She found Mort further down the hallway, leaning against a wall reading something on his phone. He glanced up as she joined him.

"How do we catch this monster?" she asked, keeping her voice low.

"I have no idea."

Which wasn't the answer she'd been hoping to hear. "What will Ozymandias do?"

"He's trying to trace the summoner. If we're lucky that'll work."

"So, we have to babysit the new graves until this looney shows up again?"

Mort's terse nod told her that was exactly the plan.

For some reason Katia felt compelled to visit the cemetery one more time. As Riley had predicted the magic-induced headache had returned and banged away inside her skull like a jackhammer. The usual over-the-counter pain meds had been useless. Breakfast hadn't helped, either.

A quick stop at a grocery store scored her a bouquet of flowers, two candy bars, a liter bottle of water and a smaller one of Pepsi. To some that might seem blasphemous since this was Coca Cola's hometown, but Katia didn't care. She liked the stuff and so that's what she drank.

The cemetery hadn't changed much since earlier that morning, only hotter. Katia replaced the flowers in the vase on Anna Lanier's grave, added fresh water from her bottle, then tidied up the now dehydrated roses another mourner had left behind. It felt right, even though she'd never met the woman. If not for a winged miracle named Ori, she would be doing the same for her brother's grave.

To her surprise, Mr. Means' casket was still there. Wouldn't someone from the cemetery have picked it up by now? When it had exited the grave, the dirt around it blasted outward in a geyser, the clods falling as much as thirty feet away. The lid had speared itself into the earth, like a surfboard wedged in grass and clay. It would have been funny if she and Riley hadn't been in the middle of that destruction.

The casket itself was lying on its side near another gravestone, the once highly polished walnut scored and muddy. No doubt Mrs. Means would be livid about that.

Katia stepped up to the grave and peered inside. The vault

itself was still there, though the lid had disintegrated. Literally. Squatting down she touched the dirt, then quickly yanked her hand back with a yelp. The ground was still tainted with magical residue, both from the protective circle and the thieving necro.

Since the cops had already investigated the site, she gave the casket a shove, flipping it over. Filthy white satin now covered the interior. A small, open drawer on the side of it caught her notice. Her grandmother's casket had one of those and Katia had placed a special treasure inside that drawer.

This one was empty with no family mementos. Or if there had been, they were lost in the destruction. She shoved it back in with a click. Disappointed, Katia wandered around the site, unsure of what she'd hope to find. The grass was beaten down now, more than just when the cops had been here.

There were marks in the dirt, equidistant, like a three-legged stool. *Or a tripod.* The man who'd been with Mrs. Means hadn't had one, so someone had come back after everyone had cleared out. Maybe a news crew?

Voices came from the parking lot and they belonged to a couple of guys climbing out of a truck sporting the cemetery's name and logo. Probably here to collect the casket and close the grave.

Katia met them on the way to her car, their hands full of shovels and rakes.

"Lots of weirdos hang around this place," one said.

She rolled her eyes and kept walking. Then halted and spun around.

"Ah, hi. You said a lot of weirdos hang around here. Can you tell if there were any in the last few days?"

The guy who'd made the comment gestured at her in lieu of an answer.

"Besides me."

"Well, the day we opened the grave for that dead dude," the other man said, gesturing at where Means had once rested, "there was a guy who looked like he spent most of his time inside, if you know what I mean. Real pale."

Pale? "Young or old?"

"Young. He just hung around for a while and asked questions about our job. I figured he was just an oddball. We get them now and then."

The first guy chimed in. "You one of them necromancers?"

"No. I was watching the grave last night when the summoner showed up. I'd like to know how he stole Means from inside a Holy Water circle."

"Voodoo," the man replied, nodding his head knowingly. "Gotta be Voodoo."

"Yeah, that's it for sure," the other guy replied.

She debated about warning them about the residual magic, but then decided not to. She suspected they wouldn't even feel it, not like she had.

Katia thanked them and headed for the car, thinking through what she'd just learned. Someone had shown an interest in Means' burial site *before* the funeral. Could it have been a relative or someone who wanted to claim the man's body a couple nights later? Their description, a "pale" guy, wasn't much help. Lots of people had inside jobs or were serious about using sunscreen in the Deep South.

While chomping on one of the candy bars and washing it down with swigs of Pepsi, Katia sat in the cemetery parking lot with the car windows rolled down. It didn't help that much.

Surfing on her phone gave her the information she needed: According to Means' obituary, Beesh Funeral Home had overseen his final arrangements. Their office was in one of the suburbs north of the city which meant there'd be a lot of traffic.

She knew what big cities were like because Kansas City was less than an hour away from her hometown. When she was in high school, she and her friends would head there to get away from their parents and the endless scrutiny of their nosy neighbors. And yet, the KC metro area was about two million people while Atlanta's population was over three times that. Those extra bodies made a difference.

A glance at her phone said she had enough time to get there

and then back to the trapper's meeting. With a sigh, she snapped her seatbelt in place and headed out. Behind her the two cemetery workers hauled the coffin toward their truck.

"Sorry guy," she said, as if Means could hear her. And who knew, maybe he could.

SIX

Eventually she found the right street and the funeral home was easy to spot. Stately and dull, it was a tan brick building with two white columns at the entrance. There was the usual Stars and Stripes on a pole, and a big parking lot. What was not usual were the two police cars in that lot.

Katia parked her car further along the road, then hiked up to join a knot of onlookers clustered on the sidewalk in front of the building. Didn't matter if it was a small town or a metropolis, people were naturally curious.

Even before she could ask what was going on, one of the ladies said, "Yeah, old man Beesh doesn't look happy." She angled her head toward an older man talking to the cops. He waved his hands around, then pointed to the open door on the side of the building, probably the one used for their "customers."

"You know him?" she asked.

The lady gave her a quick glance, then nodded. She looked to be in her fifties and wore a sundress covered with bouncing purple rabbits. It actually looked nice.

"I'm a neighbor," she said. "Beesh and his family have had a funeral home here since the sixties. This is the first time the cops came, though."

"What happened?"

"Someone stole one of the bodies. Made off with it sometime last night."

What?

"They didn't steal it," one of the other bystanders said, an older guy with an Atlanta Braves cap. "I heard one of the cops say there wasn't a break-in. It's *The Walking Dead*, I swear it," the man insisted. "You know, like that TV show. The bodies are just gettin' up and takin' off."

A couple of the others chuckled at his suggestion.

Katia did not. The *takin' off* part was too close to what happened when someone underwent reanimation. They just found out the body was missing?" she asked.

The lady shrugged, causing the rabbits to dance around. "If the coffin was closed they wouldn't know, would they?"

"I bet it was demons," another man suggested. "They do stuff like that. Take bodies, you know."

"Hellspawn aren't interested in dead people," Katia replied.

"You sure of that?" the second man asked, frowning over at her now.

"Yeah, I am. I'm a Demon Trapper."

"Why would a girl do stuff like that?" the first man asked.

"A job is a job," she said, ignoring the *girl* part. "Any idea whose body wandered off?"

There were shrugs all around.

"Did any of you see a thin guy hanging around the funeral home? Pale, like he didn't get out in the sun much."

There were head shakes until it came to the lady in the sundress.

"I did the other day. He was sitting in a car in the parking lot next door, just watching the place. I almost called the police, but then he drove off and I never saw him again."

"What did the car look like?"

"Black. Nothing special. I didn't see the license plate."

"Why did you ask?"

Apparently, these folks hadn't seen this morning's news headlines. "Because this isn't the only body that's gone missing."

"I told you!" the first man crowed. "Give it a few days and there'll be even more. They'll take over this entire city, you just wait."

She left them debating whether it was a zombie invasion or if someone was selling the bodies for their organs. Neither of which were realistic, but everyone would have a theory. And none of them would be right.

The trip back to the Guild meeting did nothing for Katia's nerves. It was as if all of Atlanta's irrational drivers had decided to come out at once, but it was the middle of rush hour. Or as Simon had patiently explained, rush *hours*.

This was her first trappers' meeting in her new home. There'd been two others, but she and Simon had been at exorcisms and missed them both.

The church where the meeting was being held had a large parking lot which was currently full of trucks and the occasional SUV, the kind that were expensive to run even though a couple had solar panels on their roof. At least the price of gas had continued to drop.

It was easy to tell these were trappers because of the cages. The demon decals on the sides of the vehicles were another big clue. Riley's car sat a few slots down from where Katia parked, Simon's a few rows over.

Over the last seven and a half weeks, it had slowly sunk in how bad it'd been for her in Lawrence, and how many of her coping skills hadn't been intelligent, or survivable. The heavy drinking had scared her, which was why she'd backed away from alcohol since she'd arrived in Atlanta.

She'd used booze to deal with her brother's coma, the trauma of losing a master she'd really liked, and then the nightmare that had come with the one that had taken his place.

One night she'd finally admitted to Grand Master Stewart what she'd been doing. She'd expected him to criticize, but instead he'd told her that sometimes, in the middle of a crisis we make decisions that weren't that smart. That was human. He'd done the same, he said.

But if she craved that next drink, then she needed help to avoid what Master Harper had suffered all those years. Stewart's kindness and honesty had made all the difference. Now that she was working in this crazy city, Katia felt no need to bury herself in a bottle of vodka. And that was a blessing.

After retrieving her trapping bag from the car, she made sure to lock it. She'd miss having the ability to get around on her own without asking Simon or Riley for a ride.

Apartment first, then car. It'd become a mantra now.

Then she wanted to join a gym. Maybe one of them would have a bōjitsu class. Unlike back home, here she had so many things she looked forward to.

Once Katia trudged up the long set of stairs to the church entrance, she paused and turned around. Something had happened here, something bad, she could feel it. Something demonic. It was like oil sheeting across her skin, along with the faint stench of sulfur.

"Hi, are you Breman?" a voice asked.

She turned to find a young guy standing behind her. He was probably in his early thirties, tall, tanned, and with muscles in all the right places. With that long blond hair he could easily be a model. She could just see him clad in armor and toting a sword on the cover of a romance novel.

Katia dragged her mind back to the conversation. "I am Breman." *Please don't be a jerk.*

"I'm Reynolds," he said, smiling at her now.

That was a name she'd heard more than once, and all of it had been positive.

"Good to meet you, Reynolds," she said, relieved. "Can you help me? I have no clue where to go for the meeting."

"I'll show you."

"Thank you." But she didn't move, still trying to figure out why this location bothered her. "What happened here?"

"Here, like . . . " He pointed at the ground beneath them.

"Yes. Something to do with Hellspawn. I can feel it."

Reynolds blinked in surprise. "Really?"

She nodded, not sure if she should have said anything. If he told the other trappers then she'd get a reputation for being crazy.

"Ohhkay," he said. His cheerful expression had vanished now. "Master Blackthorne killed an Archfiend down there," he said, pointing at the bottom of the concrete stairs. "Maybe that's what you're sensing."

That was it. "How long ago?"

"Ah, last December. It was the third one she'd killed." Reynolds huffed at that point. "The dickhead from National got unstuck about that, ran his mouth in front of all of us, right here," he said. "He had the balls to tell her that no matter how many Archfiends she killed, she'd never be a master." A big grin appeared. "No surprise, Riley proved him wrong. You do not mess with that woman. *Ever*."

Katia matched his grin.

Reynolds looked down the stairs again. "You can actually feel things like that?"

"Only if it's really strong."

"Huh. Not me. But I am *not* complaining." He paused and then added, "So, what do you think of Atlanta?"

It was a smooth change of topic, and she appreciated it. It seemed everyone asked her that question and her answer was always the same.

"I like it. Different, but not boring." *So not boring*.

"Like last night in the cemetery?" he asked, eyeing her as they made their way toward the church's front doors.

"Heard about that, huh?" A nod returned. "Scared the hell out of me."

"Would have done the same to me. That's why I never grave sit. Too damned many creepy things out there as it is." As they reached the entrance, he added, "You already have a good rep with most of this crew because of what you did with Simon. You know, saving those kids. Don't let any of the assholes bother you."

That she hadn't expected. "Thanks. It's good to know that."

Carefully stepping over a thick line of Holy Water at the double doors, though why they'd do that in a church she didn't know, Katia followed Reynolds into the building and then down a long hallway. Like most churches there were bulletin boards on both sides. They listed various activities, like a quilt group, a schedule for a local food pantry, then there were drawings from the little kids and the occasional Bible verse. For a moment Katia felt like she was back in Lawrence.

Eventually they entered a large room where there were rows and rows of folding chairs, along with the scent of fresh-brewed coffee. At the front of the room were two chairs placed up on a small dais. She guessed those were for the masters.

Not knowing if there was any order as to where people sat—there certainly hadn't been in Kansas—she followed Reynolds to the front and chose a place at the end of a row. After a nod he wandered off to talk with other trappers.

"Hey, Katia!" She turned to find one of Riley's apprentices taking a seat right behind her. "How's it going?"

"Hey, Jaye. Good. Well, mostly. Nothing bad in the trapping part of my life, at least."

"Yeah, I heard about the grave robbing. That had to suck."

"It was nasty, that's for sure," Katia said. She could still feel the scorching burn of the magic as it left her body and flowed into the earth. Eager to change the subject, she said, "I hear your journeyman's exam is coming up."

Jaye's smile dimmed. "I'm really worried."

"You shouldn't be. You'll do fine." Riley had casually mentioned that if anyone could ace the exam, it'd be Jaye. Katia certainly hadn't.

"I hope so. It's really scary."

"Riley will make sure you do well. Don't doubt it."

Jaye gave a nod, then was distracted by another trapper walking up to chat with her.

Katia looked around and found Simon talking to a couple of guys. He glanced at her, then turned away as if he hadn't seen her. But he had, and his reaction was odd. Usually, he was a lot more polite.

Master Jackson climbed up the stairs onto the dais. He was followed by Master Harper who parked himself in one of the chairs. He gave her a penetrating glance, then shifted back to watching the other trappers with that same intense stare that made most people squirm. Katia always did.

She plucked a pamphlet off the chair and sat down. It was a religious tract so she set it on the empty space to her right, then waited as the others settled into their seats. There were murmurs around her, and she heard "Kansas" and "Breman" a couple times.

"Okay, people. Time to get started," Jackson said, shuffling papers on the lectern in front of him.

What followed was various bits of good, or less-than-good news delivered in the master's calm tone. Someone's elevation to journeyman was announced and there was clapping and cheers, at least from most of the trappers. A small group of them along the far wall were noticeably quiet. Katia made a mental note to ask Riley who they were.

It was eventually her turn to be introduced. She stood, trying not to look nervous.

"Let's give an Atlanta welcome to Journeyman Katia Breman. She's working with Simon during the exorcisms and doing a damned good job," Jackson said, smiling down at her.

More unexpected praise, and she wasn't quite sure how to deal with it. She heard a couple of grumbles about "Kansas" but she ignored them. If this had been a Lawrence meeting mentioning Georgia would have had the same reaction.

"They have any demons in the sticks?" someone called out. It was one of the guys along the far wall.

"Yeah, we have a few. Not like here, though," she said, not wanting to make any enemies.

"That's for sure," another voice called. "Welcome to Atlanta, Breman. Not your fault you used to live in the middle of nowhere."

Katia ignored that one. Of course, there were laughs, then she was no longer in the spotlight and the meeting moved on. The main topic of discussion shifted to how there appeared to be fewer Hellspawn in the city now.

"Probably having a meeting in Hell," someone called out. "You know, like ours only with more screaming."

That'd be about right.

Katia could just imagine the Prince giving all his fiends a pep talk. More likely he'd execute a few just to improve morale. From what she'd seen of him, that'd be his style.

"Ask the new girl. She's been there. Or so they claim," another voice called out.

She refused to take the bait.

"Hey, new girl!" a guy called out. "You really been to Hell? What's it like?"

They weren't going to back down. "Zero stars," she called back. "It pretty much blows. And don't get me started on the smell," she said, hoping that would be the end of it.

"Yeah, told you. It's all b.s.," another trapper said.

"Adler doesn't lie. Can't do it even if he wanted to," someone insisted.

Oh yes he can.

Still, it was always smart to have someone underestimate you.

"What about it, Adler?" one of the trappers asked.

Simon rose. "Been there. It's Hell, what more can I say?" Then he sat down.

That was abrupt even by his standards.

"Right now, we have no idea why the demons are thin on the ground, and once we do, we'll let you know," Jackson said. "Frankly, it's puzzled everyone, even the grand masters." He looked out into the room. "Harvey, you got a question?"

The man lowered his hand and stood. "I do. We have that winged bastard roaming around the city now. You know, the one that works for Hell. He's killing demons that we should be trapping. How do we stop that? He's cutting into my trapping fees."

"I'm thinking you mean Ori, and the last thing we want to do is try to stop him. You challenge him and you'll end up dead. And the word is he's not working for Hell anymore, so he's on our side," Jackson said.

"Not if he's keeping me from earning a paycheck."

Riley rose now. "I talked to him a couple days ago about this. He's agreed to do most of his hunting outside of Atlanta because there aren't that many demons. He realizes what that means to us. He's only going after the really dangerous ones."

"You believe a Fallen? That's just nuts.'

The master frowned. "Yes, I believe this *formerly* Fallen angel. Because he's the reason this city isn't a smoking crater full of burned up corpses."

Jackson cut in now. "Okay, thank you. One last thing—according to National our dues will be going up the first of September, so don't be surprised if your license renewal fee rises as well."

There were groans, which Katia joined in. The last thing she needed was more expenses.

"And now Master Blackthorne has news for us," Jackson said, nodding at Riley. She rose and walked up to the front of the room.

"The summoners have an issue that shouldn't be a problem for us, but if you see something odd going on, let me know."

Then she delivered a shortened version of what had happened at the city's cemeteries, that the summoner involved wasn't a local, and that the mayor wanted something done *now*.

"Not our problem," someone called out. There were mutters of agreement.

"Might not be right now, but weird crap tends to spread. Just let me know if you see a summoner doing something they shouldn't be doing. I don't want one of us in the crossfire if something goes wrong."

More muttering, but some agreement now. She nodded to Jackson, then returned to her seat.

"And finally," Jackson continued, "the number of unlicensed trappers in the city has shot up in the last couple of months. We're working with the city authorities to deal with that. It's tough enough making a living without having someone else steal your paycheck."

"There's only one way to deal with those assholes," a man called out.

"Keep it legal," Harper said, the first time he'd spoken during the entire meeting. "That way it doesn't blow back on us. Because if it does, then I'm going to nail whoever crosses the line. Got it?"

More murmurs, followed by nods.

And then it was over. Katia sighed in relief, then turned to talk to Jaye, but she was already gone.

Reynolds rejoined her. "Was this like back home?"

"Pretty close. Except no one was complaining about which football team lost their last game."

"Wait for it, it'll happen soon enough." He hesitated. "Maybe someday you and I can go get a drink together?"

It took longer than it should have to realize what he was asking.

"Sure, sometime down the line would be good. Things are kind of strange for me right now," she said. Nothing about Reynolds made her nervous, but she'd still check with Riley just in case.

"Cool! See you later, Katia."

She watched as he headed for the door, which took a bit longer than he probably would have liked as trappers wanted to talk to him. Clearly the guy was popular.

"Let's see if I can read your expression," her master said as she appeared at Katia's side. "You're wondering if Reynolds is on the level," Riley said. "He is a nice guy and is even hotter now that he's ditched his full beard." She paused, then continued, "He is also a *player*. Not in a bad sort of way, but he doesn't stick with one girlfriend for long."

"Understood. Having a drink with him is fine, anything beyond that is probably not an option."

"Who knows, you might be the one keeper in his hoard of lady friends."

Katia laughed at that thought. "Not likely. I've got enough

going on without all that."

"There's been rumors about you and Simon hooking up."

Katia stared at her boss. "No, we're just friends."

"And that's what he needs right now—a good friend." A pause, and then, "And maybe more."

Rather than follow up on that, she went with something Stewart had mentioned a while back. "Simon's qualified to take the master's exam. Why hasn't he?"

Riley raised an eyebrow, showing she knew that Katia was purposely changing the subject.

"I think he let it slide because he felt awful how everything played out between us. Then by the time he returned to Atlanta he was an exorcist. He's been flat-out busy ever since then. Why?"

"Just curious. Grand Master Stewart thinks it's a good idea."

"I agree." Riley paused, then added, "You two could study for the exam together."

"Me? I haven't killed an Archfiend."

Unlike you who has killed three.

"Not yet. The way things are going it's only a matter of time. Oh, and you should work on fighting with a sword."

"I'm not that great with edged weapons."

"You could be. Have Simon teach you. He's good with a blade."

No way.

"Oh, you said to tell you about anything odd. There was a body snatching at Beesh Funeral Home today. The neighbors said the deceased just waltzed right out of there. And that there's been a pale dude who was watching the place. It sounds like the same guy who was asking Means' grave diggers a lot of questions before he was buried."

Riley grew thoughtful. "Huh. I'll pass that on to Mort in case he's not in the loop. Another body. How many does this guy need?"

Katia shrugged. "If I hear anything else, I'll let you know."

"Thank you. And yes, you do need to study for the master exam. Don't argue with me on that, Journeyman."

Having delivered her sermon, Riley left her on her own. Katia did a quick check for Simon, wanting to hear how his family thing had turned out. He was already gone. He'd known how worried she'd been about her first trappers' meeting, but he hadn't bothered to acknowledge her existence. It was a slap in the face, or at least it felt that way.

"Not good, guy. Not good at all."

With a growl she headed for the door.

SEVEN

It'd been a one-two punch.

The first blow had been the conversation with his parents about the family issues, the primary one being Deanna. His eldest sib had thrown a major fit since Simon wasn't playing the part of the subservient younger brother. His mother cautioned him that other things were going on in Dee's life, which is why she was overreacting.

He wasn't so sure about all of that. Still, he'd managed to hold his temper and agreed to try to work things out with his sis, though he knew that wasn't going to happen. Not this time. And his parents knew it as well.

The second hit was from his employers. What he hadn't told his folks was that his work life had just taken a major hit courtesy of Rome's institutional paranoia. Simon had not looked at any of his emails from the Vatican, wanting to wait until his sabbatical was over. Tonight, he'd caved and read them before going to his parent's house. Now that he knew exactly what was going on in Rome it left him hurt, and truly angry.

Father Rosetti had tried to soften the blow, but until someone evaluated his ability to create a protective circle through visualization, Simon was forbidden to use that method. Instead, he'd been ordered to use the older method of pouring Holy Water on the ground, and then invoking the protection.

That was what they taught at exorcism school and it worked fine if you weren't being immediately attacked by Hellspawn. In his case, often more than one fiend at a time. Rosetti acknowledged this point but said that there were some in Rome who felt the visualization he used was of magical nature and that wasn't something they could tolerate.

Simon had read through the email three times, hoping he was wrong. That hadn't been the case. He had to use the old method or his time as a lay exorcist was over. Rosetti always read his reports, knew what Simon faced when he did his exorcisms. How dare Rome second guess him?

He'd known this was coming. He'd been careful not to create a visualized circle in front of a witness, at least not one who wasn't currently inhabited by Hellspawn.

Then TrapperCon happened. When demon Azagar had descended into the hotel's atrium in all his self-absorbed glory, Simon had created the circle on instinct. There'd been hundreds of witnesses as well as videos uploaded to the internet. It was only a matter of time before one of those reached Rome. Creating the circle that way had kept them alive when he and Katia had been dragged down to Hell. No, he'd never regret that decision.

Knowing that the Vatican would eventually hear about that, Simon had carefully explained the technique to Father Rosetti. He'd hoped that would be all that was needed. His gut told him otherwise, and he'd been right. Now everything he did was under the Vatican's intense scrutiny.

What if they permanently forbid that method, ruled it magic and therefore heresy? Then he'd have a decision to make. He'd either risk his life or walk away. Could he do that?

In some ways he was ready to resign even after the sabbatical. He was weary. The eleven days he'd been away had done little to reduce his mental fatigue. In his heart he knew it went soul deep.

If he ceased being Atlanta's exorcist, he could still trap demons and still work with Katia. At the same time, he'd be walking away from those who truly needed him. People would die or lose their souls to Hell if he allowed his pride to rule.

"Dammit."

Tonight, he'd purposely ignored Katia at the trappers' meeting, though it was hard to do that. If he had spoken to her the bad news would have poured out of him and then the trappers would know what was going on. Some already resented him because he was no longer "one of them," as if being an exorcist was somehow more prestigious than being a trapper. It was stupid, but those who believed that nonsense would love to see him fail.

Rather than going home and facing his irate partner, because she wouldn't cut him any slack for being rude, Simon took himself to where his pride had nearly cost him his life.

It was well after nine-thirty now and the sun had set, and yet the city still buzzed with activity. Someone walked their shaggy dog along the street, talking on his cell phone about his job. Another couple strolled along, hand in hand. A jogger trotted past, arms pumping.

These people were why he was an exorcist, why he risked his life to keep them safe from the fiends in Hell. Now his job was being threatened and it made him ill.

The ruins of the Tabernacle had been cleared and now wildflowers rose where the rubble and bodies had once been. Amid this huge city it was a reminder that man was as transient as any other living being, no matter how much they'd like to believe otherwise.

Simon paused in front of the brick arch, upon which were engraved the names of the dead. If not for Heaven his would be there as well. He took time with each name, remembering that person as they had once been, then offered a prayer of peace for all of them.

Finally, he wandered along the stone path that led into the sea of flowers and sat on one of the benches. Despite the noise of the city his mind reverberated with the sounds of the battle, the cries of the dead and dying, the howls of the murderous fiends. The scars on his abdomen flared to life, burning in memory.

"Why did you let me live?" he whispered.

He knew part of it was because Heaven wanted to strong-arm Riley into stopping Armageddon, but why *him* in particular? Why not one of the other trappers? Had it been because they'd been dating? Or was it because his pride had made him the ideal target?

He felt the angel's presence before he saw him.

"Do you mind if I join you?" Ori asked quietly, standing a few feet away.

"No, I do not mind." Because often wisdom came from unexpected sources.

The Divine joined him on the bench, then leaned his forearms on his knees, bending forward. It was such a human pose for one from the Upper Realm.

"Taking a break from demon extermination?" Simon asked.

"Yes. At least in Atlanta. There are very few of the dangerous ones here now."

"Any idea why that is?"

"No. And that troubles me." Ori looked over at him now. "Your thoughts are extraordinarily strong this night. I tried not to hear them, but I sense your turmoil. If you prefer not to speak of what troubles you, then we shall not. The choice is yours."

In response to the increasing darkness, lights began to glow along the walkway. Any other time it would be pretty, but not tonight.

"Since you heard my thoughts, you know what I face."

"Old prejudices are preventing you from using a weapon that keeps you alive."

"That's it exactly."

"Perhaps this is what you mortals call a *teaching moment*. Perhaps you can show your superiors that the Light may be used in other ways, and that not all of those are magical in nature."

Simon gave him a long look. "You think that's possible?"

"Since it's you, I'd say you have a better chance than most. They know your work, they know what you've faced, and overcome. Use that knowledge, for that is part of your many strengths."

He'd never thought of it that way. "You're saying I should have a strategy for all this?"

"Yes. The Church understands the use of power, it's why it's survived all these centuries. You have power of your own if you choose to wield it. If not, they will lose one of the best weapons they have against the Prince. Inhibiting you is a mistake."

"I think Father Rosetti knows that. His email had a different tone than usual, as if he was being instructed on what to write to me."

"It sounds as if you have at least one ally. I am willing to bet you have more than that." Ori rose, then hesitated. "I do not know what's happening in Atlanta, but it feels unlike the norm. Don't let your worries about Rome blind you to other dangers."

That sounded familiar, at least the danger part. "You're the second angel to say that to me. As always, thank you, Ori."

"You have suffered much to protect the innocent."

"I can say the same of you."

With a nod, the Divine set off down the walkway and then onto the sidewalk heading north. For once he hadn't just flown away, which told Simon that Ori had his own troubles.

The text message pinged at just after midnight, pulling Katia out of a deep sleep. She stared at the screen until the words finally sunk in.

EXORCISM IN 15 MINUTES. WILL NOT WAIT FOR YOU.

Below that terse message was the address.

Katia swore as she tore around the bedroom pulling on her clothes. Even at this hour getting anywhere—the address was in Decatur—would not be quick. Once she was dressed, she collected her gear and ran out the front door of the house like a thief. It was only then she realized that Simon's car was not in the driveway.

Katia didn't have time to worry about that, so she pushed the speed limit as much as she dared while complaining about idiots in general, and Simon's replacement in specific.

It'd taken several weeks before the Vatican could line up someone to cover Atlanta's exorcisms while her partner was on sabbatical. They said they were that shorthanded. The first guy from Dallas had been okay. Decent at what he did and not a jerk. This latest one? He really was pushing her buttons. He'd just arrived yesterday and was already causing trouble.

Katia had no doubt the fool would start the exorcism without her. If it went well, she'd get the "I told you so" speech. If it went bad, there'd be lots of questions from the guys in Rome, and the masters here in Atlanta. Worse case they'd be shipping the exorcist's body back home for burial.

To her relief, Katia found the door to the two-story house unlocked. She hesitated, then retrieved the small vial Simon had gifted her right before he'd left. Attached to a long cord, she kept it tucked under her T-shirt.

Unscrewing the top, she placed a tiny dot of Papal Holy water on her finger and then transferred it to her forehead. After a quick prayer she recapped the vial and dropped it back under her shirt. Maybe someday she'd be able to create one of those quick circles like Simon did.

Katia found the substitute exorcist in the kitchen, and to her relief he hadn't started without her. Instead, Lay Exorcist Snyder from California was methodically laying out his paraphernalia on the kitchen table: brass cross, aspergillum, vial of Papal Holy Water and two bottles of the locally sourced version to create the protective circle. The metal box that would hold the demon after exorcism sat at his feet.

Simon said he'd used the same gear when he'd first started, but now he was down to his cross, the metal box, and his unshakable faith. He said he felt all the rest just slowed him down, and he was right. Snyder appeared to be Old School, but then she guessed most of the Vatican's exorcists were like that.

As usual, Hell's Remodeling Crew had turned the kitchen into a trashy mess. The refrigerator had been emptied and tossed on its side, the open-door alarm still forlornly dinging away. Spoiled milk and orange juice dripped down the walls. Broken dishes and glassware, ripped up cookbooks, knives imbedded in the ceiling. Every cook's worst nightmare.

The other nightmare in the room stalked back and forth near the far wall. The possessed woman had hot pink hair curlers hanging from her graying hair and wore ragged yoga pants and a ripped top. Her now five-inch claws dug holes in anything they touched.

The instant the possessed saw Katia, she hissed that low sound that grated against your bones. Or more correctly, the demon inside her hissed.

"Katia Allyson Breman," it announced.

"Fiend," she replied. "How are things in Hell these days? Still sucking up to the boss?"

That got her a quick glance from the exorcist, then a frown. He must have thought she'd not make it here in time. Teaming up with a trapper wasn't common, and she guessed that part of his attitude was because he didn't know what to do with her.

As Simon had taught her Katia did a quick inventory of the room for potential demonic weapons. The news sucked. Pots and pans hung on a wrought iron rack secured to the ceiling. Two wooden cutting boards, a knife block riddled with stabby items, and various small electronics, including a heavy-duty expresso machine. This was a demon's dream come true. No wonder they loved kitchens so much.

The lay exorcist ignored her, moving to the cleanest part of the room and then pouring out a line of the local Holy Water for a protective circle. The Papal stuff was far too valuable to waste on wetting down a floor.

As Katia moved closer to the area, Snyder stepped inside and closed the circle with the final bit of liquid. A quick invocation and the circle went live with a bright flash of light that made the fiend, and Katia, wince.

Snyder's eyes met hers. He'd done that on purpose. He should have allowed her sanctuary inside that circle but instead he was letting her know what he thought of having a trapper as backup. She could still enter the circle if she framed her thoughts in the proper way, but she might destroy it in the process.

"It's kinda good for both of us to be inside that," she said, wondering how he'd spin this.

"I'm not going to need your help. It's a waste of time for you to be here," he said, then turned his back on her.

The whole point of having the trapper *inside* the circle was in case something caused that protection to fail. That way the person with the weapon could stand in front of the exorcist and keep them alive.

But no . . .

Katia shifted her attention to the fiend. It was grinning now, the kind of sickening and gut-twisting expression that said it was really enjoying itself. No surprise, it was playing them, or at least the solemn jackass inside the circle.

She took a position to the right of the exorcist and swiftly created her own circle with a bottle of Holy Water. Snyder registered his surprise that she knew how to do that.

"I'm ready when you are," she said, ensuring there was enough snark in that announcement that even he would get it. Fortunately, the demon hadn't taken advantage of the situation and lobbed missiles at them while they were getting ready for the actual exorcism. Most of them were smarter than that.

To her immense relief it all went smoothly: The fiend was pulled from the hair curler lady and then firmly imprisoned in the cross-adorned metal box, ready to be destroyed. As she'd expected the knives, pots and the fancy espresso machine had all gone airborne, but no one had been injured. This guy did have talent as an exorcist, but he was nowhere near as powerful as Simon.

The formerly possessed, a middle-aged lady named Adelina Rodrigues, was so shocked at what had happened to her and her house that she fled. After more hunting, Katia found her in the closest bathroom. The water was running so hopefully after she'd cleaned up, they could talk.

When she returned to the kitchen, Snyder had his gear packed and headed for the door.

"Aren't you going to bless this place first?"

"No. She can call the local priest. That's not my job."

"What about that?" she said, pointing at the demon inside the metal box.

"You can handle it. That's what demon trappers are for, right?"

Then he was gone, off to call a cab and return to his hotel.

What a self-righteous ass.

Now what? Simon had been adamant about clearing a structure immediately after an exorcism. He said the previous demon's inhabitation made it more likely another one would check the place out unless all the taint was destroyed. The only time he hadn't done that was during the unreal day when Azagar had been holding those kids hostage. Even then, Simon had instructed the wife of the former possessed author to get their priest to the house immediately. And she'd done just that.

Lay Exorcist *Not My Problem* Snyder had just become Katia's problem. He knew the priest who handled this kind of thing was down with the flu because the Archdiocese had sent them both texts with that news.

"It might not be your problem, but it sure the hell is mine," she muttered.

With a long sigh, Katia headed for her car to retrieve more Holy Water as well as the large wooden cross Simon had loaned her so she could perform the blessings. Now that she thought about it, maybe he'd seen this coming.

EIGHT

It was almost four in the morning when Katia finally returned to Simon's house. This time his car was in the driveway and the lights were off inside.

The Rodrigues' house hadn't been huge, but it'd still taken a couple hours to cleanse all the rooms, offering prayers and anointing each space with Holy Water, all the while hoping she'd done it right. Just to be sure Katia ran a line of the liquid across each entrance into the structure. Every window, door, and vent. Thank God the woman didn't have a fireplace. And then she'd sent a note to the Archdiocese suggesting they have a priest come and bless the house again.

Mrs. Rodrigues had finally crept out of hiding, then lost herself in a sea of tears over the state of her kitchen, and her life. Katia had stayed to help the lady clean up because her grandmother would rise from her grave if she didn't do the right thing. And then she'd driven the lady to her sister's house, and finally the demon to the monastery. Once it was destroyed, she made her way back to Atlanta in the dead of night. Tempting as it had been to just catch a nap in the car out in the quiet of the monastery grounds, that wouldn't work. If Snyder was called to another exorcism, she needed to be in town.

Still furious over how everything had fallen out, she'd stopped at one of the many Waffle Houses on the way back from the monastery, slurped down some coffee and eggs, and handwritten her report, line by line. Once she'd dropped all that on the page she finally headed to Simon's place.

The owner of the house was asleep, so she stripped down and fell into her bed, exhaustion and anger boiling around in her. It was a volatile combination fueled not only by how the exorcist had behaved, but also everything that had gone down at the cemetery.

Maybe after a few hours' sleep she'd be able to rewrite her report, at least if Riley thought she needed to make changes to avoid hassles with Rome. She had been totally honest about what had gone down, and that honesty had been brutal.

No matter what, Lay Exorcist *Not My Problem* was going to regret messing with this demon trapper.

†✳‡✳†

Simon's cereal had grown soggy, his coffee cold. Katia had been gone when he'd finally come home at a little after one. He'd heard her return about four but decided to wait until this morning to pass on Rome's edict. Now it was after eight and he was getting angry again. Just what Hell would love happening to an exorcist, even one still on sabbatical.

He heard her bedroom door open and then she marched out to join him. Her frown told him her life wasn't any better than his.

"Morning," he said.

She walked past him with a murmured "morning" of her own, then returned with a small plate bearing a bagel, one smeared with cream cheese. A glass of orange juice was placed beside it, and then she sat across from him.

"Some reason you blew me off at the trapper's meeting?" she demanded as she picked up the bagel.

It appeared he wasn't the only one pissed off right now.

"Yes." He shoved the printout of Rosetti's email across the table. "Bad news from Rome. Got it right before I went to my parents' last night. I wasn't ready to talk about it at the meeting."

Katia dropped the bagel back on the plate and retrieved the paper. He watched as she read it, her frown deepening with each additional line.

"What the hell? Are they crazy?" she said, looking up, then

back down at the offending document. "The only reason we're still alive is because of your quickie circle thing."

"They are worried someone will say 'Hey, why is magic bad when one of your own is doing it?'"

"It's not magic! You know that. You told them that. They should believe you." She shook her head now. "Is this why you didn't talk to me at the meeting?"

"Yes, because I couldn't trust I wouldn't blow up. I didn't want to say anything in front of the other trappers."

"Okay, well *next time* send me a text that says you're going to be an asshole and ignore me, and then I won't get so wound up."

Simon grimaced. He'd handled that badly. "I will. I promise. I'm sorry." He owed her that. "What's going on with you, because you look as angry as I feel."

She shook her head. "I'm not telling you why I'm being a bitch. Maybe later. So, what are you going to do when we have an exorcism?"

"Use the old method until Rome gets someone over here to see how the invocation technique works. I don't have a choice."

"How long will that take?"

"A few days, a few weeks, a few months. They're still making decisions about things that happened in the 18th century. so God knows."

Her frown grew. "This sucks, Simon. Really, really sucks. I'm furious that they don't trust you when you tell them something."

"Same here."

Without a further word she ate the rest of her bagel, downed her OJ, then took off out the front door with her trapping bag in hand. She'd left behind the plate and glass. which was not her usual style.

"Yeah, something's definitely going on with you."

†✶‡✶†

It felt good to get a few rays of sun before the day heated up which is why Riley had lobbied for a patio set at the office. Located to the right of the main door, the table was large enough to handle four people and had an adjustable umbrella to shield you so you didn't roast. Even the padded chairs were comfortable.

Initially Master Harper hadn't been impressed with the idea but Riley had seen him out there a couple times late in the evening when she'd driven by. He'd been leaning back in one chair, feet up in another, drinking a soda. By the grumpy master's standards that was a huge thumbs up for the new furniture. Not that he'd ever admit it.

Today it was serving as a makeshift classroom for the final apprentice from the first batch Riley had mentored. Though the other two had already passed their exams and become journeymen, Jaye's exam was in a week. It wasn't because she hadn't been a great student.

The delay had come because of her mom's medical issues. Now that Mrs. Lynn's health had improved—she was on a kidney transplant list—Jaye was back to worrying about her exam. That test was anything but easy, designed to weed out those who "phoned it in" because someone who was sloppy could get you killed.

Riley had just finished reviewing the fundamental steps of how to deal with a Grade Five Geo-Fiend when she saw Katia pull into the parking lot. A glance at her phone said that the journeyman was late, which wasn't usual. The instant Katia exited the vehicle she could tell something was wrong.

Jaye looked over at their fellow trapper and smiled. Then the smile dimmed. "She doesn't look happy."

"No, that's the Someone Has Pissed Me Off look. Katia's usually better at hiding it."

"I like her. She's cool," Jaye said. "She doesn't act like she's a big deal, but she is."

"Yes, she is." Though the Kansas trapper didn't quite realize that. She was a hard one to read, and more than once Riley and Beck had discussed the best way to mentor the city's newest trapper. They still weren't sure.

Instead of unloading the instant she reached them, Katia pulled out a chair, then a bottle of water, and leaned back to watch Jaye labor through another question.

"We're working on the Grade Five trapping section for the exam," Riley said, pointing at the papers in front of them.

"Ugh," was the prompt reply.

"What if you can't ground the Geo-Fiend?" Jaye asked.

"Then you're in deep trouble," Riley said. "Remember to use whatever is at the scene—fences, anything metal."

"Cars don't work well because of the tires. They just tend to blow up," Katia said.

"Had that happen?" Riley asked.

"Not to me, but to my first master."

"So how did he ground the fiend?"

"Total luck."

Jaye went back to studying the sample questions on the sheet in front of her.

"You need to talk something out?" Riley asked, her eyes still on Katia.

"Yes, but I don't want to interrupt what you're doing here."

"I'm good," Jaye said.

"Okay, then let's go talk because I'm willing to bet whatever you have to tell me is going to be great fun."

The snort that returned told her it was going to be anything but.

Since Harper was at an AA meeting, Riley raided their refrigerator stash, collecting two sodas, then she took a seat at her desk, indicating that Katia should join her. "So, what happened?"

There was a long sigh as the journeyman rummaged in her trapping bag. A manila envelope came Riley's way, and inside was a handwritten report.

"I'll type it up, but I wanted you to see if first. Because, well . . ."

Riley parked herself in her chair and read through it. The further she read, the less she liked what it said.

Failure to allow for adequate time for trapper to reach exorcism site? Check

Failure to include trapper inside Holy Water circle? Check

Failure to offer counsel to demonic victim, cleanse the structure, and transport fiend to the monastery for destruction. Check for all three.

Riley tapped the bottom of the report on the desk to even it up, a sure way of getting the journeyman's attention. Then she laid it down.

"I need to know if I'm letting my anger go too far, or if this is what Father Rosetti needs to know," Katia said.

"The fact that you didn't immediately type this up and email this to him says you're not sure."

She nodded warily.

"I'm thinking you might want to give yourself a day to cool down, then we can look at this again and decide what Rosetti needs to know. This might be a onetime thing with this guy. Or not."

"Okay. I can do that." She sounded relieved Riley had made that suggestion.

"Did you tell Simon about this?"

"No. Not yet."

There seemed to be more going on. "Anything else I should know about?"

Katia's eyes lit with fire. "Yes!"

Rome. Their usual paranoia. Katia unloaded about all of it and how they had ordered Simon not to use the quick Holy Water circle thing until the Vatican determined if it was magical or not.

"Can you believe it? They're willing to risk his life because they don't trust him!"

Oh yeah, Katia was incredibly angry, and she bet Simon was the same.

This was another thing she and Beck had discussed because they both knew Rome wasn't likely to approve of how the exorcist set his wards now.

"They get nervous about stuff like this. They sure didn't

know what to do with me when I told them about the Angel of Death. Or the fact that I wanted to study with magic users."

"But you were right about all that."

"Yes, but that doesn't make it any easier for them to accept."

She reviewed what Katia had told her. "So, the order is that *he* can't generate a quick circle, at least for now. Did the email say *you* couldn't?"

"No, it didn't mention me. But I've not been able to do it. Simon showed me, but it just doesn't work."

Aha. "Our favorite exorcist is great at many things, but he might not have the right approach to this technique. I think he's still a bit unsure about it."

Katia gave her a sidelong glance. "You're being diplomatic, aren't you?"

"Yeah, I am. Simon fought me on this until he realized that there was no magic involved. Well, maybe a little, but I didn't bother telling him that. In his case, it's the power of his faith that makes it work, not a spell."

Katia shook her head. "I'm not as religious as he is."

"No, but you have strong willpower or you wouldn't have been able to offload that spell last night. I think it might be enough to make this work."

The journeyman's expression said she thought this was total b.s.

"Think how surprised he'd be when you create your first circle for him. You can keep him safe, at least until Rome gets things sorted out."

She'd already noticed the friendly rivalry between them and was pleased it existed. Simon, for all his strengths, needed a good friend, someone who would watch his back no matter what, and tell him he was being an ass when needed. With Katia by his side during the exorcisms, her fears for his safety had dropped to a level that was almost bearable.

In return, Katia needed someone who wouldn't undermine her confidence because too much of that had happened with her former master. Together Journeyman Breman and Lay Exorcist

Adler were a formidable team, so formidable that even the Prince of Hell had tried to take them down. And failed. Riley still smiled every time she thought about that.

It took about an hour, with frequent telephone interruptions from the public to report demonic activities, and Jaye asking questions about the review content, to finally get Katia comfortable with the circle visualization technique.

Once Katia understood the process, she rocked, setting seven out of the ten practice circles straight up. Which was better than Simon's first attempts. Even more impressive was that they were using the everyday Holy Water, not the special variety from the Vatican.

"There you go," Riley said, pleased at what they'd accomplished. "I wouldn't do this around any of the other exorcists, not until Rome gets a clue that it's okay. At least you have a backup if something gets really dangerous."

Katia's face lit up with what had to be her first smile of the day. "I'm honestly not trying to make trouble for Snyder. He's just a jerk."

"Possibly. Or maybe there's something else going on. You'll know soon enough. Oh, and ask Simon if he'll share some of his papal Holy Water so you always have some on you."

At that Katia pulled a chain out from under her T-shirt, then waved the small vial at the end of it. "Ah, he already did."

Go Simon.

Chuffed by the progress they'd made they rejoined Jaye to help her review the Legalities and Liabilities section for the upcoming exam. Jaye was sure she'd blow it. Riley knew otherwise. And now Katia knew how to set a protective circle without fussing with the big bottles of Holy Water.

No matter how the day played out, that was a win-win.

NINE

Once Jaye's study session was done and Master Harper had returned from his daily meeting, Katia headed into the office to organize June's paperwork. Copies of all this had already been sent to the National Guild, weekly.

But the pencil pushers insisted on yet another lengthy report categorizing all the trappings for the previous month by type of fiend, location, extent of public damage, and so forth. Katia had never gotten this far into the minutia of trapping while in Kansas, and now she was grateful for that.

Still, working with Riley and listening to her mess with Master Harper's head was always fun. Simon had hinted that Harper had once been an abusive SOB, but since he was dealing with his alcohol addiction he'd been fairly decent to work with. There was a lot Simon hadn't said and that made her wonder just how brutal Harper had been.

As she finished yet another entry about a Techno-Fiend screwing up the computers at a primary school, the door to the office creaked open and a man entered. Tan Shirt, tan pants, running shoes. Probably here to report a demon sighting. He headed toward her and Riley, ignoring Master Harper entirely, which was odd. Usually, they insisted on dealing with the sole male in the room.

"Riley Blackthorne?" he called out as he approached them.

"Yes?" her master replied from behind her desk. "Can I help you?"

In lieu of an answer he handed her an official-looking envelope. "Katia Breman?"

"Yeah?" She got her very own envelope in return.

"Congratulations, you've both been served."

And then he was out the door making a hasty retreat.

"Served?" Katia said, not understanding.

Riley opened her envelope and unfolded the documents, then muttered a couple choice words in Hellspeak. "She did it."

Since her boss rarely swore, Katia ripped open her envelope and was met with legalese, none of which made any sense.

"Getting sued?" Harper said, frowning.

"Yup, courtesy of the late Mr. Means' obnoxious widow," Riley replied.

"Then she's just being a stupid bitch," Harper said and went back to his paperwork.

"That's it exactly," her master murmured as she stuffed the documents in the envelope, then pushed it aside. "Oh well, we'll deal with this later."

"Ah, but how?" Katia asked. She had no idea what you did when you got sued.

"First thing, don't talk to that woman or any of her legal people. Especially not the press. It's a court case now so we don't want to give her any ammunition. And you and I will talk to Fireman Jack to see what can be done about this."

A grunt came from Harper, which sounded like approval.

"Fireman Jack? The demon trafficker?"

"Jack's also the Guild's lawyer. He'll know what to do." Riley paused and then added, "Okay, back to work."

How does she do that?

There was so much to admire about her boss, but Master Blackthorne's ability to compartmentalize trouble had to be a superpower, one that Katia did not possess. She already saw all the money she'd saved for an apartment being burned up in lawyer's fees just because some necromancer just had to have another corpse.

As if she could read her mind, Riley added, "It'll be okay. Fireman Jack is a seriously good lawyer. Do not let this spook you. It's not worth it."

"If you say so."

Yeah, definitely a superpower.

A little after five, Katia's phone dinged to report another exorcism, this time in Midtown. Lay Exorcist Snyder had supplied the address and nothing else, no further information as to whether this was a structural or a personal possession. With a sigh, she typed back that she'd be there in about twenty minutes.

This time Exorcist Snyder waited for her outside the house, pacing back and forth, clutching his phone. By the time Katia joined him his call had ended. There were tears in his eyes now.

"Are you okay?" she asked, putting her gear down. Because even if he was a jerk something was going on.

"I . . . my daughter. She had cancer. *Had* cancer. The chemo worked. We just got the test results. She's in remission. It's all gone!"

No wonder the tears. Katia would be blubbering by now.

"I couldn't be there for the tests. They were scheduled after I got here. I wanted to be back home with her, but . . . "

There was no one else who could take his place.

"How old is she?" Katia asked, feeling her own emotions kick in.

In lieu of a reply Snyder handed over his phone. The image on the screen was of a girl of about ten and she sported a huge grin. She was bald, no doubt from chemotherapy, and in her arms was an adorable Labrador puppy, all fluffy and huggable.

"That's Lesley. She's our only child. And now . . . " His voice broke.

Katia smiled, blinking back her own tears. "And now she has a future."

Snyder nodded, a fat tear rolling down his cheek. "Thanks be to God." He hesitated, then added, "I'm so sorry I was an ass during the last exorcism. I've never been that way before. I was so worried about Leslie, and I took it out on you. I put you in danger. That was very, very wrong. Please forgive me."

There *had* been something else going on, just as Riley had suggested. It was good she hadn't submitted that report. She'd make sure that the revised one wouldn't cause any problems with his bosses.

"Your apology is accepted. I admit I was really angry at you," she said. "But I know what it's like to be so afraid you'll lose someone you love. Nothing else matters at that point. Nothing."

He cocked his head. "Was it someone in your family?"

"My baby brother. A demon put him in a coma for six months. He's awake and doing great now."

Snyder smiled. "There is much to praise God for, isn't there?"

She nodded and sent another thanks to that angel who'd saved Kevin's life.

After finding a tissue in a pocket Snyder blew his nose, then straightened up. He glanced toward the house behind them. "Alright, let's go do what we do best, Journeyman Breman."

She liked this guy more by the minute.

"You got it, Lay Exorcist Snyder."

It was late for supper but Beck didn't seem to mind. He had worked his way through a full plate of Mama Z's ribs, with all the sides, and was leaning back in the booth with a sated expression. Riley, on the other hand, had picked at her food and then offered him what she hadn't eaten. Those ribs vanished as well. Instead of massive amounts of protein she'd opted to nibble on the potato salad and coleslaw.

As Beck eyed her across the table, she knew questions were also on the menu. He took a long sip from his beer, set it down, then turned the bottle so the logo was facing him. He didn't know he did that when he was uneasy about something.

"Go on, tell me what's on your mind," she said.

His deep brown eyes rose to meet hers. "The number of demons in this town keeps droppin'. Whatever's goin' on is gettin' worse. I'm hearin' that the fiends are spooked about somethin'.""

"Something going on in Hell?" she asked.

"Don't think so. The problem is here."

"Serrah, maybe?" Perhaps Atlanta having a new guardian angel was what was making the fiends skittish.

"Don't think it's her, either. What's the angel say?"

The angel being Ori.

She sighed, setting her fork aside. "I hunted him down this afternoon and asked him a few questions. Did you know he likes to hang out on top of one of the skyscrapers downtown?"

"Really?" Beck said. "Why?"

"He tracks demons from up there. Go figure."

"Takes all kinds."

She chuckled at that. "I sent him a mental text sort of thing asking to talk to him and a few seconds later I found myself on *top* of that building."

Beck straightened up now, frowning. "What?"

"Yeah, sixty stories up. Almost a thousand feet tall. I looked it up on the internet once I was on the ground again."

"Was it the buildin' that you said looks like a pencil?"

"No, the SunTrust one. Ori apologized for 'the abrupt movement of my person' as he called it. He claimed he was looking for a particular fiend and was having trouble finding it. That bothered him." She shrugged. "So, we sat up there, him glowering down at the city, and me asking him a bunch of questions while trying not to throw up."

"Did he actually answer any of yer questions?" His sharp tone said that her husband wasn't happy with his wife being spirited off by an angel. But then those two had a history of butting heads.

She smiled at his reaction. "Sorta. Ori is as worried as we are. He insists that something has changed in the city. He asked Serrah about it, but she has no idea what's normal for Atlanta since she hasn't been its guardian for long."

"It's odd all the time, but sometimes it's just damned odd," Beck replied. "Did he give you anythin' to work with?"

"Not really," she replied, then began picking at her potato salad again. It was the kind she loved, all creamy with great spices, but she just couldn't do it.

"Riley?" he nudged.

A shove moved her plate away. "He's as confused as the rest of us. He insists that it has nothing to do with Hell, so that's good news. But he can't figure it out. I ask the guy who's been alive forever and should have all the answers, but he's just as clueless as anyone else. I don't know what we're going to do."

"What about Mort?"

"He's still looking for the necromancer who stole those corpses. He's checking to see if this kind of thing has happened anywhere else. So far the answer has been 'no.' The ability to bust someone out of their grave while *inside* a Holy Water circle has thrown him and Ozymandias both. They're thinking a spell was placed inside the grave. But when? If that was the case wouldn't Means have been snatched the first night?"

Beck thought for a moment, then circled back around to something she'd said earlier. "What about that demon Ori was tryin' to find so badly. Did he say why?"

"I didn't think to ask about it, I was starting to lose it up there. It was hard to concentrate when all I could think of was that I didn't have a pair of wings like the guy sitting next to me."

"I'd be the same. I'll call Angus tomorrow mornin'. He's back at the manor house now so maybe he can check the records to see if this has happened anywhere else."

"There's another couple problems."

Then she told him about Mrs. Means' lawsuit and Rome's latest nonsense. Both of those resulted in a swear word muttered under his breath.

"How's Simon handlin' that?"

"Katia says he's really upset. She is too. Oh, and I taught her how to set a visualization circle today so at least she can keep them safe during the exorcisms."

Beck thought that through as he took a sip of his beer. "And if Rome has a problem with that?"

"They can bitch all they want, and it won't matter," Riley replied. "Katia's not an exorcist, so they have no control over what she does."

"And if they say that trappers can't work with their people anymore?"

She frowned. "Then they'll lose Simon, for sure."

"Yeah, and they should if they pull that kind of crap."

Abruptly he rose, scooped up the check and headed for the counter to pay. Riley took one last bite of her coleslaw, then followed. Maybe tomorrow would give them some news that'd be of value. Her instincts told her they were facing something unusually nasty. Unfortunately, those instincts were rarely wrong.

TEN

At her master's insistence, Katia was to take the day off unless there was an exorcism. No trapping, no paperwork at the office, none of it. Considering there were fewer demons in the city than usual, she didn't argue. There wasn't much to do anyway. She could hardly complain about the downtime when she'd been nagging Simon about his inability to chill out.

By the time she crawled out of bed he was gone, which meant she'd have to wait to tell him about her training session with the Holy Water. Because this was Simon, he'd left her his itinerary for the day propped against the napkin holder on the kitchen table. Mass, then his parents' house to help his mom in the garden, then off to the gym. It was obvious that he was trying to keep himself busy so he didn't have to obsess about the Vatican thing. It wouldn't work.

Katia had just finished her breakfast when Fireman Jack's email arrived. She quickly read it, then read it again.

"Yes!" she shouted, executing a fist pump.

Jack's email said that according to Georgia law, those who sat vigil over a deceased individual were exempt from civil litigation providing their actions did not cross the line into "gross incompetence."

He insisted her and Riley's actions the night of the corpse napping *did not* fall under that clause, and that it was best to just let this play out through the courts. Also, all legal fees incurred *would be covered by the Summoners Society.*

"Thank you, Mort." That was his doing for sure.

She sent a quick text to Riley and a short time later she received a response which said "Told you. Now go have fun. It's your day off."

With that order in mind Katia began working through her latest list of potential apartments. This was now officially An Ordeal, her brother's favorite term when assigned tasks he despised. For him it was the Ordeal of Cleaning the Garage, or the Ordeal of Math Homework. Kevin would always finish those tasks but there was always a significant amount of complaining involved.

The first landlord she'd called had asked what she did for living and when Katia had said, "I'm a demon trapper," he'd hung up on her. She drew a line through that listing and moved on.

The second landlord had asked her the same job question and this time Katia replied, "pest extermination." Which wasn't exactly a lie. He then launched into a long monologue about how he expected to always have access to her apartment for spot inspections, any hour of the day, without any prior notice.

"Not happening. If I rent a place, I expect privacy."

"Not if you rent from me."

"Understood." She hung up on him.

Landlord Number Three wanted seventeen-hundred and fifty dollars a month, utilities not included, for a one-bedroom apartment. And he wanted three months' rent in advance, part of which was a damage deposit. That meant she'd have over five thousand dollars invested even before she moved in. She passed on that one. It appeared she'd be staying at Grand Master Stewart's house longer than she'd planned.

After lunch Katia dove back into the Rental Olympics. This time there was a "perfect" apartment located in a modern complex, one bedroom, one bath, parking space, community swimming pool and exercise room, all for far less than she'd expected. It just sounded too good to be true so she gave them a call.

"You can't afford to wait," the lady on the other end of the line insisted. "This will go fast. If you want to hold it, I just need the first month's rent and security deposit."

"I'd need to see the apartment first. Any chance I can do that today?"

"No, it won't be until next week. I'm not in town right now. But the deposit will hold it for you."

Huh? "And if I don't like the apartment?"

"Then I'll refund the deposit, no problem. I just need you to fill out a form for me and email it back. Usual background check stuff, you know."

Which would include Katia's birthdate and social security number.

"No, I'd need to see the place first."

"You will be sorry," the woman said. "It's a wonderful place. Top floor in a high rise, splendid view. You can't do any better in the Atlantic Station neighborhood."

"Maybe not. Anyway, thanks for your time." Then she ended the call.

Part of her wondered if her lack of trust was overblown. The other part said the whole conversation felt off. Trusting her instincts, she decided to move on. Then she received a text from the far-too-perky landlord.

I'VE JUST HAD ANOTHER COUPLE INTERESTED IN THE APT. SEND THE DEPOSIT IN THE NEXT 20 MIN & IT'S YOURS! YOU WON'T REGRET IT!

The text included photos.

"Oh, you shouldn't have done that." Images could be traced on the internet. "Let's find out if I'm being paranoid."

Within those twenty minutes she'd been given before she lost the deal of a lifetime, Katia had sourced the apartment's photos to a Buckhead real estate agency's website. There was the apartment in all its glory, room after room professionally staged and looking awesome.

But it was *for sale*, not for rent, and the real estate agent's phone number wasn't the one who offered her that wonderful "deal."

"Well, look at that."

A quick email to the agency let them know someone was running a scam on one of their properties. She included her phone number in case they wanted more information. Within minutes Katia was talking to a nice agent guy telling him where she'd found the bogus listing and the phone number of the fake landlord.

"Maybe this time we'll get lucky and someone will go to jail," the man said.

"Happy to help. Go get 'em!" There was a laugh. "Do you manage rental properties?"

He did, but the prices he was quoting were way beyond her budget. She thanked him and gave up for the day. She'd just started researching what types of flowers could survive Georgia summers when her phone rang. It was her favorite exorcist.

"Hey! How goes it with the gardening?" she asked.

"That plan got bagged," Simon said. "Mom had to cover for someone who called in sick."

"She's a nurse, right?"

"Nurse practitioner. I'm headed to the gym. I need to punch things that aren't people. Then I'll be going over to this new dojo that just opened. They have a longsword class there. I want to find out what it involves."

Longsword? "From what I've heard, the pointy end goes *toward* the other guy."

He laughed. "Really? So that's what I've been doing wrong."

She returned his laugh. "Do you mind if I come up with ideas for the flower beds in your backyard?"

A pause. "Go for it. You're the pro."

"Okay, might do a few different options and get you cost estimates. Do you want any vegetables back there?"

"No need. My mother has a huge garden, and she shares all that with the rest of us."

"Okay, flowers it is."

"Sounds good. And I know what you're doing, trying to keep me from worrying about what's going on with the Vatican.

I owe you."

"Right back at you, my friend. Oh, something you should know: Riley taught me how to set a Holy Water circle using that visualization technique. Just in case we might need that or anything."

There was silence on the other end of the call.

"She suggested I shouldn't use it in front of any other exorcists, but I needed to know it for backup. Like if things go south."

"And she's right," he said. "We'll do it the old way until we have a ruling from Rome, but knowing you can do a quick circle makes me feel a lot better. Thank you."

"No sweat. Now go have fun with the pounding on something that isn't people," she said.

"I will. Later." Then he ended the call.

Sword fighting?

The guy never ceased to amaze her. And he'd taken the news about her ability to make a circle on her own without any pushback. That was a good sign.

Katia rose, intending on measuring the flower beds so she had a clue how much square footage was involved. That activity didn't require a lot of brain power so she could think through all that had happened over the last two days. As she headed for the back door, her phone pinged a text from Summoner Alexander himself.

HI. RILEY GAVE ME YOUR NUMBER. IS IT POSSIBLE
FOR YOU TO COME TO MY HOUSE SOMETIME TODAY?

I HAVE THINGS WE NEED TO DISCUSS AND I DON'T
WANT TO DO THAT ON THE PHONE OR IN AN EMAIL.

She tapped her chin in thought. "Hmm, let's see. I can dig in the dirt, in the blazing heat, or hang at a necro's house with A/C? Maybe figure out what's going on with the stolen bodies."

That was a no-brainer and she let him know she'd be there

in about and hour.

The copper archway that led to Summoner Alexander's home hummed today, a low vibratory sound that she couldn't ignore. Its warning inscription, *Momento Mori*, seemed to glow like a beacon. Even Katia with her limited Latin knew what it meant. Yes, she remembered that someday she would die. Being a trapper didn't allow you to whistle by that graveyard.

Even as she walked under the arch the intensity of the magical buzz didn't diminish, instead it kept zinging across her skin. She was tempted to plunge her hand into a nearby planter of colorful zinnias to offload that buzz. But with her luck someone would catch her doing it, which would require an explanation, and probably kill the flowers as well. She gulped down more air and kept moving.

On her left and partway down the cobblestone street was the witches' shop, Bell, Book, and Broomstick. Riley said it sold items for both the wannabees and the genuine practitioners. Her master had often spoken of her friend, Ayden, who had fought in the great battle at Oakland Cemetery. Katia had met a couple witches in Lawrence, but they didn't seem to be the kind to wield a sword and lop off the heads of Hellspawn. Or at least they'd never acted like it.

Sitting next to the entrance to the shop was a cat, a calico whose fur was a riot of apricot, gold, rust, and black. Two emerald-green eyes studied her as she approached. This feline had a distinct white outline. Not a demon, but something else. But then this was Little Five Points.

The shop's door opened and a woman bustled out, a shopping bag hanging from an arm. She didn't appear to notice the cat just a foot or so away which confirmed Katia's suspicions that the feline was unique.

"Thank you so much," the lady said, addressing someone who appeared in the doorway now. "I really want that lizard out of my house and this will do the trick."

"You're welcome."

The woman in the shop's doorway watched her go with a bemused expression. She had her auburn hair in a loose bun, no doubt because of the heat. She wore a multi-patterned blue top and a long, pale blue cotton skirt. The top was low enough to reveal a large tattoo on her neck and chest. It appeared to show the inside of a cave, but why one would want that on their skin made no sense.

"Is it a real lizard?" Katia asked, curious.

The woman studied her for a time. "She sees it, so it is real to her."

That was an interesting idea. "Are you Ayden Marshall?" A nod returned. "I'm Katia Breman. I work with Master Blackthorne."

"Riley has spoken of you. Often, in fact." Another meow, which caused them both to look down. "Yes?" A long meow, then the cat stretched and headed toward Katia.

She knelt as it approached. "Your cat is so pretty. What is its name?"

There was a brief hesitation. "Her name is Esme, short for Esmerelda. Not everyone can see her."

"Then I'm just lucky, I guess."

The feline halted a short distance from Katia, still eyeing her.

"Is it okay if I pet you?" she asked.

A chirp was the response and then the creature turned tail and marched back toward the witch.

"Sure, ignore me," Katia said, laughing as she stood. "Typical cat."

"Are you here to see the Summoner Advocate?" Ayden asked, gesturing down the street toward Mort's house.

"I am."

"Good. Tell him if he has any questions to call me."

Then the witch was back inside the shop with the door closing behind her. The cat remained outside, licking a paw, then vigorously applying it to an ear.

"Bye, Esme, it was nice to meet you," Katia said as she continued toward Mort's place. It was only when she was some distance away that she muttered, "Ghost cats. Now I've seen everything."

She'd been inside Mortimer Alexander's home once before, the day she'd arrived in Atlanta. During that visit there had been a mild tug of magic as she'd entered the house. This time the tug was more like a body slam and sucked the breath out of her.

Mort noticed her reaction and winced. "Sorry. I ramped up my wards. I'm a bit on edge, for obvious reasons."

"No sweat," she said, then took a very deep breath to let the sensation pass. "Better than a guard dog."

He didn't reply but bolted the door behind her and then led Katia down the hallway to his terrace. It felt cool there despite being open to the backyard. A high-tech ceiling fan stirred the air from above but that shouldn't have made much of a difference.

"Have a seat," Mort said, gesturing to one of the wicker chairs.

Like the last time the chair was comfortable, and she settled into it with a sigh. But unlike the last time there wasn't any food on the side table. Nor any drinks. Mort was all about hospitality so that showed how wired he was.

"How bad is it?" she asked, pulling her water bottle out of her trapping bag.

"Bad." Then he noticed her drink. "Sorry. I should have had something laid out for you."

She waved him off. "We've got bigger stuff to worry about, so no problem."

Mort sank into the chair nearest hers. "Well, before we get into all that, I have contact information for someone who can teach you how to handle your ability to channel magic. Her name is Claúdia Santos and she lives in Savannah. That's about four hours south of here on the interstate."

"This lady is okay with helping me?"

"To be honest, she's reluctant. She doesn't like people knowing she's a chaîne."

His tone implied there was more. "And?"

The summoner leaned back in his chair. "Offloading a magical spell is dangerous. If you do it wrong it can kill you, or make you wish you were dead. The process needs to be *very* precise. You were lucky because Riley and his lordship helped you."

"So doing this without the training is a dumb idea?" she asked.

"If you have a choice between being bespelled, or trying to ditch the spell, do it. Just know that the process robs your body of essential minerals. If those minerals get too low you can have a stroke, a heart attack, or a seizure."

Katia blinked at that. "Oh good. That's lovely news," her sarcasm ringing through every word.

Did she have a choice? *No.* Just because she might never grave sit again didn't mean someone wouldn't throw a spell on her for whatever reason. If she had this ability why not learn how to use it?

"Yes, I'd like to talk to this lady. If she's not good with helping me, that's fine. It's her call. I probably won't ever need to offload another spell anyway."

"One never knows," Mort replied.

Then his warning clicked into place. "To teach me how to do this means someone has to throw spells at me, right?" The summoner nodded. "That's why this lady's uneasy."

"She's more than uneasy. Her last pupil didn't survive the training."

Didn't survive the . . .

Katia would worry about that later. "Are we up to the bad part of the news yet?"

He sighed as if the weight of the entire world was on his shoulders. Which it probably was, at least in Atlanta.

"As of now, nine people have been reanimated. Five of those were stolen when the necromancer overwhelmed the grave sitters. Three had their graves explode, destroying the protective circle, like what happened to you and Riley. One reanimate came from a funeral home." He paused and added, "Riley said you told her about that one."

"And the pale guy."

He nodded. "He isn't the necromancer, I'm sure of that," Mort said. "I've been trying to find a pattern but—"

"You're so wiped you can't think straight."

A slight smile said she was right.

Katia retrieved her legal pad and a pen from her trapping bag. "Then let's work through them, one by one. Maybe we can see something they have in common, something we missed."

Mort seemed to relax for the first time since she'd arrived. "I've got notes as well. Let me get them."

A little over an hour later they had a detailed list of all the missing reanimates, dates of death, their home addresses, occupations, who had handled their funeral arrangements and where they were buried. To put all that data in some form that made sense, Katia created a grid. It was second nature to her after all the years of landscape planning, and it helped her sort things out in her own mind.

Mort studied the listings, then tapped a finger on the page. "I used to be a mortician, so I have experience in the business." He put small check marks by five of the businesses listed. "I know the directors at these funeral homes personally. I'll call them to see if there is anything they remember that seemed odd."

That was a good idea. "You want me to do the others?"

He shook his head. "I'll get further with them than you will."

"Then maybe I need to find the guy who was at the funeral home and at the cemetery."

"He might be a relative of Mr. Means."

"Well, if he is I can't really talk to him since we're being sued."

He blinked at that. "Good point. You know, there's one thing we don't have on this list," he said. "We need to know who was grave sitting those bodies. I can find out the names of those who were injured, but I don't know the others. I'll check with Riley about that."

"Maybe get the names of everyone who watched these graves, not just the ones the night the bodies were stolen. Maybe there's a pattern?"

"Good idea." He made a note of that.

Katia took a photo of the grid with her phone. "You need me for anything else?"

"Not unless you'd like to stay while I make those calls. It might take some time, though."

"No, I better get back to Simon's place. I owe both Riley and the Vatican a couple of exorcism reports. Don't dare get behind on those."

As he placed his first call, Katia let herself out the front door. In her jeans pocket was the name and phone number of the lady in Savannah. Maybe someday she'd contact her. But not today. Not with Alex's future on the line.

ELEVEN

"Go!" he shouted. And still the dead just stared at him. "Go, please, just go!"

It was useless. All his plans had failed. *Again.*

"Why can't you do what I command?" he demanded.

Nine dead faces stared back at him, some blank, some bewildered. Only one seemed to comprehend what Mathias was trying to do.

"You want us to go into that other world again?" the one named Means asked.

"Yes. Go there and bring something back to me."

"But we can't go," Means replied. "It won't let us in."

And that was the problem.

Mathias had opened a gateway into that other world, bright and shimmering with energy. Or at least he'd thought it was the entrance until he'd been tossed out on his ass. Entry refused. The doorman, or whatever the hell that was on the other side, refused to deal with him. He'd tried again and been slung back into his own realm. And warned never to try that again.

So, he'd sent in the dead. Whatever that was on the other side couldn't have any problem with them, right? The first few he'd reanimated weren't lucid enough to do what he needed, so he reanimated even more bodies, carefully choosing those he thought might be capable of the task.

His assistant had helped him weed through the obituaries, and the last few had been a lot brighter. Means, in particular. Those that made it through the portal were immediately tossed back into this world.

Just like me.

Mathias Burnley Chaffin, a summoner with considerable power, a wearer of the darkest navy robe, was a failure. If the stakes hadn't been so damned high his pride would have been hurt. But that wasn't important, not when Her life was on the line.

Mathias waved his hand and the portal vanished, revealing the dirty wall of the abandoned factory.

"I need someone strong enough to cross the barrier and get past that damned gatekeeper," he murmured, pacing now. "Someone who has done it before."

He needed them to bring him an object of power or the one he loved would perish. Even now She was dying, he could sense it. Dying with all her people because of the evil that had invaded their world. An evil that should never have been there in the first place.

He'd been naïve, so sure he could save them all. Now Mathias had no choice but to send someone who was still alive, and he knew who that had to be. Something about that strange girl at the gravesite told him she might be the one. Not the summoner, she would be too much of a hassle.

No, it had to be the trapper, the one who'd resisted his magic but didn't have any magic of her own. The one that his lover said had walked the realms.

Was it true? Could the trapper get past the menace at the doorway? Only one way to find out. But first he needed leverage to ensure she'd make the journey and return with the object he needed, because she wouldn't do it otherwise.

Mathias knew stubbornness when he saw it.

"Who would you risk your life for?" he mused.

He stepped away from the Deaders and made the call.

"Yeah?" the voice on the other end said.

"It's . . . Magus. I need you to check someone out for me. I need to know who her closest friends are, her family, who she'd be willing to fight for."

"I thought I was done," his assistant complained. "People are starting to ask questions. Someone saw me at one of the funeral homes."

"I don't care about that."

"Well, I do," the voice insisted.

Mathias gritted his teeth. "Think about who you're talking to."

There was a sharp intake of breath as reality hit home.

"Yeah. Sorry. It's not been easy."

"It isn't easy for any of us, Hawkins. Check out the trapper at Means' grave. Her name is Katia Breman. I need the info *tonight*."

"Okay. But this is it, right?"

"Yes, this is it." Because if what he planned didn't work, he was done.

"I'm grave sitting right now. I planted the spheres just like you asked."

"Fine. Whatever. I won't be needing them." *Not now.*

Mathias ended the call. It was only then he realized the reanimate was still standing nearby, watching his every move. Means looked over at the other Deaders, then back.

"Can you send them home now?" he asked as he gestured toward the others. "They can't help you. They need to be at peace."

Mathias wasn't a bastard, or hadn't been one until recently.

"I'll free a few of them, but not all." He needed some for leverage against his fellow summoners. "I'll give them a restorative and then send them to the cops. The police will make sure they get to the proper people."

"Thank you." Then Means shuffled over to rejoin the others. There was murmuring among them, and one of the dead started to cry.

As the weeping continued, Mathias closed his eyes, thinking again of the one he was trying to save. If She and her people died, then he didn't care what this world would do to him. They could rip away his magic. Kill him. It simply would not matter if She didn't survive.

In that case, dying would be a mercy he did not deserve.

†✳‡✳†

Katia headed downtown after her time with Mort. Having a full day off didn't happen that often so if she didn't get called out to an exorcism, the afternoon was hers. For once, she'd decided to do something touristy. How often could she take a real Atlanta Demon Trappers tour?

Because her face was all over the news, both in electronic and print, she'd opted for a disguise. A pair of sunglasses covered part of her face and the Six Feet Under restaurant baseball cap, a present from Riley, hid her hair.

When Riley had initially mentioned the tour, Katia had brushed it off. Then her boss had routed her to the tour's website which said thirty-five percent of the fees were donated *directly* to the local Guild's Orphans' Fund. There was even an official letter from Master Harper that stated tour guide Gary Bates was for real. She suspected that it'd been Riley who'd engineered that endorsement.

Gary's website bio said he was a former journeyman trapper who had quit the business right after the Tabernacle massacre. He'd been there, been injured, and now the thought of trapping Hellspawn gave him endless nightmares. Instead, he'd decided to educate people on what trappers did, what Hellspawn were really like, and how it wasn't at all like Hollywood's crazy hype.

Now she was downtown listening to Gary restate all of this at the beginning of the tour, just in case someone hadn't read the fine print on his website. That honesty earned him major points.

They'd begun in the heart of the city.

"The trappers call this part of town Demon Central," the guide said to the group as he gestured around. He looked to be in his early fifties, but you could see that the job had worn him down.

"Though it's not generally known, Hellspawn infestation has moved around over the years. At one time it was closer to Little Five Points, which is northeast of us," he said, pointing in that direction. "When the witches and necromancers moved into that area about twenty years ago, the demons shifted here."

Which made sense. The fiends would always go after easier prey, especially those who couldn't toast them with magic.

"Will we see one today?" one of the group asked hopefully.

There were fifteen of them, a few from the area but most were here on vacation. It appeared that the good folks from New Orleans, Boise and New York City were eager to see Atlanta and its Hellspawn.

"We may see some. Maybe not. I always hope we don't," Gary said.

Katia eyed the worn denim bag on his shoulder, big enough to hold a few bottles of Holy Water, a magical sphere or two, and a steel pipe. Gary might be out of the trapping business but he was no fool.

After stopping at a few more locations where famous trapper events had occurred—Terminus Market and the former site of the Tabernacle, now a memorial—they took a break inside a bar formerly known as the Armageddon Lounge. It'd been a favorite haunt for fiends until the new owner had renamed the establishment.

It was during this stop that Gary worked his way around the group, talking to them as they enjoyed their drinks and got out of the broiling heat for a bit.

When he finally reached her table, he smiled. "Journeyman," he said, keeping his voice low. She was sitting on her own, so she smiled and removed her cap. So much for the disguise.

"How did you know?"

He sat across from her, a beer in hand. "You have a trapping bag," he said, pointing at the item at her feet. Then he grinned. "And I was at the meeting the other night."

"You got me," she said, smiling back. "I notice you don't take the group to Oakland Cemetery."

He shook his head. "There might be questions I wouldn't be able to answer."

Katia nodded in return, knowing exactly what kind of questions those might be. Was it true that both the Prince of Hell and the Archangel Michael had been there? Why were demons on holy ground? Did Master Blackthorne really stop Armageddon like folks claim?

"You enjoying the tour?" he asked after another sip of his beer.

"I am. I needed to get an idea of the city's trapping history. You're helping me do that. And Master Blackthorne recommended your tour."

"Bless her. Hope I've helped. Well, better get back to it."

A few minutes later Gary gathered up his flock and they headed out the door. The next stop was in front of an abandoned building. According to the guide this is where the local trappers and the Vatican's elite Demon Hunters had fought with Hellspawn. To escape they'd had to jump off the roof of the building, landing on a tarp a few stories below.

Katia looked up at the roof then let her eyes follow the path down.

"No way," she muttered, shaking her head.

But it was for real. She'd seen a video online, one with Riley, Beck, and the Vatican's guys leaping off that very same building.

"No way," she repeated.

The final stop on the tour was a place called The Gulch, a large parking lot located near the huge Mercedes Benz stadium. Katia listened intently as Gary explained what had happened here, and to what he *didn't* say.

How to do you admit that one of Heaven's angels had gone batshit crazy and decided to destroy a major city? You didn't, at least not without getting into big trouble with the religious authorities.

That meant the actual story had been spun in a more acceptable direction: Vicious Fallen angel comes to destroy Atlanta; two trappers and another angel take it on. Bad angel destroyed and city saved. High fives all around. It sounded like a made-for-TV movie. From what she'd heard someone was already working on a screenplay. She bet Riley just loved that.

As more questions came from the tour group, Katia tuned

them out. Instead, she studied the location. She'd watched the YouTube and news station videos, replaying the battle. Battles plural, because Grand Master Beck and Ori the Fallen had taken on a bunch of big-assed demons, a kind she'd never seen before. At least not until she'd been in Hell.

A shiver from that memory rolled through her. She still couldn't believe they'd survived that journey. Simon felt the same way.

The tour wrapped up and Gary called out his thanks. Katia waited until all the tourists were gone then offered him a ten-dollar bill for a tip and thanked him for his time.

He waved off the money. "No tip needed from a fellow trapper. Glad you came on the tour."

"Can you give it to the orphans for me?" Gary nodded his agreement and pocketed the bill. He paused for a moment and then asked, "You regret coming here to Atlanta now that you know what it's like?"

That wasn't a question she'd been expecting.

"No," Katia said, shaking her head. "It's been . . . unreal, but no. I *belong* here. I didn't do well in Lawrence. You probably heard about that."

"I heard you had a bad master who stole from you and the others. And now he's getting nailed for it."

"He is. Gotta love it," Katia replied, grinning.

The guide laughed. "Works for me. So, I'll see you at one of the trapper meetings," he said. "I like to go and catch up with my buddies."

"Sounds good. And thanks, Gary. This was great."

With a smile he trudged off toward the city, his limp more pronounced now.

This area had a different vibe so she wanted to figure out what that meant. Turning back to the battle site, Katia closed her eyes and let her senses loose. Concentrating proved hard to do because of the city's background noise. People chatted on cell phones, car doors closed and engines started, followed by the sound of the vehicle headed elsewhere.

Despite the heat radiating off the pavement Katia wandered around until she was at a part of the lot that had more sensations than the rest. Here the pavement appeared newer than the surrounding area.

Then she felt the Divine. She looked over her shoulder to find Ori walking toward her. He was still wearing all black, which somehow didn't feel right.

"Katia Allyson Breman," he said as he joined her. Angels were always big with the full name thing.

"Ori the Divine," she replied.

His gaze shifted to her in an instant as if waiting for something more, something judgmental.

"Riley told me you were no longer Fallen. That's as it should be. When I look at you now, you are brighter. Not as gleaming white as Serrah, but not as grayish as before."

He studied her for some time, then gave a nod. "Your inner sight is true."

"Congratulations for giving the Pit Boss the middle finger."

A shrug returned, though he seemed pleased by her enthusiasm. "There are downsides."

"Ha! Always skeptical. You sound like me."

"We are much alike in that way."

Katia gestured at the area around them. "This place feels strange."

"It has changed since the Angel of Death was here."

"*Ha mashhit.*" That's what Riley had called it, its name in Hebrew. "The Destroyer. But why did it choose to come *here*?" she asked, pointing down.

"At one time this was the heart of the city."

"Alright. What about those big demons that came after you? What were they?"

"Retrievers. They're the Prince's personal guard. He sends him to bring his enemies back to the Pit for torture."

"Enemies like you?"

"Yes. And now, you and the exorcist as well."

"Go us," she muttered, and Katia swore she heard him

chuckle.

In front of them was a stained section of pavement. A couple bouquets of wilted flowers sat in the middle of it. "Is this where it died?"

Ori's expression turned to one of sadness. "Yes."

There was gray, grainy material that glistened in the sunlight. "Are those The Destroyer's ashes?"

"No, it was returned to Heaven." He stepped closer, examining them, then frowned. "These are the ashes of the beings it sent against Riley Anora Blackthorne and the grand master. She destroyed them."

Katia moved closer, then knelt to study the particles. When she reached out to touch them Ori was instantly at her side, his hand catching hers. "Not a good idea."

"Why?" she asked, looking over at him.

"Because those should not be here."

"Okay, then I won't touch them."

His hand reluctantly retreated as she left hers above the stained bit of pavement, palm down. There was life in those particles, she could feel it. Life where there should be none.

"These cannot stay," Ori said, and with a wave of his hand they vanished. Then he was gone, just like the ashes, as if their presence offended him.

Katia shook her head as she rose. "Sure, don't mind me. I was just trying to figure out what's happening here." She huffed. "Let me guess, you had to go press your wings or something."

No reply. But then she hadn't expected one.

She gave a quick look around, but no one seemed to care what she and Ori had been doing. At least in a big city if you did something strange people just ignored you. Not like that in her hometown.

Her phone rang. It was Riley. "Hey, Boss, what's up?"

"Sorry, I know it's your day off but some of the missing reanimates just showed up at a police station. They said they were told to go there by the summoner who stole them."

"He set them free?" she asked, incredulous.

"He did. I need you to go there and make sure no one walks off with those dead folks until we talk to them. Mort and I will be there as quickly as possible."

"Got it."

"Thanks. Sending the address now."

After one last look around, Katia headed for her car.

Why would a necro steal a bunch of corpses, then turn them loose?

Katia hadn't spent much time in police stations, though a few of the pranks she'd pulled as a teen should have rated a lengthy stay in one of Lawrence's jails. She'd been lucky.

This precinct was bustling, but that wasn't a surprise. After getting herself through the front door past two young ladies complaining about a parking ticket, she made her way to the desk. The older woman behind the barrier looked tired and Katia felt for her already. She laid her trapping license on the ledge between them, pushed it toward her, then smiled.

"Hi. I'm Journeyman Breman. Master Blackthorne said some reanimates showed up at this precinct. She has asked me to stay with the Deaders until she and the Summoner Advocate can get here."

The cop eyed her. "Why would you do that?"

"Because we need to know who stole them."

"You the trapper that was at that grave robbery the other night?"

"I am. Now you know why we want to nail this bastard, *hard*."

A hint of a smile came her way. "Give me a moment."

"Thank you."

A phone call was made, her license returned, and finally a young detective made his way up to the front desk. He was probably in his late thirties, wearing a navy suit, though his tie was loosened in deference to the heat. He looked as tired as the lady at the front desk.

"I'm Detective Brighton," he said.

"Journeyman Breman."

"Come this way, then."

The reanimates were seated in a tidy row of folding chairs in a room at the back of the station. They each held a plastic mug full of a liquid that glowed, something like a necro might give them. There were four of them, so five were still missing. Mr. Means was not in the room and Katia kept the groan to herself. More fuel for The Widow's lawsuit.

"They just showed up," the detective said, rubbing a hand through his short brown hair. He sounded frustrated. "They said they'd been told to come here."

"Was someone with them?"

"We didn't see anyone. Probably dropped them off a block or two away, but I can't say for sure. They just walked in the front door."

"Okay. Once Master Blackthorne and the Summoner Advocate get here, we'll start questioning the reanimates."

"Good luck with that. I've tried but got nothing back. I'm not sure how you'll do any better."

She shrugged, feeling sorry for this guy. "We'll give it our best. We'll let you know if we learn anything."

"You do this every day?"

"No, usually I'm trapping demons. This isn't my thing."

"Not mine either." He looked back at the sad faces. "God, that has to be hard for them and their families."

"It is," a voice replied.

It was Mortimer, and he was in his black robe looking exactly like a senior summoner. Riley was at his side, in trapper garb.

Introductions were made and then one of the reanimates was taken to a separate room to be questioned with the detective present. To her surprise, Riley stayed with the others, insisting that Katia help Mort.

The questioning went quickly because it was clear they had little knowledge of what was going on. Each had been bespelled which pretty much wiped out their memories after the point of reanimation.

"Can you break it?" Katia asked as they waited for one reanimate to shuffle out and another take his place.

"I could, but it will harm them even more," Mort replied. "They've been through enough."

"That's for damned sure," the detective added.

They lucked out on the next-to-last reanimate, a lady named Alice Laine. She clutched her drink as if it was a lifeline, and it probably was. Ms. Laine remembered an old factory, a summoner, and a shimmering wall. What did all that mean?

"Thank you, Ms. Laine. We will get you back to your family."

She nodded, then walked out, dragging one foot.

"He did take care of them, but dammit he shouldn't have stolen them in the first place," Mort said, shaking his head. "I just don't get why he did this."

After a call to the Summoners Society, plans were made for the reanimates to be returned to their individual funeral homes. There a summoner would reverse the reanimation, which apparently took a good bit of magic. Then the dead would be consigned to their graves as their families grieved once more.

A while later Riley and Katia walked out of the precinct barely missing being ploughed into by a drunk under arrest. A low stream of Hellspeak curse words came from her boss.

"You okay?" Katia asked, giving her a worried look.

Riley shook her head. "Too many memories of my dad's reanimation."

"This had to be really hard for you."

The master trapper's eyes reflected her inner turmoil. "Someday when I'm not so angry I'll tell you the whole story. But not now."

Then Riley headed off on her own. There hadn't been the usual "good night" or anything like that as she trudged up the sidewalk to where her car was parked.

Yet another reminder that Master Blackthorne had been through things that would have broken Katia. "I don't know how you do it."

Her phone pinged and she found it was Reynolds, checking to see if she wanted to go trapping with him. This she could do, despite all the drama tonight. She told him to count her in and then headed to her car. The dead would have to sort themselves out on their own.

TWELVE

The Evil never slept. It was the kind that knew it held more power than those who dwelt in this world, knew it held their lives in its blood-stained claws.

It appeared to be female, but Mathias wasn't sure about that. Despite his many magical talents he'd never been good at seeing through glamour spells. It was well over six feet tall, and his gut told him that was *not* glamour.

The face looked human, but not quite. The eyes were too wide and the cheekbones too sharp. Its hands weren't human, not with those claws. It had hair, but it was coarse and gray. No matter what it was, it was far too powerful. How else could it have made its way into another realm and taken control of this world?

He called it the Unholy Terror, though he dare not say that aloud or someone would die. He'd seen it kill once. The death had been astoundingly cruel, a slow torture as the victim's life force was ripped out of each cell of its body. When it was over only a dried husk remained.

All the while the other beings in this realm had mourned and pleaded for mercy. It had made no difference. And then the Unholy Terror had licked its lips and smiled. It was then he knew it had to die.

The other inhabitants of this world were dangerous, but they were outclassed. And dammit so was he. The only reason he was here was because of the one with the bright red hair, the one he had grown to love.

Once again, he stood in front of the monster, for this was one realm he could enter without difficulty. Yet again he'd been summoned as if he were a pet on a leash.

The Unholy Terror's eyes studied him as if deciding just how much skin could be flailed off his bones and still keep him alive.

"You are a disappointment," it said, the voice like the bone-chilling cold that drifts across a grave at the stroke of midnight. "You have a task. Why are you not fulfilling it?"

Part of him wanted to shout, demand to know why the hell it couldn't go into the other realm and get the damned thing itself. But if he did someone would die. Someone his own love cared for. So, he bowed his head, seemingly contrite, though murder was in his heart.

"I cannot get into that world. The dead I've summoned can't get into it. The thing that guards the doorway refuses to let us in."

"I do not care for your excuses. You will retrieve the ring. You will deliver it to me or I will kill again. And again." Its crimson eyes went toward the beings nearest to it, all on their knees in obeisance. Most shivered in fear. "Who should I choose?" it said. "Perhaps the one that you care for? The one with the flaming hair?"

No, not her!

The one who held his heart was fading, he could see it. Her eyes had dulled, her usually white skin now a pale gray. The ferns in her hair were dead, falling away every time she moved. But the fear in her eyes is what drove him forward, for her kind weren't weak. He had to find a way to kill the Unholy Terror and make things right again. He still didn't know how this evil knew about the ring or why it wanted it so badly. Something told him not to ask.

"You don't have to hurt anyone," he insisted. "I will send another into the realm. Someone who is still alive. Perhaps she can get what you need."

"Who is this?"

"She has experience with the fiends in the Pit. She is a demon trapper."

The creature tensed now. "This one is not welcome here."

"She doesn't have to come *here*. She'll get what you want and bring it to me," he replied. He was unsure if Breman could pull this off, but knew he was out of options.

A nod came his way, condescending as always. "This is your last chance, wizard. Fail, and all in this realm will die. *All* of them!"

Mathias spun around and headed for the portal that led back to his own world. Just as he crossed over the barrier into his world, he swore he heard the sobs of the beloved he'd left behind.

It was after nine when Simon's phone rang. For a second he thought it was Katia, but instead it was a grand master.

"Hey, Beck. What's up?"

"Thought you might like to know that I had an off-the-record chat with someone at the Vatican about yer upcomin' review."

Simon frowned. "How did you—"

"Katia told Riley, and my wife told me."

"Of course they did." He wasn't sure if he liked that or not.

"I know, you'd like to keep this to yourself, but you can't do this on yer own. You've got allies in Rome, and one of them wanted you to know that Rosetti is pullin' for you, as are some of the others. Even though this looks bad, don't give up, at least not yet."

"There's nothing keeping them from saying I'm doing magic and kicking me to the curb."

"Then there will be nothin' keepin' you from tellin' them to go screw themselves and become a master trapper."

"You just had to say that, didn't you?" Simon grumbled.

"Sure did. Because it's all true."

Simon bet it was Captain Elias Salvatore, the former head of the Demon Hunters, who'd offered up this information.

"Was the person who called you at Oakland Cemetery during the big battle?"

"Yup, he was. And that's all I can say. It works best if his superiors don't know he's pullin' for you."

He made a note to thank the man if they ever met again. In private.

"Did Katia tell you she can set one of this Holy Water circle things with her mind?" Beck asked.

"She did."

"Good. That means you got backup until the Vatican gets with the plan. Use it." He paused. "Hang in there, Simon. We'll get this worked out, one way or another."

"Understood."

After the call ended, Simon debated about calling Katia. Check in on her.

"Maybe not." She was trapping with Reynolds and that meant she'd have someone watching over her.

Simon leaned his recliner back and closed his eyes. He'd wait until she was home, safe. Maybe someday he'd tell her how he felt about her.

But not tonight.

Journeyman Reynolds was in good humor and kept firing jokes her way. Katia made sure to laugh, his jokes were funny, but her mind was elsewhere. Today had been odd even by Atlanta's standards. She was still unnerved by finding those ashes in The Gulch. As she saw it, Ori's abrupt departure after that discovery was an admission that he was just as uneasy.

She and Reynolds were currently wandering around Demon Central, and so far there had been no sign of any Gastro-Fiends, no Pyro-Fiends, nothing. They'd met up with a couple other trappers and they'd had the same bad luck.

"If this keeps up, I'll have to raid my savings account to pay the rent," Reynolds grumbled.

What if she did find an apartment and then her paychecks were cut in half? She didn't have enough money laid back to handle that loss of income. She'd be damned if she couch surfed here like she had in Kansas. Not that Simon or Riley would let her do that, but still the thought made her nervous. At least the exorcism income would continue for the time being.

They'd just rounded the corner onto yet another abandoned street when a sleek rat raced by them. Then another.

"That's a good sign," she said. Rodents knew they were an easy meal for a Three and always took to their feet if they smelled one nearby.

Reynolds removed his steel pipe from his trapping bag. "Let's see what we got."

The further they walked the quieter it became, an oppressive sort of silence that made Katia's skin crawl. Another rat raced by in what appeared to be blind panic.

"I'm not liking this," her companion said, looking back over his shoulder as if something was sneaking up on them. It appeared her fellow trapper had his own set of "this is just wrong" instincts as well.

Her early warning scar flared to life. "I'm thinking we need to back out of this."

Reynolds nodded. "I'm with you on that. Let's get out of here."

As they turned, the closest brick wall flared with a yellowish light, spiraling as if spun by an unseen hand.

"What the hell is that?" he said, stepping back.

A rank smell came now, something like three-day old fish if left to rot in the Atlanta sunshine.

"Oh my God, that's awful," she said, trying not to gag. "That's not Hell. I know what that's like."

"But then what—"

The yellowish light faded and darkness filled the wall as if they were staring down a long tunnel. Something appeared out of that darkness. Something long, narrow, and pale orange. Katia backed up, her steel pipe in hand.

"Is that a beak?" Reynold asked, incredulous.

"Yeah, I think it is."

Multiple amber eyes appeared now, each set in a broad

forehead covered in white feathers.

"That is *so not* a demon,' she said, backing off even further. Reynolds did the same, then gave a quick check in both directions.

"We can run for it. There's nothing in our way."

It was an option, except something kept her in place.

The eyes stared at them, never blinking, then after a rusty, grating squawk, the head retreated into the darkness. A few seconds later the swirling began again and then they were looking at an old brick wall.

"What in the fuck was that?" Reynold said, shaking his head in disbelief. "I wasn't hallucinating, right?" He sighed, letting his shoulders relax. "No one is going to believe us when we tell them what we saw."

"Riley will." Of that Katia had no doubt.

The brick wall remained unchanged as if something totally alien hadn't just poked its head out and had a look around. Katia moved closer, then gingerly touched the bricks. To her relief they felt like they should.

"I'm thinking we should lay Holy Water down just in case it comes back for another visit," she suggested.

"I agree, but how do we know that'll stop it? If it isn't from our world the Holy Water might not do a thing."

Reynolds was right.

Riley. Yeah, this would need the sacred liquid *and* her boss.

"I'm going to call Master Blackthorne. She'll know what to do."

"Amen to that."

They retreated further down the street while she made the call. Her boss sounded cranky about being awakened until Katia mentioned the "and then a hole appeared in a brick wall and some alien creature stuck its head out. And no, it wasn't a demon." The call ended shortly after that.

"She'll be here in twenty minutes," Katia said.

"It'll be closer to fifteen."

"What are you willing to bet?" she said. Because you could never pass up a wager with a fellow trapper.

"Five bucks."

"You're on." They slapped hands and then walked a short distance away. As they waited a rat sauntered by, eyed them, then continued on its way.

It looked like they were safe for the time being.

When Katia finally pulled into the driveway, the lights inside indicated that Simon was still up even though it was just past eleven. Part of her had hoped she wouldn't have to tell him what had happened tonight; just to let it slide. She didn't want him to worry. It didn't look like she had that option. At least she'd won the bet with Reynolds so she was five bucks richer. She made a mental note to buy the trapper a beer down the line.

Simon met her at the door looking like he should have been in bed a couple of hours earlier.

"Hey," he said, then gave her a soft smile. Was that relief she saw in his eyes?

"Hi. Been a long day."

"That I can see. You hungry? I can make you a sandwich."

That sounded good. "Yes, please. I don't remember the last time I ate." Lunch? Maybe.

She closed the door behind her, flipping the lock as if that could keep the bad things out. It was a childish thought but she went with it.

By the time Katia had stashed her gear in the guest room and run a washcloth over her face and arms, Simon had created a meal for her. The sandwich was on rye bread with ham, cheese, and mayo. A sliced apple sat on a separate plate, along with four oatmeal cookies. Then he added a glass of iced tea to the feast. She looked at what he'd done for her, then up at him.

"You rock, you know that?"

Simon shrugged and sat at the table with her. She noticed he had a glass of water, not his usual beer.

"Beck called to tell me I have folks on my side in the Vatican.

Someone went out of their way to let him know that."

"That's good news, then."

"I hope so."

Now would be the time for Katia to tell him about her adventure in Demon Central, but she wasn't ready. Instead she demolished the sandwich in a few bites, then crunched on the apple slices while trying to figure out a way to explain what she'd seen.

Simon held his silence, which was one of his best weapons. Eventually you just had to tell him things no matter what.

"Reynolds and I had something weird happen tonight," she began, returning one of the apple slices to the plate. Then she laid it all out, including the part where Riley and Beck had shown up to check out the scene. How her master had laid Holy Water in front of the wall and how they all hoped that would be the end of it.

Simon frowned. "Did the creature make a sound?"

"Just a screech, like a bird would. Mostly it just stared at us and then the portal closed. It wasn't a Divine or a fiend. It was something I've never felt before."

"What did Beck say about that? I mean those guys know stuff we don't."

"All he said was 'Well hell, that's not good news.'"

Katia popped the last of the apple slices into her mouth, then loaded up the oatmeal cookies in a napkin to take to her room. It was a holdover from when she'd not had enough to eat. She wondered just how long it would be before she no longer felt that need. As she reached for the dishes, Simon waved her off.

"I'll clean up," he said. "Get some sleep. We'll talk more in the morning." Which meant he wanted to think about what she'd just told him.

Katia paused at the doorway. "Thank you for supper. You'd make someone a great roommate, you know that?"

"Depends on the person," he said, watching her intently.

Katia wasn't sure how to respond. "Good night, Simon. Thank you for everything."

"Same to you, Katia. Thank God you're safe now."

It was only when she was in her room, after her shower, that she realized she hadn't told him about the stolen reanimates.

Mathias scanned the information on his phone, the report he'd received late last night. Hawkins had done as asked and now he knew more about the trapper from . . . Kansas. He huffed at that. Miles and miles of flat ground, that's all he remembered of the road trip through that state when he was a kid. Back before everything had changed.

According to Hawkins, Katia Breman was a journeyman demon trapper who worked with Simon Adler, a lay exorcist for the Vatican. On paper she didn't appear to be anyone special, but somehow she'd withstood Mathias' attempts to make her break the Holy Water ward. That meant something. And his lover insisted that Breman could move between the worlds. But could she get past the doorman?

He reviewed the video his lackey had forwarded him of the exorcist and Breman at a local convention a couple months back. One minute they'd been there, the next they'd vanished, along with a big demon. Rumors said they went to Hell, which was definitely another realm.

"Yeah, Breman is exactly what I need."

Damn this whole situation ate at him. If he didn't do what the Unholy Terror said more of his beloved's kind would die. *She* might die. Because at the heart of his enemy was a malicious evil that ripped worlds apart and gloried in their destruction.

"But am I much different?" he whispered as he leaned against the factory wall. He had ripped bodies out of graves causing untold suffering for their families. He'd put other necromancers at risk from the government. He'd almost killed one, and the trapper as well, during Means' reanimation.

"No choice. Dammit, no choice." That was what hurt the most.

Mathias looked over the remaining reanimates now. From what he'd seen on the news, the ones he'd sent to the cops were being returned to their graves. Everyone was calling for his blood.

Can't be helped.

It was time to take the war to the Unholy Terror. If he was lucky, Breman would give him the weapon he needed to survive that last battle.

THIRTEEN

It was just her, Riley and Harper in the office, which meant another morning of wrangling paperwork. Katia had her own pile and was slogging through it page by page. At least she was being paid for this torture.

This was not how she'd imagined spending her twenty-fifth birthday. No, she'd always figured she'd be on a beach getting some sun, not assembling trapping data that pinpointed the exact geographic location for each of those captures. Per type of Hellspawn and time of day.

Just shoot me.

One of the benefits of all this drudgery was that Katia was learning the names of the other trappers, one report at a time. Some of those reports were meticulous, some were the bare minimum.

At least the hardest part was already behind her. After he'd had a cup of coffee, Master Harper had listened to her and Riley's report about the weird portal thing.

He'd just frowned and muttered, "What is it with this town?" Then went back to his paperwork. At least he hadn't said that she was making things up. That wouldn't have been the case in Lawrence, not with Master Kelly. But then karma was stomping all over his butt right now and she couldn't think of a better birthday present.

She'd already answered her brother's and sister's birthday messages. Her dad's had arrived a few minutes ago as he was always an early riser. Nothing from her mother. Somehow that was not surprising because her mom was still annoyed Katia hadn't resigned her job and moved back home by now. She'd probably send one later.

There was a creak as the office door opened and a man entered. He paused for only a moment, then shut the door behind him. The quality of his suit suggested he was a lawyer.

"Can I help you?" Riley asked.

"I'm here to talk to Riley Blackthorne and Katia Breman."

"For what reason?"

The man flicked a glance toward the senior master, then back to them. Harper leaned back in his chair now, watching this play out. She had no doubt he'd intervene if needed.

"I'm representing Mrs. Albert Means. I need to speak to you both about the lawsuit she has filed. The suit regarding your egregious behavior the night her husband's corpse was stolen."

At this point Katia did the same as Harper, leaning back in her chair. This was going to be fun.

Riley shook her head. "No comment from either of us. Talk to our lawyer."

She rummaged around on her desk and found Jack's business card, but instead of walking it over she let it float across the open space, courtesy of her magic. When it hovered in front of the lawyer, he snatched it out of the air.

"That does not impress me," he said.

"It wasn't supposed to." She pointed behind him. "Unless you'd like to report a demon sighting, the door is that way."

"You need to answer my questions."

"No, we don't."

The shark in the suit looked over at Katia now. "It would not be wise to let her speak for you in this matter."

"Yeah, it would."

"I was going to offer you a chance to settle. I won't be doing that now."

"Oh, what a bummer."

Riley made shoo'ing motions with her hands. "Off you go."

"You will regret that." And then the dude was gone, purposely letting the door bang shut behind him.

"God, I hate lawyers," Harper said. He heaved himself out of his chair and headed for the kitchen to refill his coffee.

"I'll let Jack know we had a visitor," Riley said, tapping away on her computer now. "He'll find that amusing."

Katia's phone pinged and the text was from Simon.

HAPPY BIRTHDAY! WELCOME TO 25!
THERE'S ICE CREAM, CAKE & A SURPRISE WHEN YOU
GET HOME.

She swung toward Riley. "Did you tell Simon it was my birthday?"

"I did," her master said, grinning. "Happy Birthday, Journeyman Breman. We should celebrate the good stuff when it happens. At least if Hell isn't raining fireballs on us at that point."

Another grunt from Harper along with a "That's the damned truth.'

"Thank you," Katia said.

What would Simon's surprise be? Had he bought her a present?

She typed out a reply.

YOU ROCK, MR. TOO-MANY-NAMES ADLER. ALL OF
THAT SOUNDS GREAT. YOU ARE THE BEST FRIEND
EVER!

That wasn't a lie. She'd had friends, but none like him. When there was no reply she dug back into the paperwork, still smiling. Who knew, maybe later she'd get a message from her mother and then this day would be perfect.

By the time Simon finally crawled out of bed, Katia was gone. A note on the kitchen table said she would be at the trapping office this morning, and thanked him again for the meal he'd made for her. What she hadn't said was that today was her birthday. Not a word. Luckily, Riley had warned him ahead of time.

In some ways Katia was as guarded as she'd been the day she'd arrived from Lawrence. Well, maybe a little more open, at least with him.

"I'll just have to feed you more sandwiches," he said.

He sent off a text wishing her a Happy Birthday, and was waiting for a reply when the doorbell rang. He expected it to be Mrs. Carmody, the neighbor lady who insisted on complaining about everything, Simon included.

Instead it was his oldest sister on the doorstep, and from her frown this wasn't going to be a friendly visit. The instant he opened the door she swept inside, brushing past him. She dumped her purse on the couch, turned and glowered at him.

Her timing sucked, but then it usually did.

"I'm not happy with you," Deanna said, adopting her usual "hands on the hips" posture.

"Goes both ways," he said evenly. In the past he'd have tried to play peacemaker, but not today.

"You didn't tell me you were going out of town."

"And?"

"I should know where you are, Brother."

"If I feel the need for you to know my schedule, I'll tell you. If not, it's none of your business."

She blinked in response. "What is this attitude? Why are you being so stubborn?"

"I'm not being stubborn, Dee. I'm living my own life. I don't demand you tell me your travel schedule."

"It's what family does," she insisted.

"No, it's what an obsessive control freak does." She gaped at him now, and for a half second he felt bad. It was time to set some ground rules.

"You kept the set of keys you got from our uncle, then came *into my house* as if you own it. You moved furniture around, you took food out of my refrigerator and threw it away. You even swapped stuff around in two of my cupboards, for God knows whatever reason."

"It made more sense that the mixing bowls be near the sink than on the other side of the kitchen."

"In *your* kitchen, yes. I moved those bowls where I wanted them. This is *my* home, Dee. You have *no right* to come in here without my permission." A ping came from his phone now, probably Katia answering his text. The sooner he got his sister out the door he could read it.

Dee's eyes widened. "I was trying to help you," she insisted.

"Help me?" Simon walked a few steps away, then spun back toward her. He'd been holding all this back for far too long.

"In my job, demons mess with my head. They make me see things that *are not real*. That's part of their power. Then I come home and find that things have been moved around in my house. Is that demonic, or just my damned nosy older sister screwing with me?"

She blinked in shock, unaccustomed to his anger.

"My life is my own, Dee. You may not like what I do, but it is important."

That triggered her. "You're right, I don't like it! You almost died, and now you're out there trying to die again. Do you know it's like to hear that the kindest thing would be to take your brother off life support? I do. What is this damned martyr complex of yours? Are you freakin' suicidal?"

Before he could answer, the doorbell rang.

Who the hell is this?

His newest visitor was a nondescript older man in a very wrinkled suit. Something about him looked familiar, despite his gray pallor.

"Are you . . . the exorcist?" he asked, his voice creaking as if speaking were difficult.

Simon almost said, "No." But he couldn't. If this were someone who needed help, he'd find a way to do that, even on sabbatical.

"Yes, I'm the lay exorcist. Can I help you?"

"Simon, what's going on?" his sister asked as she joined him at the door.

The man's attention moved to her. He straightened up now, as if new energy had been introduced into his body somehow. His eyes, previously pale brown, blazed silver.

"Well, she looks like family. What luck. This couldn't be more perfect."

At that, the strange man began to murmur under his breath. Even before he could close the door, a spell struck Simon like a body blow. He opened his mouth to shout, but then lost the will to do anything at all. Beside him, his sister cried out, then fell silent.

No matter how hard he tried Simon's body was not under his control, though his mind raced in panic. Now he knew where he'd seen this man's face: He'd opened his door to one of the stolen reanimates. A Deader who was under the control of a necromancer.

"Come along you two! Lock the door behind you. You don't want to let just *anyone* inside, do you?" the darker voice chided.

Woodenly, Simon did as he was ordered as the spell grew stronger around them. Then he and his sister were nowhere at all.

It was the low murmur of voices that pulled Simon from the depths of the spell, voices that sounded as if there was no life in them. Beneath him was a floor made of stained concrete. Above him, metal trusses and a roof. The space smelled of dust and mildew.

After forcing himself to sit upright he found his sister next to him, blinking in confusion.

"What happened? Where are we?" Dee whispered.

He could only shrug, as he had no clue. It was stifling hot here, and to make it worse there was the faint smell of death.

They were in an old factory, one with tall industrial shelving along two walls. Cobweb-draped lights hung from the ceiling high above them, none of them lit. There was a lengthy line of windows up near the roof, and a few were open. Others were cracked or missing entirely. All were filthy just like the concrete beneath him.

It was then Simon saw the dead. Some were lying on the floor like broken dolls while others leaned against a wall, hollowed eyed, staring at him like they'd never seen another human before. It'd been their voices he'd heard.

One of them rose and made his way over to him at a snail's pace. It was Albert Means, the man who had come to his door and been stolen out of his grave despite Riley and Katia's best efforts.

Means stopped a short distance away, looking first at Deanna and then at Simon. "I'm . . . sorry," he said, his voice barely audible. Then he shuffled closer, a cellphone in his hand. "Here, this is yours."

Simon snatched the phone away, wondering why the dead man had it in the first place. "Why are we here?" he asked, pushing his anger down.

"He said to come for you." Means looked over at Deanna again. "I do what he tells me. I have no choice."

"Everyone has a choice," Dee replied, frowning. Did she realize he was dead?

"Not when you've had a spell cast on you."

"Spell? Is that what happened to us?" she asked. Means nodded.

Simon had intentionally not shared much with his family, especially the supernatural aspects of his job. His parents being the only exception. In the case of Deanna he'd been even more closemouthed, knowing she'd just worry. When she worried, she interfered with his life.

"Summoners can call the dead from their graves and they can also cast spells on the living," Simon said.

"Everyone knows that," she snapped.

"We were bespelled, Dee. I had no choice coming here,

neither did you."

She opened her mouth to argue, then gave a grudging nod as she studied Means. "Is he . . . ?"

"I am dead," the man replied. "I was reanimated. It is not what I wanted." He pointed at the phone. "She will come now. I am sorry for that, too."

"She?" Dee said, confused.

Who did he mean? Simon swiped the phone's screen but it stayed dark.

"We can't leave," the dead man said, gesturing toward the others. "Not until he tells us to go somewhere. You folks might be able to. I don't know."

The far doors swooshed open in a blast of air and then slammed shut once again. As the dust settled a figure appeared in a pool of murky light. He was younger than Simon had expected, probably in his early forties, clad in a dark navy robe.

To some, the necromancer might be considered handsome. He possessed a strong jaw, deep brown hair and eyes, with only a few wrinkles making an appearance. He was about six feet or so, not muscular, but not flabby either. He had a light tan which told Simon he didn't spend all his time creeping around cemeteries stealing the dead.

"Our kidnapper has arrived," he whispered to his sister "Let me deal with this, okay? This is *my* world, not yours."

Dee gave a short nod, but he could tell she was close to losing it.

The necro walked closer now. "Means, go away," he said, gesturing.

The reanimate moved back to join the others, then sank onto the floor like a well-trained dog.

"Hello, Exorcist. I've heard about you," the man said. "Your name is in the news. A lot."

"Why are we here?" he demanded.

"Well, I need you to take a journey and retrieve something for me."

"Why?"

"Because you can walk the realms. Not everyone can."

Realms? "Why would you think that?"

"You'd be surprised what I know," the man replied, a hint of arrogance in his words now.

"What are these realm things he's talking about?" Dee asked.

"I'll explain later." And just how he'd do that he wasn't sure, but that wasn't what had him worried.

Someone in the Pit had to be involved in this, someone keen to score points with Lucifer. How else would a necro he'd never met know Simon had gone to Hell, and returned?

"My sister doesn't have a clue about any of this. Just let her go."

"Of course she doesn't. She was just an unlucky bystander." The necromancer turned back to look at the doors behind him. "What we need is someone else who's walked the worlds just like you. And here she is now."

†✳‡✳†

"Why here?" Katia murmured. She checked the location on her phone and then compared it to the address she'd received from Simon. It matched.

Usually, the exorcist on duty contacted her directly about the time and location of their next assignment. But the text looked legit and had all the details she'd needed, so she'd not bothered to call Simon and double-check it. She guessed that someone at the Archdiocese had forgotten he was on sabbatical and sent him the assignment instead. Rather than telling them they'd made a mistake, he'd just sent her the deets.

She drove through the open gate, past an abandoned guard shack and then further into the industrial estate. None of the buildings looked occupied, and most had their windows broken. There was a lot of graffiti, some of it quite artistic.

There was no sign of Lay Exorcist Snyder when Katia parked in front of the building that matched the address. He didn't have a car, so he'd have taken a taxi or a rideshare here. Tempting as it was to send him a text to check his status, she decided to wait him out. A structural infestation was far less urgent than a human one.

The eight-story concrete block building looked to be a warehouse or a factory. Like its neighbors it had broken windows and grass growing up between the cracked pavement in front of the place. Usually abandoned buildings weren't high on the list for demonic possession. Why take over a rundown dump when you could possess a house in Buckhead or downtown Atlanta?

Katia fidgeted and then grabbed her trapping bag off the seat next to her. Forty minutes had passed since she'd gotten Simon's text and yet Snyder was a no-show. Growing bored, she decided to check out the building to see what they were facing. With the bag hanging off her shoulder she headed for the front doors. After a final glance at the parking lot, she turned the handle and found that the door swung open with a dry, rusty creak.

That it was unlocked either meant someone couldn't be bothered to let them in, or there were other dangers inside besides a demon. Drug addicts would squat in buildings like this, and then it'd be a human possession, not a structural one.

After a deep breath, Katia crossed over the threshold then promptly sneezed from the dust. At the same time that her left arm scar flared up, magic skittered over her skin.

"Run! It's a trap!" someone called out.

Before she could retreat the doors behind her slammed shut. A powerful force shoved her from behind, sliding her feet across the concrete floor. She fought, but the force was too strong and she fell to her knees, skidding along.

"Ah, there you are," a different voice called out. "About time."

She knew that voice. The necro who had stolen Mean's body stood a few feet away. This time it was the real deal. He was younger than she'd expected for his level of magical prowess. But his smirk was gone. Something had happened between that night and now, something big.

As Katia struggled to her feet she spied the few reanimates

he'd not set free. And then beyond them, farther into the building, two figures. One was taller than the other, a male with bright blond hair.

"Simon?" she blurted.

Snyder wasn't here. It had been a trap, just like he'd said.

Katia spun around toward the summoner now, furious. "What the hell is going on?" she demanded.

"You're here because you and the exorcist have a journey to make. I need you to retrieve something from another realm. If you do, I'll set you all free. If not, well then things are going to get bad for all of us."

"Are you nuts? You just don't wander into another realm."

"Tell me about it," he huffed. "I can't go there, but maybe you two can. After all, you took a quick trip to Hell and back."

What? "How do you know that?"

He ignored her question. "If you *don't* fulfill the quest, *this one* is going to die and be reanimated," he said, pointing at Simon's sister now. "Any questions?"

"She has no part in this," she seethed.

"She does now."

Simon swore under his breath. "You vow not to harm my sister while we're doing your damned quest?" he demanded.

"Of course."

That reply had come far too quickly.

Katia's eyes met Simon's, each weighing their options. They had none, not if they wanted to keep Dee safe.

She gave him a nod and his expression darkened now.

"We'll go," he said. "But I swear to God if you hurt her, I will hunt you down and kill you."

The necro rolled his eyes. "I'm not worried. You're not powerful enough."

"Don't count on that," Katia said. "We made it out of Hell alive. Hundreds and hundreds of demons, and the Prince himself. You best think twice about crossing us, asshole."

"Hell?" Deanna said, staring at her brother now. "*You* went to the Pit?" Simon gave a reluctant nod. "Dear God."

For a moment it looked as if their kidnapper was going to back down, then he shook his head. "This will lead you to the ring. Find it, bring it here."

Something flew toward Simon and he barely caught it.

"You have until midnight," their captor said. "Make it count."

"A ring?" she said. "Really?"

So, they'd find the thing and they'd have to haul it to Mount Doom or wherever. Because that's the way things always went in these kinds of stories. There'd probably be orcs trying to kill them. And really big spiders.

"Just the ring. Nothing else. Do you hear me?" the necro demanded.

"Yeah, we hear you." Grinding her teeth, Katia picked up her trapping bag and joined the pair.

"Simon?" his sister said, her eyes widening in fear.

He stuck whatever the necro had given him in his jeans pocket, then took hold of her hand. "Katia and I are going on a trip and get something this bastard can't. We *will* be back, Dee. You understand? We *will* come back."

"But—"

"We have no choice, Sis. He'll hurt you if we don't go. I'm sorry, Dee."

She reluctantly nodded, her body shaking as he hugged her. He leaned closer to her now. "Don't provoke him. If you see a chance to escape, go. You hear me?" A faint nod was his answer. "And I love you, Sis, always have."

"I love you, Brother. May God keep you safe."

"Same for you."

"Leave your gear here," the necro said, pointing at Katia's trapping bag. "You won't need it where you're going."

"No way I'm going unarmed."

"Leave it here," he bellowed as magic rose around him.

Furious, she slid the bag off her shoulder. "Whatever. Let's get this done."

The summoner pointed toward the back of the building, which was nothing more than a solid wall.

"And?" she said, frowning at him.

"Such a closed mind," he muttered, then waved a hand while murmuring under his breath.

The blocks slowly dissolved leaving a jagged hole in the wall like someone had taken a sledgehammer to create a new opening. Beyond that was utter darkness, the kind that ripped at your soul. An eerie wind blew toward them, scattering dust. It held no scent, not like the night before. Then the hole began to glow.

"Begone!" the summoner shouted.

Magic rolled across the factory floor, scooping them up and throwing them across the boundary between the worlds.

As Deanna cried out for her brother, the portal slammed shut behind them.

FOURTEEN

The journey from the factory to the other realm came with a gut punch, a blow so deep it nearly made Katia retch.

"Damn, that hurts," she said, bending over to lessen the pain. A glance at her partner said he was suffering as well. "Wasn't like this . . . when we . . . went to . . . the Pit."

Simon grimaced. "We were inside a circle. That might . . . have made a difference."

When she was able to straighten up, Simon was already upright, though a hand remained on his abdomen, fingers clenched. Together they stared at what lay ahead of them. To Katia it looked like an endless sea of black sand. Above it sat a steel-gray sky, with no sun, moon or clouds. A totally alien world.

"My God," she whispered.

"It's like something out of a movie," Simon said, staring in wonder.

"I'm thinking Arrakis meets Tatooine." Then realized he might not get those movie references. You never knew with him.

"If there are sandworms or Jawas, we're out of here," he replied, proving he had.

As far as she could see there were no creatures in sight. It was as if the world was only the sand and the thick slabs of ebony rock ahead of them. The rocks were probably eight or nine feet long and about three feet wide, arrayed in a perfect flat circle. In the center of that circle was what looked to be pure white sand. All it needed was a giant neon arrow pointing at that one spot.

Simon extended his hand, whatever the necro had given him sitting on his right palm.

"What is that thing?"

"A button. An old one. It's made of ivory, I think." He jerked in surprise when it promptly rotated so the pointed end faced toward the slabs.

"I'm not liking this. That open sand there?" she said, pointing at the area between them and the slabs. "*Something* has to live under that. Something that loves to eat people like us. You know I'm right."

He shot a look over his shoulder. "We have no choice. The doorway back home is shut."

She dared not look back or she'd cry. "None of this makes any sense, Simon."

Not knowing what else to do, Katia dug in her front pocket and found a quarter.

"I don't see any parking meters," he joked, though his voice sounded brittle. That was one of his many strengths, the ability to face impossible situations and keep his sense of humor. Sometimes that was all you had.

Katia tossed the coin out as far as she could, then watched as it landed with a tiny puff of sand. Then it sat there. There was no deadly whirlpool, no tentacles, no monster claws. Just a shiny coin on top of black sand.

"Give it some time," he suggested.

Sweat had started to run down the side of Simon's face and in this bizarre atmosphere it almost looked like black blood. The sight made her queasy so she shifted her attention to that long stretch of ground between them and . . . whatever that was.

The coin remained exactly where it had landed.

"Sometimes I'm way too paranoid," she said.

"Well, then I am too. Let's assume there is something there. If we walk out together both of us are toast," he said.

"Split up and run like hell?" she suggested.

"Yes. If we're lucky, that will confuse whatever might be there and we both can get to those rocks safely."

She frowned at him. "Your plan sucks, Mr. Exorcist."

He frowned back at her. "And yours is, Ms. Trapper?"

"Equally sucky because it'd be the same."

"Right." He took a deep breath and let it out slowly. "You go left, I'll go to the right. That way one of us might get there." He offered her the button, but Katia shook her head.

"You count it down," she said.

The countdown went far too fast, and then they were sprinting across the black sand. Simon chugged along to her right some ten feet away, arms swinging in time to his movement, sand kicking up in his wake.

Beneath them the ground rumbled, as if something had woken from a nap, and yet the sand remained flat. With a final burst of speed they reached the rocks and scrambled up on the closest one.

"Go us," he said, sucking in air in big gulps. She was doing the same, which meant the atmosphere was different than back home.

Behind them the sand was still motionless, no hint of anything beneath it. Even more eerie, there was no sign of their footprints.

"Yeah, I was too paranoid," she said.

As if to prove her wrong the rumble came again, but this time it was under their feet. Simon grabbed onto her hand as they struggled to stay upright. Something surfaced in front of them, sheets of dark sand rolling off it.

The creature was bulky with pebbled iridescent skin. It had a large, round head, with two rust-colored eyes and a long slit of a mouth. Two arms, also covered in that bumpy skin, ended in pale blue fingers, four to a hand. The bottom part of the beast was still buried in the sand so she had no idea if it had feet, a tail, or whatever.

The creature settled on the ground now, one of its arms rising. Caught between two digits was her quarter.

"What do we do?" she whispered.

"I have no idea," Simon whispered back.

The creature made no move toward them but brought the coin up to eye level. It studied the metal disc carefully, turning it one way, then another, like an archeologist scrutinizing a rare find. Its head moved side to side and a low humming sound began. It didn't sound angry. If anything, it seemed pleased.

Her brother Kevin would love this. It was too much like an RPG, a role-playing game. Maybe that was the way to play it.

Katia cleared her throat, which had gone bone dry. "Oh great one, the disc is our tribute for entry into your world," she called out. "We hope you find us worthy."

Simon stared at her as if she'd lost her mind.

More humming. Then an articulated blue finger pointed toward her companion. When Simon didn't react, it pointed again.

"I think it wants something from you. But not a coin. It already has one of those." As if he didn't know that.

Simon appeared to be working through his potential gift options when the digit pointed again, this time toward his chest and the wooden cross he always wore.

He touched it. "This?"

The sideways nod came again.

There was torment in her friend's eyes now. Riley said that cross had been found in the ashes of the Tabernacle, where he'd almost died. Where so many other trappers had perished. If he refused to hand it over, how would they get into the next realm? Or return to their world to save his sister? Could he give away the symbol of his undying faith?

To her astonishment Simon removed the cross. His finger rubbed across the damaged wood with reverence. Then he looked up at the creature in front of them.

"This symbolizes my trust in the Light. Consider this my gift to you. Please grant us safe passage so that we can save my sister's life."

He tossed it into the air and the strange fingers nimbly caught it, then brought the cross up to the creature's eyes for closer examination. Once that scrutiny was complete, another long hum reverberated as it sank under the sand with its treasures.

"I'm so sorry, Simon. I know what that cross meant to you," she said, touching his arm.

He did not reply, his eyes glassy.

A sound came from behind them now and they whirled around. In the center of the slab circle was an open door made of gnarled beige rock. Simon retrieved the button from his pocket and held it out on his palm. It swiftly aligned itself to that portal.

"We go together, hand in hand," she said. "I don't want to lose you."

His expression changed as he tucked away the button.

"And I don't want to ever lose you."

Hand in hand they walked through the doorway into another realm. Behind them came a low hum and then silence.

The instant her brother and the trapper were hurled through the wall, the necromancer strode out of the factory, the doors banging shut behind him. That was a smart move or Deanna would have tried to strangle his ass.

"What the hell was all that?" she grumbled. A glance at the dead people didn't give her any answers.

Tempting as it was to break down in tears, she wasn't going there. At least not until she got out of here. Her brother was in danger and that's all that mattered. And he owed her an explanation, especially about the trip to Hell stuff. Not even her parents had mentioned that bit and she bet they knew about it.

How much had Simon been hiding from her over the years? Did they think she was too stupid to understand what that meant?

Dee sighed, shaking her head. She had to figure out how to bust out of this place because she bet those front doors were blocked by magic. Calling for help wasn't an option—her phone was in her purse at her brother's house. From the lost expressions in the dead peoples' eyes, they were going to be no help at all. Which meant she'd have to do this herself.

It was then she spied the bag the trapper had been forced to leave behind. Simon had often spoken about the gear he had to tote around. Maybe something in there would give her a means to escape. She hustled over and grabbed the bag—it was heavier than she'd expected—and then hauled it over to the closest wall. There was no place to sit but on the dirty concrete, so she parked herself and began to dig through the bag's contents.

A steel pipe came out first, which would make a great weapon though it felt heavy in Dee's hand. There was a glass globe nestled inside a Styrofoam shell, a couple of liters of Holy Water, a few protein bars, a small First Aid kit, a short length of rope, and a cell phone, which didn't work at all.

She knew that Holy Water could hurt demons, Dee doubted it would do much to the necro. The steel pipe might be a possibility, but she'd never get that close. At the bottom of the bag were two plastic bottles of drinking water so Dee pulled one out, cracked the seal and gulped some down. Capping it, she rose. It was time to do reconnaissance.

Her brother was counting on her.

Riley leaned against her car as she watched Mort's vehicle arrive. Though Greenwood Cemetery dated from the early 1900s, it still accepted burials and so there was still the need for grave sitters.

About an hour earlier her fellow summoner had called her, all excited. During his survey of local funeral directors, one of them remembered a pale young man during a visitation. That visitation had been for a woman whose body had been stolen later that night. Armed with that info, Mort had done more digging and come up with the name of the sunlight-challenged grave watcher: Harry Hawkins.

Mort found that Hawkins had a pattern to his grave sitting. He was never there when one of the bodies was stolen, but he'd always sat the shift right before the thefts. Coincidence? Mort wasn't sure, but he felt this might be the break they needed.

Riley locked her car and joined her friend. For once, she left her trapping bag behind as they were close to hallowed ground.

"Hey Mort. You really think this might be the guy?"

"Maybe. Maybe not," he said. As he looked toward the cemetery's entrance, she could see the toll this whole mess had taken on him. "It was Katia who got me thinking about the grave watchers. She was going to check them out, but I haven't heard from her."

Riley's phone buzzed so she pulled it out. It was Beck sending his love, which was always appreciated. She returned that love then stuffed the phone into a pocket.

"I couldn't get hold of Katia to let her know what we were doing. She said she had an exorcism, but usually she will text me once it's over."

"We'll check in with her as soon as we're done here. Hopefully, we'll have good news for her."

They hiked through the cemetery's gateway and into the grounds filled with over a century of headstones. According to what she'd found online, Greenwood was home to many different nationalities and faiths, with Chinese, Greek and Jewish sections. A slice of life in 1900s Atlanta.

"Katia would like this place. The headstones are upright. She can't stand the more modern ones. She was very verbal about that."

Mort didn't reply, but abruptly changed directions and headed toward a distant circle of light. As they moved closer to the new grave and the glowing circle around it, the grave watcher looked up. He was a young guy, probably mid-twenties, very thin, and pale. His wavy dark hair went in all directions.

"That's the guy who watched Means' grave right before us."

"Which means the vigil schedule was accurate. Not always the case." Mort paused. "Do you feel that?" he asked.

Riley let her senses loose, then grinned. "It's the same magical signature as the one who's been stealing the dead."

Her fellow summoner nodded. "This is good news."

The young man's eyes widened as they paused just outside the circle. He was dressed in a plain gray T-Shirt, jeans, tennis shoes. A worn baseball cap covered his head, shielding it from the sun. At his side was a bottle of water and his worn knapsack.

As grave watchers went, his setup was bare bones.

"Harry Hawkins?" Riley said.

He blinked at his name. "Yeah?" He glanced down at the candles and then up again, as if judging whether the circle would hold against them. "Hey, I know you. You were here the night—"

"Mr. Means' body was stolen," she said. "You know anything about that?"

He shook his head vigorously. "No. No."

"Then why were you in the cemetery talking to the workers before he was buried?"

"What?" he said. "No, wasn't me."

"There aren't too many pale guys like you roaming around Atlanta."

"Don't know about that."

"And you were seen outside Beesh's Funeral Home, the same day a body went missing."

"No, not me."

"They have a security camera," she said. Riley had no idea if that was the case, but the guy's eyes widened, confirming his guilt. She looked over at Mort now. "Things are looking pretty bad for Mr. Hawkins here."

"I agree," her companion said. "The mayor's demanding someone's head, and his will do."

"It wasn't me! I didn't do anything."

"But you know who did," Mort shot back.

There was a quick look at the glowing candles as the man took a very deep breath. His panicked expression faded now, replaced by defiance.

"Or what? You going to bust me out of this circle? No way that's happening. I'll just stay here until you leave."

That was a decent threat, other than he'd eventually need food, and a toilet. Destroying the circle really wasn't a good idea, especially with the press already shouting about summoners breaking the law.

Since this guy wasn't going to cooperate and recite the phrase that would allow Riley to enter it, they'd have to pry him out of that protection.

"Toast the circle?" she asked, looking over at Mort again. She made sure her wink wasn't seen by their quarry.

There was a flare of amusement in her friend's eyes, also something Hawkins wouldn't notice. "Go for it."

Riley deftly rolled up the sleeves on her robe, raised her arms, then pushed against the circle with her magic. It immediately flared bright, as it should. She didn't push any further, there was no need. Instead, she wove a spell to create a light display which churned across the surface of the circle, and the protective shield above it. SGI, as Mort called it—summoner-generated imagery. Completely illusionary, but this guy didn't know that. Sometimes it was all about theatrics.

"Stop that!" Hawkins said, jerking his head around to follow the images as they shimmered across the circle. The spell caused the colors to morph from red to blue, then purple and finally to deepest green. Skeletal hands formed now, reaching toward the man inside.

"Hey! You can't do that!" Hawkins squeaked as he leapt to his feet, staring at her as if she was the devil incarnate.

"We're not here to hurt you or the deceased. We're here to find the truth," Mort said.

"I don't know anything," the man insisted, as his eyes darted around looking for a means of escape.

Riley pushed a bit more magic into the spell and the hands became bloody claws. Chilling howls filled the air as if the denizens of Hell were closing in. And just for the fun of it she made her robe billow around her.

"No, don't do that," Hawkins shouted, looking back at the grave, then at them.

"Tell us the name of the summoner. That's all we want to know," Mort demanded, stepping closer as his hands glowed blue. "Last chance. Is this worth dying for?"

The man's complexion went stark white and then he ran for it, right through the circle, past Riley and Mort, his feet pounding across the graveyard at an astounding speed. In his wake the circle broke, leaving the recently deceased unprotected.

"Idiot," Mort said, shaking his head. He gestured and their quarry stumbled, then fell to the ground. Though Hawkins managed to roll over onto his back, he was unable to rise, held in place by the spell's invisible bonds.

Riley changed gears, murmuring her own incantation to raise a new protective circle around the grave. Once it was in place she stepped back and rolled down her sleeves.

"Those were very nice effects, Summoner Blackthorne," Mort said while Hawkins continued to flail in a useless attempt to escape the binding spell.

"Hey, if I can't cut it as a summoner, there's always Hollywood," she replied. Her friend barely stifled a laugh.

With a gesture of his hand their captive rose in the air and then floated over to land on the grass in front of them.

"You can't do this to me. I have rights," Hawkins said, still flailing and getting nowhere.

"The cops will nail you for grave robbing, desecration of a gravesite, and unlicensed use of magic," Riley said. That last one was a lie, but this guy didn't know that.

Finally, Hawkins stopped fighting as a glare came their way. "I didn't do anything."

"I'm thinking there's no need to get the cops involved." Mort gave an unholy smile as more small blue orbs began to weave around his fingers. "I'll be happy to off this sucker just for the practice," he added.

"Then you could reanimate him after he's dead."

Her friend grinned. "Good idea. I need a new servant. The last one didn't last long."

"What was it, like two weeks?" Riley said, playing along with this charade.

"If that. They don't do well out in the hot sun. Roasts them every time."

"No," the young man shouted. "You can't kill me. He said I wouldn't be hurt."

"Well, *he* lied." The blue orbs grew larger now.

"So which spell is that—the *burn the body like a pinecone* one, or the *boiling intestines* one?" she asked, struggling not to laugh.

Mort was having the same difficulty. "Both. I combined them," he replied. "I've been eager to try it out on a live subject. The last one only took about ten minutes to die. I'm hoping it'll be longer this time."

"Oh my God, you can't! I didn't do anything," Hawkins cried.

Riley gave him a "really?" look.

"Okay, okay, I put something in the dirt on the graves. That's all I did."

"What kind of something?" Mort asked.

"There were four glass spheres with powder inside. He said they contained spells. He told me to bury them a foot or so down, right above the vault."

"All together?"

"No, he wanted them to form a square. He said that he would trigger them and then the dead guy would be free." Hawkins sucked in a breath. "He said I was to do it before he came to get the bodies. That way if he couldn't make the grave watchers break the circle, the spell would. And since I wasn't there, I wouldn't be blamed."

"Well, what do you know," her fellow summoner said, "I never would have thought of that tactic."

"But you didn't do that because you were sick the first night Katia watched Mr. Means' grave," Riley said, putting it all together now.

"Yeah. He was really pissed about that."

"Are there any of those spheres on this grave?"

Hawkins nodded. "When I talked to him last night, he said he didn't need them anymore."

Had the necro finally stolen enough corpses or was something else going on?

"What's the summoner's name?"

Their captive shrugged. "He said I should call him Magus,

so I did."

Which was just another word for necromancer. "And you did this because . . . ?" Mort asked as the glow on his hands faded now.

Hawkins groaned. "He said he'd teach me magic. I want to be a necromancer. I want to raise the dead. I want to *be* somebody." His defiance vanished and he sobbed. "I just want to make enough money to have a place to live. Food. Stuff like that."

Mort issued a long sigh at this news, trading a quick glance with Riley. It appeared their villain wasn't as evil as they thought.

"Where can we find him?" she asked.

Another shrug. "He only calls me when he wants something done. The number changed every time."

"Of course it did," Riley muttered. "Anything else you can tell us?"

Hawkins sat up now, a sign that Mort had released the binding spell. He brushed the dirt off his T-shirt, then looked up at them, his face set. "The magus wants something in another world. Some realm place or whatever. He said he had to have it soon or lots of people would die."

"Realm?" Riley said, shooting her friend a worried look.

"Yes, but he couldn't go there himself." Hawkins glanced toward the circle and then back. "Look, I'm sorry. I just wanted to do something better than starving, you know? I thought magic was the answer." He shook his head in dismay. "It was a stupid move."

As Summoner Advocate of Atlanta, it'd be Mort's decision if this fool was sent to the cops, or worse.

"Anything else? Because now is the time to be totally honest. It might save your life," Riley said. "I'm not kidding about that, Hawkins."

He grimaced. "Ah, yeah. The magus asked about the trapper that was with you that night. The Breman girl. He wanted to know everything about her, about her family, friends, her job, all of it."

"Why?"

"I don't know. But he doesn't ask for something unless it's really important to him."

"When was this?" Mort asked.

"Yesterday. I sent him the info late last night."

"What did you find?" Riley asked.

"That people thought she went to Hell and came back. I'm betting the magus guy was all over that news."

And she's not answering her calls . . .

Mort stalked away as he contacted someone on his phone.

"It all sounded so cool, you know?" Hawkins continued. "Then I realized I couldn't shake free of this guy. He gave me the creeps. Really powerful, though."

"You have family here in Atlanta?" Riley asked.

"No. I'm from Michigan."

"Why are you so pale? Are you anemic or something?"

He gave a quick nod. "I've been donating blood a lot."

Selling his blood because he had little money. Katia would see this guy as a kindred soul.

"Where are you staying?"

"I'm crashing with someone I met at a bar. She's weird, but okay. Well, sorta okay. She's even creepier than the necro. She keeps asking me to find her cat corpses."

Ewww.

Riley set a circle around him. "Don't try to break out of this or it'll hurt."

He blinked, then nodded. "No reason to run anymore. It's done." He looked over toward Mort now. "Really done."

Riley walked over to where her fellow summoner was just finishing his phone call.

"Learn anything else?" he asked, looking back at the man who sat slumped inside his magical prison.

Riley explained exactly how the guy had been living hand to mouth, as her father would say.

A nod returned, as if that didn't surprise him. "Summoner Andrews has agreed to babysit him for the time being. I'm afraid if he's left on his own, the rogue necro will kill him because of what he knows."

Riley didn't bother to hide her sigh of relief. "Oh, good, I'm not the only pushover in this cemetery."

Mort smiled at her. "Not even close. I will need time to remove the spell on the grave just in case our rogue is still collecting bodies."

"Okay. I'll call Katia again. And I'll find someone to watch this one overnight."

"Sounds good."

When Mort delivered his verdict to Hawkins, the guy stared in astonishment, then fought back tears. "You're not going to kill me?" he blurted, looking back and forth between them.

"No," Mort replied. "I wouldn't have. I was just messing with your head so we can find this thief and stop him."

Hawkins slumped in relief. "Oh, okay. I deserved that."

"Yes, you did," Riley replied. A thought occurred. "Did you call Mrs. Means to let her know that her husband had been reanimated?"

Hawkins looked away, then nodded. "I thought she outta know."

"But you didn't do that for any of the other families," Mort said.

"Honest, I was feeling kinda bad about all these bodies walking off. But I didn't dare tell the magus I wouldn't help him. He's not someone to cross."

His conscience had finally kicked in. That still didn't explain why Mrs. Means was dressed to impress for her trip to the cemetery in the wee hours of the morning. Maybe she was great at putting makeup on in a car. Who knew?

Riley removed the spell around Hawkins and then he was waved over to join the senior summoner. This was going to be a complicated process as Mort needed to magically levitate the first few feet of dirt from the grave to find each of the spheres. Knowing him, he'd also raise the vault's lid to double check that there was nothing else magical placed near the deceased.

Then all that had to go back in place without a hint of it being disturbed.

Riley turned her back on the activity, mentally working through a list of trappers who were skilled at grave sitting. There weren't many, most were too wary to even try. Then she smiled and hit the proper contact on her phone.

"Hey, boss. What can I do for you?" Jaye Lynn asked.

"Want to earn some money watching over a grave?"

"Ah, any chance that might earn me a visit from a body poacher? Like what happened to Katia?"

Riley looked over her shoulder. As magic poured from Mort's hands, the soil covering the grave rose a few feet above it, followed by four spheres. Those floated a short distance away and then settled on the ground while Hawkins stared in awe.

"My guess is that there won't be a rogue summoner tonight," she said. "Not for this grave at least."

"Then count me in," Jaye said. "The extra cash would be great."

Her next call was to Katia and once again it went to voicemail.

"Call me. We found the pale dude."

Now they just had to find Hawkins' boss.

FIFTEEN

Chilling cold enveloped Simon's body as his lungs labored to take a breath. When he was sure he'd suffocate, the immense pressure suddenly ended. He sucked in air, his heart battering in his chest. Katia was next to him, but they were no longer touching.

Where the other place had been barren, this one was lush, but in a way that grated against his senses. Grayish brown moss spread out around them. No, not moss, not when dragging his shoe over it made a sound like he was breaking glass.

There were trees, if trees had leathery trunks and branches that moved even though there was no wind. The sky was an unusual shade of brownish red, as if someone had sprayed blood into the air and it had dried there. The air itself was heavy and so thick it was hard to breathe.

His sister Amy loved urban fantasy novels, and she'd talked about places like this. The more bizarre and otherworldly the better. In those places were outrageous monsters, magical heroes and heroines. For a time Simon enjoyed reading those books as well, until he became a trapper.

Then the monsters had become too real.

"Duck!" Katia called out.

His swift reaction saved him from being shredded by a creature that swept past them in the air, claws extended. It wasn't a bird, more like a two-foot-wide butterfly thing. Its wings were razor sharp. They tracked it as it headed deeper into the forest beyond.

"What was that?" Katia said.

"I'm guessing it's the norm for whatever this place is."

"Well, that blows," she said. "What does the magic button say?"

Simon held out his palm and the thing spun a few times, then stopped. Once again it pointed directly into the heart of the grim forest beyond.

"Remind me to beat the hell out of that necro if I get a chance," Katia said.

"We both will, if Dee hasn't nailed him already." A chuckle returned.

Rather than immediately heading into those woods, Simon took the time to apply Papal Holy Water to his forehead, followed by a prayer for protection. When Katia saw what he'd done she did the same. Her prayer was quick and to the point—"Don't let us die here, okay?"

"Ready?" he asked, seeing the apprehension in her eyes. He felt the same. He faced demons for a living, not creatures in unknown worlds.

"Yeah. Let's do this," she said. "The sooner we are out of here the better."

As they walked toward the darker part of the forest his senses went on full alert. That proved a blessing when Katia tripped and would have fallen face first into the glittering moss if he'd not caught her.

"Thank you. I'm not usually this clumsy."

No she wasn't, and neither was he. It had to be the effects of this realm, or the journey here. Once they found the ring, how the hell were they going to get back home?

It quickly became obvious that this realm's time was out of sync with their own world. Daylight changed to twilight in a matter of minutes. Then nightfall and back to full daylight. It was like an ornery toddler kept playing with this realm's dimmer switch. On. Off. On. Off.

While the light and dark alternated, as if days had passed, so did the landscape. The forest now had lush orange bushes and head-tall amber fronds with trumpet-shaped flowers. Those flowers were dangerous and she'd made sure to keep away from them. Especially after nectar had dropped from one of the blooms and the moss beneath it had melted into goo. She figured the same would happen to them. She made sure to point that out to Simon.

"The trees aren't moving here," he said.

"Yeah. Noticed that." Was that good or bad?

Urrrrrrrrip!

Katia jumped at the shrill sound, hunting for the source. "Where is that coming from?"

Simon pointed to their right. "There."

High up in one of the trees were about a dozen figures clustered along a thick branch. At first she thought they were crows. But these were composed strictly of bones with not a feather in sight. There were no eyes inside those skulls and yet they acted as if they could see both her and Simon. One stretched out a bony wing and then tucked it up again.

Urrrrrrrrip! Urrrrrrrrrip!

In unison they all leaned over the branch now as if monitoring their progress.

"Damned glad those things aren't in our world," she said, shuddering.

Urrrrrrrrip! Urrrrrrrrrip!

They hurried onward and eventually the skeleton birds fell silent. Simon checked their progress with the button and found it still pointed forward. Once again it was daytime but that seemed to shift the moment they entered an area devoid of trees.

Here there was no spiky moss, just pale brown dirt that appeared to move on its own accord. The same tall fronds they'd passed earlier encircled the open space. Something flew by one of the fronds only to be encased in liquid and whatever it was melted away in screeching agony.

"Dear God, get us out of here," Simon whispered, then crossed himself.

In the very center of the open space was a rock. It was almost like an altar, large, flat, and surrounded by fronds. In the very center was a skull. She guessed it was a male from the size, and it was human. Katia could feel something emanating from it. Something incredibly powerful.

"The button says this is the place," Simon said, the item lying on his palm pointing directly at the rock.

"I don't see a ring."

"Maybe it's under the skull."

"Riiight. So, we're supposed to just roll up there and grab that thing? Does he think we're idiots?"

"I'll go," Simon offered.

"The hell you will," she said, glowering at him. "That is a trap. Even you know that."

"I do. But what other choice do we have?" he shot back.

The increasing darkness flowing from that thing made her want to run. Simon had never been as tuned into stuff like that, but then his expertise was exorcisms, not random skulls in the middle of nowhere.

Not this. Evil. Evil!

Katia frowned. She'd last heard that voice the day she'd arrived in Atlanta. What was The Lady doing here?

As she stalled for time to think this through, Katia turned in a slow circle to ensure nothing was sneaking up behind them. There was no sign of The Lady, though she knew she'd heard her.

"Check the button again."

With a huff Simon extended his palm and it still pointed at the skull. "See?" he said, frowning. "We have no choice. The ring must be under that thing."

Before she could reply the button abruptly veered to the left, away from that rock and its prize.

Simon stared at it. He shoved it back the way it'd been and after a time, it veered left again. "How did you know that would happen?"

"Gut instinct," she said, because now was not the time to explain The Lady and how they'd met. Things were freaky enough.

Simon grumbled under his breath as the new direction took them out of the clearing and away from the rock. From behind her she could still feel its pull as if it was stalking them. When he staggered, she caught his arm.

"You okay?"

Simon shook his head. "Feel weird." He paused, then straightened up. "It's better now. Let's get out of here."

They pushed on as the button routed them deeper and deeper into the woods. If The Lady meant for them to die here, this was an ideal way of leading them to their graves. But there wouldn't be any graves. No one except Deanna would know they were here, and even she had no clue *where here* was. Katia's parents, her brother and sister, would never know what happened to her. And neither would Simon's family. They would just disappear, forever.

"We survived Hell, we'll survive this place," she said under her breath.

In the distance came a faint agonized cry. They picked up their pace. Near the far edge of the clearing was another tree with the same leather bark and the same oddly shaped branches as the others. What was different were the two leg bones lying on the ground in front of it. Every bit of skin and flesh was gone,= as if the tree had just gulped down a passerby. A ripped robe was nearby, a solid black one.

"A necromancer?" Katia guessed. "But who would come here unless they were forced to?"

A quick glance at the button told them this was their goal.

Be of care. Much evil, The Lady whispered.

Simon hadn't moved. Then he pointed to yet another tree, another set of skeletonized legs, another black robe.

"What is this place?"

He didn't reply, but The Lady did though her voice was softer now.

Evil ones here. Get ring. Flee!

Katia sucked in a breath. "You're going to have to trust me on something. Can you do that?" she asked, watching her partner's face in hopes of reading his inner thoughts. If they were like hers they were totally confused.

"I'm getting a . . . feeling that the person in that tree is major evil. All we need is their ring. Nothing else. Just the ring."

His steely blue eyes locked on hers. "Do I want to hear how you know this?"

"Not right now." Because if she was wrong they were both history.

"You'll explain all this when you can?" he pushed.

"Yes." Simon was owed the truth one way or another. And if they were dead, it wouldn't matter.

He considered her for a moment longer, then nodded. "Okay. Ring only. Got it."

She stared at him in astonishment. "You're trusting me on this?"

"I am. You sense things I don't. And we're running out of time here." He held up the button which was noticeably smaller than it had been when they'd entered this realm.

"Oh, shit."

"Yeah.' He tucked the thing away, then eyed the situation. "I'll pull on the legs and hopefully that will get the body free so I can find the ring. Keep an eye on those branches for me."

"That works."

She realized he would need some sort of protection to keep from being sliced up if that tree proved hostile. Which it would since everything else in this realm seemed that way.

Scooping up the tattered robe, she shook it out and then wound it around her right arm. To her relief no magic remained in the fabric. That wasn't the same for whatever was in the tree. A low moan came again, but how could that be if the necro was dead?

"Ready," she announced.

Simon grabbed both leg bones and tugged. Then tugged even more. One of the feet promptly snapped off in his hand as a scream came from inside the tree.

He tossed the foot aside, then repositioned himself and pulled again. The body of whoever it was slid forward inch by agonizing inch as the bones creaked and cracked.

Then the tree went crazy.

The first swipe of a branch barely missed crushing Simon's skull. Katia stepped forward as the next one swept sideways and she purposely let it hit her arm, gritting her teeth as the shock of the blow vibrated throughout her body. Positioned as she was, she couldn't see her companion, and she worried she'd step on him.

Two more branches came at her, working in tandem. She parried one branch, then spun to let the other bounce off her. This time it drew blood as it sliced through the robe and deep into her arm.

There was more grunting, another muffled cry, and then "Got it!"

She glanced down to find Simon hastily scrambling away from two dislocated legs and an arm. On instinct she ducked as the nearest branch barely missed her.

"Asshole," she said, then backed off even further. She was so tempted to give the trunk a stout kick, but that was probably how the necro had been trapped in the first place.

He held up the ring. "I can't believe we found it."

"Neither can I."

They'd gone only a few steps away when a groaning sound made them turn. The tree had begun to expand, the bark pulsing like it had a heartbeat of its own.

Run! The Lady shouted.

"Run!" Katia echoed.

They sprinted away but only made it a short distance before the tree exploded and spears of bark flew toward them. Both dove to the ground, but still a few hit their target. Simon swore and pulled a shard from his shoulder, tossing it away. Katia did the same for the one that had hit her forearm.

The fronds nearest them began to shift and dirt flew as they uprooted themselves from the soil.

"What the . . . " he said, jumping to his feet. Katia did the same only to find the fronds skittering across the ground toward them, their blooms glistening with the acidic nectar.

They ran for their lives. Soon they were in the domain of the skeleton birds and this time the things no longer just screeched their fury, but flew toward them, scraping at their heads and faces with their razor-sharp talons.

This world hadn't liked them on the way in, now it hated them because they were trying to leave.

"It's because we have the ring. I swear it!" she said as they continued their flight.

The moss was taller now and digging at their ankles, ripping their jeans and their flesh as the trees swung their branches in ever-closer attacks.

A choir of voices rose, a hellish chorus of pain, anger and sorrow. They burrowed into Katia's mind and made her stumble. Simon did the same, his face ashen gray and glistening with bloody sweat.

Save us. Free us. Free us or die! the voices cried.

"Holy Father, drive away the darkness and danger," Simon called out. He sucked in another breath, still running with Katia by his side. "Clear our path and shelter us with your Light. Take us home!"

In response, the realm doubled its efforts to kill them; even more eager to rip the flesh from their bones.

"Come on, help us!" Katia called out. "You want this damned ring, help us!"

Go. Go now! The Lady called out.

In a dazzling flash a light appeared in front of them illuminating a stone path. The closer they got, the brighter that light grew.

"Faster!" Simon shouted as they pelted across the open ground. A quick look over her shoulder showed the darkness growing steadily behind them.

Katia reached the shimmering light first. She had no idea what was beyond it, only that whatever was waiting there couldn't be any more dangerous than what was hunting them. Simon was right next to her now, sprinting as fast as possible.

Something tripped her and as she began to fall he caught her. Once she regained her balance he jammed the ring into her hand. "Go!"

Katia turned to reach for him only to see him being dragged backward.

"Go!" he shouted as he fought whatever had gripped his leg.

"No way!"

As she hurried toward him she slipped the ring on her thumb to keep from dropping it. The instant the ring was in place its magic wound around her and she hit an unseen barrier. When she struggled to reach Simon it held her back, then slowly began to pull her away from him.

Katia tugged frantically on the ring but it refused to budge. Simon cried out, fighting against whatever had grabbed onto him. She managed to take a few steps forward, the magic tearing at her with each movement. She kept fighting it and reached out. He stretched out his hand for hers, his eyes filled with terror. Closer, closer, a few more feet.

Then to her horror he jerked backward as something reeled him in. When she tried to grab him, the magic doubled, enveloping her, lifting her into the air.

"NO!"

She sailed over the ground and through the portal, landing hard on the factory floor. When she stopped rolling, someone grabbed her arm and pulled her up to her feet.

"Where is he?" his sister demanded. Then Dee looked back where the wall should be and saw the void that was just beyond. "Simon?" she shouted.

"No, don't!" But before Katia could stop her she leapt through the portal and was gone.

The doorway snapped closed. Simon and his sister were gone.

SIXTEEN

"NOOOOO!"

Katia pounded her fists against the rough concrete blocks. She could feel the residual magic in them, but there was no way she could make that portal open once more.

"God no, Simon. You damned fool."

There had to be a way to get him back, and Deanna as well. *The ring.* She looked down at her hand, but it was gone. "Where is that damned thing?" It would be the leverage she needed to make the necro retrieve them.

"I have it."

She whirled around to find the summoner near the front doors, the gold ring in hand. His expression wasn't triumphant, but saddened, as if he knew exactly what price had been paid for its retrieval.

"Bring them back!" she demanded, pointing at the wall. "Bring them back, now!"

The summoner gestured. The wall glowed, but nothing more. He tried again, shouting some magical words. The glow faded and died.

"I . . . can't," he said. "I'm sorry. I'm really, really sorry." There was truth in his words. "You removed something from that world and now it's closed to us. I didn't realize that would happen."

He looked down at the band resting on his palm. It seemed so ordinary, made of gold with a ruby setting. "I must go now. If I don't, she'll die. I can't let that happen. I'm truly sorry about the others. If there is a way . . . " Then he glanced over at the Deaders now, Means in particular. "I'll set you free, I promise."

As the doors behind him swung open, the summoner strode through them. Then they banged shut.

Katia's jaw dropped. "You bastard! You can't leave them there!"

But he had.

Her mind ran rampant, desperate for a solution. The only way she could get back into that world was through a powerful summoner. Mort or Lord Ozymandias. Either one might be able to do it.

Katia spotted her trapping bag resting by a wall so she sprinted to it, then dug inside. Her phone was in there, but of course it didn't work. The necro had probably set a spell to keep that from happening. She jammed it in her back pocket, then rose again.

"I have to get out of here."

Tears burned tracks down her face, the truth as painful as any wound she'd ever received.

Simon had known that ring was pulling itself into this world. He'd given it to her, on purpose. He'd sacrificed himself to ensure she survived, never anticipating his sister would try to rescue him. Be trapped with him.

The tears slowed and she knuckled them away, cold fury filling her.

"You will come home. Both of you," she whispered. "If I can't do it, I'll find someone who will. I will make this happen, or I will die trying."

The vow hung in the air, taking on a strength of its own.

A shuffling noise announced the approach of a reanimate. Mr. Means stopped next to her, then gently touched her arm, his face gray and his eyes dull.

"I'm sorry. It's . . . . not . . . . right," he said.

Maybe this man knew more than he thought. "Why did he reanimate you?"

"He thought we could enter that other place, get the ring."

"Why?"

"He said he needed it to save someone he loved."

Loved? "Who?"

A sad shake of his head was the reply.

"How do I get the hell out of here so I can find us help?"

"You cannot crawl out the lower windows. There is magic on them."

Wards.

"The other lady couldn't go up the stairs. But maybe the spell is weaker the higher you get. I don't know."

And if she did make it to the top of the stairs, then what? Shout from one of the windows until someone called the cops? Well, it was better than waiting for the asshole to come back. Or starve to death if he decided to abandon them.

If I can get up on the roof . . .

She took one deep breath, then another. Her muscles ached, her wounds burned, and her head throbbed. But the fury deep within her propelled her forward.

I will not let you die because of me.

A plan began to form, a long shot, but at this point that was all she had. After taking a deep breath to let some of the adrenalin drain off, Katia retrieved one of the bottles of the sacred liquid from her pack and waved Means over to join the other Deaders. Then she carefully laid a circle around all them and invoked the protection. The circle flared bright as a smile appeared on Means' face. He knew what she was doing.

"Stay inside this circle. I'm not sure if this will keep you safe, but it's better than nothing. I'm afraid I might trigger a magical backlash or something if I break out of here and I don't want you hurt." She handed him the only other bottle. "Reinforce it if necessary. You understand?"

He nodded. "Where are you going?"

"To find someone to help us."

Means gave another nod, then sank onto the floor with the bottle of Holy Water clenched in his hands.

Katia exited the circle, taking great care to keep it intact, then picked up her bag and headed for the nearest set of stairs. There was no guarantee she'd be able to escape the building, but she bet the necro hadn't planned on having a free agent wandering around inside, at least one that wasn't a Deader.

As Means had said, the stairs were not an option, warded at the top where they reached a door marked Office. Retreating to the factory floor she methodically checked every potential exit, though the reanimate had said he'd already done that. All were warded. That left only one more way out of here.

That choice sucked. She dug out an unopened bottle of water and took a long pull of the refreshing liquid. Once she'd recapped it, she set it aside and tucked a power bar in her pocket. More time was involved re-tying her shoe laces.

"Just get it done," she muttered.

After another glance at the Deaders inside their circle, she headed for the shelving on the far wall. Like everything in this place it was old, grubby and not in great shape. Once she found a section that felt firmly bolted to the concrete blocks she began to climb.

When Katia'd been in high school, she'd religiously scaled a climbing wall at a local gym to strengthen her arm and chest muscles. At first it'd been impossible, but eventually she could scale that wall like a monkey.

But this was nothing like that.

The shelves were dirty and slippery with both dust and a thin film of oil. Worse, a few of them wiggled more than she'd like. It took a while before she developed a rhythm: Right foot on the closest shelf, left hand on the shelf above that, then move upward switching limbs. Once Katia was in the zone, she made substantial progress until her left hand met something on the next shelf up.

When the rat trap snapped she nearly fell, then swore in a stream of both English and Hellspeak. It took work to pry the thing off her fingers while dangling one-handed above the factory floor. When it came free and fell at least thirty feet, then executed a series of energetic bounces across the concrete, shocked gasps came from her audience inside the glowing circle.

"It's all good," she called out, trying to reassure them.

It wasn't, but they didn't need to know that.

There were at least eight more shelves so she kept moving. Her arms and back throbbed as her face dripped sweat. The higher she went, the hotter it got.

After what seemed like days she reached the top shelf. She tested it, then crawled up on it, balancing precariously. A forgotten box of dusty gears sat nearby, the bleached-out address label catching her notice. This package had been shipped fifteen years earlier. Katia had been ten. She'd spent that summer skateboarding in Lawrence or at her grandmother's farm to avoid arguing with her mother.

"I miss you, Gran," she whispered. "You wouldn't be doing this crazy shit."

But her gran would be cheering her on. She always had.

Now, all those years later, she was spending her birthday trapped in a factory with some very dead people. Gran would have had a good laugh about that.

The twitching of her over-worked muscles made it feel like something was creeping all over her arms, legs and back. And of course, there had been a spider or twenty and she was ignoring the wasps' nest tucked high in the rafters. So far its occupants had been ignoring her.

A sneeze began to build and despite her efforts to stop it, it burst forth. Katia clung to her perch as her nose tried to rid itself of all the dust she'd sucked inside. When the sneezing finally ended, she wiped her nose on her T-shirt and studied the line of windows above her.

Even as her nose continued to drip, Katia tried to judge how much magic was present. To her relief, it appeared to be none. Madman Necro hadn't bothered to ward the area near the windows and the roof girders. Why would a reanimate try to climb up here? They wouldn't, not when they were under his control.

But Katia wasn't one of his minions.

"*That* was a mistake, dickwad."

A quick check of her mashed fingers proved they weren't

broken or bleeding, just hurting like hell, which meant it was time to get out of here.

Katia carefully stood, bracing herself against the wall and peered out the closest window. There was nothing outside, no walkway, no railing, nothing but a sheer wall.

"Really?" she said, shaking her head.

She shoved at the window and it creaked open, spraying rust and dirt in all directions. Leaning out she found a metal stairway further down the building, one that extended downward from the roof. Not a fire exit, but likely used to access the roof if repairs were needed. It would be a way out if she could figure out how to get to it.

It was either that or yell her head off and hope someone heard her. The industrial estate remained as silent as when she'd arrived. She saw no cars or people so that meant she could shout until the end of the world and no one would hear her.

Which left that exterior stairway as her only other choice. To reach it, she'd need to move to the next set of shelving to her right. Shelving that was at least eight feet away and stacked with mangled boxes and even more dust. She narrowed her eyes trying to study the bolts securing that section to the wall. They didn't look good.

"Stop whining. Simon wouldn't be whining. By now he'd be out of here, the necro in chains. Get it done, Breman."

After another sneezing fit, she evaluated her next steps. Climbing across to the nearest shelving unit wasn't an option, there was too much space involved. She could try jumping over, while praying the whole unit didn't head for the floor. That would be such a stellar way to die.

Above her was a thick metal chain. It dangled down from a winch secured high in the ceiling. No surprise, that chain was rusty. At least her tetanus shot was up to date.

Praying that it was still strong enough to hold her weight, Katia leveraged herself out from the shelf, then grasped on the chain, kicking off from the unit. A shaky glide got to the next shelving unit as gasps came from the reanimates below.

"That worked," she said, immensely proud of that bold maneuver.

Until she heard the unmistakable sound of a bolt shirring off. Then another and another as her weight made the shelving system increasingly unstable. Metal ground against blocks as the entire section began to free itself from the wall. Boxes slid off the shelves, racing to their demise below.

"Dammit!" she cried, then leapt upward and grabbed onto the window above. Tucking her feet up as tight as possible, Katia watched as the entire metal structure executed an impressive swan dive to the factory floor.

Rather than collapsing on itself, it fell forward like a drunk, a corner of it striking the Holy Water circle. As the reanimates cowered inside, it held, exploding in a flash of light. What followed was the screeching impact of rows and rows of metal shelving, and their supports, raising a thick cloud of dust and rat droppings.

With a final burst of strength, Katia pulled herself up and kicked through the closest window, glass shattering. Once it was reasonably clear she ducked through the opening to freedom. As she sucked in a huge gulp of air she let her mind clear, her body still shaking.

To her relief, the stairs were right below her so she eased herself down on the first step in case the whole thing was as rotten as the shelves inside. They held solid.

Euphoric, she clattered down the stairs at a near run, only coming to a halt when she found she had run out of stairs at least ten feet above the paving below.

"Come on, there has to be way to get down there."

Fire escapes often had a built-in extension that retracted to keep people from accessing the building without permission. Maybe this one did as well.

Katia parked herself on a step while sucking in more air. She hadn't realized how foul it'd been inside that old factory until now. It took some fiddling, along with more cursing, until she finally located the twin latches that dropped the remaining stairs.

The second latch fought her, but she got it done and the stairs clunked downward, rattling as they descended.

Katia zipped down those like a horde of demons were on her tail, then once at ground level she bolted across the pavement. It was only when she had gotten at least forty feet from the factory that she stopped and turned around, still coughing out the dust and whatever else had invaded her lungs. A minute ticked by, then another, and yet no magical something came after her.

"I did it!" she shouted, executing a fist pump. Then another because it felt good even if her back was screaming at all the exercise. After more coughing and a few more sneezes, she dug a hand in her front pocket. Then realized what was missing.

"Oh, damn! Dumb, dumb, dumb!" she growled.

She'd left her car keys in the trapping bag. The bag that was still inside the factory.

With dirt and blood-smeared hands she pulled out her phone, which had somehow managed to stay in her pocket. It lit up the moment she swiped across the screen.

Katia Breman was back in the game.

SEVENTEEN

Simon knew he was going to die.

The claws that were hooked in his leg kept dragging him across the ground, and though he desperately tried to free himself his efforts were useless. To slow the inevitable he dug his fingers into the dirt, and prayed.

"Let. Him. Go!"

There was a solid whack, followed by an ear-splitting shriek. Then another solid blow. After another shriek the claws set him loose and retreated. Simon scrambled to his feet and found himself staring at his sister's sweaty face. She held a steel pipe dripping with dark blood.

"What the hell are you doing?" he shouted. How had she gotten here?

"Saving my little brother. Now get us back home, will you?"

He shot a quick look at the way they'd come. He'd feared this would happen. His sister didn't realize the portal had closed behind her.

"Dee, we're stuck here for now."

She whirled around. "What? But didn't that bastard want you to get something for him?"

"I did. Katia has it."

"And she just left you here?"

"I didn't give her a choice."

She glared at him. "What do you mean?"

He shook off the question. "It doesn't matter."

"You really do want to die, don't you?"

"No, I don't, but—"

Rustling came from the forest behind them.

"Let's keep moving," he said, taking her arm and tugging her forward.

"Shouldn't we stay near where the door was?"

"I'm thinking that way is closed for us."

The rustling grew louder.

"So where do we go?"

"I have no idea. But let's get moving."

As they hiked away, silence fell between them. He kept checking and was surprised he didn't see whatever was making that noise. In his distraction he would have missed a different gateway if Dee hadn't pulled him to a stop.

"There! Can we go there?" she asked, pointing at it with the pipe.

Just another dark opening in the middle of the forest with no hint of where it would lead. He bet it wouldn't be back to the factory. No, they needed to stay here. It increased their chances of being rescued if Mort or one of the other necros came searching for them. At least that was his prayer.

"We're not going through any portal unless we're sure it's safe."

His sister gave a look around. "You mean as compared to here?" He followed her gaze to see another tree with a mangled skeleton trapped inside its trunk. No summoner's robe this time, so was this just a random traveler? It was then he noticed the legs were bound together with chains, as if this had been a prisoner sent to their execution.

Shuddering, Simon turned back to his sister. "Yes, we need to wait until someone comes for us."

"How long?" she demanded.

His patience ended. "How the hell should I know? Time doesn't mean anything here."

Dee stared at him as if seeing something unexpected. Then she reluctantly nodded. "Okay, we wait. But if it gets bad let's not let something eat us if we have other options."

"Agreed." As they moved away from the portal, Simon asked the question burning in his heart. "Why did you come after me?

You were safer there."

The glare that came his way should have singed his skin.

"And just what was I going to do there? Sit on my butt and then tell our parents you died in some godawful wherever the hell this is? No way!"

He opened his mouth to argue, then knew she was right. She was an Adler. He would have done the same for her.

"Okay, got it."

"I saw you give something to the trapper. What was it?" she asked.

"A ring. It was pulling me into our world. When I got grabbed I knew it was the only way she'd survive. It wouldn't give her a choice to stay behind with me."

Dee studied him more closely now. "I always said my brother is a hero. Who knew?"

"Just trying to keep up with my sister." The smile he received was almost worth all this horror.

Now Simon knew exactly what he needed to do. "Let's find somewhere I can make a sacred circle and we'll hunker down."

"And then what?" she asked.

"Then we wait."

Dee looked around again, eyes wary, then nodded. She still clenched the steel pipe, her fingers blanching white. "This is your thing. I'll do what you tell me."

His always-in-charge eldest sister had just let him take the lead. God help them both if he screwed this up.

It took time to find a spot that didn't sport any of that flesh-ripping moss and wasn't close to any of the cannibalistic trees. He explained what he was about to do, then created the circle around them using the papal Holy Water and his visualization technique. At least Rome wouldn't know about that. When the circle flared to life, Dee's surprised expression reminded him of just how much he'd kept from her. From most of his family.

If they survived, he'd need to change that.

Then it was a matter of waiting and praying that someone would come for them. They sat in the dirt as the light around them faded. Occasionally something would check them out, but most of the creatures kept their distance. A raccoon-sized orange beast with crazy yellow eyes wasn't as cautious and trotted up to poke its spiky nose at the circle. With a sharp yelp it took off at top speed.

Simon heaved a sigh of relief. He hadn't been sure if a sacred ward would work here, but so far it had. It made sense—God had created the entire universe after all. This was just a distant corner of that cosmos.

Once the beast had cleared off, he pulled out the button to find it was even smaller now. He quickly stashed it away because he didn't want to explain what that meant. Instead, he turned his attention to his sister as she watched the area around them. The steel pipe was at her feet now, but still within easy reach.

It was time she knew it all. "Go on. Ask your questions. I'll try to explain," he said.

Dee blinked at him, telling him she hadn't expected him being so candid.

"Okay. Where are we? How did this happen?"

In a low voice, Simon told the tale, pausing every now and then to organize his thoughts and to study the area around them. More creatures wandered by, but none of them were bold enough to touch the circle. All of the things were nightmare fodder.

Dee's frown deepened. "So, we're in another realm place and the only people who know we arc here is the trapper, that damned necro, and a bunch of dead people?"

His sis always had a way of cutting right to the heart of a situation.

"That's it. You don't know Katia, but I can promise you she's working on a way to escape that factory. Once she does, she'll call for help from the other summoners."

Dee shook her head. "There's no way out of that place. I tried. It felt like something was clawing the skin off my bones."

"That would be a spell. Katia is really sensitive to those, so she'll find any weaknesses. In the meantime, there isn't much we can do."

"Except starve?" she asked.

"Feel free to trap your own dinner. I'm not leaving the circle and I'd recommend you do the same."

"What if no one comes for us?" she asked, her voice thinner now.

"Then we'll find a way out."

More silence. Something screamed in the woods, making them both jump.

"This place sucks," she said, moving the steel pipe closer now. Then she eyed him. "You know, you were always different than the rest of us."

"How so?"

"Well, when you were small, maybe three years old, you would sit and watch Amy and Josh play. Sometimes you'd join them, but usually you just watched them. It wasn't because you didn't know how to play, it was that you didn't want to. You haven't changed."

Simon had no idea what to say so he held his silence.

"Mom said that was the way you were. It wasn't that you were sick or didn't care, but that you had a different relationship with us and the rest of the world."

"I still do," he admitted. He'd always been one to stand back and observe, to weigh and measure events and people.

"That's obvious. But all that quiet serves a purpose, I think. Not sure what, but it's so you." She hesitated. "You're having trouble with your job, aren't you?"

He blinked at her observation because she was right. "Yeah, I'm burning out already. Too many demons, too fast."

"And like when you were a kid, you're trying to figure that all out rather than just saying, 'screw this, I'm outta here'."

As if he could. "You got all the sass in the family, Sis."

"Ha!" she said, shaking her head. "No. But whatever isn't working for you, you need to change it." And then she frowned, gave a look around, then nodded to herself. "Same with me, I think. Yeah, same with me."

If God were merciful, when this was over she'd be alive to

move stuff around his house and complain when he missed one of the family dinners.

†✳‡✳†

After the discovery of Harry Hawkins' role in the summoner's thievery, they'd hit a wall. Hawkins had given them everything he knew, and it still wasn't enough. Riley wasn't the only one frustrated, not from the expressions of her two companions as they sat on Mort's veranda. Their host kept muttering to himself while Ozymandias had remained stubbornly silent. Probably because he hadn't been able to track the rogue summoner by magical means.

"Come on, answer your phone," she said, crossing her fingers as she dialed Katia's number yet again. It swiftly went to voicemail. "No luck. Where the hell is she? It's been hours."

"Maybe try Simon again?" Mort suggested.

No answer either. She'd already left one message, but tried again.

"Hey, Simon. Call me as soon as possible. Thanks, bye."

"This does not bode well," Ozymandias said, crossing his hands over his chest.

"What are the chances of survival if she goes into another world?"

"It depends on the realm. The journeyman did survive Hell, but that's entirely different than some of the other worlds. And given that she is a chaîne, it would depend on how she interacts with that realm's magic."

"What's there that this summoner would want?" Mort asked. He had a glass of iced tea in front of him, but he'd been ignoring it.

"There are magical artifacts stored in certain worlds to keep them out of the hands of those who would misuse them. Those items augment one's existing abilities. There are those who would use such an item to gain power or to exact revenge."

"I hate to think that's what this guy is doing. He's enough of a threat without a magical boost," Riley replied.

Her phone rang and she snatched it up, studying the screen. "It's Katia!" she said, relieved. "Hey. Where have you been?"

"I need help. Is Mort with you?" The journeyman's voice sounded hoarse as if she'd been coughing.

"Yes, and Lord Ozymandias too," she said, glancing over at the two of them. The latter's eyes were open now, focused on the conversation. "What's going on?"

"Put me on speaker."

From her ragged breathing, Katia was barely holding it together.

"Okay, you're on speaker. Tell us what's happening."

"It's Simon and his sister. You have to help them, or they'll die."

Before she could respond, Katia continued, "They're in another realm. The necro snatched us up and sent us there. Simon and I were coming back and then he got stuck there. His sister went in after him and the portal closed. You have to help them!"

"Where are you right now?" Mort asked.

"I'm at an old factory in Duluth. The other Deaders are here. The asshole necro was sending them into this other world, trying to find this ring."

Lord Ozymandias shot Mort a concerned look. "What did this realm look like, Journeyman? I need you to give me as much detail as possible."

"Well, the grass was this spiky glass stuff. The trees looked like they were made of leather and there were these skeleton sort of birds. They made a really weird noise and attacked us. The flowers had acid dripping out of them. Oh, and there were human skeletons stuck in some of the trees."

His lordship grimaced. "I know this place well. I will head there now and try to find them." He paused, his eyes growing distant. "I make no promises, Journeyman. That realm is *particularly* dangerous for all mortals, especially summoners. It was meant to be that way."

After one last troubled look he strode into the house, his robe flowing behind him. Riley gave Mort a raised eyebrow and he just shrugged.

"I need a ride," Katia said. "My car is here, but the keys are inside the factory and I can't get back in. I forgot to grab them before I climbed out."

Climbed out? There had to be a story there.

"Where are you?"

"I'll send you the address. This was supposed to be an exorcism, but that was fake. This was a trap and I walked right into it."

So that's why you disappeared. "Just stay put. Someone will be there to pick you up as soon as possible."

"I don't care about me. Just get Simon and Dee out of that place. That's all that matters," Katia pleaded. The panic in her voice hadn't lessened. If anything, it had grown.

"We'll do what we can," Mort said.

"He . . . . Just help them. Just help them get back home." Then the call abruptly ended.

"I can go after her," Mort said. "I'll need to deal with the reanimates anyway."

"I think we need her here quicker than that, especially if she has any injuries." Riley thought for a moment, then knew who could help them. She concentrated, waited a bit, then nodded again. "Ori will bring her here."

"Ohhkay. I'll dig out the First Aid kit."

"Do you think they're still alive?" she asked.

Mort's expression grew grave, which was answer enough.

Ozymandias swept by them with his staff in hand, his sigil blazing on his forehead. He stopped in the middle of the backyard. The power coming off him blazed like a bonfire.

"Good hunting!" Mort called out.

With a wave of his hand a portal opened. Ozymandias stepped through and then vanished.

"Good hunting," she whispered.

EIGHTEEN

Katia parked herself in the shade near the building and scrolled through all the messages she missed. Still no birthday greeting from her mom. She sighed.

There came the sound of wings flapping, large ones. With her luck it'd be one of Hell's crew dropping by to offer Katia the ultimate deal: Her soul in trade for Simon and Deanna's lives. And God help her, she wasn't sure if she'd turn down that offer.

To her relief it was a Divine instead. As Ori's feet touched the pavement, and his wings tucked close to his body, he gave her a quick look.

"I have been tasked with bringing you to Mortimer Beaumont Alexander's dwelling."

Riley must have made that request, and he didn't look pleased being asked to haul her all over Atlanta. "Yes, please. Today has been a total bitch so far."

"A portal to another realm has been opened and closed nearby," he said, his tone more severe than usual.

"You can sense that?" A nod. Was it possible . . . "Can you go through one of those doors?"

He shook his head. "Divines are forbidden to journey into other realms. But that isn't preventing creatures trying to come here."

Like the thing in Demon Central.

"Can you stop them?"

"Maybe, once they are in this realm."

Ori offered his hand. When she took it she could feel the callouses on his fingers. At one time she'd had the same, but she doubted his came from wielding a shovel.

"You should close your eyes," he advised.

"Why?"

"Because if you have any issues with heights—"

She slammed her eyes shut and then felt the air move around them as they shot upward. A few minutes later her feet once again touched solid ground, and that was a reassuring feeling. They were now in Little Five Points, standing in front of Mort's front door.

A rideshare with wings. My brother would be so jealous.

Ori didn't reply, but let go of her hand and rapped on the door. It opened immediately revealing Mort who looked as worried as she felt.

"Oh, good, you're here. Thank you for bringing her."

Without waiting for a reply Ori shot into the air like a rocket, winging his way back into the city. In the past the angel had always been civil, but not today.

"He's spooked or he wouldn't be so abrupt." Mort gestured. "Come in. You look awful. And what did you do to your hand?"

"It was a rat trap."

He blinked at her a couple times, then ushered her inside. Katia was so tired she just let Mort take command. His first task was sending her to a bathroom to wash out all the wounds, at least those she could reach.

Her clothes were filthy, and so was her mood. She stripped off her T-shirt, leaving the sports bra in place. She ran warm water in the sink, but then hesitated. The washcloth and hand towel were the decorative variety, not the kind used to clean whatever the hell it was in her wounds.

A tap on the door, followed by "It's me," led to Riley's entrance. She eyed her, assessing the various wounds. Katia pointed at the towels and her master immediately understood the problem.

"Give me a minute and I'll find something you can use."

"Thanks."

As Riley went on her quest, Katia leaned on the sink, so tired she wasn't sure if she could remain standing. The cuts on her arms were darker now, which meant that whatever was in them was trying its best to kill her. The injuries from the tree weren't much better.

Simon's will be the same. And he had no way to treat them.

Riley returned with a roll of paper towels, a dark towel, a washcloth, a pair of scissors, and a box of latex gloves.

Katia kept gripping the sink, despite how much it made her left hand hurt.

"What if they die?" she said. "What if I never see him again?"

"Ozymandias will hunt for them until there is no hope. You can count on that."

Katia met her master's eyes in the mirror. "Simon sacrificed himself for me. We found the ring the necro wanted and he knew it was pulling him into this world. Something grabbed onto him and he *gave it to me*. That's why I'm not there with him. Dee just jumped in to try to help him, and that's why she got caught."

She sucked in a breath, trying not to sob. "Why did he do that? Why?"

After donning a pair of gloves Riley ducked the washcloth in the sink, then rinsed it out, as if the movements allowed her time to weigh her words.

"I'm thinking you already know why he did that. But you haven't dealt with what it means yet. You'll have time when he returns."

When he returns. It was like a prophecy.

No matter how hard Riley scrubbed on the wounds the black stuff wouldn't wash away. When all the injuries on her upper body were as clean as possible, she dried them with a paper towel. Then she stepped back.

The next step involved trimming Katia's jeans to shorts level and then cleaning her leg wounds. They were equally nasty, but didn't have the dark drainage.

"I sat near Beck's bed when he was dying after Sartael wounded him," Riley said, her voice quieter now. "I tried not to lose hope. I knew he was strong, that he had something to live for. He came back to me." She gently touched Katia on her shoulder. "Simon is strong. Doubly so because his sister is with him. Do not give up hope."

Katia nodded, tears dripping down her cheeks. "I won't."

A careful hug was delivered and then Riley herded her out to the veranda where Mort had already laid out a large First Aid kit on the table. He pointed to a chair and she readily sank into it. Once she was settled, a glass of liquid was handed over. It was orange and foamy.

"What is this?" she said, sniffing the contents dubiously.

"An electrolyte solution. I'm guessing you were moving magic around and probably didn't realize it. If not, this is a nice top up."

Katia took a sip, then took an even bigger one because it tasted good and helped clear out the dusty film in her throat.

While she enjoyed the beverage, the summoner examined her mangled fingers. At least it was her left hand.

"Don't appear to be broken," he observed. "Some bruising and skin scraped off, but nothing bad. Have you had a tetanus shot recently?"

"Yes." It was required if you work at a landscaping firm."

"Okay, then that's good. This treatment is going to sting."

The liquid he applied didn't sting, it burned like Hell's deepest infernos.

"Oh my God, what is that stuff?" she demanded, waving the hand in the air in a futile attempt to stop the scorching.

Mort chuckled. "A witchy version of liquid fire. It'll stop hurting in a bit. It really does work, trust me."

She was about to argue that fact when the burning suddenly ended. She tentatively flexed those fingers and found they moved properly. Some of the swelling had gone down, as well.

"Huh."

"Told you," he said, smiling. "We disagree with the witches about a lot of things, but they know their herbs. This is a special potion and it's not available to the public."

"What Mort isn't saying, because he's modest, is that he's earned the trust of his magical neighbors. That's not common,"

Riley explained.

The summoner didn't blush, but he came close. "Ayden and I have had a lot of spirited arguments, but we respect each other and that's vital."

He eyed the various cuts on her arm and began treating them.

"How did you get this one?" he'd ask and she say it'd been a ravenous tree, a skeleton bird, or the sharp moss. And in one case it was a thin slice courtesy of the window at the factory. Riley sat across the table watching the process, wincing in sympathy whenever that incendiary stuff was applied to a new site.

"How long will it be before his lordship returns?" Katia asked. Sweat had broken out on her forehead and she felt lightheaded.

Mort hesitated, gave Riley a quick glance, then sighed. "I really don't know. His lordship stopped walking the worlds because it was taking too much of a toll on him. I hope he can handle it one more time."

That was too honest but she needed to hear it. "Will they come through a portal here or somewhere else?"

"Most likely here."

A yawn snuck up on her and she barely covered her mouth in time. "Sorry." She set down the now empty glass as he taped one bandage and then began to work on another.

Once the wounds on her legs had been treated, Katia looked like an advertisement for a bandage supply company.

Another yawn broke free.

"I have a spare bedroom," Mort offered.

"No, I'll stay out here, wait for them."

He looked like he was going to argue, then nodded his understanding that she would not be moving until they returned. Because they just had to.

Mort packed up the kit and left her on her own. She noticed that he'd taken the First Aid supplies with him, which said he wasn't convinced that anyone else would be needing his care in the next few hours.

Body aching courtesy of her shelf climbing and the murderous trees, she stretched out on a lounge chair on the veranda. The ceiling fan above her slowly moved the muggy air around, swirl by swirl. Bees clustered around a flower out in one of the raised beds, humming happily at their colorful find.

It was impossible to fall asleep no matter how exhausted she was. Instead Katia kept an eye on the backyard, and then every few minutes shifted her attention to the sundial. It was a pretty one with a fancy filigree thing on the dial. Though it wasn't as accurate as the clock on her phone, in its own way it reminded her that time was passing. Time neither Simon nor his sister had.

"He needs your help," she whispered. "Please show them the way home. Please, for me."

About a quarter of an hour later, Mort headed to the factory. He'd promised to return as soon as possible once the dead folks were rescued. That meant he would have to de-activate the building's ward and the one around the Deaders. She wished him luck with all that.

Katia watched the sun slowly shift across the grass, blade by blade. She knew how to sit vigil because she'd done it for her brother when he'd been in a coma. Watching for any little sign that something was happening. But like that vigil in Kansas this one was the same: Nothing changed as the night grew closer with each passing minute.

Riley eventually joined her, sitting in a nearby chair. "How are you doing?"

"All I want to do is hug him and know he's safe."

Her fellow trapper took a deep breath and let it out slowly. "When he comes back, talk to him, find out where his heart is. I'm sure he thinks of you as more than a friend or he wouldn't have done that."

Katia instantly shook her head. "We *can't* be more than friends."

"Why not? If you say you're not going to trust him because of your ex back in Kansas, that's not going to work for me. Before I dated Beck, I had an abusive boyfriend. Nasty dude, though I did find out why he was so bad, and I understand him better now. Not that it gave him the right to hit me."

"But—"

"You trust Simon to keep you alive during the exorcisms, but you don't trust him for anything else?"

"But—"

Riley held up a hand, cutting her off. "How long are you going to let the ex screw up your future? Because he's taking up a lot of headspace, and he's not worth it. I know how that works. Oh, do I."

After that uncharacteristic scold, her boss retreated into the house, leaving her alone with her doubts.

"Ouch," Katia whispered. That hurt almost as much as the witchy medicine.

Noah had never been physically abusive, but he'd had his own way of jacking with her head. He would always make her the villain, even when he'd clearly done something wrong. It was always her fault. *Always*. It wasn't until she'd arrived in Atlanta that she realize what he'd been doing. There was a term for it—gaslighting. Noah had been a master.

Riley was right: She and Simon would have to talk this out.

But first he had to stay alive.

When Mathias hadn't been able to re-open the portal to retrieve the exorcist and his sister, he'd panicked. So, he'd nearly cried in relief when the door to his lover's world opened without any difficulty. He wore the ring now, the one that came from his immensely powerful ancestor. From what he'd read about *that* Chaffin, he'd been an evil bastard. It appeared this bit of metal recognized his bloodline because it felt heavier now, far weightier than a circlet of metal should.

One of the small male-like creatures met him when he crossed into the realm. It was short, maybe two feet tall, clad in clothes that were covered in moss. Its face was that of an elderly man, wrinkled, pale and sad. The fear in the little one's eyes was even greater than the last time he'd been here.

It was a captive, a minion, not much different than the dead he'd reanimated, which only made Mathias feel worse. At least he'd set the first batch free, and the ward on the factory would soon fade so that the second group could escape. Means would see to that. That was one of the reasons he'd not set that reanimate free with the first group because Means was much smarter than the others.

The unexpected loss of the exorcist and his sister troubled him. He'd never intended to harm them, despite his blustery warnings. Now they were trapped in a world he couldn't reach. At least not yet. Maybe if he could defeat the Unholy Terror then he could find a way to bring them back. He owed them that.

The little man beckoned him forward, and it was then Mathias saw the scarring around his neck, the moss ripped away. More of the Unholy Terror's handiwork.

The path they followed showed the continual desecration of this once bountiful world. The trees resembled willows, but now they were dying, their barren branches touching the ground as if in sorrow. No small animals skittered around, and there was no sound of birds roosting in the branches. It was as if this realm knew it was doomed.

The clearing where he'd spent many an hour with his lady was crowded with the inhabitants of this world. Some looked Fae, others not so much. Tall, short, mossy, hairy. All different. No doubt they had been summoned to witness his arrival, and his demise. If the ring on Mathias' finger wasn't powerful enough, he'd be another source of food for this horror.

This had to work. There was no Plan B.

His enemy sat on a low throne made of hewn stone. This time the hood on the dark cloak was up, obscuring its face. It wasn't a summoner, that much he knew. He didn't think it was a witch, either. The spell it'd woven kept him from seeing through the glamour.

Mathias halted about twenty feet from the throne. His adversary ignored him, attention riveted on a small creature lying in the dirt in front of her. It looked like a fawn, with pale beige fur, tiny horns and cloven hooves. Its tongue hung out of its mouth, its eyes glazed. From the way its muscles had contracted it had just died in agony.

The Unholy Terror's head rose and it sniffed the air as if it could sense the ring's power. "Bring it to me."

He glanced at his lover, memorizing her face for what might be the last time. Then he pulled on the magic buried deep in the metal, channeling it into himself.

"Bring it to me!" the Unholy Terror commanded.

Mathias smiled. He had prepped the spell even before he'd stepped into this world, and now he cast it directly at his enemy. He'd spent hours crafting it, designed it to strip away her power, then kill her.

It enveloped her and the throne raising a torrent of fire and energy around her. A low screech rent his ears and still he kept pouring everything he had into the enchantment. The ring grew hot, almost scorching.

To his horror the Unholy Terror stood, the flames his spell had created now forming around it like a shield. Somehow it'd shifted that spell to one of protection. No one should be able to do that.

With a blast of energy the spell broke and the rebound struck him. As Mathias tumbled backward, he heard his lover cry out. When he struggled to rise a heavy black boot stepped on his arm. His foe glared down at him.

Before Mathias could stop it, the ring slid off his finger and rose in the air, hovering for a moment in front of the Unholy Terror. Then the evil slipped it over a claw and onto a finger. A low hiss came now, for it'd just felt the surge of power that came with that circlet.

"Ah, I know this well, just as I knew your ancestor. It holds much dark power. It calls to me."

How the hell had it known of *that* Chaffin? What was the connection?

The Unholy Terror turned its hand one way and then another, studying the ring. With a nod, it crowed. "It will be mine now."

Movement began beneath its cloak now, and it seemed to grow wider somehow.

The foot retreated, and for a second Mathias thought he might escape death. The Unholy Terror stalked a few paces away, then turned back. And laughed.

"Why are you doing this?" he demanded. "What has this to do with my ancestor?"

"So stupid. He was not like that. He knew which side held the power."

After a barked order many hands seized him. Soon he was bound to one of the dying trees as his foe retreated to her throne.

"Cut him," it ordered. "I will taste the blood, I will taste the pain, and I will grow stronger. Then none may stop me." It pointed at the one being he'd hoped it'd forget. "You! You will cut him."

His lover shook her head, her pale blue eyes pleading.

"You will do as I command. What will it be? Him? Or them?" it said, gesturing at the horrified bystanders.

Mathias's eyes met those of the Fae who held his heart. "Do it. Save your people. I have failed."

She was given a knife, then slowly made her way to him now. As his robe and shirt were ripped away, she blinked up at him in tears.

"Know that I will always love you," he whispered.

"Live. Live for me," she pleaded.

And then with a cry, she made the first long slice across his chest.

When Mort returned, he brought Katia's trapping bag with him. Then he handed over her car keys and said the vehicle was parked down the street. How he'd done that she didn't know, but she thanked him nonetheless.

"How'd it go?" Riley asked.

"The spell had weakened by the time I got there. It didn't

take much effort to break it."

"He said he'd free them," Katia said. "And after the portal closed he tried to reopen it, but he couldn't. Now that I think about it, he was really upset about that."

Mort sank into a chair. "The reanimates are staying with Summoner Norman while their families are being notified. Oh, and Mr. Means asked me to thank you, Katia. He said you saved their lives with the Holy Water circle. He told me about how you climbed the shelving and escaped."

"Someday you'll have to tell us the full story," Riley said.

Katia gave her a nod and resumed staring at the backyard. In time, Mort drifted inside the house and Riley joined him. While Katia rejoiced that the Deaders were free, each passing hour felt like torture as time continued its relentless march forward. Darkness fell, yet the backyard remained illuminated with soft lighting. Now that it was useless to stare at the sundial Katia stared at nothing at all, hoping for the return of her friend, his sister, and the most powerful necromancer on the East Coast.

Eventually both her host and Riley returned, sitting nearby, talking quietly among themselves. If they thought she couldn't hear them, they were wrong.

"Ozymandias is never gone this long," Mort said, his voice thick with worry. "Each trip has been harder on him, and it takes him longer to recover."

"You think he'll find them?"

"He won't give up until he does, or he's forced to return. Too long in one of the other realms and your magic fades."

"Will he be too weak to cross back here?"

"It's possible. In some realms there are things that live on magic. They will devour him."

"Oh, God."

Katia closed her eyes and began to pray.

NINETEEN

The sacred circle was fading, its power ebbing with each passing minute. Simon had tried to create another one but it failed. He tried again with the same result.

Why had the first one held for as long as it had?

"We're running out of time, aren't we?" his sister asked as the circle's slow demise was easy to see.

"I'm thinking so," he said. Perhaps it was time for more honesty. "You know, I've always been in awe of you, Sis."

"Me?" Dee replied. "Why?"

"Because you never allowed anyone to run right over you. Not like me."

She laughed as if his suggestion was ridiculous. "Oh, you're wrong there. So wrong, Simon."

Before he could reply there were noises in the forest behind them, followed by a lengthy howl. Then even more howls. Simon took the steel pipe from his sister and rose.

A beast came out of the woods, shouldering one of the trees aside as if it were a mere nuisance. It stood at least ten feet tall with a pair of spiny heads on long reticulated necks.

The mouths gaped open and were filled with multiple rows of jagged teeth. Each of the tongues glowed green in the dim light. One of them dropped down to the ground, slid along, and then captured something. A small creature screamed in terror as it was lifted and then dropped inside one of the gaping mouths. Chewing ensued while both heads stared at them, as if sizing up their next meal.

Simon glanced down to find the circle was gone now. "If we run, it'll chase us."

"And if we don't?"

"We're going to be eaten like that little thing it just snarfed up."

"So running away is the plan," Dee replied as she got to her feet. "Your job *really* sucks, did I mention that?"

They began to back up, one slow step at a time. Simon gave a quick look over his shoulder and then swore. A smaller version of the lizard thing had moved in behind them. The first one set up a howl, followed by the second one. Their tails lashed the air and spit flowed out of their mouths.

"Please tell me they're going to ignore us and fight each other instead," she said, her attention swiveling between one threat, and then the other.

The shift of the larger one to the right, followed by the smaller one going left suggested that his sister might be correct. This might become a fight for dominance. Or a mating dance.

Simon was about to suggest they angle away from the pair when the bigger beast charged straight at its opponent. The other lizard rushed forward as well, and he was sure they were going to be trampled between the two monsters. Then just as quickly both beasts turned toward him and his sister, eyeing them.

"Run!" he shouted.

Dee easily kept up with him, sheer terror making her move at top speed. Behind them came the bellows and the crashes of brush and small trees as the pair of lizards tried to run them down.

Simon leapt over a thick branch, only to be caught by another branch further on. As he started to fall, Dee caught his arm, yanking him up. A bellow came from ahead of them now, identical to the ones behind them. They were being herded to their deaths.

"Adler!" A voice shouted. "Adler!"

Frantic, Simon searched until he found the black robe and the glowing sigil.

He came for us!

"This way!" Ozymandias cried out, beckoning.

They sprinted toward him. There were more beasts on their tail now and Simon swore he could smell their fetid breath. A flash of light heralded the opening of a gateway just as something struck his back. Simon sprawled into the dirt, then stumbled up on all fours, then to his feet to catch up with his sister.

"Go! Go!" he shouted. At least she might get out of here alive.

Dee went through the opening first, a small flash of lightning heralding her passage. As he drew closer to the summoner he felt magic build behind him, raising the hairs on his neck.

Simon dove into their world, Ozymandias on his heels. The moment he had crossed the opening the summoner launched a spell, the sigil on his lordship's forehead blazing like a lighthouse in a turbulent storm.

"None shall pass!" he cried, striking the portal with his staff.

Lightning blazed, thunder roared, and then there was only green grass where there had once been a doorway. Simon fell next to his sister, unable to go any further. His lordship joined them on the ground, panting as if he'd used every bit of his power to bring them home.

This was Mort's backyard. They were truly safe.

Someone cried out his name.

Katia.

She was alive, which meant that all his prayers had been answered.

†✻‡✻†

Caught up in their discussion neither Riley nor Mort had noticed the tiny glimmer of light, how it began as a small dot out of nowhere. But Katia had and she bolted out of the lounger as that small light exploded into a gaping hole.

Deanna staggered through first, making it a few steps before falling to her knees.

"Simon?" Katia shouted. But there was no sign of him.

And then there he was, limping, his face pale, and his clothes torn as he staggered through the doorway.

"Ozymandias!" Mort shouted, moving closer. "Get out of there!"

Finally the elder summoner stepped through, then banged his staff against the portal. As it closed something bellowed on the other side, furious at losing its prey.

They had made it home. Someone had heard her prayers and brought them back.

"Simon?" Katia called out.

Riley knelt next to Deanna now, talking to her, then slowly helped her rise. The woman shook, so terrified that she stared at nothing. Then she saw her brother and began to cry.

Mort put his arm around his lordship's waist, and with significant effort hefted him up. The light on the senior necromancer's forehead was dark now. They slowly moved toward the house, Ozymandias stumbling twice on the flat ground. Only his fellow summoner was able to keep him upright. Riley and Deanna followed them, each step full of effort.

That left Simon. He had leveraged himself up on his knees now. His arms and face were streaked with dried blood. The instant his eyes met hers a true smile appeared. He had no idea how furious she was with him. It was time to fix that.

"You damned idiot!" Katia shouted. Then she shoved him as anger overrode every other emotion. "What *the hell* were you thinking?"

Simon's bloody palm gently touched her cheek. "You had to survive. Nothing else mattered."

That was not what she wanted to hear. "Me? What if you never come back? What if you'd died? How could I live with that?"

He smiled. "But I didn't. And neither did you."

She shoved him again, just because. This time he landed on his butt, that idiotic smile still in place.

She's alive.

Katia had several bandages on her arms and legs, but she

looked better than he'd hoped. He saw her anger and knew it for what it was: She had truly feared she'd lose him.

"You are an idiot," she murmured, sinking onto the grass next to him. Then to his surprise she laid her head on his shoulder and let the tears fall. He placed his arm around her and rejoiced. A miracle had been granted them and he would always be grateful for that.

Riley found them like that a few minutes later. She edged closer, then cleared her throat as if unsure she wanted to intrude.

He looked up at her, still smiling.

"Hey, you," she said. "Your sister is okay. Freaked, but okay. She only has a few cuts. Mort called Ayden and she sent down one of the witches. Tastra's a healer." From her cautious tone she expected him to argue about the witch's involvement, but he just nodded his approval.

"Oh, and your sis wants to go to your parents' house once she's sure you're okay."

"What's to keep the necro from hunting her down?" he asked.

"Nothing. Which is why Mort thinks she should stay with Summoner Canhoto. At least until this is over."

"I'm not sure Dee will go for that." Because she'd want to be with their family after all she'd been through.

"Then maybe you should talk to her," Riley suggested.

That was ironic: An exorcist's sister would be safer with a magic user than with her own brother, or her own family.

Simon reluctantly rose, his head spinning. His various wounds pounded in time with his heartbeat, and he swore he had the beginnings of a fever. "I'll do what I can."

"You might find her more receptive than you think."

He had no idea what that meant, so he left Katia sitting in the grass and followed Riley into the house. His sister was in a back bedroom along with a woman with long mahogany brown hair. The witch was winding a bandage around Dee's arm.

"Put this ointment on it twice a day. If it starts draining, let Summoner Alexander know immediately. I don't see that happening, but it's always good to be cautious. Fortunately, the wounds aren't that deep."

"Thank you."

"Happy to help. I hope I was able to answer your questions."

It was only then that Deanna noticed he was at the door. "Simon," she said, her voice guarded.

The witch looked over her shoulder. "Hi, I'm Tastra. Your sister is going to be fine."

"Thank you for helping her."

"I'll leave some of the ointment for you, too." A pause and then, "You should know it was created with magic, though."

Which meant there had been a discussion as to *who* he was and what that meant in terms of treatment options.

"Okay. Thank you for letting me know that."

After a quick nod Tastra departed. It sounded as if his sister had been quizzing the witch, though about what he wasn't sure. As he saw it he had two ways of dealing with this: Go hardline as to why it wasn't wise to hang with magic users—and acknowledge that didn't seem to apply to him—or accept that his sister had her own path.

Dee beat him to it. "I asked her about herbal medicine. I'm, well, interested in natural healing and I'd been told the witches know a lot about that."

"They do. Riley swears by it. She would know."

A series of emotions crossed his big sister's face now: Surprise, confusion and then relief as if she'd expected a stern lecture. Which told him just how much of an insufferable ass he'd been, even with his own family.

Simon leaned up against the door frame because standing was getting harder by the minute. He was trying to ignore that the wounds on his arms were turning black.

"Look, I don't like magic, but I've also seen it save lives. Like both of ours today. If his lordship hadn't come after us, hadn't stopped those lizard things, we'd be dead. Or wishing we were dead."

There was hope in his sister's eyes now. "So, ah, if I wanted to study with the witches to learn about herbal medicine, that wouldn't make things bad between us?"

He sighed. Yeah, he'd really been a jerk over the last few years.

"It's your life, Deanna. My job means I deal with the supernatural and with magic users. Last year I thought they were all evil because I was a total self-righteous hypocrite. I learned my lesson the hard way, that often the evil we think we see in others is really our own."

His sister was off the bed and hugging him before he could move. His injuries protested and he barely kept the agonized groan to himself.

Once Deanna had stepped back, he asked, "So what brought on this interest in herbal stuff?"

Her eyes flared. "Because I hate my damned job." She stepped even further back, clearly upset. "Two days ago I was informed that I needed to *take on even more responsibilities* because the morons I work for aren't going to replace one of the staff members who just quit."

She strode back to the bed, plopping down on the mattress. "I'm already working ten to twelve hours a day and even more on the weekends, and not getting paid *for any* of that extra time. There's no acknowledgment of my efforts, or any chance at promotion. When I do what they ask, I just get more work shoveled at me. I'm damned tired of it!"

It slowly dawned on him that maybe Dee had been micro-managing his life, because she felt she had no control over her own.

"I wondered what was going on. You've been stressed out over the last few months. I wasn't sure if it was because of me, or something else."

The anger in her eyes dimmed now. "Part of it was me worrying about you. Most of it was my crappy life. I want to do something that helps people, not just file papers and make sure I hit all the damned corporate goals for the quarter so I can get a pat on the head like a good little girl."

Oh yeah, she was pissed. "Then do what makes you happy.

If nothing else, I've learned life is too short to be miserable. I'm betting Mom and Dad told you the same."

Dee nodded. "They did." After a long sigh, she added, "I love you, Bro, you know that, right?"

"I do. And I love you right back. Well, unless you're rearranging my kitchen cabinets."

She delivered a mock frown. "It really did work better; you have to admit it."

He shrugged, not willing to concede that. "You're forgiven. I hope you'll forgive me for being a self-righteous dick for all those years."

A crooked smile appeared now. "You know, I'm thinking you hanging with that new trapper is a good thing."

"I certainly have more to talk about every time I go to confession."

She laughed. "I bet the Vatican would love to know what sins you've been committing. I know *I* would."

He wasn't going there. "Mort really feels you should stay with one of the senior necromancers in case this crazy comes after you. He might do that, Dee. If you're at our parent's place . . . "

She nodded her understanding. "Yeah, bad news. Especially if the little ones are at home. Okay, get me somewhere safe and then nail this bastard," she said, brightening up.

"You got it."

Simon headed back to the courtyard, running on empty now. Once she saw him, Katia pointed at a chair near the wicker table.

"Shirt off," she said, then added a reluctant "please."

He did as ordered, trying not to moan at the pain the movements caused. Sitting with his back to her he could feel the air on the wounds, and it made them throb even more.

"Oh, God. These cuts are deep. And they're oozing black stuff."

That explained the nascent fever. "It was one of those skeleton bird things." He'd tell her about the lizard things later. *Much* later.

"Yeah, well, that's why we are going to have to use the witches' treatment first because washing them out doesn't work. We learned that with mine. And yes, there's an extra something in this but if you don't ask what it is I won't have to lie to you."

He could refuse it, or he could just let his wounds be cleaned by something that might counteract whatever crud those birds had dug into his skin. A lengthy shiver zipped through him reminding him that dying was stupid.

"Go for it."

There was a relieved sigh. "Fair warning, this will hurt like a bitch."

"Go for it," he repeated.

He nearly jumped out of the chair when the mixture touched the first wound. "What the hell is in that stuff?" he growled.

"I'm thinking acid, ground glass, and napalm," she said. "I did tell you it hurt like a bitch."

He swore under his breath in Latin, grimacing as whatever it was charred itself into the wounds.

"Okay, then, that really worked. The black junk dried up and now it's flaking off. That's amazing."

"Not from where I'm sitting," he said through gritted teeth.

"Suck it up, dude. I survived it, so will you. Here goes another one."

By the eighth application Simon's clenched jaw ached and he'd run out of Latin swear words. If she kept it up, he'd have to move onto the Italian ones.

"Done." She studied him for a moment. "I'll go get some soap and water to wash them out. I'm thinking you're not in any shape to stand at a sink right now."

She was right about that.

"They already look sooo much better, Simon. Honest, I'm not kidding."

A glance at his arm showed she was right. The black goo was gone, leaving glistening reddish-pink wounds behind, the kind that would eventually heal.

As she set off to find the supplies, Riley joined him. From

her grin she'd known exactly what he'd been saying in Latin, even if Katia didn't.

"Impressive vocabulary. Learn that in exorcism school?" she said, her grin wider now.

"Some of it, but not all."

"You'll have to teach me a few of those."

Maybe not. "My sister gone?"

"Yes, she is." There was a pause and Riley's voice grew quieter. "Katia told me what you did."

He ignored that. "What happened to her? How did she get free?"

"You saw the inside of the factory?" He nodded. "Apparently, she climbed up the shelving and went out one of the upper windows."

What? "But that was sixty, seventy feet up . . . " He shook his head in wonder. "And I was worried about her."

"It went both ways, my friend."

Katia returned carrying a blue plastic bowl filled with soapy water. A washcloth and towel lay over an arm.

"Don't they look great?" she said, indicating the wounds.

"Much better," Riley agreed. "I'm thinking you might have a few more scars, though."

Once the wounds were clean and treated with the ointment Tastra had used on his sister, dressings were applied. Simon already felt better. The ointment numbed the pain, and he swore he could feel those cuts healing already. And then suddenly he was supremely exhausted, whatever adrenalin he'd been running on was gone. He could tell by the dark circles under Katia's eyes she felt the same.

"Any chance we can get some sleep before we go to war?" he asked, trying to keep his tone light. Because there was going to be a battle once he found that damned necro.

Riley pointed toward the house. "Beds are ready for both of you. It'll be a while before Ozymandias is strong enough to talk strategy. Mort said the most important thing is to rest. It'll help the healing. We need to be at our best to take down this guy."

Simon led the way and was pointed down a long hall by Mort's reanimated housekeeper. Katia followed him. They reached the first bedroom when Riley called out, "Just got a text—your sister is at Summoner Canhoto's house."

"Thanks," he said, wiping that worry off his lengthy list. And then it was only him and Katia. To his astonishment she leaned over, gave him a light kiss on the cheek, and then headed into the closest bedroom. The door shut behind her.

With a weary smile he touched the spot where the kiss had landed. God had been merciful today. He would always remember how angry Katia had been when he'd returned. How she'd been afraid she'd never see him again.

Perhaps she cared for him as much as he did for her.

TWENTY

The nightmares ended when morning arrived. Somehow Katia hadn't screamed during the worst of them, but it had been close. Watching someone you cared for being torn apart by monsters was an unholy torment, even in a nightmare.

Staring up at the bedroom ceiling in Mort's house, that fear drained away. Simon and his sister had survived. Hopefully, Lord Ozymandias was regaining strength as they'd need him for what lie ahead. Because no matter what, this wasn't over.

Yet it felt as if one of the nightmares wasn't hers. It had been the necro, the one who had thrown them into that other world. He had been fighting something, screaming in agony, pleading for help. She shook her head. That was ridiculous. The bastard had risked their lives for some old ring.

When Katia finally sat on the edge of the bed she found her suitcase on a chair near the door, the same one that had been at Simon's house. Her guess was that Riley had something to do with that.

Despite feeling like she needed another twelve hours of sleep, she took advantage of clean clothes and running water. Maybe in a few days she'd be able to shower once all the wounds were healed. The fingers on her left hand were considerably less swollen and she made a mental note to apply more of the witchy ointment after breakfast. Not that she was hungry.

At least her brain felt less empty, and her feet moved without having to tell them to. Still, the face staring back at her in the bathroom mirror was of someone older than twenty-five. Was that a side effect of walking in other realms? Or just all the hell she'd been through over the last few months?

"Gotta stop doing this shit," she muttered. Like that was going to happen.

To her immense relief she found Simon sitting in a chair on the veranda, coffee cup in hand. He still looked tired. He gave her a smile and she returned it. His phone sat in front of him. She guessed Mort must have found it at the factory. Riley sat next to him, a cup of tea in hand, and pointed to where a mini buffet had been laid out on a long table. Katia claimed her own cup of java, a few slices of orange, and some cheese. More than that she didn't think she could handle.

"That's all you're going to eat?" Simon asked as she sat next to him.

"I'll start with this." She'd be lucky to finish it.

Sounds came from inside the house, low conversation, and then Mort exited. Following behind him at a snail's pace was his lordship. The older summoner eased himself down in a chair and then accepted a tall glass from Mort. The swirling twinkles above the glass suggested magic was involved. And yet, the glowing thing on his forehead was still dark despite all of Mort's efforts. Sitting there he looked like a very tired, old man.

Katia was handed a similar glass but with no twinkles.

"More electrolyte mix," Mort said.

She jerked her eyes up to the summoner now. "But I haven't been bleeding off any magic, not like I did at the cemetery."

"You have. You just don't know it," he replied. "Now that you sense it you're automatically shoving it away from you, even if you aren't touching the earth. Your body doesn't care either way—it just reacts by screwing up your electrolytes. And that other world would have registered as magic to your system, so there you go."

While she digested that bit of news, she took a sip and let the orange, lemon, and whatever else do its thing, which didn't seem to be much. She noticed that Simon was staring at her now, which meant she'd have to explain the "shoving away magic" thing eventually.

After a final frown in her direction, he took a deep breath.

"Thank you for risking your life for us, your lordship," he began. "You paid a heavy price to do that. If you hadn't, my sister and I would be dead. I am in your debt. I sincerely mean that."

"Even if the Vatican might not approve?" Ozymandias asked, raising an eyebrow.

"It's not their concern," Simon replied. "You could have left us there, but you didn't. That is the mark of a good man, even if he does wield magic."

Ozymandias gave a gracious nod, acknowledging the complex emotions behind that statement. "Don't shortchange yourselves. You did well in there. Most do not survive even a few minutes, let alone hours."

He accepted the compliment with a nod. "My earnest prayer is that I never have to see that damned place again."

"May it be so for all of us."

"Do you guys have any idea what this is all about?" Katia asked. "Because I sure as hell don't."

The two senior necros traded looks and it was Ozymandias who answered.

"First, please tell us how you came to be in that particular realm."

Simon looked over at Katia, and after her nod, explained what had happened to him and his sister. Katia could just imagine it: Mr. Means at the front door, the spell being cast and then finding themselves at the factory with no clue what was going on. No wonder Dee freaked out.

Ozymandias shifted his attention to her. "What brought you to that location?"

"I got a text from Simon about an exorcism there." She looked over at him. "It seemed weird since you're on sabbatical, but why would it be a lie? I mean, it looked like you'd sent it to me."

"I wondered why the reanimate had my phone. The necro must have made him send the text." Simon turned back to the others. "He came after me to use as leverage against Katia. My sister just happened to be there when the spell was cast," Simon added.

Mort frowned now. "Then why all those reanimations? What was the point?"

"Means said that the necro had tried to send the dead folks into that world and they couldn't get through. That something stopped them," Katia replied.

"Probably what we ran into," Simon said and she nodded. "We were told to bring something back. A ring. The summoner gave me an old button and it worked as a compass once we were there. It was the only way we would have found it. But first we had to get past the gatekeeper or whatever it was guarding the entrance."

"Gatekeeper?" Mort asked, puzzled.

Katia continued to sip her beverage and ignore the remainder of the orange slices as Simon told them about the being that had vetted them before they'd entered the other realm.

"I wondered what had happened to your cross," Riley said.

Simon looked down where it had once sat on his chest. "I didn't want to give it up, but I don't think we would have been allowed to enter otherwise."

"I have encountered this sentinel, as we call it," the older summoner replied. "It keeps those out who have no business in certain realms. I have been denied entry into others myself."

"I didn't feel threatened by it," Katia said. "It just seemed very interested in who we were."

"It's not surprising a reanimate was unable to make the journey. They have enough difficulty navigating *our* world. Fortunately, none of them were lost that way."

"Thank heavens for that," Mort added. "We're taking enough heat as it is."

"Because of this, we will not be at liberty to reveal why they were stolen in the first place. The public cannot know about the other realms."

"That is definitely going to be an issue."

"Mort and I found the pale guy that everyone was talking

about," Riley said. "His name is Harry Hawkins. He might be the reason the necro knew you could go into other realms. That and a certain video at TrapperCon."

"Of course," Simon groaned.

"Oh, and we found out why Means' grave exploded." And then she explained the magical technique and why it didn't happen that first night.

"Huh," Katia replied. "Tell me he's in jail right now." Because that idiot had almost gotten her and Riley killed.

"No. There are mitigating circumstances. I'm taking personal responsibility for Hawkins from now on," Mort replied, giving her master a quick glance. Katia noticed he didn't ask for the elder summoner's approval, so this was already in the works. She could be pissed about that, or just move on. She chose the latter.

"Not all of us are capable of walking the worlds," Ozymandias said softly. "For good reason." He took a long sip of his drink. "Do you still have the button?"

"Yes." Simon dug in the front pocket of his jeans and laid the now smaller item on the table between them. The senior summoner rested his hand above it, palm down, and held it there for a time.

"As I feared." He turned to Mort. "We need to do an online search of the Society's archives."

Their host immediately headed into the house and then returned with a large silver laptop. Once he was back in his seat, Mort waved his hand over it while murmuring something under his breath.

"You put spells on your computers?" Katia asked, intrigued.

"Yes, but you didn't hear that."

"What happens if someone tries to steal it?"

"Nothing good," was the quick reply.

After a short session of rapid typing, apparently logging onto the site Ozymandias had mentioned, he turned to his lordship. "Who do you want me to check out?"

"Lord Chaffin. We need to see a picture of him. In particular, any that show a button on his clothing."

More typing and then Mort turned the laptop around so they could see an image on the screen. "Look familiar?" he asked.

It was a close-up of an antique button, identical to the one on the table.

"That's it," Simon replied.

Ozymandias finished his magical drink and set the glass aside. His eyes seemed brighter, though the sigil remained dark.

"You said you brought back a ring." He looked over at Mort who had accessed another part of the image. The gold ring sat on a man's finger, the garnet stone dark like dried blood. "Is this it?"

"Yes," Simon said.

"Where was it in that other realm?"

"On a skeleton trapped in a tree."

Now the image had zoomed out to reveal an older gentleman with mutton chop whiskers and bushy beard. He was clad in a black suit and a dark waistcoat. The buttons on the latter were just like the one in front of them.

His lordship gestured at the picture. "This is Elias Burnley Chaffin. He lived in nineteenth century Boston. Before he supposedly died, he broke all the rules. Well, at that point there *were* no rules and he's the reason they now exist. Though they're obviously not working as intended."

His fellow summoners huffed their agreement.

"Chaffin was the son of a prominent banker, a magical terror by all accounts. He was known to bespell his family's business rivals, causing them to go insane and commit suicide. Sometimes he'd have them butcher their whole families first."

Riley gasped. "That's awful."

"His final act was calling up the dead from one of Boston's oldest cemeteries. He ordered the reanimates to march through the streets to City Hall, intending to take charge of the city. Many of the deceased had died during the Revolutionary War so the reanimation was considered an immense sacrilege. That act caused a lot of grief."

"You said 'supposedly died'?" Katia asked.

"Caught that, did you?" Ozymandias said. "Chaffin had so much power it took an extraordinary effort to shut him down. The public was told he died of a heart ailment. In truth, his fellow summoners exiled him because he was nearly impossible to kill."

Simon sighed at that. "Let me guess—they exiled him to the realm with the skeleton birds."

A nod returned. "I checked in on him every few years to ensure he was still on the other side. Even there, he was just as dangerous as ever. He's dead now, for that was his skeleton in the tree. I found him there the last time I visited that world."

Ozymandias paused, then added, "I spoke with him once, while he was still breathing, and that conversation was pure insanity. He kept telling me that *his time was near*. If I knew what was best I'd side with him when he returned to exact his revenge. That all would pay for defying him."

His lordship took a breath and then continued, "Right before he crossed over the Veil, my mentor, Lord Zimmer told me all about Chaffin and warned me that he was still a threat. I honestly thought he was exaggerating until I finally visited the madman."

Mort studied the senior summoner intently now, as if this was a tale he hadn't heard before. "So that's why you kept disappearing into the other realms?"

"Part of it. I was also searching for knowledge. It was a very bold, and ill-advised plan. It is good that the other summoners at this table have not been so daring."

Riley shook her head. "No way I'm doing that. My one trip to Hell was enough for me."

"That guy wasn't the only body stuck in a tree," Katia said. "There were others."

"One had chains around its feet," Simon added. "Which means that's a prison for your kind. For the really scary ones."

His lordship didn't respond at first, then reluctantly nodded.

Mort's mouth had fallen open at this point. Riley looked just as shocked.

"What? I thought we just stripped the bad ones of their magic and let the civilian authorities take it from there," their host said.

"We strip the magic of those less powerful. But for the ones like Chaffin there is no means to render them magically inert, so they were exiled into that realm. They are unable to return, and in time the realm kills them. In this case, it was one of the trees rather than one of the beasts."

"But why was he more powerful than the others?" Katia asked.

"It is rumored that Chaffin sold his soul to a Fallen. That wasn't confirmed, but it's likely given how much power he wielded. I was lucky that Sartael wasn't interested in mine, at least not at first. If he had survived, I suspect that would have changed."

"That makes sense," Simon replied. "A Fallen would love having someone like that on its leash."

"Exactly. That is why the worst of our kind are secured in that world by a spell. So far none of them have figured out how to break it. You were able to retrieve the ring because you were not one of the prisoners. If you'd helped one of them escape, you would have died instantly."

"That place still went nuts when we tried to leave," Katia said. "So, whose skull was that? It was just sitting on a rock. The button pointed right to it."

Ozymandias attention instantly shifted to her. "Did you touch it?"

"No way." She gave Simon a look now.

"I was going to check it out," he admitted. "I thought the ring might be underneath it, but Katia insisted that wasn't what we were after."

"It felt evil," she added. "Really evil."

"It is good you trusted your instincts. I must insist that none of you speak of that realm's purpose to anyone. It *must* remain secret, or others will try to access it if they can find a way around the sentinel. There are immensely powerful objects stored there." He was still staring at her. "Like the skull."

"What does it do?"

"Nothing good."

"But how did this rogue necro know where to find the ring?" Riley asked. "I mean, if this realm is a secret and all that?"

"My guess is a family connection," Ozymandias replied.

Mort tapped away on the keyboard, doing just such a search of the family's history. "There are only a few Chaffins in the U.S. that are registered through the Society," he said. "How old do you think this guy is?"

"Forty, maybe a bit older?" Simon replied.

"Okay, there's one in Cincinnati, but he's seventy-two. Another in Philadelphia who is fifty-six." Mort kept eyeing the screen in front of him. "Ah, here's a possibility." Once again he shifted the laptop so it faced them. "This guy look familiar?"

"Yes! You got him," Katia said as Simon nodded his agreement. Though the summoner looked younger in the photo, it was the man who'd so callously thrown them into another world.

"Our rogue necromancer is Mathias Lynley Chaffin and he's the . . . great great great grandson of Lord Chaffin. He's forty-four and has been awarded a dark navy robe. Got some serious power behind him, but not as much as I'd have thought given what he's been up to. Single, last address was in Charlotte, North Carolina."

"And now he's here," Riley said. "How did this guy know his great, great whatever was in this other realm?"

"Someone was working on the Chaffin family history a while back. It might be this man or someone he knows. If so, he may have heard what really happened to his ancestor," Ozymandias replied. "The Summoners Society was not as closemouthed back then as it is now."

It was at this point that Katia realized that the most senior summoner on the veranda was still watching her closely.

"Is there more you'd like to tell us, Journeyman Breman?"

Damn.

"Katia. Just Katia."

"Katia, then. Tell us why you were leery of the skull. And yes, I know you sense magic but I believe it's more than that. Now is not the time to hold anything back, no matter how odd it might sound."

Simon wasn't going to be happy with what she was about to tell them.

"Okay, there's another person, well another someone involved in all this. I call her The Lady because I'm not sure what she is. I first met her at TrapperCon." She looked over at her partner now. "You were in the restroom at the time. I was hanging in the hallway when someone tapped me on the shoulder. I turned and there she was."

"What does she look like?" Mort asked as he closed the laptop's lid, his focus on her now.

Katia pulled up the memory. "Her skin is pure white, like alabaster. Her eyes are steel blue, her hair bright red and she has ferns and flowers growing in it. She's what I think a faerie would look like."

A cup of water appeared at her elbow courtesy of Riley, and she nodded her thanks. After a long sip she continued. "The Lady winked at me, put a finger to her mouth to tell me not to say anything, then she just sailed over to the closest wall and went right through it."

"And you never thought to mention that to me?" Simon demanded.

Yeah, he was upset just like she knew he would be.

"We'd just met that morning so you wouldn't know if I was on the level or totally wacko at that point. We had Azagar and those kids to worry about. Things were bad enough."

He grumbled under his breath, but she could see she'd made her point.

"But that wasn't the only time you saw her," his lordship said.

She shook her head in amazement. "You know, you're really scary when you do that mind reading thing."

"I don't read minds. I read faces."

"Well, you're damned good at it. And you're right. I saw her again in downtown Atlanta the night we fought off a Big Mouth demon."

Her master blinked at that news. "Where was she?"

"In the alley, after the fiend was dead. She looked ill. Her ferns and flowers were dying, and her skin was gray. Something had happened to her since the con, something bad."

"And?" the senior summoner pressed.

This guy is scary. "I hear her in my head sometimes. When we were in the skeleton realm she warned me away from the skull. She kept speaking to me while we were trying to escape, helping us get out of there."

"You sure she wasn't there as well?"

"I didn't see her, no." She hesitated because what she was about to say did sound crazy. "The summoner said something about doing all this *for* someone. Last night I had an awful nightmare with him in it. He was screaming in pain, and I saw a lot of blood. I know he's the bad guy here, but I swear something else is going on."

Ozymandias shifted in his chair, pensive. "It would help if we knew if this Lady is fae or not. Would Ayden be willing to help us with that?" he asked, looking over at Mort. "My knowledge of their world is miniscule, at best."

"Same with me. I'll text her," Mort said and then set about doing just that.

"But why did she choose you?" Simon asked, still fixated on Katia. "Out of all the people at that convention, why you?"

He wasn't going to let this slide so more personal history was needed.

"My grandmother said she spoke with the fae. I never really saw them, but I always felt that someone was watching me when I was walking in her woods. Flowers would appear on her doorstep, out of nowhere. She had a little shrine in the woods and sometimes left them gifts. Feathers, stones, things like that."

"And you're named for her," Riley said. "They might know of your connection to the one who believed in them."

"But here, in Atlanta?"

"For them, geography is no big deal. They're everywhere, or at least they want you to think they are."

Simon seemed mollified at her explanation, though she suspected there'd be more questions later. As they waited, Katia kept poking at her food. It held no interest. After he rose to refill his own plate, a half of an apricot muffin was set in front of her.

"Eat," he mouthed. She rolled her eyes at him. He immediately repeated the command.

"Yes, Dad," she muttered, then took a bite of the offering. It tasted good, better than the fruit, so she quickly finished it off. All the while Simon was doing his best not to look smug, and failing.

When Ayden joined them on the veranda she carried an embroidered bag on her shoulder. She held it close to her body as if protecting it. Her eyes swept everyone at the table, pausing on Ozymandias. "Ouch. Walking the worlds again?"

"Yes. I do not recommend it."

The witch arranged herself in a chair, then removed a white velvet cloth from a satchel and laid it on the table. It was followed by a thick leather book with an ornately embossed burgundy cover held closed by a silver clasp in the shape of a star.

Ayden looked at each one of them in turn. "Fae come in all kinds. Small, big, clever, wicked, devious, you name it. Just like people." Then she laid her palm on the cover of the book and closed her eyes while murmuring something under her breath. The metal clasp snapped open though the book remained closed.

"Katia, please place your hand on the cover. Imagine what this being looked like when you met her."

Katia dusted off her hand on her jeans, then laid it palm down on the leather. Closing her eyes she recalled the first time she'd met The Lady. How unbelievable that moment had been. Underneath her fingers, the book began to move on its own. She yanked her hand back and watched as it opened, then flipped pages. Finally, it stopped.

"Ah, I see," Ayden said, studying the page in front of her.

"She is definitely one of the Kindly Ones."

She turned the book around and then carefully held it up so all could see.

Katia stared at the image. "That's her!" A few lines of calligraphy sat below the colorful illustration, far too small for her to read. She wondered what it said.

"We do not know her name," the witch added. "She has not shared that with us, at least not yet. Did she with you?"

Katia shook her head. "I call her The Lady."

"That works as well as any. They don't reveal their real names if they can avoid it."

"So, I'm not nuts."

"No. I'm guessing this goes with your ability to see angels." *And spirit cats.*

"Katia said her grandmother had an affinity for the fae, so maybe it's in the bloodline," Mort replied.

"Very likely."

"Could this necro have met her somehow? I mean, how else could she have known where the ring was in that realm?" Katia said.

"Ring?" Ayden asked.

Mort quickly brought her up to speed on what had happened in the other world without once mentioning the word "prison."

After mulling over that information, Ayden shifted her gaze to the most senior summoner. "You took a big risk retrieving those two."

Ozymandias shrugged, though it didn't look like a gesture he made that often. "You would have done the same if you could travel the realms."

The witch nodded reluctantly.

"You think there was contact between this Lady and our thief before all this began?" Mort asked.

"Not sure, but he seemed driven to help someone," Katia said. "Could she have talked him into getting the ring for her? Wait, that makes no sense. If she knew it was there why didn't she get it herself? Damn, I'm so confused."

"Perhaps there was a reason the summoner had you fetch the ring instead of The Lady, as you call her. You're assuming that she could enter that realm, which might not be the case," Ozymandias said.

"And if she's like Ori, she can speak to you without being physically present. He does it to me all the time," Riley said. "I bet the fae can too."

"Whatever is going on, be on your guard," Ayden advised. "The Kindly Folk have their own rules. If your necromancer has gotten enchanted by one of them, it would be dangerous for you to interfere with that relationship."

"Or dangerous if we *don't* interfere," Ozymandias said.

The witch nodded in agreement. "That's the problem. You never know where you stand with them."

Riley's phone pinged. She took a quick look at the message, straightened up, and then read it through a second time. Then she tapped out a reply. "Speaking of Hellspawn, the police want us to check out some dismembered demons. Like *totally* dismembered. They usually wouldn't contact us unless it's something odd."

"Like the other day?" Katia asked.

"No, that was just someone playing games with the cops. This sounds real." She glanced at the phone again. "It's downtown, in The Gulch." Riley looked over at Mort now. "Can I send this to you? I think we need to see this on a bigger screen."

"Go for it."

The photo transferred via email and then Katia found herself staring at absolute slaughter. The bodies had once been Gastro-Fiends, but exactly how many of them was hard to tell from the picture. She saw at least two heads, maybe more. Limbs torn off, gnawed on, entrails looping across the dirty pavement.

Something about the scene called to her. "I'm in. I'm not sure why, but it feels important."

"I'd like to go, too. I trust Katia's instincts," Simon said.

Riley looked over at her fellow necromancers. "You guys okay if we check this out?"

"The timing is good as I need more rest," Ozymandias admitted. "Lots more rest."

"We'll let you know what we find out. Might not mean anything."

"Thanks, Ayden, we really appreciate your help," Mort said, rising.

The witch nodded as she packed up the book and placed it back into the satchel. Then she hesitated. "If the Kindly Folk are involved, you may need our expertise when it comes to dealing with them. Let me know if that's the case."

"We will. Again, thank you."

As he helped the older summoner to his feet and slowly escorted him back into the house, Ayden trailed behind them.

"Let's go see what the cops have found," Riley said rising. "I'm hoping it's no big deal."

In the Gulch? No, this was something important.

Katia could feel it deep in her bones.

TWENTY-ONE

There were things you expected to find in a city parking lot. In this case, cars and trucks, the occasional motorcycle, empty beer cans, maybe a discarded lotto ticket or diaper. But not savaged demon corpses.

"Looks like something tore them apart and ate all the insides," Katia said, eyeing the grisly remains.

"Now that's a disgusting thought. Can you imagine what that tastes like?" Riley said.

"Rancid chicken mixed with slimy motor oil." At her raised eyebrow she added, "I got a face full of the stuff in Lawrence once. I couldn't stop gagging for over an hour."

The master trapper shuddered. "Just, yuck. So, we have at least four mature Gastro-Fiends, a good hundred pounds each, who have been ripped apart and then partially eaten." She moved closer, staring down at a pile of intestines. "No flies. You'd think this mess would be covered in them."

Chunks of the demons' matted and filthy fur was scattered around what was left of their bodies. One of the arm bones displayed gnaw marks.

"There's defensive wounds on some of these. They fought back," Simon said.

"Then this is something bigger, or quicker, than a Three," Riley mused. "Or something way more vicious, which is hard to imagine." Then she frowned. "No slicing marks on the bones, so this was a physical assault, not one with bladed weapons."

"And that leaves out . . . ?" Katia asked.

"Archfiends, for the most part. They love their scimitars. A Fallen could easily tear these guys apart, but frankly they couldn't be bothered. And if they did, they wouldn't eat them. Not their style. No scorch marks so that means a Pyro-Fiend isn't an option."

"What about a Big Mouth demon?"

The master pondered on that. "Maybe. I could see one of those grabbing these guys and chomping on them. But I would have thought there would have been torn-off tentacles or something when the Threes fought back."

"Yeah, good point."

"Check this out."

That had come from Simon who was about ten feet away, staring at something on the ground.

"Whatcha got?" Katia asked as they joined him.

He pointed. "To the right of the demon's head."

"All I see are guts, guts, more guts," she said, then stopped. One of the entrails lay next to a claw attached to a scaly arm. The arm was at least six feet long. "Could that be from a demon?"

Riley didn't reply, but murmured something under her breath that made the arm rise out of the carnage and float over to a body-free section. It landed on the ground and then she stepped closer to it.

"Not a demon," she said, looking up at them.

"Something from another realm came out for a quick snack?" Katia asked.

"That's my guess."

Simon kept eyeing the scene, section by section. "There's another something that doesn't look demonic," he said, pointing again.

A severed wing. It sure wasn't from an angel.

It was then something pressed against her mind, a strong nudge that made her skin crawl. As the sensation increased Katia became oblivious to whatever the other two were discussing, at least until Riley touched her arm. That touch made her jump.

"Hi. You're off in that little world of yours when you're seeing stuff the rest of us don't. I only feel the Hellspawn, or whatever's left of them. What about you?"

Was this a test? Her last master had been great at exploiting her mistakes, at least until she realized he was purposely setting her up for failure.

She glanced at Riley, then back at the corpses, taking a few more steps forward. Whatever had happened here was so wrong she couldn't put it into words. Was this an invasion that had failed, even if it was only one monster?

"Katia?" When she still didn't answer, Riley moved closer. "You do feel something, don't you?"

She had no choice but to answer. "I'm not sure."

"Not sure of what you're feeling, or not sure if you want to tell me?"

Atlanta's youngest master was too damned perceptive.

"I want to think about it before I say anything," Katia hedged.

"Your call. I trust your judgement on this." Her master stepped away from her now, giving her space. Somehow Riley knew when to do that.

Trust.

It always came back to that, didn't it? Two months into her new job in Atlanta and the past still haunted her, still affected every decision. As if what had happened in Kansas could happen here, and again it would be her fault. It hadn't always been that way, not with her first master because he'd known how to guide her.

But after his death Master Kelly had destroyed her confidence in a short period of time. Her ex-boyfriend, Noah, had only contributed to her insecurities. If her grandmother had been alive she'd have been able to fight back. But she'd died and Katia's brother had almost done the same.

It'd been as if the universe had decided she was worthless.

And I let it happen.

She jerked back to the present as something kept tugging on her senses. A few dozen steps took her across the pavement away from the others, past another piece of dead demon, this an eyeball. Again, no flies. The trail of black blood continued and Katia followed it for about twenty-five feet, then it abruptly ended. There was more of that Do Not Enter feeling, so she headed back from where she'd come, cold sweat covering her arms now.

Behind her, Riley chatted with the pair of cops who'd summoned them. Their relieved expressions said they were thrilled the corpses were no longer their problem. Sure enough, they walked back to their patrol car and drove off without bothering to look back. The police were always happy to drop anything Hell related into the trappers' laps. It was only fair.

As Riley walked back toward them, she texted someone, then paused to wait for a reply. When the phone beeped, she nodded and stuck it away in her pocket. "Fireman Jack will send someone down to collect the corpses. Sorry, but there won't likely be any money off these things."

Katia hadn't figured there would be. "This is where it happened last April."

Her master looked over at her now. "If you mean 'the Fallen Angel Tried to Destroy Atlanta' thing, then yes. It was just over there," she said, gesturing toward the west now. "This area is called The Gulch, in case you're wondering."

Gary the Tour Guide had mentioned that. "Simon told me what really happened. It wasn't a Fallen Angel."

Riley took a quick look around to ensure there was no one nearby other than the exorcist, who was methodically studying each pile of demon carcasses for whatever reason.

"Okay, then this is where the Angel of Death met its end, almost taking me, Ori and Beck with it. It was a near thing. *Very* near."

Katia had watched the videos of that day and they'd made her cringe. "Do you think that will happen again, another angel going crazy?"

"If I'm lucky, not in my lifetime. Or anyone else's." Riley hesitated, then pointed toward the south now. "What do you feel about that building over there? The abandoned one? Any impressions?"

It was the building where Riley and Beck had jumped off the

roof. "Gary the tour guide took us there."

"Okay, but what kind of feeling do you get from that place?"

"I sense demons and magic. Weird magic. Not sure what kind."

Riley studied her for a time and then smiled. "Wow. You have an amazing gift. The demons in that building *were* different. They couldn't die. No matter how hard we tried to kill them."

Katia stared at the building, trying to imagine what that was like.

"I'm guessing for you it's not a "here's a bit of magic" thing."

"No. It's more like having my skin sandblasted, depending on how strong it is. What about you?" she asked, looking back at her master.

"I'm better at sensing Hellspawn and how much power they have. I can sense most magic spells, but not all of them, at least not yet. So yeah, I'm feeling fortunate compared to what you put up with."

"It's not all bad," Katia blurted, then wondered why she had. "I felt the evil in a woman once. I told my teacher, but no one believed me until she tried to kidnap one of my classmates."

"How old were you?"

"Six."

"Six?" Riley blurted. "That had to be so scary."

"It was, because I didn't understand why I felt that way. My mom didn't know how to deal with someone like me, so she said I was just imagining it. It was always that way when I told her stuff like that."

"Did *anyone* believe you?"

"I think my dad did, but he didn't say much because mom would get mad. My gran *did* believe me. She said it was a gift. I don't see it that way."

"Your grandmother was right. What you have *is* a gift, though it's hard for you to bear. It is from the Light, that I can guarantee. I would sense if it was otherwise. You should trust it. And even more, trust yourself."

Katia felt the prickle of tears, so she turned away, not wanting her boss to see her weakness. Her eyes met Simon's, and he nodded in response. She hadn't realized he'd joined them, so caught up in the conversation.

"She's right," he said. "Let what happened in Lawrence stay there. You have a new life here now."

She wasn't sure about that.

A van pulled up, white with no markings on the side. Nothing special. The two men who climbed out dressed in jeans and T-shirts, just like they were doing a delivery.

"Hey, Sam, Zeke, how goes it?" Riley called out.

"You stick us with all the crap jobs, you know that?" one of them called back, but he didn't sound upset. "Do we need bags?"

"Oh yeah, and gloves. And a strong stomach."

The guys traded looks, then sighed. "One of those, huh?"

"Yes, and I'm sorry about that. But this time we didn't do it, so that should count for something."

"Aha."

A voice called to Katia now. One that pleaded with her, begging.

Save him!

She turned back toward the pile of demon bits, then listened again.

"Katia?" Simon said.

"Hold on," she said. Closing her eyes she shut out the world around her, listening.

Here!

It was The Lady, that much she knew.

"Katia?" Riley called out.

She ignored everything but the voice. The further she went from the carcasses, the stronger the sensation became, more urgent. Katia's stomach lurched and she nearly heaved. Then it faded as if she had crossed an invisible barrier. Forcing herself to keep moving, she spied something in the distance. It was a body. Lying next to it was a tattered navy robe.

"Oh, shit."

A broken staff lay next to the summoner, Chaffin's face a

mask of blood, his body no better. And yet, to her surprise, his bare chest moved with each shallow breath.

"Katia?" Simon shouted.

When she looked back at her companions, they weren't there.

"You are Between," the voice said. She turned and found The Lady watching her. She was battered as well, her face streaked with mud and green fluid, perhaps her version of blood. Her hands were red.

"Tried to save us. He could not." A tear ran down her face. "So brave, but not strong . . . enough. Help him. For me."

Then she turned and vanished into the darkness.

It had taken all of Katia's strength to drag the comatose summoner from the Between back to her world. Her shoulder and arm muscles complained, as well as those in her back, and she knew that a couple of her wounds had reopened.

None of that mattered. Katia had seen the grief in The Lady's eyes, seen more than that. She'd done the only thing left to do— she'd found a way to pull this dying man back to her friends using his robe.

The instant she crossed whatever barrier was in place she heard Riley gasp. Katia let go of the robe, then staggered a few steps, only to fall on her butt, strength gone.

"Help him!" she said, waving at the injured summoner behind her. "It's Chaffin. He's hurt."

Riley sprinted up to the injured man and knelt next to him. "Oh yeah, not good. Not good at all," she said. "Simon, I'll need your help getting him into the car."

"Why?" he demanded, glowering at them.

The question hit Katia like a fist to her jaw. "Why? Because he's hurt."

"Why should I care? He didn't give a damn when he sent us to that other world to die."

She forced herself to her feet, glaring at him. He glared right back, making no move to help.

"How about you stick your wounded pride up your ass and help this guy. Because trust me, there's more going on here than we know and he's the only one who can tell us what it is."

Simon stared at her, then looked as if he was going to argue.

"She's right, and if we let him die we'll never figure it out on our own," Riley insisted.

With an angry grunt, he stomped over and grabbed one end of the robe when Riley took the other. As they moved him across open ground, a low groan came from the wounded necro. One of the guys tasked with collecting the fiends' remains offered to help, but Riley shook her head.

"Thanks, but no. You're covered in demon guts and this guy is in bad enough shape as it is."

Katia managed to make it to the car first, so she opened both rear doors. It took a lot of maneuvering, but finally Summoner Chaffin was in the backseat, laying on his side, on a blanket. A makeshift pillow had been created from another blanket. Throughout it all he'd done nothing more than moan and leak blood from each of his many wounds.

Riley's car wasn't big, so Katia sat in the back with him, his booted feet lying across her lap.

"Hospital?" Simon asked tersely.

"No, Mort's house," Riley replied. "Call him and let him know we're inbound."

As the call went through, Katia kept an eye on the necro, watching his chest rise and fall. Whatever had attacked him had done so with incredible precision, the cuts on his chest and arms at near perfect intervals. Slice after slice.

He's been tortured.

Now the immense sadness in The Lady's eyes made even more sense.

Mort had them bring the summoner in the back door, not down

the lane past far too many nosy people. He'd insisted that Riley put a glamour on Chaffin so that it looked as if they were carrying a rolled-up carpet, not someone who was rapping on death's door.

Once the rogue was inside the house, Katia headed for one of the chairs on the veranda and fell into it, so tired she could hardly move. In time voices came from inside the house, one of them being the witch who'd treated Deanna.

Simon eventually joined her, his face still set in a frown. He got this way sometimes, just closing off from everyone. Was it because he'd been willing to let Chaffin die where they'd found him, or was it something else? There was only one way to find out.

"Why did you want us to leave him there?"

His eyes studied her, brilliant blue and cold. So cold she almost shivered. This was a part of Simon she rarely saw.

"I would think it was obvious."

"Nothing about this is obvious. You're mad at him because your sister could have died, right?"

A grimace replaced the cold stare. "Yes."

"Okay, that I understand. But it made no sense to let him croak without finding out what made him do what he did."

No reply.

She'd had enough, so she rose and headed for her room. Maybe by morning he'd have gotten over whatever was bugging him. Or not. And at this point she didn't care.

Riley tapped on her door a few minutes later, then wandered in without waiting for a reply. "You need help with that?" she asked, pointing at the open wound on Katia's arm which she was in the process of re-bandaging. Somehow she'd lost the first one during Chaffin's rescue.

"Yeah. I can probably do this one myself, but it won't be as neat."

The master sat on the side of the bed, added a small mound of gauze over the top of the healing wound, then began winding on the bandage. "Couldn't get Simon to help you?"

"Didn't want to ask him. He's being a jerk."

"Why do you think that is?"

"Because he's mad at the necro."

"That might be part of it."

"What other part is there?"

Riley's eyes met hers now. "Oh, maybe the part where you ploughed on ahead without us? Without telling us what you are seeing, or sensing? Leaving us behind and worried about what was happening to you after you disappeared? Something like that, maybe?" she snapped.

Oh.

Katia had done exactly that. Rather than explaining to them what was going on, she'd just done her thing, never considering she might need backup. What if she'd gotten to Chaffin and found it was a trap? She'd had no one to watch her back.

"Waiting to hear your thoughts on this, Journeyman," Riley replied. And from her tone she was just as upset as the exorcist.

"I'm not used to working with people. At least with people who aren't trying to screw me over."

"Do you think we'd do that?" her master asked.

"No."

"Then, as my husband would say, 'Y'all need an attitude adjustment'."

She even sounded like Beck.

"Because if you don't, one of these days this solo act thing is going to get you dead, and that will piss off a lot of people. Like me." She tied off the bandage. "Understood, *Journeyman*?"

"Yes, Master Blackthorne."

Riley's expression softened. "It's hard to trust when you've been treated badly, but that changed the morning you got off the bus. Suck it up, get used to working with us, and that way you won't get Simon's jerkiness or my lectures. Because I hate sounding three decades older than I am."

"Got it. Ah, does Beck really say 'Y'all need an attitude adjustment'?"

"He does, though his version is a bit more colorful."

After washing her hands, Riley paused at the door to the hallway. "Get some sleep. Chaffin will either live, or not. Either way we have a problem, and we're going to need your help with it."

The door closed behind her with a noticeable click.

Katia whistled under her breath. "Damn."

She'd just gotten her butt kicked, at least verbally.

"And I totally deserved it."

TWENTY-TWO

The longer Simon spent at Mort's the more he knew it was time to go home. He was too angry to be around anyone. He was likely to say stuff he'd regret, especially to good friends. He told Mort's housekeeper he was leaving and to have her employer let him know if he needed him.

Then he bailed.

It was only when he was outside that he remembered his car was at home. Going back wasn't an option, so Simon kept walking until he was on one of the main roads, and then used technology to complete the trip. Fortunately, his ride-share driver didn't want to chat, which was fine by him. Part of it might have been because of all his bandages.

To his relief, his house looked like it had the last time he'd been here, which only conjured up a memory that made him even more upset. Instead of coming in through the kitchen, he went to the front door, making him use the entrance from where he and his sister had been kidnapped. Forcing himself to deal with the emotions that act had generated. He didn't dare push those emotions down, not like he'd done after his near-death experience last year. Instead, he had to deal with them. So he did, furious that some bastard had dared violate his home.

He'd expected there would be magical residue on the front porch, but there wasn't.

Riley.

Simon bet she'd done something to remove the taint of the foul magic because nothing like that brushed up against him, not like he'd anticipated. The interior of the house was no different, just as it had been before, without any indication that a powerful spell had been tossed at them. It was as if nothing had happened. But it had.

There was a note on his dining room table that said his sister's purse had been returned to her and that the house was "clean" of anything magical. As he'd anticipated, Riley had signed the note. She never stopped watching out for him and his family.

Working around the bandages, he'd gotten as clean as possible then dressed and headed to the one place he knew he'd feel safe; the only place now his home had been invaded. Perhaps attending Mass and spending time in prayer would help him calm his soul. If not, it'd be a really long night.

After Simon returned home from Mass, he found himself listening for Katia's car to pull in the driveway. It never did. Instead, she'd sent him a text that said she was staying at Mort's tonight. There had been no further explanation and Simon knew he didn't deserve one. He acknowledged her message and then swore under his breath. This was his fault.

There were times he could be so damned cold-blooded, and the moment he'd realized that the wounded man was the thieving necro, he'd been willing to let the bastard die.

But at the heart of those emotions was fear, and he knew it. He had been powerless in that other world, or at least it had seemed so. It reminded him of the attack at the Tabernacle, that sense of defenselessness. It was why he was so determined to be the best exorcist possible. If it'd just been him in that realm, that was one thing. But having Dee and Katia there, in danger, brought out his bloodthirsty instincts.

When he grew tired of sitting in his recliner, staring at nothing, he moved to his backyard. A beer rested on the small table next to him. A beer he'd opened a half hour ago and never touched.

"I'm a damned mess," he muttered. And he missed Katia so much.

He checked his phone and realized it was too late to call. If she was as tired as he was, she was probably in bed. But he could send her an email. That wouldn't wake her up.

He hesitated, trying to find a way to say what was in his heart. Then realizing he couldn't reveal all of that, not yet.

Finally, his fingers began to move.

You were right. I was wrong. I'm sorry.

Right before he was about to hit Send his pride flared, but he pushed it back down. A man admitted his mistakes, and he'd made a big one. He was human, as Father Rosetti had often reminded him. We all endured a lifetime of lessons is what the priest had said. It appeared he still had more to learn.

Simon hit Send and then finally took a sip of his beer. Once it was gone he headed for bed. Maybe tomorrow they'd find out why a powerful necromancer had risked their lives for a damned piece of jewelry.

† ✻ ‡ ✻ †

Katia woke to a knock on the bedroom door. With effort she managed to sit upright. She was still tired, even after many hours of rest.

Riley stuck her head in the room. "Chaffin is awake and wants to unburden his soul."

"This better be damned good or I'll haul his ass right back to where I found him," Katia growled.

"I'll tell him that. I let Simon know and he'll be here in about ten minutes." The door closed.

More effort was required to wash her face, get her hair tamed, and dress. It was only after she was heading for the door that she checked her phone and found the email.

You were right. I was wrong. I'm sorry.

The message had come in a little before midnight. Simon wasn't finding it any easier to sleep than she had, not after what had happened between them.

"And I'm sorry for scaring you," she whispered.

Summoner Mathias Chaffin looked like he'd been given the deluxe tour of Hell. Dressed in a baggy black T-shirt and pants, likely borrowed from Mort, he sat rigidly in one of the chairs, his scabbed hands in his lap. His eyes were hooded and bloodshot, his whole demeanor one of defeat. Gone was the arrogance Katia had once witnessed, leaving behind a broken man.

As testament to the witch's skills the cuts on his arms and hands were already healing, though there would be noticeable scars. Someone had really worked this guy over, one slice at a time.

At the same table was their host, Lord Ozymandias, and her master, all of them grim.

Katia eyed the rogue necro, then pointedly addressed the most senior summoner. "This guy isn't going to be tossing spells around, is he?"

His lordship shook his head. "We've called a truce for the time being. The magical inhibitor he's now wearing will keep him from breaking that agreement."

"What he said." Chaffin raised his left arm. Encircling the wrist was a wide metal bracelet inscribed with magic symbols. Surprisingly, he didn't seem upset about that addition.

Katia heard steps behind her and looked up as Simon joined them. "You got my email?" he asked quietly.

"Yes. Your apology is accepted. We'll talk about mine later." Because she'd been at fault as well.

That seemed to confuse him as he sank into the chair next to her. Then he gave a nod to the others.

"That's all of us," Mort said. He looked over at Chaffin. "Now is the time to tell us everything."

"I will. I'm a dead man anyway," he said, coughed, then clearing his throat. A glass of water sat in front of him and he took it in both hands and then carefully sipped. As he put it down, he cleared his throat again.

"I don't give a damn what happens to me. I honestly thought I could deal with the threat, but instead the threat damned near killed me."

At this point, he eased back in the chair and closed his eyes as if collecting his thoughts. A few moments passed and then those weary eyes reopened.

"About five months ago I was visiting Atlanta and I met someone not from this world. She is . . . incredible," he said, his voice filled with awe. "We spent a lot of time together, sometimes in a park or in the woods. I knew she was fae, but that didn't matter. We became lovers and then she granted me entrance into her realm. It was *so* beautiful there."

"Describe her for us," Mort said.

"She has eyes of blue, her hair is fiery red, and her skin is pure alabaster. She is ethereal, a vision. She is everything I ever hoped for."

That was The Lady. "What is her name?" Katia asked.

"I'll not say it as it might gain you power over her."

"Fair enough."

He gave her a weary smile. "My lady likes you. She said that one of your family was a friend of their kind and that's why she revealed herself to you."

"That would be my grandmother. She was always a bit different, and I guess I am too."

"It's not easy to earn their trust." He paused. "When we first met, my lady was all joy and happiness, with a smile that made my life worth living. She likes our world. It fascinates her." He looked away for a moment, then back. "And no, I've not been bespelled. I would know if I was. We genuinely love each other. Then *it* came and began to destroy her world."

"It?" Riley asked, her expression guarded. Katia wasn't sure if her master was believing all this or not.

"I call it the Unholy Terror, but I don't know if it has a name. I think it's female, but I'm not sure. It's a being with great magical powers, though one I'm not familiar with. But then I've not had that much experience with otherworldly things, at least not until I encountered the fae. This thing crossed into my lady's realm and began destroying it."

"Is that why her ferns were dying, the ones in her hair?"

Katia said.

"Yes. Imagine that same effect on a world."

"What does this creature want?"

"Destruction," Chaffin replied. "It thrives on chaos and pain. One day my lady didn't show up at the park like we'd planned. I got worried so I went into her world. The Unholy Terror was there." He shook his head at the memory.

"I could tell I wasn't powerful enough to stop it, and it knew it too. Then out of nowhere it commanded me to bring it that ring. Told me if I didn't, it would kill more of my lady's people." His eyes dimmed. "I have no idea how it knew about my ancestor."

"But *you* knew the ring existed," Ozymandias replied.

"I did. There'd been whispers in the family about it, but most of us were happy it'd gone missing, along with its owner. It's why there aren't many of us Chaffins who become summoners now. Too much family history there."

"How did you learn where to find Lord Chaffin's remains? That's *not* common knowledge."

"A few of the older members of our family claimed he'd been exiled, though I never believed it. Some of his personal possessions survived, hidden away so they weren't destroyed when the good folks of Boston burned his house to the ground. Not that I blame them for that." He shook his head. "Lord Chaffin was one twisted bastard, that's for sure." At that point he seemed to realize he'd not answered the question.

"I made a trip to his birthplace, found his waistcoat in a local museum and 'borrowed' one of the buttons. Then I did a rather complicated 'find me' spell because I didn't trust the Unholy Terror when it said that the ring was 'not of my world', whatever that meant. The spell took forever to get right. I figured the ring had to be somewhere in North Carolina. Ha, not even close. But how did that monster know that?"

That was a good question.

"I heard The Lady talking to me when we were in the other realm. Was she there and I just didn't see her?" Katia asked.

"No, she wasn't. You two have a strong connection which is

why you hear her speaking to you. I'm guessing she steered you to the ring."

"She did. And saved us from something far worse."

"I can see her doing that. My lady refused to touch it. Said it would kill her. That's why I wanted the dead to retrieve it because I didn't want anyone to be harmed. But they just couldn't enter that realm."

"So instead, you kidnapped us?"

Chaffin reluctantly nodded. "She said she could sense that you'd been in other worlds. I had someone check you out and that's how I saw the video, the one at that convention. One minute you're there, then you're gone. I figured if anyone could bring me the ring it'd be you." He looked over at Simon now. "I never wanted your sister to get caught up in all that. It was just supposed to be you two, but by that time I was panicking. I wouldn't have hurt her. I'm so deeply sorry."

Simon just glared at him.

"We found Harry Hawkins," Mort said.

The necro winced at that. "I'd hoped he'd escaped your notice. Please don't punish him. Hawkins isn't the bad guy here. He just needed to earn some money and wanted to learn magic. I take full responsibility for all this."

"Have you been opening portals anywhere else in Atlanta?" Riley asked.

"No," he replied, surprised. "Why?"

"Because we've had a couple appear out of nowhere and then something tries to creep across."

"No, that wasn't me."

"Of course not, that would have been too easy. So, you got the ring but it didn't work," Riley continued.

Chaffin looked down at one of the long slices on his arm. "Despite my magical abilities and the boost from the ring, that creature nailed me. It took over the spell I cast and slung it back at me. I had no way to fight that."

"It tortured you," she said, quieter now.

The summoner's expression saddened. "No, it forced the

one I love to torture me. I still remember the tears in my lady's eyes as she cut me, over and over."

"Oh my God," Katia said, her hand going to her throat.

"I'm alive because the Unholy Terror has a limited attention span, and when it was no longer amusing to watch me suffer, it ignored me. It was too enthralled with the ring. I lost a lot of my magic, but not all of it. I crawled my way out of that world and back to my own. I wanted to die here. I didn't want the one I love watch me take my last breath."

"Dear God," Simon whispered.

Chaffin carefully shifted positions. It was obvious he wouldn't be upright for much longer.

"I know the penalty for stealing corpses, and I'm willing to accept it. But for the love of God, please stop that thing from hurting my Lady and her kind. Stop it from growing any more powerful. Because if you don't, it now has the ring and the power to move out of that realm and into ours. It'll do the same damned thing here. Its evil has no bounds."

Looks were traded around the table now. That was the dilemma—as long as the monster remained in the other realm, they were safe. Not our problem, right?

But monsters never stopped destroying, never stopped killing. It would be naïve to think it would stay in The Lady's world and not search out more victims. Otherworldly, demonic or mortal, all monsters were insatiable.

"*Your* enemy may eventually be *our* enemy," Ozymandias said, summing up the issue succinctly.

Chaffin nodded. "I fear so. Or it may go to other realm. Once it's drained my lady's world dry, it will move on." He took another long sip of water. "There was so much I didn't know. I figured I'd be able to save them. I can cast powerful spells. I can open portals to other worlds. What could possibly be stronger than me?" He shook his head in despair. "God, I was so stupid."

"That trait is not yours alone," his lordship said. "I, too, have made such mistakes."

"Then we're all fools."

"Is the door to The Lady's home world near where I found you?" Katia asked.

"Yes, if the Unholy Terror allows you entrance."

"I'm betting it will. Only one way for me to find out." Simon was already shaking his head before she'd finished.

"If you confront it, what stops this evil from forcing you to do its will? Force you to bring it *into* our realm?" Ozymandias asked.

"He's right," Chaffin said. "That's how it entered my lady's world. It took control of a fae, one of the more belligerent ones. He brought it into their realm and it returned the favor by killing him. No matter how hard they fight the creature, they always lose," Chaffin said.

"This thing is not only brute force. It's cunning. Somehow it knew about your ancestor and his ring, and then purposely found a way into the fae realm," Simon said. "That means someone told it about you and your lady. It needed leverage to get you to do what it wanted. And the fae were it."

Chaffin gave a hollow laugh. "Ironic, isn't it? That's why I kidnapped you and your sister, just to have leverage." He hesitated, then sighed. "The fae that brought the Unholy Terror into their world had been following my lady and myself for some time. She said to ignore him, but I think he was jealous."

"This Unholy Terror found a weak link and exploited it," Mort suggested.

"It did. Nothing would keep it from doing the same to you, Ms. Breman."

He was probably right.

"It might. But I have to do something because this horror needs to die."

"You are convinced this is the only way to proceed?" Ozymandias asked. She nodded. "Well, I see. I would join you in this fight, but I cannot at this time. My strength is not sufficient," he replied, his voice full of regret. That much was obvious since the sigil on his forehead was barely lit.

"Are you sure about this?" Riley asked. "You're still hurting from the last trip."

"I am," Katia replied.

"Anywhere else and I'd go with you. But not another realm, not after my trip to Hell," her boss said. "I'm not even sure I can walk the worlds. That was Ori's doing, not mine."

"You have to have a particular mindset for that sort of travel," Ozymandias said. "You're correct, Riley, that it *was* the angel that took you into the Pit, not you."

"I can't do it," Mort said, trading a look with his superior now. "I tried once. It just didn't work. And up to this point, I've not regretted it. Until now."

"Please, think this through. You'll be on your own," Riley warned.

"No, I'll be with her," Simon said, looking over at Katia now. "Don't bother to argue with me."

As she began to refuse his help, her master cut in. "Remember the conversation we had yesterday? You need someone to watch your back, Journeyman. This isn't just about you."

Katia did remember that convo, and she knew Riley was right. She was grateful for Simon's support, but she feared what that might cost her friend if this went wrong.

"Alright, we go together," she said, because she wasn't suicidal.

Simon's tense posture immediately eased. "

"They are running out of time," Chaffin said. "She won't be alive for much longer. I can feel it."

"We go tonight?" Katia asked, eyeing the exorcist.

"Tonight," he agreed.

"The best we can do is reinforce our side of the portal in case you're not . . . successful," Mort said. "We'll need to prepare counter spells to stop this creature if it tries to come here." He turned to Riley and added, "I'll need your help with those."

"You got it. I'll let a certain grand Master know what's going on."

"Please do so," Ozymandias replied. "We might need his help if this plan fails."

Chaffin closed his eyes for a few seconds, and when they reopened they glistened. "If you can save their world, save her, and keep that thing from coming here, then it will all have been worth it."

Riley's eyes swiveled to him. "Not so fast. All of this is on you. We are just cleaning up your mess. You own this; everything."

With a nod of understanding, he rose and slowly shuffled back into the house, a broken man.

TWENTY-THREE

Once their plans had been laid, Katia returned Stewart's car to his house, leaving it in the driveway and the keys on the kitchen table. Her timing had been good as Mrs. Ayers hadn't been home so no explanation for the early return was necessary.

Since she was there, Katia took a few minutes to check out the newly painted rooms and found them to be as nice as she'd hoped. The old house had been renewed, and only a faint paint smell still lingered. One of the ornate cornices had been painted white now and it was perfect. Grand Master Stewart would love this once he got back home. If Katia survived her encounter with the Unholy Terror tonight, she'd be back here to enjoy it as well.

It was close to six that evening when she and Simon finally had a chance to talk. Once again, they were in his backyard, neighborhood noises filtering in from beyond the high cypress fencing. Someone was playing badminton and having a grand time of it. Just normal everyday activity. It felt good.

As she'd savored the sounds, Simon had spent the last few minutes staring at the fencing, silent. It didn't look like he was going to start the conversation, so she did.

"I owe you an apology," she said, and that drew his eyes to her now.

"About what?"

"About taking off on my own when I found Chaffin. I should have told you and Riley what I was going to do. I didn't. That was my bad."

He looked away, then back again. "Is that what she meant

today?"

"Yup. She was right. She gave me hell for it. And I think that's part of the reason you were so angry with Chaffin. Some of that was because of me."

A slow nod came her way. "That was part of it. Also, I let my heartless side show. It's not pretty when I do that. I can be really cold sometimes."

"We all can."

"Your apology is accepted."

"Thank you. I'll try to do better." She noted he didn't acknowledge that other people had their hardass moments as well.

"This is likely to be a one-way trip tonight. You saw what happened to Chaffin."

"Any crazier than exorcising fiends or going to Hell to chat with the Infernal Asshole?"

He shook his head. "The first we know how to handle. The second, we got lucky. I'm feeling really bad about this whole thing, Katia. We have no clue what we're facing over there."

"Then why did you offer to go?"

It took Simon a few moments to reply as if he was weighing his answer.

"Because I saw Chaffin's expression. He's in love with The Lady and he risked his life to save her. Not for his ego, but for her and her kind. As much as I want to hate him, I just can't. And I won't let you go alone. I couldn't do that."

"I can't hate him, either."

"The penalty for necros who steal corpses is to have their magic ripped from them. Most of them go insane and are put in an asylum somewhere, staring at the four walls and drooling. If they're not insane, they go to prison. Or he might face exile into the skeleton bird realm. I'm not sure what would be worse."

"Still, he risked all that for her,' Katia said.

"He did." More shouts came from the badminton game, triumphant ones as if someone had just won a match.

"I think you should talk to your parents before we go. In

case . . . " he trailed off.

In case we don't come back.

There was no way she could keep the worry out of her voice, and she didn't dare tell them what she and Simon were facing. Then there was the matter of her move to Atlanta.

At first, her folks had been really upset. Her brother had said they were better now, but that she doubted. Maybe her father had chilled out, but her mother had always been a hard one to understand. They had never been able to find common ground, not since that day that she'd discovered that Katia was anything but normal.

"No, I'm not going to talk to them. That means we both have to survive this nonsense. What about your folks?"

Simon immediately shook his head. "I'm not telling them. They know what I do has a lot of risk involved. They can't know about the other realms, at least not yet. It's bad enough my sister knows about them."

"Okay, so we're going to do this," she said, letting that sink in. "I think we should take our usual gear. Well, not the metal box thing because this isn't a demon, but some Holy Water. And my steel pipe."

He blinked in response to her comment, as if something had just occurred to him. "I never gave you . . . " He rose. "I have something for you that might be better."

Simon walked down to the garage, unlocked the side door and slipped inside. When he returned, he carried a long wooden staff. A bō.

"Happy Birthday," he said, then to her surprise he knelt on one knee in front of her, his arms extended, offering the staff like a knight would to his queen.

"Simon . . . "

Those brilliant blue eyes met hers. "If you haven't figured it out by now, I'm really into you, Katia Breman. Sure, we work together, but that's not only how I see you." He glanced down at the staff and then back up again.

"Please don't shoot down my fantasy that someday we might

be something more than friends. I need hope for what we're facing tonight." He swallowed, hard. "Please just accept this gift and smile. That'll be enough."

She knew that eventually they would need to talk about whatever was happening between them. But not tonight.

Katia took the bō, smiled, then tried not to cry because this was so much more than she'd anticipated. Why was she so emotional right now?

"Oh, this is wonderful!" She examined the staff, running her hands along the smooth oak. "How did you know?"

"Riley showed me your video. I hope you don't mind, but I shared it with an instructor at the dojo up north. She helped me pick out your presents."

"Thank you so much. I meant it!" Then she paused, confused. "Presents?"

As if by magic, a black case appeared in his hand. She'd been so fixated on the bō she hadn't seen it. This time he just handed it over, skipping the bow.

"Sometimes you'll need a long staff, sometimes you'll need a collapsible one. Now you have a choice."

Katia unzipped the case and then stared. The bō inside was blue, the color of his eyes. She'd always wanted one of these.

"Oh my God, Simon." She removed it, still staring. "One was enough."

"I wanted you to have a choice."

A choice.

Since she'd become a trapper, she'd had no choice but to do things that didn't make her life any easier. And yet this guy who'd she'd only known for a brief time, understood she needed those choices. He knew her better than her own family.

"Which will you take with you tonight?" Simon asked, rising. After dusting off his knees, he settled back into the lawn chair. He seemed genuinely pleased at her reaction to the gifts.

"If the Unholy Terror is fae, it won't like the metal. But an oak staff gives me other options. I'll have to think on this."

"While you're thinking, can I have a demo? I mean, the video is great, but seeing your skills in person would be even better."

That she could do.

Katia chose the collapsible bō, curious how it would feel. Extending it with a snap of her wrist, she moved into the center of the yard and took a relaxed stance. After a few deep breaths she began to move, to let the staff talk to her because each of them had their own personality.

The first test move was more awkward than she would have liked, but Simon didn't comment on that. The next few moves smoothed out. Soon she was flowing *with* the bō, becoming one with it.

She began with ten overhead strikes, followed by a high block, then one to the left and then the right. As her body warmed up she went for a side kick. It wasn't at all graceful, but the next three were better. And then she moved into the spins, a grounded block, a reverse hook kick, and then an uppercut.

After a few more spins she let the staff come to rest, sucking air into her lungs as fast as possible. She hadn't exercised like this in over six months and it showed. And yet, when she looked up, she found Simon staring at her in awe.

"My God, you're incredible," he said, then gave her a huge smile. "You rock, Katia from Kansas. You know that, right?"

No, she didn't. But hearing it from him made her think it might just be true.

"I'm kind of rusty at this."

"You'll get there. Like my sword fighting skills. One tiny step at a time. You make mistakes, then you learn. It's how life works." He was so right about that.

"Ice cream to celebrate?" he asked.

At her nod, Simon headed inside the house leaving her alone with her amazing presents and his astounding confession. Was it possible that they had a future together, one even more than just friendship?

"Maybe," she whispered. *Maybe.*

† ✳ ‡ ✳ †

For Katia, Atlanta at night was a wonderland of lights, sounds, and smells. The Gulch, the heart of the city, only seemed to magnify those sensations. The buildings around her were lit like blazing candles as traffic streamed along. Lively music came from a bar nearby. She listened for a bit longer, then smiled. There was a bagpipe in there somewhere.

As it was close to ten most of the cars were gone, the commuters tucked in their homes and apartments for the night. That left a few locals wandering around, some in groups of four or more, as well as the occasional stray cat. One had two kittens trailing behind her as they went in search of a meal.

For Simon and the others this was home. For Katia this was foreign territory. Unlike at home or in Kansas City, she could feel the undercurrents of magic and the presence of the fiends as if they were just another scent in the wind. Less of the latter in the last week.

Lucifer was no fool. He knew something was playing out here and he'd pulled his fiends out of the way. Well, not all of them or that pile of Threes wouldn't have happened.

When her phone buzzed and she knew who it was even before she read the message. When he'd gone to take a shower, she'd left Simon a note telling him she needed time on her own. That she'd meet him in The Gulch. What she hadn't said was that she needed a chance to put things in perspective before they entered the unknown.

The gifting of her presents, and what he'd said about her, had stirred up feelings she'd thought long forgotten. What would it be like to be loved by someone like him?

And if they dared take that step, what would happen if that relationship failed? Dare they risk losing such a deep friendship? As if reminding her of his commitment to her, Simon's text read:

BE THERE SOON. PLEASE DON'T GO WITHOUT ME.

She texted back, promising to wait for him, and a smiley face was his reply. Clipping her phone back on her belt, Katia hefted her trapping bag and tucked her oak staff under her arm. She set off toward the one part of this big parking lot that called to her more than any other area.

This time there were no gray ashes on the pavement, no Ori the Divine. Just the city and the sense that what had happened here had changed Atlanta in ways that few understood. And that included the angels.

Setting her gear down, she put her hand over the top of the pavement where the remains had once been. The asphalt still radiated heat from the day's high temperature. If she was right, it radiated more than that.

Katia had done a lot of thinking about the Angel of Death and what had happened here. It seemed that its job description was not complicated: Kill everyone, burn everything. Job done.

And yet when it'd been in Atlanta it hadn't left a black seething mass of destruction behind it, not like the videos she had seen from other countries. Italy's visitation had been unbelievably horrific.

Here the angel had left behind those ashes, the remnants of the warriors it'd used to distract Riley and Beck while it fought with the other Divine. Ashes that had not been taken back to Heaven with the angel after its death.

But why would that matter?

"Because that's not the way it was supposed to work," she murmured.

It was doubtful that God's executioner would only be confined to *this world* when it came to smiting the wicked. No, the Angel of Death would need the ability to go to any realm created by the Almighty, which many believed was the entire universe. If that was the case it should be able to *walk the worlds*, like some of the necromancers.

That was probably part of its essence, a built-in ability that didn't require any magic at all. At least not the kind Katia was familiar with. Since those gray fragments had once been part of the executioner . . .

"Could that be it?" she whispered. "Is that why other realms can open into ours now?"

As if on cue she felt Ori's presence again, and she turned to confront him. "Am I right? Is this why the other realms are connecting to ours?"

The angel's mouth formed a grim line. His face said he was weary, and he lacked his usual vitality, as if all this upheaval was taking a personal toll.

"Well?"

"I can't answer that question."

"Why not? You're not working for Heaven anymore. You should be able to tell me the truth."

Again, silence. His eyes were darker now and she could feel his anger, though it didn't seem aimed at her.

"Can Serrah tell me?"

He shook his head. "She's still finding her own way here, just like you."

"Okay, here's a question maybe you can answer. Was the Angel of Death able to walk the worlds?"

A cautious nod came her way.

"And those gray ashes were created by it?"

Another nod.

"So that stuff can probably move through time and space, just like the Angel of Death."

He nodded again, his eyes deeply troubled. "Riley Anora Blackthorne destroyed those."

"But did she get all of them?"

No reply.

She shifted topics because this wasn't helping her and Simon's chances of survival tonight. "You said angels like you aren't allowed to walk the realms. Can you break the rules and do it anyway?"

"No. At least not to my knowledge."

"Well, so much for Divine backup tonight," she muttered. "You know where we're headed? What we're facing?"

"Yes."

"Any suggestions how to stop something that lives on pure

life force?"

Again, no reply. That pissed her off.

"Are you here to just stare at me, or are you going to tell us how to keep ourselves alive? Because if you're not here to help you can just go the hell away."

Ori looked away for a time, his shoulders high and tight. "I cannot help you in the way you would like."

"Wonderful," she said, making sure the sarcasm rang through. "Unless we're incredibly lucky, we won't be seeing our friends or our families ever again. Chaffin was systematically tortured, Ori. His magic was drained. I figure we'll be given the same treatment. Hopefully, we'll die quickly. If not . . . "

Another look into the distance, then his posture grew less rigid as if somewhere someone had spoken to him.

"I cannot tell you much that might help because of certain restrictions, but . . . the skills you and the exorcist possess are *especially important*. Remember *what* you are and what strengths you both possess. That may make all the difference."

Ori turned now, gazing at the headlights of an approaching taxi as it crossed the parking lot. "He is here." The angel looked back at her, his face full of worry. "Do not fail him."

Then the Divine was gone, vanishing as if he'd never been there in the first place.

Katia swore under her breath. "Really helpful suggestions, dude."

Go with the Light, Katia Allyson Breman. It will never desert you.

With a deep sigh she nodded her understanding, for that much was true.

She caught up with Simon near where the piles of demon corpses had once been. That area was now as tidy as it could be in the middle of a parking lot. Someone, probably Fireman Jack's guys, had even given the pavement a quick scrub.

And I think my job can be bad.

Simon carried a sheathed sword, but no trapping bag. He was in a black T-shirt, black pants and hiking boots, almost exactly what Katia was wearing. The small silver cross hanging on his chest seemed so different than the one he'd sacrificed so they could make the trip into the skeleton bird realm.

"You okay?" he asked, concerned.

She could just imagine how angry she looked.

"As good as I can be. I just needed space to get my head straight."

"Did it help?"

"Not really." If anything, it was worse after her time with the angel. "Ori said we should remember what we are."

"That's it?"

"Yeah. I don't think he was allowed to say much more."

"Great," Simon muttered.

"You didn't bring your car."

"I thought it was best if it was at home."

Which meant he didn't think they'd be alive when this was over.

Two cars pulled up now. One of them was Riley's and she exited hers as Ayden and Mort climbed out of the other one. Somehow, they'd timed their arrivals, which was a miracle in this city.

"Magical reinforcement," Simon said.

The passenger side door of Riley's car opened and someone in a navy robe stepped out. Using a cane for support, the rogue necromancer slowly moved forward until he was a few feet away from them. Chaffin still looked like crap, but not as fragile as this morning.

When Katia gave her master a questioning look, Riley shrugged. "He insisted he had to be here."

"I do. I have no choice." Chaffin took a deep breath. "If you can't get into my lady's realm, come back here. Then maybe I can walk you in."

"You think the Unholy Terror is going to let you go a second time?" Katia asked, surprised by this offer. If he went back, he'd die for sure.

"It won't matter. *Do not* let anyone in that realm hear your full name. That's *especially important*."

Katia and Simon traded looks.

"I could never really get a fix on what the Unholy Terror is, but the power it has feels slimy, if that makes any sense."

Slimy magic did sound familiar, at least when it came to demons. But if angels couldn't do inter-realm hops, the Death dude being the exception, neither could Hellspawn. No way would Heaven allow that to happen.

"Then it's an unknown evil until we figure it out," Simon said.

"That's the best way to think of it."

Riley moved closer now, then enveloped her in a tight hug.

"Use those strengths of yours, and not just the physical ones. You are a warrior, Katia, and this battle is yours to win. Go there, kick ass, then come back to us. You hear me?"

"I do."

Then it was Simon's turn. Their embrace went on longer, but then he and Riley had been closer at one time. Then he stepped back, his expression troubled.

"I wish I could do more," Mort said, shaking his head.

"Same here," Ayden added. "Do not discount the fae. If they can help you, they will. Their world is in danger and they're biding their time to get revenge."

"Just guard the door," Simon said. "If we can't kill this thing, make sure it doesn't get into our world. That will be the best revenge I can think of."

After a nod from Chaffin, they gathered their gear and headed toward where Katia had found the injured necro.

The air around them began to change. "The barrier between the worlds is really close," she said.

"I can feel it now." He hesitated and added, "Hold on for a second."

She waited as he anointed himself with the Papal Holy Water, whispering a prayer as he did so. Though she wasn't sure if it would help, Katia did the same. Then she anointed her bō on each tip and in the center because it felt right.

Simon watched her, one eyebrow raised, then did the same to his sword.

"Can't hurt," he said, re-sheathing the blade in its scabbard.

After one last look behind them, they walked through the void and left their world behind.

TWENTY-FOUR

The moment they stepped into the new realm, it felt like she'd been run down by a semi. Katia took a few deep breaths, using her staff to keep her balance as her head spun.

"Well, that was special," Simon mumbled.

Once her vision cleared, she stared at absolute darkness, the kind that absorbed both light and sound.

"Looks like someone wants to meet us," she said. The darkness continued. "Right now, it'd be great to be a necro and have one of those bobbing light things."

"Or we could use a flashlight," he said, digging in his pack.

Of course he'd be prepared.

"Let me guess—you were a Boy Scout, right?"

"Yup." He clicked on the light and an entrance appeared in the gloom, one that led to a tunnel that had been constructed by someone who had zero masonry skills. The stones were ugly brown, not uniform or nestled flat in the wall, but just jammed in there as if someone hadn't cared one way or another.

"Is this real?" he asked, moving the light around to examine the various stones.

"Not sure."

"Then let's keep going until we figure out what *is* real."

As they moved forward, the glow of the flashlight bounced off the walls. Beneath their boots, the black dirt had bits of gravel that crunched as they walked. Katia gave a quick look over her shoulder and then winced.

"Where we came in is all darkness now."

Her friend murmured under his breath, a prayer perhaps.

"I talked to Ori right before you arrived."

"Good news or bad?"

"I'm thinking bad." Then she related what the angel had said about their journey here, and how to fight the evil they'd encounter. She purposely didn't mention the ashes. Simon had enough on his mind at the moment.

"You think he knows what this is?" he asked.

"I'm not sure. If he does, someone higher up told him to keep quiet about it."

Simon sighed, moving ahead, the crunch-crunch of his boots the only sound. She knew he was parsing out what she'd just told him and was probably as pissed as she was.

He suddenly halted, turning toward her. "Are we walking into a trap?"

She hadn't even thought of that possibility.

"Chaffin didn't act like he was setting us up. He seemed on the level."

"He might not have known," Simon replied.

With no other option they pushed on. The walls of the tunnel were still the same, and it occurred to her that maybe they were just going in a big circle. Before she could mention that a mist formed around them, white and clingy. Katia swore she felt it inside her mind, digging around, searching for something. She shoved it away and the sensation ended.

"What was that?" she asked but got no reply. "Simon?"

Finally, the mist thinned enough that she could see he was still standing next to her. His expression was blank. She touched his shoulder and got no reaction.

"Simon! You okay?"

He blinked a few times. "I think so. It felt like something was inside my head."

"Same with me."

The mist gradually evaporated revealing a new scene. It was the smell that hit her first, the stench of sulfur. Oh yes, there were the flames billowing upward from the cavern floor, the tortured faces in the walls screaming in agony. Small demons skittered around as bigger ones leered at her and Simon with their bright red eyes.

The edges of the scene wavered as if it wasn't solid. "It's an illusion," she said. "Not bad, but not the real deal. Probably why we got the mind probe thing."

The cavern gradually revealed itself: High, wide, full of Hellspawn, just like the other place. And just like the Pit there was a throne, and it was occupied. This time there were no massive Hellspawn guarding the occupant.

Remember what you are, Ori's voice echoed in her mind.

The figure that rose from the throne wore a long cloak, its face obscured by a hood. The Unholy Terror, as Chaffin called it. When it raised its head, burning red eyes glowed at them. The kind of eyes she'd seen countless times in the past.

"You're kidding me! A demon? Here?" she exclaimed. "That can't be right."

Simon stared at the figure. "Remember the necro said one of the fae brought it here. If they can possess mortals, why not a fairie?"

Her mind still couldn't quite make the leap. At least they knew how to kill the thing, which was what Ori had been trying to tell her in his own subtle way. Hopefully, she'd get the chance to ask him why he hadn't bothered to tell her that right up front.

"A Four, you think?" Simon nodded. "But how could Chaffin not know it was a demon?" she said, puzzled.

"Most of them don't have much to do with fiends. Mort and Ozymandias are exceptions. If it didn't reveal itself, he wouldn't have known."

"Huh."

Simon eyed the threat, no doubt trying to work out a strategy.

"You dare to enter my realm?" the Hellspawn said, moving closer now. It was nearly seven feet tall, but then that might be what it wanted them to see. The cloak around it fell away now, revealing something even more frightening.

They'd thought this was a Hypno-Fiend, a Grade Four Hellspawn. Trappers called them Mezmers as they were skilled at jacking with your head. A creature that sucked life out of others. But this was more than that. Bigger, wider, heavier. The beginnings of wings jutted out of its back. There were more than two eyes and far too many serrated teeth. This was Hell's version of an orc.

"Oh, God," Simon murmured. "It's morphing into an Archfiend."

She'd heard Mezmers could do that if they got enough power. This one certainly was. "Did the ring do that?"

"I'm thinking so. That's why it wanted it."

Keeping an eye on their foe, Katia pulled the trapping bag off her shoulder and let it settle on the ground next to her. The one thing they really needed—the metal demon prison—was back in Atlanta.

Next time we bring everything. Providing there was a next time.

"Did you own the soul of Elias Burnley Chaffin?" Simon said.

A hiss. "Yes. He summoned me and then he was mine."

"But the necromancers exiled him to that other realm, along with his ring, because that Chaffin was too dangerous. And you couldn't get to him there."

The fiend shifted on its feet, its many eyes glowing. "*They* took him away from me!"

Now it made sense. "So, when you saw the current Chaffin in Atlanta you realized who he was," Katia began. "Then you found out he was in love with one of the fae. That meant you could blackmail him into getting the ring."

Simon nodded in agreement, glaring at the monster now. "You took possession of one of the Kindly Folk and walked right in here. Because here the Prince can't touch you," he said, pointing at the ground beneath their feet. "If you'd tried that in Atlanta, Lucifer would have cut you down, and you knew it. How many Retrievers does he have looking for you right now?"

The Unholy Terror hissed louder, which said that the Prince's hench demons were doing just that.

Time to push harder. "Speaking of Hell, where you down

there when we came for a visit?" she said. "You remember, with Azagar? Oh wait, he's dead, isn't he? So sad."

Simon snorted at that.

The flames shot higher around them, but their adversary didn't do anything stupi*d*. Usually, you could bait these things into making a mistake.

"Were you one of his flunkies?" Katia nudged.

The eyes flared brighter now. "I served him until his death. He was a fool."

No argument there.

"I'm surprised you let us come here," Simon said.

"You are the enemy. Enemies must die."

It was right about that.

"There's only one option," her partner said, shooting her a quick look.

"Understood." Not having the cross-covered box with them meant this thing had to die. "Remember the warning."

He gave a nod and after a deep breath, he called out, "I am Simon . . . Adler. I am a Child of God, a Follower of the Risen Lord and of the Light." He took a deep breath. "*We* are your doom, fiend."

"You do not command me, *Simon Michael David Adler*. No one commands me. This is *my* world now."

So much for not revealing one's full name.

Though their foe didn't move, the illusion began to shift. One by one the demons vanished, and then the cavern was gone, along with the flames and the nauseating smell.

As the fae world began to appear, Katia gasped. She could only guess what it had been like before the Four had come. The forest was a wasteland, the towering tree trunks cracked open, leaking moldy sap. The breeze brought the thick stench of decay. The Mezmer gestured with a clawed hand and corpses appeared now, randomly discarded in the dying meadow, the remains of the inhabitants of this realm. All fae. All dead.

This was a charnel house of a world.

The fiend moved closer. "Now you are mine as well."

A glint of gold on its left hand caught her notice.

The ring. "Do you see it?" she whispered.

Simon nodded. "And when you've drained every bit of life from this place?"

"Then there are other worlds that will be mine. No one will stop me. *He* cannot travel the realms, so I am safe."

Which meant their world would be spared because Lucifer was waiting for this fiend if it ever went back home. But other realms were in jeopardy because these things were insatiable.

Simon shifted on his feet, his eyes alight, hand resting on the pommel of his sword. "You are the evil that destroys all that is good. You blame your master, but the darkness is yours. How *dare* you come into this world and claim it? How dare you harm those who have never harmed you?"

The Hellspawn bristled. "These beings are nothing, just as mortals are nothing," it said. With a gesture at least a dozen fae collapsed, writhing in torment as the Four tore the life out of them.

"Your battle is with us, not them," he shouted. "We're your enemies, not them!"

"So it shall be."

The demon made another gesture and the torture abruptly ended. Now it knew that they would sacrifice themselves to save the beings in this world. The damned thing had manipulated them like a pro.

Out of the corner of her eye she saw one of the fae dart forward. For a moment she thought it was headed toward her and Simon, but it veered at the last moment. With a bloodthirsty cry it charged the fiend, dagger in hand.

"No!" she called out, moving forward.

With a sweep of its hand, the fiend slashed its claws across its attacker, then plunged them deep into its chest. It freed the heart and held it up high as the others in the clearing cried out in horror. Crushing the organ in its hands, it turned its eyes on them.

"I will feed on your soul for eternity, Simon the Betrayer. It calls to me, even now. I crave the Light for it tastes of power."

"Bring it," he said, drawing his sword. "Or are you too scared?"

With a roar the demon charged forward. Katia clipped it with her staff, snapping its head back, and in response a fiery sword appeared in its hand, one like the angels wielded. With a curse she ducked, barely missing being sliced in two. Allowing her momentum to carry her around she reversed the bō and slashed across where the fiend's knees should be, missing them entirely.

"Move!" Simon shouted.

As she complied, his sword thrust just past her shoulder and struck home. The fiend bellowed and retreated. As she shifted into another position, Katia's legs began to tremble, and she felt her strength ebb. A quick look at Simon said he was feeling the same. The fiend had begun to drain them. All it had to do was wait them out.

As if he'd come to the same conclusion, Simon's expression grew grim. "May the Light give us victory," he said.

Katia came in from the left, he from the right. She usually fought alone, not with someone who had a blade. It cramped her moves, but between them they began to beat the demon back, step by bloody step. She swore she heard a cheer from somewhere near them. A cheer that was quickly hushed.

"Death is yours!" it shouted, though there were wet patches on its robe and its arms.

Another sword strike and suddenly a spell blossomed around it, enveloping the Mezmer. As if realizing their peril Simon attempted to sever the hand with the ring, but the blade was immediately repelled.

"Dammit!" she shouted, then executed a vertical strike, followed by a solid side kick. Both hit the fiend, hard, and it staggered back. If she could just drop it to its knees Simon would decapitate it.

Flames burst up around them now and they were not an illusion but true Hellfire. Simon fell back, trying to shield himself from being burnt alive.

With a scream she threw herself at the demon, staff whirling so fast even she couldn't see it. Then she was also on her knees, driven there by the power of that damned ring.

The Mezmer's hoarse laughter echoed around them. "Not so mighty now, mortals?"

Another mist rose and it shrouded them from their foe. A sharp spear of demonic magic rammed itself into her mind and she cried out. When the pain ended she blinked away tears.

"Remember it all. Live it all again. Suffer in agony!" the fiend cried out.

The Mezmer and the dying world were gone, and instead she and Simon were inside an old building. There was no stone here, but an arched ceiling rose high above them, constructed from wood.

The structure was two stories, had a stage at the far end, and seats on the second floor. It looked like a concert hall, until you saw the stained-glass windows.

Slowly the mist rolled away, revealing that they were not alone. In front of them were thirty or forty people. They sat around tables, listening to someone speak.

"What is this place?" Katia asked. It looked familiar, but she couldn't place it.

Simon's mouth dropped open. "It's the . . . Tabernacle."

"What? But it's gone, destroyed."

And yet they were inside a building just like it. And so were Beck and Jackson, and the other trappers.

"It's an illusion. It wants me to relive that night," he said, his eyes filling with fear.

The trappers turned toward them now, but she knew they couldn't see her or Simon. Riley gasped in shock when a man approached the group.

"Dad?" she called out.

"Run . . . Riley," the man croaked. "Run. Too many."

"Demons!" someone else shouted.

The howl of a fiend on the hunt came from behind them, a warning of the horror to come.

Simon's face went deathly pale. "Dear God, no. Not again."

†✻‡✻†

It seemed like they'd been waiting for days. Katia and Simon had entered that other realm and then . . . nothing. Once Mort and Ayden laid out a series of magical traps just in case The Unholy Terror decided to visit the city, the summoner began pacing. He'd been doing that for the last fifteen minutes.

To keep herself from doing the same, Riley texted updates, or the lack thereof, to Beck. Chaffin just stared at nothing, both hands resting on the handle of his cane.

"How long should this take?" Ayden asked.

Riley shrugged.

Something ran out of the darkness, something small. Mort's hand came up instantly, a blazing light surging around his fingers.

"No, it's one of them," Chaffin said, moving forward.

A little figure came to a halt in front of them, tears running down into its beard, its body shaking.

"Wizard, help us!" it pleaded.

"The mortals? Are they still alive?" Ayden asked.

The little one peered at her. "Enchanted. Will die if you do not help."

Then it looked directly at Chaffin. "*All* will die."

The necro took a deep breath and then sighed. "As I figured." He turned to Mort now, holding up the arm with the magical inhibitor. "I need to go into that world. I might not be able to save them, but I have to try. Remove this so I have a chance."

Mort gave a nod. "His lordship thought it would come to this." He waved a hand over the bracelet, and it fell to the ground. Then he tugged something out of his pocket, a small sphere.

"This will give you a burst of power. It won't last long. Use it carefully."

Chaffin took it, then tucked it away. "Tell his lordship know I will honor the trust he has given me."

Then he turned on his heel and limped toward the darkness,

the little man at his side.

"Go with the Light," Riley whispered.

Another howl, then a deafening chorus of them. Out of the dark came Gastro-Fiends, their furry bodies racing toward the trappers. One of them threw itself against the Holy Water ward, repeatedly. More joined it.

As Katia watched the ward broke, and the slaughter began.

"Pyro-Fiends!" a trapper shouted, pointing upward.

They crawled along the ceiling, raining down Hellfire on the trappers below. When one of the Threes came too close, Katia slammed her bō into it. It swiped at her, and what should have been an illusion proved to have claws that drew blood.

"Oh, shit!" she said, drawing back. "They aren't real, but they can hurt us? How does that work?"

When Simon didn't reply, she turned to find him immobile, caught in the hellish replay of the night when he'd nearly died. When so many of his fellow trappers hadn't survived.

"Hey!" she shouted, shoving him. It did no good.

If she could find the Mezmer, break its concentration, this nightmare would end. It had to be nearby to feed off their fear, their screams, their life energy.

"Where are you, you mother—"

Hit from behind, she managed to turn during the fall, only to find a Three raking its claws toward her throat. She jammed her staff in the way, cutting off its attempt. The stench of its fur and its breath made her gag as she fought to push it away. Then it was gone, slung away by her partner. As he pulled her to her feet, she could see he'd been wounded, blood streaming down his arm.

"Run!" he shouted.

Then he was gone, dragged away by a Three who threw him down and began ripping at his chest and stomach. Simon's bloodcurdling screams filled the air as he fought in vain to free himself.

This time Riley didn't come to his rescue.

But Katia could. With a vicious thrust she jammed the bō deep in the fiend's back. To her stunned surprise it vanished in a burst of bright fire, its tortured howls filling the air. She wasn't sure if it was because of the Holy Water or what, but that shouldn't have happened.

Simon didn't stop writhing in agony. As she reached for him, more wounds appeared on his chest, moving steadily down to his stomach. The demon's magic was killing him, wound by wound. He groaned, in agony, lying on his side, clutching his gut, unable even to pray.

She had to stop that spell. But how?

Then she knew. Would it work? Mort had told her how dangerous it was, but there was no other way.

Using the Holy Water on her forehead to set a protective circle, she cried out in relief when it came into existence. The area beneath them was no longer the floor of the doomed building, but the dark soil of this world. That gave her hope.

With her right hand, Katia grasped Simon's closest arm, and when he tried to jerk himself free, she held on. No more wounds had appeared, but he still bled from the existing ones. The lacerations on his abdomen almost made her vomit.

"Hey! Do you hear me?"

His eyes finally opened.

"This is a spell. It can be grounded. I can do it." Or at least she prayed she could. "Just keep fighting."

He stared at her, then shook his head. "No."

"Sorry, you don't get a vote on this."

Placing her left hand on the soil beneath her, Katia took a deep breath to prepare herself. She had one shot at this.

"Simon?" His eyes opened again, his face gray. "I need you to visualize the spell leaving your body. Push it out, you hear me?"

"You'll . . . die."

Which meant someone, probably Mort, had told him what

her gift entailed, and the downsides. She certainly hadn't.

"Not if I'm careful." Which was a total lie, but she said it anyway.

Katia looked up through the smoke and the flames, still hearing the screams of the dying as well as the triumphant roars of Hellspawn. To her right, Beck ran through the carnage, leaping over dismembered corpses. When he reached an exit he found the door padlocked. Prying on the lock with his steel pipe got him nowhere, so he took off in another direction, desperate to flee the inferno.

She took a deep breath and let it out, shutting off her mind to everything but her task.

"I am Katia Allyson Breman." Because at this point she didn't give a damn if anyone knew her full name. "I am a chaîne, a conduit, a path. I channel the Light, and I destroy the Darkness. Help me! Help me, now!"

Closing her eyes, she located the spell, the one killing her best friend, and pulled on it. Nothing happened. Panic set in. What if she couldn't do it?

Trust your gift. It was something her grandmother had always told her. This was one of her gifts, so she willed herself to make it work.

"Come to me. Come to me now and flow to the earth. By the Light, I command it," she cried.

An incandescent spark ignited where her hand touched Simon's arm, then she felt the spell begin to move *through* her fingers, inch by painful inch. It radiated up her right arm, across her chest, dug into her heart and lungs, then wound around her neck like a python, tightening.

As she gulped air, in her mind she saw her skin weeping darkness. Down her left arm the spell marched, to her elbow, then to her wrist and fingers. Finally, it flowed out, a sickly black ooze trickled into the earth.

Though Katia's fingers grew numb, she kept her palm pressed onto the soil. Her heart stuttered, skipping beats, as her lungs fought for her next breath. If she fainted she'd lose contact and Simon would die.

The spell continued to flow from him to her, wave after wave. Simon let out a tortured groan and then took a deep breath. She forced her eyes open and found that his wounds were gone, as if they had never been.

It's working.

As Katia felt the last of the enchantment drain away into the soil of this foreign world, she bowed her head in gratitude. She had done the only thing she could do, though it would cost her everything.

TWENTY-FIVE

The constant pain was gone, the feeling of something tearing into his chest and abdomen had faded. Simon forced himself to sit up, his mind clear of the spell. He was not bleeding to death like he had been at the Tabernacle. There were no demons around them now, no building, no fire, no screams. Just the withered world of The Lady and her kind.

He found the trapper lying next to him, her face pale, pulse pounding at her neck. "Katia?"

"I did it," she said, smiling weakly. "Now go kill that thing, will you? Kill it for me." And then she fell back into the dirt.

"What have you done?" a voice demanded.

It was their torturer, blazing sword in hand. The cloak was gone. To his relief it wore no armor. The sacred circle, their only protection, had broken when Katia fainted. It was up to him to protect her now, just as she had watched over him.

Simon rose, his own sword in hand. He squared up with the fiend, placing himself between it and the woman who had saved him.

"When I kill you, will your rotten soul return to your master?" he asked, his voice unusually calm. "And what will Lucifer do with you? Will he torture you like the traitor Sartael?"

The demon reared back in shock, telling Simon it knew exactly how the Archangel had suffered in Hell at the hands of their master.

His bones ached and his body trembled, but he would not step aside. With each minute renewed strength flowed into him. He had no idea where it came from, but it was of the Light and that meant everything.

He gestured. "I'm still waiting. Or are you all talk and no action?"

The Four didn't hesitate, but surged toward him, sword sizzling in the air. He ducked at the first swipe, then returned one of his own, catching the fiend high on the shoulder. A bellow came his way, along with another quick slash, one that barely missed his chest.

The duel continued, the hissing of the demon and the crackle of its blade filling the air. The fiend's wounds were no longer bleeding which meant it was drawing energy from some source. It was moving too fast for him, and he'd nearly been gutted, twice. He wasn't winning, not when the fiend was using magic to heal itself.

A throat cleared to his left.

When Simon turned to confront the new threat, he could only stare. Mathias Chaffin had followed them into this realm. In his hand was a cane, but no other weapon. Was he here to help, or to side with the fiend?

"That thing is not playing fair," the summoner said, shaking his head at their foe. He glanced down at Katia and frowned at what he saw. "Oh, that's not good."

He tossed his cane aside and picked up her bō. "Ah, that's better." Ramming the end of the staff into the ground, he pulled a sphere out of his pocket, gripping it tightly in his left hand. A surge of magic flowed from the hand, across his chest, and then up the bō.

"Let's see if this works."

His spell flew across the open ground and into the demon. The Four trembled and then its wounds began to bleed once again.

"Ha! It *did* work," Chaffin said. "It can't pull life force from anyone right now, but this spell won't hold for long. You're up, Exorcist! Make it count."

Simon stalked closer to the Mezmer and the battle began anew. True to the summoner's words his next blow drew blood. Now it could be injured. Now it could be killed because Chaffin had bought him a little time.

As if in reply, the earth beneath the fiend began to shift. Vines surged upward, ripping at it, distracting it, upsetting its balance. It clawed at them, furious, but they kept trying to ensnare its legs.

The fae had entered the battle.

The ring on the monster's finger flared to life and Simon felt a punch to his chest. Blood streaked down his torn shirt, as if claws had been drawn across his body.

"The ring! It's making it stronger," he said, rolling across the ground to avoid another strike.

"Not for long." Chaffin raised both his arms and began to chant. For a time nothing happened, and then the Four began to jump up and down, desperately trying to pull the ring off its finger. The stench of burned flesh filled the air. Finally, the circlet went flying and landed in the dirt at Chaffin's feet.

"Now!" the summoner shouted.

As Simon took off at a run, trying to time his stroke, the vines retreated. The Four met his blade with its own, knocking it aside, still so extraordinarily strong. He whirled around, then began another series of strikes.

Moving as if it had a will of its own, his blade lined up perfectly, piercing the fiend's thick skin. It reared back, and then with a move that his instructor would have envied, he put all his weight behind it and sent the blade toward the Four's thick neck. The slice was perfect, shearing through flesh and bones, fountaining black blood into the air. Some of it hit his face and he nearly gagged.

His enemy's head broke free and catapulted across the barren meadow, rolling over and over, gathering dirt and debris as it went. When it finally halted the Mezmer's lifeless eyes stared at nothing.

They had done it.

"You owe us one, Lucifer," Simon murmured.

At first there was silence, then came a chorus of weak cheers. Then small bodies scampered out from hiding to stomp on the flames inching through the dry grass.

"Damn, that was impressive," Chaffin said, leaning heavily on the staff as his spell faded away. His face was colorless, and Simon could tell he'd used every bit of his strength to help even the odds. "They teach you that kind of thing at the Vatican?"

"Not quite."

No, it'd been his instructor at the dojo who had taught him all that, and he'd had no clue his pupil would be using those skills quite so soon. Especially not on one of Hell's own.

From behind the savaged tree trunks small faces peered out at them. One of them, bigger than the rest, had pure white hair and brilliant blue tears on her cheeks. She made her way toward them now.

"So that damned thing was a demon. I did not think that was possible. But then, I don't know much about them."

"It was a Hypno-Fiend. It gets into your mind and can also steal your life force."

"That's for sure."

Behind them Katia groaned. He hurried to her, laid the bloody sword aside, then knelt to pull her into his arms. Her lips were too pale, her breathing labored.

"Katia? Can you walk?" There was a faint shake of her head. "Then I'll carry you." He looked up at Chaffin. "You staying or going?"

"Staying, if they let me," the necro said, leaning even more on the bō now. The Lady was next to him, holding onto his arm. The look of love in her eyes told Simon all he needed to know.

Chaffin held out the ring. "Give this to his lordship. He'll know what to do with it."

Simon slipped it into his pocket. Then despite his injuries he managed to lift Katia up into his arms. She was lighter than he expected, but it still took a bit to adjust to her weight. The trapping bag, his sword, and her staff would have to be left behind. At this point he didn't care. Only her survival mattered.

"May God go with you," he said, then set off in a direction he hoped would lead them home, because right now he had no clue.

In the end he need not have worried because he rated an escort of three small figures. They moved like their joints ached, bits of moss kept dropping off them, but still they led him through the forest. To his surprise one painstakingly dragged along Katia's trapping bag though it probably weighed more than it did.

They didn't go back through the tunnel, but deeper into the forest. Apparently the stonework had been an illusion. The trio didn't move fast enough for him, their strides short, but still he welcomed their assistance. Their job was to ensure he and Katia left this realm as quickly as possible. He was totally down with that.

When they reached the barrier between the realms the wee men followed him across. Once in his home world, they set the trapping bag on the ground and then backed away. Each doffed their mossy hats.

Simon opened his mouth to thank them, then realized that might not be wise.

"May your world be green and full of life once more."

They seemed pleased by that, and all of them bowed. Then one by one they walked back into their world and vanished.

When Simon heard Riley cry out, "They're back!" he knew they were truly home. He carried Katia closer to the cars, then gently laid her down on the pavement. Then it was a matter of stepping away so the others could help her.

"What happened?" Ayden asked, kneeling next to the trapper.

"She grounded a spell. A strong one. The demon used the ring, and it made it even more powerful."

"Demon?" Riley said. "Really?" He nodded.

"She needs a hospital, now," Mort insisted after checking Katia's pulse. "She's going to crash if she's moved all that magic."

"The trapper's clinic is closer," Riley said. "We can call them on the way, let them know what's going on. They'll take care of it."

"Then let's go," the summoner replied.

"Her trapping bag is back there," Simon said, pointing. To his relief the witch set off to collect it.

"Where's Chaffin?" Mort asked.

"He's staying in the other realm." He dug out the ring and handed it over. "He said to give this to his lordship."

"Consider it done."

After Riley supplied the phone number, Mort called the clinic, pacing back and forth in rare agitation. Once he was connected, he related the situation to whichever doctor was on duty.

Simon insisted on lifting Katia into the back of Riley's car. He climbed in, laid her head on his lap, then covered her with a blanket.

"She could have a seizure," the master warned as she started the car. "You know what to do if she does?"

He nodded, his hand resting on his partner's neck, feeling her heart pound as it skipped beats.

A few minutes later, the situation worsened.

"She's having more trouble breathing," Simon warned. He gently turned Katia on her side, but that didn't seem to help.

"We're almost there," Riley replied, then cut in front of another car which earned her a sharp honk of a horn.

As the streets rolled by, he kept a prayer on his lips. Katia had to survive. He could not face a day without her smile, her gentle ribbing, her strength.

She shuddered, and for a second he thought she was beginning to seize, but the moment passed. Then finally they were there, screeching to a halt in front of the clinic. People in uniforms poured out the front door, two rolling a stretcher. He pulled himself out of the car, carefully laying Katia's head back on the seat, then stepped away. He had done what he could. She was truly in God's hands now.

Dr. Carmela Wilson glanced over at him, grimaced at what she saw, then turned back to their patient. She usually had a smile for him, but tonight there was only grim determination. They moved Katia to the stretcher and whisked her inside the building.

He followed, exhaustion and heart-breaking worry in each step. Once he was inside, a nurse led him to one of the curtained cubicles, which didn't make much sense until she pointed at his chest and arms. The fiend had managed to cut him in multiple places. There were also deep burning scratches, which meant they were already infected.

"I'll be back in a bit," the nurse said, then pulled the curtain closed. Simon sank onto the gurney, though he was filthy, his clothes covered in that other realm's dirt. He didn't care because all he could hear was the doctor issuing orders in the cubicle next to his, the one where they were working on Katia. Something about an I.V. line, electrolytes, oxygen. More words he didn't understand.

The curtain pulled back as Riley joined him. She tugged it closed behind her, then moved nearer to him.

"How bad is it?" he asked.

Her eyes saddened. "Bad. Her heart is racing, she's having trouble breathing, her blood pressure is too high. Everything Mort warned her about if she channeled magic without knowing how to do it."

"Dammit," he said, shaking his head. "She did it to save me. She knew she shouldn't, and she still did it."

"Like you giving her the ring so she'd be safe?"

He nodded. "Yeah."

"Tell me what happened there."

Simon began to explain what they'd faced in that other world: How the demon wove a spell based on the night the Tabernacle burned, how it was rapidly morphing into an Archfiend, how Chaffin had help him kill the monster.

There was increased activity next door.

"She's seizing," someone called out.

Simon's voice faltered, then he closed his eyes and began to pray.

†✳‡✳†

It seemed to be hours before the voices on the other side of the curtain were less strident. He could still hear a beeping noise, a rapid one, and he guessed that was probably a heart monitor. So far they hadn't had to use a defibrillator, which meant there was still hope.

To his relief, Riley remained with him and held his hand, staying silent as he went through every prayer he could think of. His rosary was in his jeans pocket, but he hadn't taken the time to pull it out. Her presence helped and when he whispered that to her, she gave him a tired smile.

"She'll fight to survive," she said. "Katia never gives up. Even when sometimes she should."

He looked over at his former girlfriend now. "She *can* be stubborn, but she can be so kind. So strong."

"Have you told her how much you care for her, or are you being the strong and stupidly silent type?"

His smile came despite the desperate circumstances. "I sort of hinted how I felt about her when I gave her my presents. I think I blew her mind with that. You know me, way too serious when I shouldn't be. I just should have kissed her."

Riley raised an eyebrow. "Knowing Katia, the fact you didn't was probably wise. Her last boyfriend was a jerk. She hasn't given me details, but from what I heard, he's a master at gaslighting."

That explained a lot. "There are a few of us out there."

"Not just guys, either." He nodded at that. "Maybe once she's feeling better, you should lay it all out, let her know where your heart is. Then it's up to her to decide if you're worthy."

He sighed, understanding. "If I'm worthy. God, that's the truth."

"You are," she said, squeezing his hand. "I should know. And if she's smart, she'll see you are truly a wonderful guy, the best she'll ever meet."

Simon closed his eyes for a second, letting all that sink in.

When he opened them again, a nurse was at his side. She was young, only a few years older than him, with light blonde hair. Her name tag said she was Heather. She looked worried, but not panicked, which was good since she'd probably been working on his friend in the next cubicle.

"Okay, let's see what you've got going on."

"Just a few demon wounds. Nothing important," he said, though some of them really did need attention. "If you're needed for Katia, I can wait."

"No, they have her covered." Heather checked out the damage. As the inspection progressed, she helped him pull off his T-shirt to check the wounds on his back, ones he hadn't even realized were there. Chest bare, he shivered, and it wasn't because the clinic was particularly chilly.

"I'll get hot water to clean these, then we'll treat them with Holy Water. A couple of these are deep. I'm not sure if they'll need sutures or not. Doc Carmela will let us know if that's the case."

"How's my friend doing?" he asked, searching the nurse's face for any sign of hope.

"She's in rough shape, but you got her here in time." Heather patted the only part of his arm that wasn't bleeding. "The doc will be here in a bit. You can ask her for more details."

Then she slipped past the curtain to get supplies.

"She's alive, that's all that matters," Riley said. "They make them tough in Kansas."

They do.

Dr. Carmela arrived a few moments later, all brisk business and no smile. She reached his gurney and was about to examine one of the deeper wounds, then paused as her eyes rose to meet his.

"How is she?" Simon asked, his heart thudding in his chest.

"Better."

"That's all you can tell me?" he said, astounded.

"There are patient privacy rules we have to follow."

Riley cut in. "I'm Journeyman Breman's emergency contact

and the Guild's form she signed allows me to make any medical decisions regarding her care," she said. "I can have a copy of that agreement sent to you."

Carmela's eyes went to Simon and then back to her because clearly that agreement didn't cover him.

"Please act like there's no one else here," Riley added. "Because whatever you tell me I'll just pass on to him."

This was stupid. They worked together. Katia had saved his life. He just needed to know if she was going to live.

The doctor gave in. "Okay, Journeyman Breman's heart is beating too fast and too erratically, her breathing is labored, and her blood pressure is in stroke range. If what the summoner says is true, her electrolytes are seriously effed up, which is why she's in this condition. Given the symptoms I'm seeing, I tend to agree."

She began scrutinizing the biggest wound, then paused again.

"But, if we can get those 'lytes back at the levels they should be, her vital signs will improve. Her wounds aren't that serious, so she has a good chance of recovery. She's still not stable, so we'll keep an eye on her, keep giving her fluids and oxygen while we wait for the lab results. I considered transferring her to Emory, but honestly I think the journey would be too much for her."

"Thank you," he said. The doctor hadn't given them platitudes, only honesty.

"Same here," Riley said, gathering up her trapping bag.

"You're both welcome."

Riley gave him a gentle squeeze on his arm before departing. As the heart monitor tapped a fast rhythm in the cubicle next door, Carmela set about working on his wounds, one by one.

It'd taken a bit of persuasion, but Simon had been allowed into Katia's cubicle and that's where he'd remained. His demonic injuries had been treated with Holy Water, and the few from the fiend's sword had been sutured. Given that he'd taken on a Four with that kind of power, he'd been damned lucky.

Three hours had passed and Katia's vitals still sucked, but at least her breathing had improved. This reminded him of his time in the hospital after he'd been nearly gutted by a Three. Those memories were still too raw, especially after the demon's hellish illusion. That thing had been too cunning.

Simon bowed his head, rosary in hand.

"My prayer is for Katia Allyson Breman, who is gravely ill. She walks in the Light, just as you command. May You guide the hands of those tasked with her care. Let Your healing power flow through her, bringing relief from pain, bringing restoration of her health. Amen."

One of the nurses entered the cubicle a brief time later.

"I'm going to turn off the sound on the heart monitor. We can still see the readings at the front desk, but it can get hard to listen to if you're watching over someone you care for."

"Thank you."

That silence was unnerving at first, but the green line continued to move across the screen. Her heart rate was 124 now, which was an improvement. Seeing her lying there wired up to so much equipment, oxygen cannula in her nose, made him feel powerless.

A section of her hair, in the front, was white now, stark against the usual black. It hadn't been there before she'd entered the other realm.

Left on his own, Simon offered every prayer he could think of, some twice. He'd just finished one when his mother joined him at the bedside.

He'd called her earlier, let her know he'd been injured, but would be fine. And then he'd asked if she could pray for Katia. She'd said she'd spread the word throughout the family, and he knew that multiple prayers were headed heavenward tonight.

Now she was here because Jeanine Adler would never let any of her children suffer on their own.

"Son," she said, then leaned over and gave him a kiss on his forehead. "You look like you're hurting."

"I am." And not just because of the wounds.

Then she studied the monitors, the various I.V. solutions, and finally the patient lying on the stretcher.

"What were her vitals when she came in?"

He said he didn't know, but they were better now.

"How did this happen?"

He straightened up, his back reminding him of the bandages.

"A Four cast a spell on me. I thought I was back at the Tabernacle. I was dying, Mom. I felt it all over again." Moisture built in his eyes now. "Katia grounded the spell. She saved me."

His mother's arms went around him, and he received a gentle hug. The scent of her light perfume was like being at home again. *Safe. Loved.* All the things he'd always taken for granted until that night when he'd almost died.

"May God bless her for being there for you," his mother said. "Everything you've told me about her says she's a wonderful soul."

He nodded, then wiped away tears with a bandaged hand.

"Oh, and when she wakes up, you should warn her that she's now officially a member of the Adler clan. No way she gets out of that."

He couldn't help but laugh. "I'll tell her. I'm not sure she'll realize what that means."

"She'll find out soon enough. Bring her over for a meal, will you? If she can stand up to Dee, she'll be fine with the rest of us."

"I will. How is Dee doing?"

"She's okay. She told me what happened with you two. It sounded impossible, but she says it was for real."

"It was. I never thought she'd get caught up in that."

He knew he'd always feel guilty for that horror.

"She knows. That whole nightmare might have been a catalyst for her to make some personal changes. We'll see," Jeanine said, smoothing a hand across his hair. "I'm guessing that you want to stay here until your friend wakes."

"Yeah, I do."

"When you're ready to come home, let me know."

"I will."

He received a kiss on the forehead right before she left him to continue his vigil. He heard her speaking to someone at the front desk, the doctor, posing the type of questions a nurse practitioner would ask.

After the response, her tone said she was pleased with her son's current medical status. She wouldn't be able to find out much about Katia's illness, not with patient privacy rules, but now they realized she was in the medical field that might ease the way.

"You have to get better," he said, looking down at his friend. "You've been invited for supper at my parents' place. You'll get to meet my younger sibs. They're . . . unforgettable." He chuckled at the irony of that statement. "All of us Adlers are. And now you're an honorary one. Sorry about that."

When there was no response, he bowed his head and began his prayers anew.

✝ ✳ ✞ ✳ ✝

A soft, murmuring voice slowly brought Katia back to consciousness. It sounded weary, desperate even. And then it cracked with emotion.

It was Simon's voice. He had lived.

The need for sleep kept tugging at her, but she tried to fight it. There was movement near her now.

"How is she doing?" he asked.

"I'm liking what I'm seeing," someone replied. A doctor or nurse perhaps. There were other noises and then steady pressure on her arm. A blood pressure cuff Finally, it deflated.

"Oh, good, her blood pressure has improved, though still much higher than it should be. Her pulse is slowing down. Her kidneys are in decent shape, and her heart rhythm is less erratic now."

"Thank God," Simon whispered and then the soft murmuring began anew.

That he was praying for her recovery told her everything she needed to know about Simon Adler's generous heart. In time, she'd have to figure out what to do about his deep feelings for her. But not right now.

First, she needed to heal.

TWENTY-SIX

Katia found herself surrounded by white curtains on three sides, like you'd see in an emergency room. She was on a gurney, and it wasn't all that comfortable. On her right was a cardiac monitor mounted on a pole which displayed her heart's rhythm, pulse, blood pressure and other numbers she didn't recognize. Another pole had an I.V. bag, along with two smaller bags attached to it. On her left was another pole, and another I.V. The more of those the worse off you were, at least that was what her grandmother had always said.

It was then she realized that someone's hand rested on her left arm, a hand with a bandage on it.

Simon.

He'd stayed with her, though she had no idea how many hours had passed. When she shifted position to ease a cramp in her back, he sat up, blinking those tired blue eyes.

"Katia?" he said, putting so much hope in that one word.

"Uh huh." Then she coughed, which only made her head hurt, a dull thumping that she found annoying.

"Thank you, God!" he said, then pulled himself fully upright. His face was red and had a sheen of sweat on it. From the number of bandages on his arms, the demon had nailed him, repeatedly.

Bits of memories surfaced—the battle with the fiend, the Tabernacle illusion which had been far too real. Simon screaming in agony.

"Please tell me that goddamned Mezmer's dead."

"It is. I sliced off its head." Then he grinned. "One swipe and it was history," he said, mimicking that move, barely missing one of her I.V. stands.

Katia grinned back at him. "Damn, I'm sorry I missed that."

"You were napping on the job. What can I say?" he said, shaking his head.

That rated a laugh.

Then he sobered. "We did it, Katia. We made it out alive."

They had.

"You were right about Chaffin. He showed up just when we needed him. He forced the demon to remove the ring. We would have died otherwise. I didn't know if you knew that or not."

"I thought I heard him, but I was pretty out of it. Please tell me he stayed there." Because returning to his world would cost him his magic, and maybe his life.

"He did."

"Good. She'll take care of him. Maybe he can help their world heal." Katia paused, eyeing their surroundings. "Are we in a hospital?"

"Nope, this is the trapper's clinic," Simon said. "You were in bad shape, and this was closer. It helps that the doc is used to dealing with weird stuff."

"Weird stuff?"

"It has to do with your electrolytes. She can explain it much better than me."

"I'm not dying, am I?"

He shook his head. "Not anymore."

Not anymore?

He didn't usually exaggerate, which meant it'd been a near thing. What was odd was that he kept staring at her hair. Before she could ask about that, the privacy curtain pulled back and a brunette entered the cubicle. She was probably in her forties, wore teal scrubs, and her name tag announced this was the doctor herself.

"Hi," Katia said.

"Hey! Look at you, all awake and everything. I'm Doctor Carmela Wilson. And this is a significant improvement over what you were like when you arrived."

"Which was?"

"Comatose with bi-geminal PVCs, which means your heart was skipping beats like mad. Tachycardia, which is your pulse racing. And you had sky-high blood pressure and labored breathing. Plus, you decided to have a seizure right after you hit our front door."

"Seizure?" she said, giving Simon a quick look. He nodded.

"Yup. You have a history of them?" Katia shook her head. "Well, that's good news, at least. In short, you were damned sick and trying hard to die on us. Exactly what I'd expect since you are seriously anemic, and your electrolytes were totally out of whack."

"Is 'out of whack' an actual medical term?"

The doc chuckled. "In this case, yes. According to a certain senior summoner, you have an affinity for sucking up magical spells and then grounding them. While that is great, your body has no clue how to handle that awesome superpower, so you burned through electrolytes like mad. Which is why you ended up here. Plus, you got a few demon wounds, but that's normal for you guys."

Superpower?

This lady was a total kick. No wonder the trappers spoke of her with a special kind of reverence. She rocked.

The doc pushed a button and the blood pressure cuff on Katia's right arm automatically inflated. "What's your usual B/P?"

"One hundred over sixty something."

Carmela waited a bit and then announced, "Well, now it's one-sixty-six over ninety-eight. Much better than before, but still too high for you."

Taking all that in, Katia eyed the heart monitor which was happily plugging away at one hundred and sixteen beats per minute. It was usually in the upper sixties.

"After I.V. fluids with some electrolyte chasers, you're slowly getting back to where you should be. Your B/P and heart rate will return to normal fairly soon. Summoner Alexander says that if you don't channel anymore magic, at least until you've learned how to do that without killing yourself, you'll be fine."

"Huh."

"You know, that was pretty much my response when he dropped all that on me. I've never seen this kind of thing before, so we treated the electrolyte imbalances and that did the trick. I'd like to give you a pint of blood unless you have religious issues against that."

"No issues. Go for it. The anemia thing might explain why I've been so damned tired recently."

"That would do it. Your Guild health record says you're AB Positive. That right?"

"It is."

"Okay, then that's a definite. We'll repeat the lab tests at noon. If all those numbers are headed in the right direction, you can go home. But we'll wait until then to make that decision. One step at a time."

Katia yawned, still exhausted. "Can I have some water? My mouth is really dry."

"Sure. You up for some ice cream, maybe?"

That sounded good. "Yeah, bring it. For some reason I'm hungry."

Simon's weary grin said he thought that was good news.

"You don't have to stay," Katia said. "You have to be as wiped as I am."

"Not going anywhere," was the swift response.

"I already tried to get him to go home and failed just like you," the doctor admitted. "Now that you're a bit more stable, we'll move you into an observation room, one with an actual door. There's a real bed in there, so it'll be easier for you to rest." She looked over at Simon now. "And a recliner that makes into a decent spot to nap, so you can rest as well."

Ten minutes later he was asleep in that recliner, tucked under a couple of blankets. As he slept, Katia downed a second small container of ice cream. It was plain vanilla but tasted like heaven. Once it was done, she set the carton aside, used the remote to lower the head of her real bed, then tugged up the covers and closed her eyes. She was still wired to all the electronics, but that was fine.

I almost died last night.

A trapper knew their job was dangerous, terminal even, but coming that close to the grave, *again*, had changed something within her. It was time to rethink several things in her life. Family issues, her job in Atlanta. Simon. Exactly where she'd start on all that, she didn't know.

One thing was sure: Katia would make sure her friend's prayers hadn't been wasted.

"Katia?"

The voice wasn't familiar. Probably one of the many nurses who'd checked on her overnight. Repeatedly. No complaints about the care here, that was for sure.

Opening her eyes revealed someone standing near her bed, someone not in the clinic's teal uniform. The lady was probably fifty something, with bright blonde hair and brilliant blue eyes.

"Mrs. Adler?" she guessed.

"That's me," the lady said, and smiled in return. "Please call me Jeanine." She raised her hand to display a paper bag from Katia's favorite fast-food place. "The doc says you can eat, and my son informed me that you love egg and sausage sandwiches and hash browns, especially if they come from this restaurant. Oh, and I have fresh-squeezed orange juice, too."

A quick glance over at the recliner showed it was empty, the blankets neatly stacked on the seat.

"Is he okay?"

"He's doing fine. I took him home about an hour ago. I insisted on it, actually. Like you, he just needs time to heal."

"Thank you," she said, relieved. "I couldn't get him to take off. I really loved that he stayed here with me, but he needed to rest."

"The only reason he's gone is because I had to use my *Mom*

Voice, so no way were you going to pull that off."

Oh, yeah, Katia remembered the Mom Voice. Her own mother wasn't that good with it, but her grandmother had been.

Jeanine placed the paper bag on the tray table, waited as she raised the head of her bed, then rolled the table over. It was only then Katia saw the clock on the far wall and realized it was just after noon, which meant she'd been here for probably twelve hours. The bill for all this care was going to be unbelievable.

Beats being dead.

A glance down at her hands suggested some cleaning was needed before she touched the food. "Ah, can I wash these first?" she asked, wiggling her fingers in the air.

"Sure. Hold on."

As she waited, the electronics showed her blood pressure and heart rate had continued to fall, her blood oxygen was good, and she was down to one I.V. Somehow Katia had missed the blood transfusion, but that was fine.

After her visitor secured some soapy paper towels, she cleaned her hands, then dried them on even more towels. Smoothing back her hair, she paused mid-move. Something felt different, like the hair had a different texture.

"Ah, is there anything . . . here?" she said, pointing at the area just above her right eyebrow.

"No. It's just the lighter part of your hair."

"Lighter? It shouldn't be."

"Hold on." Jeanine dug in her purse and came up with a small makeup mirror. When Katia held it up, she gasped. It wasn't just lighter, it was stark white. "What the hell is that?"

"That's something new?"

"Yes." She wet a finger and rubbed that section of her hair. Nothing happened. "Huh, I think it's permanent."

Had this happened when she'd channeled the spell away from Simon? *Maybe.* She remembered him staring at her now. He'd known about this and not said a word, but then there'd been bigger things to worry about. *Like me trying to die.*

Katia angled her head one way and then another, then smiled

as she handed back the mirror. "You know, I kinda like it. It looks cool."

"I agree," Jeanine said. "I thought it was something you'd done on purpose."

In some ways she had.

Her stomach growling in anticipation, Katia removed the contents of the bag. An extra-large breakfast sandwich, three hash-brown squares, and one large container of OJ. This was a gourmet meal.

"Perfect," she said. Then she remembered her manners. "Thank you so much for bringing this to me."

"Not a problem," Jeanine said, parking herself in the recliner. "You need food. You're thinner than you should be. I'm guessing things haven't been great in your life. And no, Simon didn't give me any details, but I can read between the lines."

Katia hesitated before she tore open the sandwich wrapper. "It wasn't great in Kansas. It's been challenging here, but in a different way."

She'd just opened the sandwich, inhaling the glorious scent, when one of the nurses popped into the room. The lady's timing wasn't great.

"Thank you for bringing us lunch," the nurse said, this directed at Simon's mom. "That was really good of you to think of us."

"Happy to help the cause. You guys do great work."

As Katia reluctantly held off diving into her meal, the nurse made note of her vitals, then drew what looked to be at least a thousand vials of blood.

"We'll let you know when the results are in," she said and then left.

"Thank you for thinking of them. The lunch, I mean."

"It was Simon's idea," Jeanine replied. "Which tells me that my husband and I must have done something right when we raised that boy."

Katia couldn't hold back the smile. "You did good. He's got a kind soul. He's been really . . . nice to me."

"He said the same of you."

It was more than that, but she wasn't about to share that with his mom. As she opened her mouth to take her first bite of the sandwich the door opened again. This time the newcomer was a male in a teal lab coat. He was probably the same age as Doctor Carmela, with curly red hair and a twinkle in his eyes. He smiled at Mrs. Adler, thanked her for lunch, then turned his attention to Katia.

"I'm Doctor Bergersen, or Doc B to most people. Compared to when you were admitted last night, your vitals are much, much better. If the results of your blood work are decent, I'll cut you loose. There are restrictions, however."

There always were. "Like not trapping demons for a few days?" Katia guessed as she set the sandwich back down on top of its wrapper. At this rate she'd never get breakfast.

"More like no trapping for at least a week, *or two*, depending on your vitals and labs."

She groaned. "Okay, I won't fight you on that. No way can I mess with those damned things right now."

"Exactly what a doc wants to hear." Bergersen eyed the heart monitor, then looked back at her. "Do you have someone who can keep an eye on you for the next few days? Someone to check your vitals and change your bandages?"

"Ah, not really." Simon wasn't well and didn't need to worry about her. "I live at Grand Master Stewart's house and I don't think his housekeeper knows that kind of thing."

"If you're okay staying at Simon's for a few more days," Jeanine said, "I can keep an eye on both of you."

That she hadn't expected. "You sure?"

"Absolutely. I'll send our youngest kiddos to their great aunt's house for the duration. They'll love it, and so will she." At that, Jeanine turned toward the doctor. "I'm a family nurse practitioner, so watching over these two won't be a problem. Just let me know what you need and I'll send in regular reports. If anything changes, I'll let you folks know at once."

The doctor lit up. "There you go! Can't get any better than

that. One thing, does this house have stairs?" Jeanine shook her head. "Good deal. We don't need to stress this young lady's heart any more than necessary, at least not in the short term."

It was so amazing to watch these people in action. "Thank you," she said, grinning. "Thank you for everything. You guys are incredible."

"Right back at you, Journeyman," the doctor replied. "You didn't give up, and often that's half the battle. I'll let you know what the lab results are as soon as we get them." Then after a wink, he left them alone.

Katia dove at her sandwich, refusing to be sidetracked any longer.

Jeanine quickly typed out a message, then sent the text. "I let Simon know what's going on, so he'll worry a little less, if that's possible. I'll leave you my number so you can notify me when they discharge you. Because I'm betting they will later today. When that happens, I'll swing by and pick you up."

This lady was so nice. "Thank you." The words seemed inadequate.

"I'm happy I can help. You are *very important* to my son. Now I'll go stock up on food and medical supplies for you two. See you soon, Katia. It was good to finally meet you." After gathering up her purse, Jeanine shot out the door, intent on her mission.

Simon had said that his mother was a force of nature.

He hadn't been exaggerating.

†✴‡✴†

It was silly, but Simon kept walking to his front window every time a car drove by the house. Until today he'd never realized how many vehicles that would be. He'd been doing this window thing ever since his mom sent him a text saying Katia's lab reports were in, the doc was pleased, and she was being set free.

His pacing continued, which was ridiculous as he had a fever and really should be in bed. The only reason he wasn't sitting on his porch waiting for their arrival was because the neighbors would drop by and want to chat. Including Mrs. Carmody, who would chew him out about something or other she didn't like. The length of the grass in his front yard, for instance, even though it had been recently mowed. He had zero patience for that kind of crap today.

Instead, Simon kept pacing even though his mom had told him they'd be at his place in a few minutes and that Katia was stable. His phone pinged and he grabbed it off the couch. It was a text from Riley.

THOUGHT YOU MIGHT LIKE TO KNOW THAT A DECAPITATED BODY OF A BULKED OUT MEZMER WAS FOUND IN THE GULCH, ALONG WITH THE HEAD. SOMEONE CLEANED HOUSE.

I ASKED FIREMAN JACK TO CREDIT YOU FOR THE KILL.

The fae had chucked the fiend's corpse back into our world. He would have done the same. He'd be sure to share the trapping fee with Katia.

As Simon debated just going to bed, the sound of a vehicle pulling into his driveway moved him back to the window. His mom's car. He sighed in relief, as if something might have happened between the clinic and his driveway.

"I'm an idiot."

He watched as his mother patiently helped Katia out of the car, and then walked her to the house. From the tentative way she moved she hurt as much as he did. And yet he saw that determination, that inner strength that always awed him.

"You're a godsend," he said, then opened the front door.

Once up on the porch, she sent a weary smile his way. "Hey."

"Hey."

Her face was still pale, her eyes tired, but she was here, and she would heal. Jeanine Adler would not allow any other option.

"How are you?" Katia asked as she slowly entered the house. It was only then he noticed that she was mindful of each step as if her balance was off.

"I'm sore, tired, chewed up. The usual."

"Situation normal, as Riley would say," she replied.

"That's for sure."

His mom was right behind her. "Let's get you settled, then I'll check your vitals," she said. "Are you hungry?"

Katia thought about that for a couple seconds. "Yeah, I am. That's so weird. I had no appetite for days, and now I can't get enough food."

Before Simon could offer to make something for her, his mother cut in.

"Go to bed. You look like you're going to collapse. I'll check on you once I have Katia settled."

He knew better than to argue. "Yes, Mom. Katia, we'll talk later."

After he shut the door to his bedroom, Simon sank onto the bed. He heard voices in the other part of the house and smiled. She was safe. All his prayers had truly been answered.

†✷‡✷†

They quickly fell into a routine. Every two hours Jeanine would wake Katia, let her relax for a few minutes, and then check her vitals which she typed into her phone. Then that data would make its way to the clinic and whichever doc was on duty. Since everything was headed back to normal, no action was required on the clinic's part.

After the vitals check, her wounds were inspected, and bandages changed as needed. Then there was a snack waiting for her on the nightstand, something light like a peeled orange or an apple, a few nuts, maybe half a sandwich. Beverages were there too, usually fruit juice. Healthy stuff.

There were also over-the-counter vitamins and minerals to take, along with a prescription for a special Vitamin B complex.

Katia ate the snacks, downed the meds, tolerated the dressing changes, and then went right back to sleep. From what Jeanine reported, her son was getting the same treatment, minus all the supplements.

It was that sense of ordered calm that put Katia at ease. She slept without nightmares, though she knew those would show up soon enough. It was as if being in Simon's house made the healing go that much faster. By the next morning Jeanine announced that she only needed vitals taken every four hours now.

"You're getting there," she'd said. "All of these are headed in the right direction."

"You know, I wonder if this anemia and electrolyte thing was happening in Kansas and I didn't realize it. I was really tired there, but then I wasn't eating much."

"Might have. I'd best go check on my son, who will immediately ask me a bunch of questions about you."

"He worries a lot," Katia said, laying back down in bed.

"In this case that worry was warranted," his mom said, giving her a "you know I'm right" look.

And so it went. Jeanine had made it all quite bearable. How the woman dealt with six kids she had no idea. Katia certainly wouldn't have had the patience.

On the morning of the third day after they'd been injured, Jeanine got the "all clear" from Dr. Carmela, so she packed up her gear, gave them both hugs, and headed home. In her wake she left a medication schedule for Katia to follow, as well as roast beef, carrots and potatoes simmering away in a crockpot.

Those few days had driven home just how much difference there was between Simon's mom and her own. The contrast was stark. If this had been her mom the routine care would have been delivered, but also endless criticism about Katia's job, how it inconvenienced the family, and how she was being so selfish because she refused to turn in her trapping license.

It'd been easier to just stay quiet and not argue. But what had that achieved? Nothing, as far as she could tell, other than a feeling of guilt.

In the middle of one late night bandage change, she'd asked Jeanine why it was some parents were cool, and others weren't. Why did some make it so hard to love them?

Simon's mother had paused in her wound cleaning. "Is it your mom, or your dad?"

"Mom. She's never liked me. I tried, but I never did anything right. My sister and brother, they're fine. But not me."

"That's sad, for both of you." More cleaning, then Jeanine paused again. "I'm an impartial observer, so let me just say that everything I see in you is good. You're a strong young woman, Katia. I'd be proud to have you as my daughter. I don't know what's making your mom that way." She finished the wound care, then looked directly at her.

"What we sometimes think is *our* problem, is *their* problem. It's up to your mother to deal with her own insecurities, not lay any of that on you. Once you determine where the boundaries are, you'll know how to handle her. Don't let her ruin *your* life just because she's not happy with *hers*."

Silence fell between them as Jeanine finished the bandaging, wished Katia a good night, and quietly shut the door behind her.

Don't let her ruin your life just because she's not happy with hers.

Jeanine Adler had spoken the truth about a woman she'd never met.

Her mother had always worried about what others would think of their family, all because Katia wasn't "normal" like her brother and sister. That shouldn't have made her any less worthy of being loved. But it had. It *always* had.

Over the years, she'd taken that verbal poison deep inside her. It had colored her relationships, her jobs, her entire life. Her grandmother had warned her about that, but she'd not listened.

"I'm listening now, Gran," she whispered. "And this time I understand the message."

TWENTY-SEVEN

Simon's sister arrived promptly at seven that next evening, carting three big bags of food from their family's favorite Chinese restaurant. From the size of them she was feeding the entire Adler clan. Some habits were hard to break. At least there would be lots of leftovers.

"Bro," she said, as Simon opened the door for her. A swift kiss was deposited on his cheek and then she handed over one of the bags.

"Katia will be out in a minute," he said. "She was napping."

"Good on her. I should do more of that myself." She eyed him critically. "So should you."

"I plan to. I don't have to go back to work until Monday. Lay Exorcist Snyder offered to stay in town until then."

"Good. You've earned those naps, little brother."

As they laid out the various containers of rice, the entrees and such, Dee didn't chatter, not like normal. Something was different. Trying to pry anything out of her would be a waste of time; she was even more stubborn than he was.

They had just set everything on the table when Katia shuffled in. She wore one of Simon's T-shirts and her own pair of jeans. They still looked too loose on her, which meant Dee's bags of food were needed.

"Oh, man, that smells so great," Katia said, then flopped down in the closest chair. She still looked tired, but her eyes held a spark in them now.

Then she smiled at his sister. "Hi, there."

"Hi." There seemed to be no friction between them, which was one of his concerns.

"You did something new with your hair. I like it," Dee said, pointing at the white area.

"I like it, too." Katia's eyes met his and he saw the challenge in them. He'd tell her later why he hadn't mentioned that surprising change, though he bet she'd already figured it out.

"Okay, there's spring rolls, dim sum, wonton soup," his sister said, pointing at each one. "And three different entrees. Mom said y'all needed feeding up."

As usual, his mother was right. "You will let us kick in cash for all this," Simon insisted. "This is a lot of food."

"Nope. My treat. We're celebrating,' she said, a twinkle in her eyes now. "Let's eat first, then I'll tell you why that's the case. I'm starving."

It took time before Dee finally leaned back in her chair and sighed, content. "That was really good. Their dim sum rocks."

Katia waved a spring roll in the air in agreement.

"So, what are we celebrating?" Simon asked, curiosity on maximum.

"I quit my job today," she announced.

That wasn't what he'd expected. "Freeman and Hostra is history?"

"Total history. Should have done this a couple years back, but I was too busy being a good little worker bee."

"What pushed you over the edge?" Katia asked as she ladled more Mongolian beef on her plate. This was her second helping, and it didn't look like she was slowing down.

"My boss was in my face about how I hadn't completed a report, and how I was always taking time off." Dee frowned at this point. "I've missed *two days* this year. One because of the flu and the other because I got chucked into wherever the hell that place was with the creepy trees. Last year I took a few days off because this guy," she angled a thumb at him now, "was in the ICU. But no, that didn't matter. I was *slacking*."

"Your ex-boss sounds like a total dick," Katia said.

"Oh yeah. As he's spouting all sorts of bullshit, all I could think of was how close we came to dying in that crazy realm place. This guy was bitching me out about a report he *hadn't even assigned* to me. When I pointed that out, he insisted I *should have known* I had to write it anyway. That I had to take the initiative. So, let's just add clairvoyance to my job title while we're at it. It was totally ridiculous."

"Who made bail for you?" Simon said, because knowing his sister that might have been needed.

She gave a hearty laugh at that, a sound he hadn't heard from her in far too long. "I was *so* tempted to deck him, oh my God I wanted to. But I didn't. I went back to my cubicle, typed up my resignation and put all my personal stuff in a box. Then I dropped my keys and scorching hot resignation letter on his desk. Along with a number of highly creative curse words."

Simon loved seeing this side of her.

"I told him I refused to work for a company that wouldn't pay me what I was worth. That there were a lot more important things in this world than if we made our next quarterly sales target. And that he could fuck off. A couple of my closest cube rats applauded as I left. When I got home, I typed up a report about how bad a boss he'd been and forwarded to his bosses at the head office, including the owner of the company."

"Think that will do any good?" Katia asked. She'd moved onto the Kung Pao chicken at this point.

"Not likely. They all have their heads up their asses. Their only goal is profit. I'm done with all that," Dee said, then took another long sip of her soda.

"Any plans on what you're going to do next?" Simon asked.

"A sabbatical." She looked over at him now. "I happen to know someone who did just that and I'm due for some time off. I have money stashed away, mostly because I was so damned busy working, I had no time to spend it. Now's the time."

"A religious sabbatical?" he asked, though he was just needling her.

"Nope, I'm not you, Bro. But I'd still like to hear your suggestions in case I want to toss in a cathedral or two."

"Or maybe a stone circle?"

She blinked over at him. "You went to one of those?"

"I did. I'll be happy to show you the pictures."

"Well, I'll be damned. What else are you hiding from me?" Dee asked, frowning at him now.

A lot, dear sister, a lot.

Katia had finished off the food on her plate. She barely stifled a yawn, then rose. "Congratulations on being free. And thank you for all the yummy food. There's no way I'm going to stay awake after all this, so I'll just go crash so you two can talk travel plans."

"You're welcome, Katia. Thank you for watching over this guy," she said, angling her head toward him. "I promise not to keep him up too late."

"Riiight," Simon said, but he couldn't stop smiling at how this dinner had played out.

"Please let me know how your trip goes, will you?" Katia asked. "Pictures or it didn't happen."

That seemed to please Dee and she nodded enthusiastically. "I will."

"But no pictures of trees or squirrels," she said, looking over at Simon now. "I've had a lifetime of those already."

"What?" his sister asked, puzzled.

"Ask this guy. Good night, you two."

Once Katia was back in her guest room and the door closed, Dee laid a hand on his arm. "Squirrels? Trees?"

"It's a long story."

"Okay." Then she lowered her voice. "You are amazing, my brother. And so is she. Some reason you two aren't a couple? Even mom noticed you get along so well."

He hadn't seen that one coming, so it took a while to answer. "Well, I'm hoping that will happen one of these days."

"Good. But don't wait too long. We both know that life doesn't play fair sometimes. Especially if there are demons or lunatic necros involved."

That was true. He knew it was time to change the subject.

"So where are you thinking of going first?"

As Dee began listing locations, some as far away as Asia, Simon cleared the table. Ironically, he'd led the way for her upcoming journey. It was time for her own rebirth, and he was keen to find out exactly what lie ahead for his bossiest sibling. At least if she was in Singapore she wouldn't be rearranging his cupboards.

The night before Katia was to return to Stewart's house, they found themselves sitting in the backyard pointedly ignoring the one topic they should be talking about: the proclamation he'd delivered over her birthday presents.

Instead, they joked about the small dog next door who liked to yap at everything that moved, and then discussed his family's annual picnic on Labor Day weekend. The one Katia had been invited to by his mom, who'd insisted that she was "family" now.

"How big is this thing?" she asked. She guessed it could be in the hundreds.

"Like fifty or sixty plus people. All the ancient grand aunts and uncles come out of the woodwork so they can check up on us 'young folk.' My older brother will be flying in from Germany." Simon chuckled. "It's going to be fun when a few of our uber conservative family members find out he has a steady boyfriend. Joshua's been 'out' for years, but they've just ignored that. They won't be able to now."

She matched his grin. "Ah, good on him. Lots of Adler family drama, then?"

"Count on it. And some awesome food, a chance for you to meet the rest of my sibs, and hang out with my parents. Dee is doing the event planning for this year instead of Mom. She'll be flying off on her trip soon after that. Last I heard she's starting in Japan and then going to Singapore, Australia and then New Zealand. Dee never does things half-assed."

Katia's jaw dropped. "I am sooo jealous. I've always wanted

to go to *all* those places."

He looked over at her now. "Who knows, maybe someday you will. Ever been to Ireland?"

She shook her head. "Italy. That's it. Though Pompeii was cool in kind of a morbid sort of way."

"Well, I've been invited to a close friend's wedding in Killarney next April. The invite says I can bring a . . . guest."

That was very tempting bait, and from the gleam in his eyes he knew it.

"You are deviously clever, you know that?"

The gleam grew brighter now. Of course he knew.

"Riona is getting married. I met her last year, during my travels. We were lovers for a time."

The admission just popped out there and he didn't look like he was sorry it had. She had always wondered just how sexually adventurous he'd been but had never dared ask.

"You miss her." That much was obvious from his expression.

"I do. Riona has a lot of Light in her, and she shared it with me when I needed it the most."

"You've gotten two letters from Ireland since I started staying here. She misses you."

"She does. Ree doesn't like emails so it's pen and paper for her."

"How did you two meet?"

"It was at a pub. We just started talking. She told me about the sites I should visit in the area. I hitchhiked around for a couple days and then went back to the pub, and she was there eating lunch." His voice grew softer now as he pulled up those memories. It was evident they were good ones. "We talked for hours. Then she offered to take me around, and so she drove and I played tourist."

"That sounds wonderful, Simon."

"It was. We became lovers a week after we met, and I stayed with her at her cottage for three more weeks. It was a time of rebirth for both of us. No promises were made, but a true friendship was forged. We both needed to heal in our own way."

He looked over at her now. "That's why when she met someone a few months later, I was so happy to hear he'd captured her heart. Oisin is perfect for her."

Beyond all that was the hint that his heart had been captured as well, but not by the lady in Ireland.

Katia couldn't put it off any longer. "Ah, about what you said when you gave me my presents."

To her surprise, he wasn't listening to her but staring at the backyard. "We have company."

In the grass a short distance away were three small figures. They wore green caps and clothes interwoven with ferns and moss. They looked ancient, especially with the long beards. The trio murmured among themselves, then zeroed in on her and Simon.

She remembered her grandmother talking about the Little People. Brownies, pixies, goblins, imps, and fairies. What this trio was she had no clue, nor could she guess why they were here.

"They helped me when you were injured," Simon explained. "They guided me out of The Lady's realm and into ours."

He rose from his chair. "Greetings," he said. "Welcome to my . . . garden."

One of the three stepped forward, and after a swift bow placed a metal object on the grass in front of him. It was a sword, sheathed in a scabbard. The little whatever-it-was gestured at it, then stepped back.

"That's mine," Simon said. "I never expected to see it again."

He'd already explained how he'd had to leave the weapons behind. She'd hated losing the bō but accepted why that had happened. Now here was his sword courtesy of the little folks.

Her gran had said never to thank a fae, but how did she tell Simon that without insulting them. "Ah, you're not supposed to—"

"I know." He looked back at their visitors. "By bringing me this sword, you have shown me much honor."

Had it been his Irish lover who had warned him about all

that? If so, Katia would happily send her a thank you note.

Then it was her turn as the other two little men stepped forward with her wooden bō, each carrying one end of it. They set it on the ground and stepped back, again with a kind of reverence one didn't expect to see from their kind.

She hesitated and then said, "My heart is filled with your kindness."

Apparently that was what they'd wanted to hear as all three bowed in unison, turned and marched away to disappear back into their world. Curiously, there was no swirling portal like for some of the other realms.

"They know where you live," she murmured.

"Well, you're here, so I'm figuring you're the draw not me."

"You might be right about that." She wished now she'd asked her grandmother more questions about the Good Folk.

Simon collected his sword and pulled it out of the scabbard to inspect it. "It's spotless. It had to be hard to get the demon blood off it."

Her bō was in the same pristine condition. Something was tied to it, secured by long green vines. She pulled them off and realized it was a note, handwritten on parchment in brilliant blue ink.

When she saw who had written it, she laughed.

"What is it?" Simon asked, standing next to her now.

"The, ah, Wizard sent us a note." She smoothed it out and skimmed it, trying to work through the rather arcane handwriting.

Then she began reading it aloud.

To Simon Adler & Katia Breman,

Now that the Unholy Terror is dead, my lady's world is slowly healing.

I have been granted permission to remain with my beloved. I am grateful for this second chance, one I did not deserve.

We will never forget that your courage made this new life possible.

Forever in your debt,
The Wizard and His Lady

"Wow," Katia murmured. "They saw how much he loved her and let him stay."

A faint tingle began in her fingers and then the note in her hand disappeared, likely called back to the other world so no trace of it would remain. As far as Atlanta knew Summoner Chaffin was still on the run, and she was fine with that assumption.

Simon didn't look at all surprised when the message vanished, as if he'd expected that. But his face did register surprise when he pulled his sword free of its scabbard and found strange writing engraved on the blade. He gave it a couple test swings, and then stared at it like he'd never seen it before.

"It feels different. It's more . . . lively."

Curious, Katia moved away from him and then executed a few moves with the bō. Then gaped in wonder. 'It's like you said. It's livelier now. It's the same weight and balance, but different somehow. They did something to these, didn't they?"

"Looks like it."

She looked down at the staff, then over at his sword. "We can't tell anyone about this."

"That's for sure. No one will believe us anyway."

Her boss might, but it was best that this just be their secret. As he sheathed the blade, she glanced back at where the three little beings had appeared.

"Ice cream to celebrate?" he asked, and she nodded. "One scoop or two?"

"Two."

"So it shall be," he said, heading for the back door, sword in hand. She followed him inside with her staff, knowing it was time to finish that conversation, the one that she dreaded.

A short time later he'd set their bowls of ice cream on the end table in front of the couch, then taken a seat there. Anyone else would think him totally relaxed, but she knew him too well. He was waiting to hear what she thought about . . . them, and he was worried she'd reject him.

Katia sat next to him and ate the dessert. When it was gone, she'd run out of time. Simon had finished a few minutes earlier, and now his attention was totally on her.

"If you don't feel you can talk about what I said to you, I can wait. I won't like it, but I'll deal," he said. His eyes said something different.

"No, I owe you an answer," she said. "You didn't pressure me or anything." She sucked in a breath and then let it out slowly. "Almost everything in my life has changed. I had to start over in a new city, one that is so different than Lawrence, at least when it comes to Hellspawn. It wasn't my choice but here I am anyway."

Simon held his silence, watching her intently.

"The first thing I need to do is to get used to this new situation and find where I fit in. I'm thinking I've got a good start already. Riley has been great and so have you."

He nodded his understanding.

"Then there's my family. My brother and sister are okay with what I do. My parents aren't, and that's created a lot of tension. When I was being cheated out of my wages, I went from supporting myself to not being able to pay rent and being homeless. Part of that was my own fault, but not all of it. When I asked my mother for help, she said I could move back home, but only if I stopped being a trapper."

"That wasn't right," Simon said. "Your folks should be supporting you, not issuing ultimatums."

"I know. Part of it was because they were afraid I'd get killed, especially after what happened to Kevin."

"Still, you are an adult, and this job is *your* choice. They should honor that," he replied, his voice tighter now.

"I won't argue that. No matter what I did it felt like everyone was trying to run my life. Part of that was my fault because I let them. I won't let that happen again."

He cocked his head now. "You think I'm doing that?"

"No! I'm sorry, not you. You have *always* accepted me for who I am. It's been that way since I met you that first day. That means so much to me, Simon," she replied. "But before I commit to a relationship with anyone, I need to do a few things first."

"Such as?"

Please let him be okay with this.

"I need a place of my own. Apartment, house, doesn't matter. I need my own space. Grand Master Stewart and Mrs. Ayers are great, but sometimes I just like to be alone. It's hard to do if you're living with someone."

"I understand that. I'm the same way. What else?"

"I need to deal with my family. I'm not sure if that's fixable or not, especially when it comes to my mother, but it's driving me crazy. If I can't get that worked out, I need to move on. I need my head firmly in this game, especially when the game is so damned deadly here."

She sucked in a breath. "And I need to deal with this *chaîne* thing so I don't keep sucking up magic and trying to kill myself."

"That's it?" She nodded. "You can't do that while we're going on a date or two?"

Could she? "No, not really. I only have so much bandwidth right now. If we're dating, I want both of us to be fully committed, Simon. You're far too important to me to phone this in. I just couldn't do that to you."

"You're putting a lot of weight on yourself," he replied, not looking at her now.

"I know. That's what I need right now." She shrugged. "Who knows, in a couple of weeks I might change my mind about all this life-changing crap. But right now it feels really important, like something I've put off for too long."

"You almost died, more than once. That makes you step back and examine your life, look at all the things you take for granted. I'm been there, too." His finger traced down her cheek now. "You do what you need to do. I'll wait. I want you happy, Katia. That's the most important thing to me."

Oh God, he'd meant it too.

"I think I need to get things worked out in my own head as well," he admitted. "Not about you, but other stuff. The job, mostly."

Their eyes met. "Then we'll wait for each other."

"Yes, we will."

Simon's strong arms encircled her and she curled up against him. As she closed her eyes, savoring this moment between them, another kiss was placed on her forehead. It felt like a promise of good things to come.

TWENTY-EIGHT

The next morning, Simon drove Katia to Stewart's house and left her in the care of the housekeeper. He knew Mrs. Ayers would watch over her, but it was still hard to see her go. The housekeeper had even arranged for Katia to have a room on the first floor until she was cleared to climb stairs.

Now his house felt empty. He hadn't realized how much life she'd brought to it just by being here. But at least she hadn't shut him down, told him he had no chance with her. Instead, Katia treated his feelings with respect and had let him know what she needed to do before they could move forward. That had to count for something.

She'd left behind three options for his flower beds, complete with diagrams. Once he decided which he liked best she would give him a cost estimate. It'd been fun watching her pull all that together, and it appeared that Katia enjoyed the process. All that had happened in between the frequent naps. Once he knew she was feeling better he'd decide what design he liked best, and they'd do the work together. He looked forward to that.

When Riley texted him and asked if she and Beck could drop by, he'd immediately agreed. When they arrived, the grand master's expression said this would be all business.

They'd settled on the back porch after he'd brought out one of the kitchen chairs so there would be enough seating. Beck turned down the offer of a beer and Riley wasn't interested in any iced tea. Definitely not a social call.

"We need to talk about what's goin' on here in Atlanta. What ya think about all of these portals and things," Beck said.

Riley had once told him that if the grand master used "ya"

instead of "you" he was tightly wrapped, and that was the case here. But he didn't think it was entirely because of the Chaffin thing, or the gateways popping up in the city.

Simon studied his guests' faces, then nodded. "I just finished my report to Father Rosetti about some of that."

"Ah, before we go too far," Riley said. "Do you have any issue with me using a spell to shield this conversation? I don't want to do that if you're uncomfortable with having magic used at your house."

"Go ahead. And thank you for asking." It was a little late for the "no magic" decision given what Chaffin had done at Simon's front door.

She waved a hand in a circle. Simon felt a spell brush up against him, one of the "sound booth" ones, as she called it. It did solve the problem of the dog yapping next door as a cushioned hush fell around them.

"That feel right?" Beck nodded. "Okay. I need to ask this question first: Do you have to report *everything* to Rosetti, or can you just not bother to tell him certain details if needed?"

That was interesting. "I have some leeway. But if there's a threat to the Atlanta Archdiocese or Rome, I will have to let Rosetti know immediately."

Riley seemed to relax now. "No, this isn't anything like that."

"So, what won't I be telling my bosses?"

"This afternoon the Summoners Society will deliver a video to the governor and the mayor. It will show a magical duel between Chaffin and Mort. Our rogue necro supposedly dies during that battle. It's totally fake, of course. Mort and Lady Torin created it and both the glamour and illusionary spells are solid. Ozy reviewed it and said it's the best he's ever seen."

Beck nodded. "And because the summoners asked this be kept private, by tonight that video will have been leaked to the press. Always happens that way," he said.

"Which will make it look even more legit. With Chaffin supposedly dead, the Powers That Be will stop screaming for his head," Riley added. "Also, the Society gave each of the reanimates' family a sizable check to cover their pain and suffering, and for the reburials. As long as the rogue necro stays in that other realm, we're all golden."

"Ya wouldn't know how we can tell him that, would ya?" Beck asked.

So that's why they were here.

"I have a secret too," he said, and then told them about the note that had been delivered, along with their weapons.

"Then it's all good," Beck said, smiling now. "Damn, I was worried."

"Really good," Riley added. "Mort will be happy to hear that."

"Except that we keep havin' more of those portals openin' up downtown."

"Two last night," she said. "Nothing came out of the first, but something large, green, and hairy came out of the second. Luckily, Jackson was at that site, and he hit it with a Holy Water sphere. It went back home before it hurt anyone. He's not sure if that was because of the sacred water, or just pure luck."

"This is just going to keep happening," Simon said.

"We think so too. We talked to Katia right before we came to see ya. She thinks it has somethin' to do with the Angel of Death because she found some ashes in The Gulch. She's thinkin' that they're makin' these doorways into other worlds," Beck said, giving his spouse a cautious glance.

Riley frowned at him. "And you know I took care of those during the battle." At Simon's confused expression, she explained. "The Death Angel created warriors to fight us, and the ashes of those things is what Katia believes are the trigger for the portals. Mostly because Death can go everywhere since it's, well, universal."

"You don't think that's possible?" Simon asked, intrigued.

"I took out those warriors by wetting them down, and then sealing their ashes under the pavement in The Gulch. I think I got all of it, but maybe not. It was kinda crazy there for a while."

"I saw the videos and it was more than crazy. What does Ori

think about all this?"

"He's made himself scarce, as in hard to find," Riley said. "Which means something is playing out between him and the folks upstairs. More Heavenly drama it appears."

"But wouldn't there be some of these ashes left over at the other cities the angel attacked?" he asked. "Shouldn't they be having the same problem?"

"The other sites were totally destroyed, so anythin' left behind would be burnt."

"Okay. So, what does Serrah think about this?"

"I did finally track her down and she wouldn't talk about it at all. She's still settling into her new job," Riley replied. "I know Ori, he won't let her fail, but things aren't going well for her right now."

"In the meantime, we're tryin' to figure out what is makin' our city into an 'all ya can eat' snack bar for those other realms."

Riley winced at that phrasing. "I know, I'm not happy about it either. But we'll figure it out."

"What would you like me to do?" Simon asked because he knew there had to be a request somewhere.

"Keep an eye out and let us know if ya see anythin' ya think is related to this. We gotta figure it out, soon, or more of these door things will just keep openin' up."

"I can do that."

"Okay, then, thank you," Beck said, shooting to his feet as if eager to be gone. "And, well, glad to see yer better. Ya two did a helluva good job in that other world."

"We did." He wasn't going to thank him because it was the truth. "Fair warning, next time I see Ori it isn't going to be pretty. I want to know why he didn't bother to tell us it was a demon over there. He had to know that. We could have planned ahead, taken different weapons." Not been so near death that they'd needed a summoner to help even the odds.

"Good luck getting a straight answer," Riley said. "Divines can be really obtuse sometimes."

"Most times," Beck muttered, shaking his head.

After she broke the spell they walked back through the house. Riley gave him a wink over her shoulder, then she and Beck headed to their car, talking quietly between themselves.

"Realms here, realms there." Simon frowned, then shook his head because it made zero sense. Looking up at the blue sky, he pleaded, "Any help would be appreciated."

The faint breeze crossing his front porch delivered no answers, just the scent of a magnolia tree in full bloom.

As usual, they were on their own.

EPILOGUE

There had been near universal rejoicing that Mathias Chaffin had died in a spectacular duel. Of course, there were the usual conspiracy theorists claiming he was still alive. When one of the reporters caught up with Katia at Mr. Means reinterment service and asked what she thought of those claims, she'd spoken the truth.

"Chaffin is no longer a threat, and I am happy about that," she'd said.

Mrs. Means had finally gotten the message and dropped her lawsuits. It was that or face several thousand dollars in legal bills for cases she would not win. Especially now that her husband's body had been tucked back into his grave.

That hadn't made her any less unpleasant, and she'd glared at Katia and Riley during her husband's second funeral service. Katia ignored her. Mr. Means deserved their respect for all he had done, and she made sure he received it.

As they'd left the cemetery, she'd stopped by Anna Lanier's grave one last time. A fresh bouquet of roses rested there, and the name on the card indicated that Anna's husband had paid his respects. Only a day earlier, Mr. Lanier had been released from jail after the cops had finally determined his alibi during the time of her murder was righteous. The investigation was ongoing, they said. Hopefully, her killer would be found and she could finally rest in peace.

According to Riley, Harry Hawkins, the necro wannabe, had been packed off to Wisconsin rather than facing charges here in Atlanta. He was now apprenticed to a summoner in Madison, had a place to live, a basic salary, and would begin his magical studies soon. All of that was Mort's doing. The man truly had a forgiving heart.

Mort's nephew had moved back home and was back to gaining new bruises with each new magical spell. Katia planned on razzing Alex about that the next time she saw him. And just as Riley had predicted, Jaye had aced her journeyman's exam.

Then there was the news from Rome which wasn't as good. Father Rosetti and another senior cleric would be touring the U.S. in the next few weeks, visiting various cities and evaluating the skills of their respective lay exorcists. Atlanta was on that list. Katia didn't believe that itinerary was just a "let's check on the troops" tour. Not with the way things were going here.

Simon cleared his throat, bringing her back to the present. He stood a few steps above her, on the porch of a tan house in Berkeley Lake. Katia was still on the sidewalk, trapping bag in hand. The house was a well-kept older structure, two stories with mature oak trees in the front yard. A lovely home, unless you could feel the Hellspawn lurking within.

This was their first exorcism together since their adventures in the other realms. Katia dreaded it.

"You ready for this?" Simon asked, shifting the bag on his shoulder. In his other hand he held the cross-covered box for the fiend once it was exorcised.

Katia tried to stop another yawn but failed. "Oh yeah, sure. I only slept eleven hours last night, and I might not need a nap today."

Which wasn't what he'd asked.

"You're much better than you were ten days ago," he said politely.

She'd been dying ten days ago, and they both knew it.

When she didn't comment on that observation, he pushed the doorbell.

An older lady immediately opened the door. She was in her late sixties with curly salt-and-pepper hair. She had *that* look in her eyes, the one that said she'd seen Hellspawn in person, and was frightened out of her mind. That her last hope might be the pair on her doorstep.

"Mrs. Barbosa?" The lady nodded. "I'm Lay Exorcist Simon Adler and this is Journeyman Katia Breman. We're here to rid your house of Hell's evil."

The woman's eyes clouded in tears. "Oh, thank God. Come in! Come in!" she said, frantically waving them forward.

Simon entered immediately, but Katia hesitated. She had her gear, the Holy Water was in place on her forehead. She even had her collapsible bō in her trapping bag. This was her job, the one she'd trained for.

But still she hesitated.

Even though the nightmares were beginning to lessen, they still showed her Simon's death. Never hers, just his. Hell was ruthless when it came to exploiting one's weaknesses.

Her partner reappeared in the doorway. He studied her for a moment. "You can wait in the car if you're not ready yet. I'll be okay."

It was a kind offer, a thoughtful one. But it was an offer she dare not take or she'd never face another demon again. Hell would win.

I am Katia Allyson Breman.

I am a trapper. I walk in the Light.

She climbed the last few steps, then walked across the threshold to begin anew.

The End

Author Notes

&

Acknowledgements

I really hope you enjoyed Katia's story. Much like Denver Beck, who elbowed his way into the first book, Katia did the same in LOST SOULS. I've not regretted that at all. I love the trapper from Kansas. She mouthy, insecure and has such a bright future if she's willing to risk everything.

Let's face it, Katia's personal history isn't pretty. A gaslighting boyfriend, an emotional absent mother, the loss of her beloved grandmother, and loads of guilt about her brother's near death. I'm really looking forward to what happens with her and Simon in the next story.

On a personal note, in late 2022 I was diagnosed with Follicular Lymphoma, a "chronic" cancer of the blood. There is no cure for this disease, but it can be managed. Treatment began in March 2023 and I completed six sessions of chemotherapy in the autumn of that year. The chemo worked as we'd hoped.

When I wrote about Lay Exorcist Snyder's daughter having cancer, I hadn't been diagnosed at that point. When I was, I left that in the story. It's important to acknowledge how those unforeseen challenges affect us, and those around us.

I was deeply touched by the support of my friends, my dear husband, and the medical pros at Hospital da Luz Coimbra as the cancer treatments rolled out. I continue to receive immunotherapy infusions, but hope to finish those in autumn of 2025. I count myself very, very lucky. My hematologist agrees.

My husband is the reason this book is in your hands. From the moment of my diagnosis and all through my treatments, Harold was there. He drove me to the hospital, sat for hours waiting for me to finish the treatments, then made sure I got home safely. He kept me fed, even when I had no appetite. He dealt with my exhaustion, my short attention span, all of it. Not everyone has such a strong partner, but I do. Bless you, my love.

As for the previous books, Clarissa Yeo (JoY Author Design Studio) created another incredible cover. It's always fun to work with her and I look forward to doing so in the future. Thanks, Clarissa! (https://www.facebook.com/joyauthordesignstudio)

Once again, a thank you to the kind people in Portugal who have made us feel welcome here. Our home, up on a mountain, is a place of healing and happiness. And lots of energetic swallows.

And finally, thank you for reading my books and the Light you have sent our way. It has made all the difference.

~ Jana Oliver
   August 2024

About the Author

Jana Oliver never planned to become an author. In fact, she told her sixth grade teacher she wanted to be an international spy, which sounded very cool at the time.

That so didn't happen.

After pursuing various careers (registered nurse, disc jockey, travel agent, copywriter) someone flipped a switch in her brain and stories began to pour out. There were so many stories she decided to write them down and publish them. Then someone else published them, in the U.S. and then all over the world.

She's still surprised by all that.

A few years down the line Jana's an international bestselling author with twenty some books to her credit, and has won over a dozen major writing awards, including the Maggie Award of Excellence, the Daphne du Maurier, National Readers Choice and the Prism Award.

Nowadays she can be found writing her tales in Portugal when not sharing time with her very patient husband and their cranky (ghost) Feline Overlord, Ms. Dali.

Social Media

Website: www.JanaOliver.com

Facebook: www.Facebook.com/JanaOliver

Threads: @JanaOliverAuthor

Instagram: JanaOliverAuthor

BookBub: @JanaOliver

Also by Jana Oliver

DEMON TRAPPERS SERIES
Forsaken (formerly The Demon Trapper's Daughter)
Forbidden (formerly Soul Thief)
Forgiven
Foretold
Grave Matters
Mind Games
Valiant Light
Lost Souls
Bitter Magic

TIME ROVERS SERIES
Sojourn
Virtual Evil
Madman's Dance

VERITAS SERIES
Cat's Paw
Killing Game
Broken Dreams

Standalone Novels & Non-Fiction
Briar Rose
Dead Easy
Tangled Souls
Socially Engaged: The Author's Guide to Social Media
(co-authored with Tyra Burton)

www.ingramcontent.com/pod-product-compliance
Lightning Source LLC
Chambersburg PA
CBHW070644180626
46817CB00006B/2240